THE DOG CATCHER

A NOVEL

Linda,

I am thrilled that you have bought my book. I truly hope you will enjoy it. Thanks for being open to stepping into another world!

Best Wishes)

LLOYD L. JOHNSON

DEDICATION

This book is dedicated to the millions of women who've lived it.

ACKNOWLEDGMENTS

First and foremost, I'd like to thank God for putting this story in me to tell.

I'd also like to thank: My mother for believing that I had the ability to write after all of these years; my grandparents for buying me my first dictionary, thesaurus, and grammar set; Lyle for giving me the best 18 years of my life and his support...he helped me to stay focused.

One thing I realized during this process is that not everyone wishes you well. You can tell that more so from what they show you vs. what they tell you.

The following people encouraged me to move forward even when I lacked the inspiration or was just plain lazy: My brother, Philip Trueblood; my sister, Virginia Trueblood; Grace Schmitt; Lynn Dell; Karen Masi; Derrick Greene; Jerry P; Jarek Zagorski.

I really want to give a huge thanks to the people who took time out of their lives and read my manuscript through several drafts: Nancy Roberts; Robin D; Chauntress Hill; Melissa Buccheri; Georgia Ashman; Kathryn Finney-Wright; Quish Turner.

Self publishing has been very rewarding and at times, daunting. It helps to have the right people on your side who have a wealth of knowledge of the process. These people provided their expertise in helping this book become polished: Cherise Fisher, who gave me editorial direction and introduced me to the world's greatest copy editor, Nira A. Hyman.

Thanks to Davida at Oddball Design for providing cover art that really pops! And to Tabitha Haddix and the folks at Streetlight Graphics for typesetting and formatting this book so that the world can read it!

And last but not least, I'd like to extend a huge thank you to the readers for taking a chance on me and picking up THE DOG CATCHER. I truly hope you enjoy the story.

CHAPTER

1

L ET ME GO AHEAD AND put the shit out there; men are ridiculous. Worse than that, they're dogs. They all start biting sooner or later.All the men in my life have been dogs. My daddy, dog number one, is probably the grandfather of all hounds. He finally stopped beating my mama when I turned 15, around the time we moved to Minneapolis, Minnesota, from Jackson, Mississippi.

Mama got a job as a surgical tech at Mount Sinai Hospital, but Daddy could barely hold a job that first year. Instead, he spent his days at some bar, usually the Spruce, chasing butt. Not a day went by that Mama and us kids weren't finding some strange woman's earrings or watch in the car. One time I found some lady's nasty panties underneath the car seat. After awhile, Mama stopped letting on that she knew what was happening, even though we knew she knew. She was from that generation where marriage really was, "Till death do us part." But that meant putting up with all the bullshit in between.

I don't know how she made it through all of that. Maybe it was her faith in God. She believed that everything was possible through Him. Yeah, everything but my daddy keeping his pants zipped.

By the time I turned 16, I'd had enough. Mama kept

turning her head to what was going on, and Daddy wasn't even trying to hide those bitches he was laying up with.

I got so fed up, I wanted to ask Mama why she didn't leave him. At that point she was practically supporting us all by herself, so it's not like she needed him for anything. But I knew she'd say that I needed to stay in a child's place. That's one of the things I hated about my mama. She never took the time to explain anything. If she told you to do something, you couldn't ask why, because she would just say, "Because I said so, damn it!"When my body first started changing, I don't think she even took the time to explain what I was going through, or what I could expect. The day I first got my period, I was scared. I didn't know why there was blood in my panties. When I told her, all she said was, "Oh, you're startin' to get your service once a month." Then she went into the closet and fished out a pad and said, "Here, use that."

Daddy had been getting paid under the table, working as a second-rate fix-it-man around the neighborhood, but finally got a real job unloading trucks downtown. I was just as glad because instead of him being home all day, telling me how no good I was, he'd work all day and hang out at the bar all night. But when he was liquored-up I'd hear it.

One night, I got up to get a drink of water from the kitchen. When I went downstairs I overheard Daddy telling Mama how I had all kinds of boyfriends. "Ain't you noticed anything different about your daughter?" Daddy asked, deep in the booze.

"Which daughter you talkin' about, Joshua? Cheryl or Marva?"

"I'm talkin' about Cheryl. You don't see nothin' wrong with her wearin' all that makeup?"

"Well, she's gettin' to that age, Joshua. She don't wear nothin' but a little lip rouge," Mama said."She's gonna be a tramp. You mark my words," Daddy said, taking another swig of booze.

I snuck back upstairs and went to the bathroom to run my hand under the faucet and drink some water. Then I got into bed and cried myself to sleep, because it was sad to live under the same roof with folks who were supposed to be family, and yet they didn't even know me. If my parents had taken the time to ask me, they would've known there was only one person I cared about; dog number two.

His name was Diallo Washington. I'd seen him around the neighborhood during the summer. The first time I laid eyes on him, he'd been outside his house with his friends trying to fix an old, beat-up Buick. His mama stood knock-kneed in the doorway, plump like a Thanksgiving turkey, wearing a blue, and, purple swirled, psychedelic housedress. She was telling him to go to the store to get her some cigarettes. He turned to see me standing on the sidewalk, watching him. That's when the sun caught his eyes, which shimmered an amazing green. This brotha was fine as hell. I mean, he was all that and a whole convenience store, not just a bag of busted chips.

I could tell he knew he was fine. He strutted around that yard like a peacock, showing off his green eyes. Diallo was black as night, so you know that a brotha with green eyes is gonna catch some attention.

The only other black guy I'd ever seen with light-colored eyes was Smokey Robinson on *The Ed Sullivan Show*. And just like Smokey, Diallo could sing his ass off. That's how we finally met for the first time; he was out in front of the store one day, singing doo-wop to a bunch of giggling girls. I couldn't help but get drawn into it too. I'd close my eyes and it was like Dennis Edwards from The Temptations was right in front of me.

As soon as I came on the scene those other girls no longer mattered because he made his way toward me and finished his little ditty of a song, "The Nighttime is the Right Time" as he gazed into my eyes. Realizing they didn't stand a chance, the other three girls walked off in a huff.

"Eh, what's your name, lil' mama?"

"Cheryl."

"Nice to meet you, Cheryl. I'm Diallo," he said, taking my hand and shaking it.

"Nice to meet you, too."

"You got a boyfriend?"

"No."

"That's too damn bad. You're too pretty not to have a boyfriend. Can I walk with you after you get what you need from the store?"

I nodded my head shyly. After that day, it was a whirlwind romance. He drove me to and from school in that

Buick he'd been working on. I felt supreme, being seen getting out of my boyfriend's car instead of riding around in some rickety school bus with the other students.Diallo was a different breed. He was five years older and didn't have to talk a lot of nonsense like the boys my age. I felt he was someone I could tell my troubles to. When I told him all about my family drama, he not only lent me an ear, he tried putting thoughts into my head; telling me stuff like my folks were trying to control me. But I knew that wasn't true, because Daddy was always at the bar if he wasn't at home or at work, and Mama, true to form, just turned her head away from stuff so I don't know when anybody had time to control me.

When it came to sex, he seemed thrilled that I hadn't given up my cookie yet. I tried to resist his charms but those eyes and voice of his finally worked their magic. He literally sang my panties off; singing *The* Temptation hit "I Can't Get Next to You." But my first time wasn't all precious like you see in a soap opera. He just slapped his dick against my clit a few times and then rammed it inside my pussy.

To say it hurt ain't telling the whole truth. I felt like my insides were bleeding, that's how bad the pain was. I begged him to stop, but all he said, in a sex-moan-kind of way was, "Naw, naw. It'll start feelin' good after awhile!"

Yeah right! He had no idea. He was just trying to get the pussy, and my dumb ass gave it to him. He was huge in the dick department, and eventually I got into the swing of things. Again and again, that brotha knew how to pound a pussy in. That's what he used to call it.

He was so good, that he not only owned my pussy, but my heart. At 17, I guess I could've been scared when I came up pregnant. But Diallo was my everything. I just knew he would do right by me.

What I found out instead was the quickest way to get a dog to run and hide, is to tell him you're pregnant. He stopped picking me up from school, and stopped calling altogether. He even slammed the door in my face when I went to his mother's house where he lived.

I was hurt, and every day I stood in the mirror after taking a shower, watching as my stomach got bigger, it was like feeling the rejection all over again.

Mama caught on pretty soon, even though I tried to hide my stomach by wearing some of my friend Leon's sweatshirts. She didn't yell at me or anything. She didn't have to, because she had a way of saying things with a tone that had the same effect. She just kept talking about how she was gonna get me out of the house and into this place where fast-ass girls like me went to get their situations taken care of. I knew she was talking about me getting an abortion. But I remembered how painful it was for a girl I knew at school, and how raw she felt afterward. I'd be damned if I was gonna go through that myself. This was my mistake, and I wasn't afraid to feed it or clothe it.

I waited until Mama said she had made arrangements to send me away. I told her that I wasn't going anywhere. I said that I knew of a girl in my situation who still went to school and worked at night. She was taking care of her business.

That's when Mama drew back, and I guess all the pain and embarrassment of my pregnancy, plus her own unhappiness with my daddy must have been packed in her hand, because she popped me dead in my mouth.

I couldn't believe that Mama, a Christian woman—could want me to abort my baby just to save her the embarrassment of us being seen as one of *those* families. And yet she cursed me, using language that would normally make her blush, calling me all kinds of bitches and whores. And while she's staring at me, I'm seeing something behind her eyes that I'd never seen before. I knew she saw me as a disappointment.

Of all the days he could've come home early, Daddy picked *that* day.

"Your fast-ass daughter here done got herself knocked-up!" Mama screamed at Daddy.

Before I had the chance to look at his face, I felt a fist hit the side of my head. I hit the floor. Daddy pulled me by my arms, but I was trying to turn loose, so, he grabbed fistfuls of my hair. I was afraid that I wouldn't have any hair left when he was through with me.

He started kicking me; his anger was so wild that I don't think he cared where his foot stomped me. I covered my stomach, trying to avoid the wash of stomps.

I looked up; the room was blurry through my tears as I

saw Mama watching me get beat. Then, she took her car keys and left for work.

"Now this is what you're gonna do," he told me at the end. "You're gonna go upstairs and pack your shit, and take your ass over to that nigga's house who did this to you. And he better not set foot in my house or I will shoot the motherfucker where he stands, do you hear me?"

I was crying so hard, that all I could do was mumble. In my mind I was saying, "Yeah, Daddy," but I don't think it came out that way.

I limped upstairs to the bathroom to wash the blood off my face. My lips were busted. How in the hell could he do that to a 17- year-old girl, and a pregnant one at that?

As soon as I saw my eye was swollen shut, I sank to the floor. I must have been crying in that bathroom for hours because at some point my seven-year-old sister, Marva, came in there.

Here I was slumped on the floor, and that little bitch just stands on her tippy-toes so she can wash her hands for dinner. She didn't say anything to me, probably afraid my daddy would get in her ass, too.

I called my friend Rexanne. She was in a program that gave her a place to stay since she was emancipated from her parents. They threw her out when they found out she liked females. Found out? Rexanne was more masculine than a lot of dudes in the neighborhood. You mean to tell me that it took her parents coming home and catching her with her face in some girl's pussy to figure that out?"What's the matter?" she asked once she picked up and heard me crying on the phone.

"I need a favor."

"What?"

"Can I stay with you for a while? My daddy just beat the shit out of me because he found out I'm pregnant. He's kicking me out the house."

"What the fuck, man! You ain't called the police on that motherfucker?"

"No, Rexanne. I don't need no more trouble. Can I stay with you or not?"

"Of course you can. You can stay for as long as you want."Rexanne came and got me and I moved me and my few bags to her place. Since I didn't drive, she took me to all my doctors' appointments. Here I was, seven months pregnant, hormones all out of control and depressed because I was on my own, feeling like damaged goods. I couldn't understand why Daddy not only beat me the way he did, but also threw me out the house. I thought blood was supposed to be thicker than water.

I'd started to think that she was beginning to have feelings for me. I ain't gonna lie, if Rexanne had been just Rex, meaning if she were a guy, I could have seen myself with someone like her. She acted like a real man, but she was tender, too. She thought about me before she thought about herself. No man had ever treated me like that before.

In a way, Rexanne was what I envisioned my perfect man to be. She told me a woman could eat pussy better than a man because a woman has one and knows what feels good. My dumb ass let her try and prove it.

One night, Rexanne brought some Courvoisier home. I don't know how she managed to get alcohol because she was only 18, but she was always drinking the hard stuff that could put hair on the chest of most men. Since I was feeling lower than low, I thought, "fuck everything," and started drinking. As the night wore on, Rexanne started inching herself closer and closer to me. She put her arm around me and her warm breath tickled my ear. She told me that I was beautiful, even though I sure didn't feel that way. With all the drama I had endured with the men in my life, that night, I could understand why some women preferred other women. Rexanne had been so good to me and I trusted her. I knew she liked me, and I figured since she wasn't hitting me up for any rent money, it was the least I could do, and I was a little curious see if a woman could please another woman. Rexanne was all I had at the time, and she was doing her damndest to make me forget about all of my troubles.

I was good and drunk.. As we talked, I saw her licking her lips, the way Diallo used to. "What would you do if I were to kiss you, right now?" she asked.

"I'd say do what you gotta do," I said.

I sat up, wondering for a short moment if I really should have been doing what I was doing. Her eyes were so kind, I didn't mind it when she leaned in, took my face in her hands and kissed me. Her lips were soft; I just closed my eyes and went with it.

When she tried to put her tongue in my mouth, that's when I pulled away.

"Naw, naw, baby. Just relax. You need to leave them jive-niggas alone. They can't make you feel the way I can."I felt helpless as my body shivered. She looked at me with those eyes that usually seemed so suspicious, but were suddenly loving and tender. When she unbuttoned my shirt, I became embarrassed of how big my stomach was. I began trying to close my shirt back up, but she brushed my hands away.

"Naw, don't do that. You need to get off that kick of thinkin' you're ugly. I think you're beautiful."

She got down on the floor and slid my pants and panties down. I could feel my heart beating as she ran her hands between my legs. She leaned in and blew on my pussy. At first I thought, "What the hell is this bitch doing?" but then she took her fingers and started pumping me and rubbing my clit. It had been so long since I'd had anything in there. Spasms of pleasure shot through me as I arched my back the best I could. She buried her face in my stuff and ate me out like it was her last meal.When she raised her head up from her feast, her face was glistening from my wetness. Then she tried to kiss me again, but I was like, "Oh, hell no."

She got up from the floor and sat back down next to me. I struggled to pull my panties and pants back up, and re-buttoned my shirt. She just stared at me with this shit-kicking grin on her face.

"So, how'd you like that? Am I good or am I good?" she asked, like she had just given the pussy eating of a lifetime.

"It was good," I said, not knowing what else to say. I didn't like the smile on her face. It was like she was saying, "Yeah, I got this bitch." I was doing *her* a favor.

After that night, Rexanne started acting like we were boyfriend and girlfriend; coming up behind me and wrapping her arms around me, kissing my neck, grabbing my booty. I had to fix that right away.

"Listen, Rexanne, I ain't gonna lie. I enjoyed the other night. But I'm not like you; I like guys, always have and always will."

"You weren't talking that shit when you were moanin'

my name," she said.

"I may have been moaning, but I know I didn't call out your name. Now that's just something I wouldn't damn do."

"What you sayin,' that it was just a fling?"

"I was depressed and feeling sorry for myself. It was an experiment. A lot of people experiment."

"So what, you're sorry you did it?" she asked me. Rexanne sounded hurt.

"No. You're my friend. I wouldn't have done it with just anybody. But you need to understand that it was just one time."

Rexanne smiled and said, "We'll see."

On November 20, 1974, I gave birth to a son. I named him Lawrence because I always liked that name, and I thought it would fit him because I was going to raise him to know how to treat women; a gentleman's name for a future gentleman.

I called Diallo's mother to tell her that Diallo had a son. She sighed wearily into the phone.

"Now, are you sure it's his?"

"Yes, Ma'am. He took my virginity," I said, embarrassed to have to explain myself to this woman I didn't know.

"No, you probably just gave it away. Well, that's a shame. The last girl callin' here talkin' 'bout she pregnant, was a damn lie."

"Well, I'm positive; Diallo's the father because he's the only one I've been with."

"He needs to learn to wear a rubber since he can't trust you girls to take care of your own business! Anyway, I'll tell him you called!" And then she hung up. I was made to feel dirty about something that really was only half my fault. My mother came by the hospital, but I really wish she hadn't. I couldn't forget looking up to see her grab her keys and dip out while I was getting beat within an inch of my life. She brought a bag of clothes for Lawrence. I told her she could just put the bag on the chair. I guess I said it with an attitude because when she left, she took the clothes with her. Still, there was no sign of Diallo. That fool couldn't be bothered to even come by to look at the baby.

Maybe I had it coming. But I thought that maybe when he saw the baby it would hit home that responsibilities awaited him. But no, he disappeared into a mob of his doggish friends who probably encouraged him to act like that.I decided cutting my losses with Diallo was the best thing I could do for me and my son. For our sakes it would have to be.

CHAPTER

2

I DIDN'T HAVE TO SIT through an episode of *Good Times* to know that things were bad for black folks. I lived it.

It was May of 1975, and I was walking around with a six-month-old on my hip, no job, and staying with Rexanne. There was still no involvement from Diallo, though I did run into him at the grocery store one day.He looked down at Lawrence who was sitting in the shopping cart, playing with a bag of chips. "This him?" he asked me.

"Why do you gotta ask such a stupid-ass question? Who else would he be?"He picked him up and held him. Standing in the middle of the grocery store aisle, he actually looked like a proud, new father. He offered me a ride home; this after telling me how fine I looked, and that he couldn't tell that I'd even had a baby.

"Oh? Now you wanna be helpful?"

"Come on, now. My mama's been sick," he said, avoiding my eyes. Any other time he'd proudly flash those green eyes of his."What's wrong with her?" I asked, taking Lawrence back and putting him back in the cart. I put his pacifier in his mouth because his little face had started to squinch up, like he wanted to start crying.

"She's got diabetes. Yeah, she ain't been doin' too good," he said, looking at me for the first time. "Listen, I know I

11

fucked up. My sister's been raisin' all kinds of hell, telling me what a bum I am."

"She's right," I said, laughing in his face.

When we got to the checkout line, I pulled out my food stamps. I'd put off going on welfare for as long as I could, but finally realized that I had to do what I had to do. He looked horrified and probably sensed my embarrassment. He went into his pocket and pulled out a wad of money, saying, "I got it." He looked at me, smiling as though he had just made the grandest gesture. If I was supposed to be impressed, I wasn't.

"So what about that ride home?" he said, smiling that sly, doggish smile of his.I accepted the ride home. I figured it was the least his black ass could do. I sat quietly while he tried to make small talk."Why you so quiet?" he asked.

"I don't have anything to say to you."

"Then why in the hell did you accept a ride from a nigga if all you was gonna do is be rude and shit?"

"Excuse me for not thinking you giving me a ride is anything special! I took the ride because I get real sick and tired of trying to get home with a six-month-old and a ton of groceries! I'm sick of people on the bus sitting there on their asses, looking stupid when it's obvious I could use a seat, or even a hand!" That shut Diallo right up. He just shook his head and kept his eyes on the road. When we got to the apartment, he insisted on helping me put everything away, as if I didn't know where fruits and vegetables or lunch meat went.

"Okay, thanks," I said, motioning him to the door as soon as the last piece of food was stored away. He started smiling again, as though he were hatching a plan. He started looking around the apartment like he was expecting someone to burst in.

"Where's your roommate?"

"She ain't here," I said, giving him the best no-nonsense look I could.

"You wanna do something?"

"Do what, Diallo?"

He walked in closer and squeezed my booty, licking his lips in that sexy way of his.

"Why don't you gimme some of this ass right quick," he said, his hands still on my booty.

"Negro, please! You can't even help me take care of the baby we got, but you expect me to give you some?"

Just then, Rexanne came through the door, which startled both of us. I was glad to see her because then I wouldn't have to fight him off me, or worse, let those green eyes seduce me into some bullshit. She wore shorts and a T-shirt. She must've had one of her lesbian friends cornrow her hair because it looked freshly done.

"Who's this?" Rexanne asked, all wide-eyed.

"This is Diallo, and he was just leaving," I said.

"Shake the scene, Turkey," Rexanne said, posturing like she was ready to throw down.Diallo began to chuckle like she was the biggest joke in the room. "Eh, man, who is this jive-ass, dykey broad?"

"She's done more for me than you have!" I said.

"You've been lettin' this bitch eat your pussy or somethin'?"

"Fuck you, boy!" Rexanne said as she popped him on the side of the head.

Diallo looked stunned that a female had put her hands on him. Then I saw something snap in him and his eyes got really evil looking, like the devil had entered his body. Rexanne pushed Diallo out the door, slamming it shut. Diallo beat on that door. I was afraid he was going to kick it down.

"Open up this door, bitch! Motherfucker, you wanna act like a man, I'll treat you like one!"

"Diallo, get out of here before I call the police!" I screamed through the door.

"Yeah, go ahead and do that shit! Call those pigs and tell them this bulldagger put her hands on me. Funky-ass bitch don't know who she's fuckin' with!"Diallo must have stayed out there for another ten minutes. "I'm gonna get your ass for that, bitch! Just you wait!" he screamed, kicking the door one final time before leaving. Rexanne walked around the apartment, her chest stuck out like she had won the victory.

"Rexanne, you shouldn't have hit him," I said.

"Man, fuck that punk. He had no business in my house in the first place."

"He was giving me a ride home. In case you didn't know, it's hard shopping with a baby."

"You're takin' rides from that nigga now? This, after you cry to me about how he's no good and ain't livin' up to his responsibilities. Boy or girl, it doesn't matter, I don't let anybody talk shit to me in my own house, and if you don't like it, you can run your ass right after him."

She had a point. It was her house. But she still didn't have to hit him. I was scared for her because Diallo wasn't playing. And he was right; she didn't know who she was fucking with.

CHAPTER

3

DURING THE REST OF THE summer, Rexanne began to change. Sometimes I'd catch her staring at me, like I was dog shit she'd stepped in. When I asked her if I'd done something to her, she said, "I dunno. *Did* you do something to me?"

I told her no, and she said, "All right then." If she wasn't working downtown at the McDonald's, she was spending time with her lesbian friends. I think she was talking shit to them about me because the couple of times they came inside the apartment, they looked at me funny.

I wasn't convinced that we were cool, especially the night she came home drunk, talking mess.

"Why is this house so nasty? You could clean up around here since you don't do shit else."

"What the hell is your problem?" I asked her.

"I'm still pissed that you let that lowlife into my house."

"What's this 'my' house stuff? I thought you wanted me to feel like it was our house?"

"Bitch, you don't pay no kind of bills around here. You think that little money you get from the state helps out around here?"

"First of all, you got one time to call me a bitch. Secondly, you wouldn't even have this place if your parents didn't throw your pussy-sniffing ass out! You don't pay any rent your damn self, in fact, the state pays for this apartment!"

Rexanne got quiet and started chewing on her tongue like she did when she was pissed.

"Cheryl, this ain't about a program. This is about you being so desperate for dick that you'll lay with the nigga that knocked you up, but who ain't doin' nothing else for you!"

"Rexanne, I told you, he just gave me a ride home."

"He probably couldn't fuck you no way; your pussy's probably all stretched out and shit!"

I just looked at her. All this stuff she was saying seemed to be coming out of leftfield. I could feel the tears coming, but I didn't want her to have the satisfaction of seeing them fall. I looked around for my baby, the one person who loved me unconditionally. He was just as happy to be fed and played with. He wasn't coming at me with foolishness.

I picked Lawrence up from his playpen. He looked at me with a confused look on his face. "I know it, baby. This bitch is crazy," I said in a hushed tone, hoping he wouldn't cry.

Rexanne took out a cigarette and lit up. "Yeah, your slutty ass thinks you're little Miss Goldie-Cocks and shit," she said, her voice thick with cigarette smoke as she exhaled.

"That don't make any kind of sense, what you just said," I said as I bounced Lawrence up and down in my lap. I was done. If she wanted to be nasty, then so be it, because I knew she was hitting below the belt. Maybe she thought I should be more grateful. The truth was that I was grateful. But now, it seemed like all she'd done for me had strings attached. As the days went by she became more and more jealous, starting when Diallo came to the apartment. But it didn't stop there.

There was a guy named Glenn who I'd met in July. He was a positive brotha, trying to get through school and working two jobs. He wasn't that cute, but I respected the fact that he was trying to do something besides stand on the street corners with his boys and get into trouble.

He told me that he thought it was important for my son to have a father, but since Diallo wasn't around, Glenn said he'd like to be that figure for Lawrence. Almost immediately, Rexanne started dropping attitude and scared Glenn away. I think she thought that my baby and me would live happily-ever-after with her in that cramped apartment.

Didn't she think about the possibility of me meeting someone? Forget about me, what if she wanted to date someone? All those bitches she ran through, trying to turn them out, surely she'd find someone to fall in love with. But no, she thought that because she ate my pussy one good time, she owned me.

Her jealousy inspired her to start doing some crazy stuff. I found a couple pairs of my panties in her sock drawer. It was like all of a sudden I'm missing some panties. I thought maybe some pervert in the building had stolen them from the dryer in the laundry room. But then I thought, "Let me see if this bitch got my shit." And sure enough, they were in her drawer. She was probably taking them out the dirty clothes hamper and sniffing them with her nasty, crazy ass. After that, we pretty much shunned each other. But one night, I woke up to find her all hunched over, breathing hard. I broke the three-week silence and asked, "What's wrong?"

"Leave me the fuck alone!" she screamed at me before slamming the bedroom door closed.

I waited a half hour before I crept over to her room and opened her door. When I saw her, her face was jacked up and she looked unrecognizable. Her braids looked all raggedy and her work shirt was torn and covered with blood splotches. I saw her struggling to take it off and getting frustrated with herself for not being able to. I just stood there quietly in the darkness of the hall and watched. She didn't believe in wearing bras, so when she finally got the shirt off I could see her titties and arms were all bruised. Same thing with her thighs when she pulled her pants off. She looked so pitiful that it didn't matter that we hadn't been talking; I wanted to cry for her and help.

"Girl, what happened to you?" I asked as I burst into her room.

She looked at me, startled at first, but then her face relaxed as best it could before she said, "Aw, I got into it with some niggas and I guess I got the worse end of it," she said, looking away, trying to hide her bloodshot eyes. I could tell she was trying to put on a brave front. I don't know why she bothered, because it didn't save her from getting her ass whipped.

"They were just talkin' a lot of jive, Cheryl."

"Bullshit. They did more than talk jive, Rexanne."

"I just said they whipped my ass, what else do you want me to say?"

"Did you call the police?"

She shook her head no.

"Do you want me to call the police?"

"Naw, I want you to get the fuck out of my room. Ain't shit changed, bitch!"

I felt like my feet were stuck. I just stared at her, not knowing who this crazy broad was anymore. I was sad that this had happened to her, but me and my baby didn't need this shit. I knew then and there we had to move.

As far as Rexanne, I didn't bother to ask her anything else. If she wanted me to know what happened then she could tell me when she was ready. But I wasn't gonna hold my breath.

CHAPTER

4

REXANNE WAS STILL ACTING CRAZY. I wasn't allowed any visits or calls unless they were from females, and besides Rexanne, I didn't have any female friends. I always felt girls were bitchy, insecure, and dramatic. You know, like thinking that you're trying to take their man. But I figure it this way, if you gotta be worried about some other woman coming along to take your man, he ain't meant for you to have; maybe *you* ain't doing something right.I'd been feeling trapped, but the last person I thought I'd call was my mama. She hadn't seen Lawrence since she came to the hospital, so she invited me over to the house.

"Let me hold my grandbaby," Mama said.

"Be careful with him," I said as she yanked him out of my arms.

"Girl, please. I got three chil'ren of my own and all ya'll are alive."

I just smiled. "Where's Marva at?"

"She's down the street playing with her friend. I told her you were coming."

"It'd be nice to see her."

"Are you still over there with Roxanne?"

"It's *Rexanne*, Mama."

"Whatever her name is, are you still over there?"

I couldn't answer her. She was being so nice that I didn't want to ruin the mood by talking about my problems. But mamas know. As she held Lawrence, she stared at me like she was trying to read my face.

"Ya'll ain't getting along?"

"Mama, she's crazy. She must think she's my man or something."

"You had no business taking your behind over there."

I just rolled my eyes. Maybe if *she* hadn't been so quick to run off when Daddy was beating me, he wouldn't have kicked me out and I wouldn't have had to leave in the first place.

"You know, I feel as though I've done the best that I can do with you and I can't do any more. I'm just gonna send it up to God in prayer."

As Mama spoke, my stomach hurt. I felt the way I did a year before my son was born. She was always judging me; always talking that religion. As if that ever made anybody's life better. Most Christian folk I knew were hypocrites. They'd be the first ones to tell me that my soul was lost for having my baby outside of marriage, yet Daddy sat and drank with most of them Monday through Saturday at the bar.Even if I was going to hell, I knew these same so-called Christians would lead the way, and probably bust the gates wide open.

I knew Mama meant well, but how could she say she did the best she could when she couldn't even talk to me about boys, sex, or even how to use a tampon?

"You need Jesus," she said to me, bringing me out of my thoughts.

"I got Jesus, Mama."

"Girl, you ain't even saved. God forbid something happens to you, where do you think you'll spend eternity?"

"I think I'd go to Heaven."

"How you figure that? You ain't been baptized yet."

"I feel like God knows my heart."

"That's all right. Just know that in the last days when Jehovah swings His mighty scythe, all you heathens are gonna be sorry. You're about as lost as two left shoes."

Just then, the doorbell rang. I was glad too, because I didn't know how to respond to that. The ladies from church had come over for Ladies Bible Study. Mama had a nice spread of turkey breasts, ham, fried chicken wings, green bean casserole, and deviled eggs. For desert, she had made a sweet potato pie.

As the ladies started to arrive, I had to put on my happy face. I hadn't seen many of them since Daddy kicked me out. I was so busy trying to survive that I didn't have time to go to church.

The ladies made me laugh. They had that old lady smell that they tried to cover with too much perfume. And the old hags loved to get up in other people's business. While Mama set up her little film projector, the ladies got down to talking about a woman who wasn't there named Juanita Alexander. They said her daughter was selling her butt down on Hennepin Avenue to support her drug habit. They said something about her having some nasty women's disease. Then they started in on how Juanita always expected somebody to pick her up for church service, but she never came out her pocket to offer gas money. They said that her breath stunk like something died and lay rotting inside her mouth. Mama let them say what they felt like saying, but she never commented. I guess she figured, those that gossip to you will gossip about you, and she didn't feel comfortable gossiping with people she made extra money off of by selling cosmetics.

Daddy came home from work and started acting like a rooster around a bunch of old hens. He smoothed his wavy hair down with the palms of his hands, like he wanted those women to know that he had good hair. I guess that pomade and stocking cap paid off.

Since he felt he had an audience, he acted thrilled to speak to me.

"Cheryl? Is that really you?" he said, like he hadn't seen me in years.

"Hey, Daddy," I said as he hugged me tightly. I put on a fake-ass smile as I stood stiff in his embrace. When he kissed me on the cheek, I wanted to throw up.

While the ladies passed Lawrence around, I took the punch bowl into the kitchen to refill it. Daddy came in there, and the smile on his face disappeared.

"Don't get too comfortable," he said as he pulled two cans of beer from the fridge and stuffed them in his pants pockets.

"Still drinking, I see," I said.

"Bitch, don't you worry about what I'm doin.' You just track down the daddy to that bastard son of yours," he hissed. "That is, if you can keep your legs closed long enough to look!"

"Old man, I hope your fucking heart blows up in your chest," I said, trying to keep my voice down.

He raised his hand like he wanted to slap me, but then Mrs. Moore came in. Just in time, too.

"'Scuse me, baby, but do ya'll have any hot sauce? I just love your mama's cooking," she said.

Daddy lowered his hand and pretended like he was picking something out of my hair.

"Cheryl, Baby-love, it looks like you got something in your hair," he said as he gave my hair a hard yank.

"Thank you, Daddy, I got it," I said, leaning back from him. I quickly opened the cabinet and got the hot sauce.

I knew that nigga thought he was slick, but Mrs. Moore wasn't a dummy. I could tell from her face that she knew she'd walked in on something.

"Cheryl, we're old, baby, we ain't tryin' to die of thirst," she said, giving me a wink.

I picked up the filled punch bowl, but couldn't help but turn around to see my father, standing there, looking pissed off.

"Cheryl, I'm fixin' to go upstairs and take me a nap. You probably won't be here when I wake up, will you?"

I knew what Daddy was trying to say in a roundabout way. "Nope," I said, clutching the punch bowl.

Later when my mama's Bible study was winding down, I saw Mrs. Bagley sitting by herself, sucking on a chicken bone. She looked up at me sweetly and said, "Darlin,' who's the baby's father?"

"His name is Diallo," I said, noticing the sudden hush in the living room.

"Where he at?"

"Don't know, don't care."

"They're just having a little spat. You know how these young kids are. Today they argue, tomorrow they make up," Mama said.

"Mama, you don't have to make excuses for us. You know Diallo's jive-ass ain't shit."

When I said that, it looked like the blood had left Mama's face, but the ladies giggled.

After everyone left, I helped Mama clean up. Mostly I cleaned up and my mother played with my son. I was trying to finish quick because I didn't want Daddy waking up to start more arguments. As soon as I was done, Mama reached inside her pocketbook and handed me two twenties.

"Here, take this," she said.

"Thank you," I said, taking it quickly as though she was gonna change her mind.

"I'm gonna pray for you. You don't see it now, but God has a plan for you. So you keep holding on to His unchanging hand."

"Yeah, okay, Mama."

"You did a good job cleaning up. And all the ladies told me how pretty you look."

"That's nice. Tell them I say thank you."

"Listen, Cheryl, don't pay your daddy no mind, you hear?"

"I ain't thinking about Daddy."

"He's just a little disappointed right now."

"Like you?"

"You're my child and I love you. Maybe I could have handled things differently, but what's done is done."

"Yeah, it's too late to go back."

"But your daddy loves you, in his own crazy way," Mama said chuckling.

"I can't tell. Stomping me half to death ain't a love I want."

"What you need to do is just *let go, and let God*, baby. You got too much anger in you."

Once again my mama was turning her head from shit. "You need to pray that God will soften your daddy's heart."

"That ain't gonna do no good. Look what he's put you through." As soon as I said that, I regretted it, because Mama bowed her head in shame.

"Just do this for me, make sure you find you a decent man who will respect you and not put you through all kinds of changes like your father did me." She pointed her finger upward as though I didn't know who she was talking about.

I reached in and gave her a hug. It felt good to be back in her good graces. I didn't understand a lot of what she did, but I understood the spirit she did it in.

I could hear Daddy snoring upstairs as Mama went into the family room to lie down. I thought about her request, which made me think of my son. He needed a father, and I needed someone I could stand still with; someone I could depend on. The question was: Did I deserve any better, or was I doomed to a lifetime of Diallos?I hoped the God my mama believed in, and that even I believed in to a degree, would bring me somebody. But the first thing I needed to do was get my act together. I knew I needed to go get my GED if I was gonna go to nursing school. But just as important, I had to get me and my baby the hell away from Rexanne— and quickly.

CHAPTER

5

DIALLO'S MOTHER DIED THAT FALL, and I guess he decided to step up to the plate and be a man. He wasn't giving me much money, which wasn't a surprise, but at least he was in his son's life, and there were times when he would drop his son off with a bag of clothes and toys. Thankfully Rexanne wasn't there.

I wasn't jumping for joy and praising him for something he should've been doing in the first place. But, if it took her dying to get him to do what he needed to do, then that part was a good thing.

~ * * * ~

I had started dancing at the Land-O-Ladies strip joint. It wasn't anything I'd set out to do, but the tension and stress of living with Rexanne had gotten to such a high point, I wanted to make some quick money so that I could save for a place of my own, just in case social services couldn't help me.

I was on my way to catch the bus after talking with my case worker, when I saw this greasy-ass, fat, balding white man standing outside the club talking with some of the customers and smoking a cigarette. Dewey was his name.

He had a bushy mustache and one of those hardened, beet-red faces that made you want to throw cold water on it. He stopped me dead in my tracks and told me that I looked like "chocolate delight." He said that they didn't really have any black dancers working in his place, but he'd received a lot of requests for them. He asked me if I didn't have anywhere else to be at the moment, could I come in to talk.

When I went in that club, it was lit with red lights. There was a small bar off to the side with maybe four men sitting there smoking and drinking. The two girls trolling around there looked like a hundred miles of bad road. I mean, those bitches were walking around with stretch marks on their belly fat that hung out like they had just given birth. I could've sworn that one looked like she had cigarette burns all up and down her legs.We sat at a table near the main stage, which looked like four or five, rickety, big, black boxes pushed up against one another.

He cut to the chase. He told me that he believed in the civil rights movement and liked women from all across the rainbow. He said that my name should be "Chocolate Drop."

"I can already see you'll be one of my biggest money makers," he told me.

"There's nobody in here, though," I said, looking around the room at the pitiful attendance.

"Well, it's the middle of the day, sweetheart. Now listen, you're one sexy lil' mama, but before you debut in front of a full house, I gotta see if you have anything to show."

"What, right here?" I asked.

"Yep. Just climb up on the stage so I can see what you're working with."

"Wait a minute. Before I do all that, how much money can I make?"

Dewey sized me up with a smirk. "I'd say about a couple hundred a week."

I smiled at him. That was a lot of money to me, seeing as how I didn't have a job and was on welfare.

Working in that business, he'd seen plenty of girls strip before, so he didn't seem fazed. He must have sensed that I was nervous because he put his left hand on my shoulder, almost like a father would a daughter. I noticed he had a wedding ring. His fingers were like Vienna sausages and it looked like the ring was cutting off his circulation.I took off my blouse and bra and stared straight ahead, trying to ignore those fools sitting at the bar, who had turned from their drinks and looked at me like they'd never seen titties before. I imagined myself on a fashion show runway, like Naomi Sims or Beverly Johnson. I was nervous as hell. I glanced down at Dewey, who had a smirk on his face. He was enjoying the fact that I was uncomfortable; I wouldn't have been surprised if his dick was hard from it.

My first dance was a little rough, I ain't gonna lie, but, he must've liked what he saw because he gave me the gig: dancing for ridiculous-ass men who couldn't get laid, or, who had their suburban life but wanted a thrill, or guys who'd rather put their child support in a G-string than do right by their kids.

After working at Land-O-Ladies for two months, I had made pretty good money. I even had a few regulars.There was this white guy named Alex who always asked for me. If any of the other girls asked for a dance, he'd say, "No, I'm waiting for Chocolate Drop." He was straight-laced, wore glasses, and looked like a college professor. He was very respectful and talked to me like I was a human being and not just a piece of pussy to be had. Sometimes we talked about his loneliness, me wanting to be in the medical field or my son. He told me that he was happy that I wanted to do something productive with myself and even offered to help me go to school. He told me he could see us together, and that's when I knew he had feelings for me. I never thought of myself with a white man. He wasn't bad looking at all, but he wasn't my type. I liked the bad boys and Alex seemed stiff and needy.That's about the time when a lot of the other girls' jealousy came out, like it was my fault they couldn't get any of those men to buy a dance from them. Instead of getting their own acts together, a lot of them were self-medicating; in the back doing lines of cocaine, or out at the bar drinking and getting faded alongside the patrons. I don't know how they expected to be able to dance for somebody, looking all sloppy and shit.

But for some of the girls, it wasn't about the dancing. They were selling themselves. And to look at some of the men who came in there, you could tell that to them, a hole was a hole. And, it didn't matter what was attached to that hole as long as they could get their dicks wet in it.This one girl went by the name "Vanilla Fudge" because she was mixed race. She was pretty, like me, but she was one of the main ones turning all kinds of tricks. And she wasn't even trying to be discreet with hers, neither. She'd get fucked in people's cars, or suck somebody's dick out back by the dumpster. One night she came in with cum all over her mouth. She was dabbing at it with a Kleenex, trying to be dainty about it, but I could tell she was strung out. I don't know why Dewey let her walk around like that, but he must've known what he was doing, because he never got raided by the cops—at least not while I was there.

Alex came over to me and asked me for a dance. He was different though. He looked and acted like he was on something. He kept trying to kiss me, and even tried to stick his finger inside my G-string. I slapped him in his face and ran away. Why did these men think that because they gave you a little piece of money they own you?I ran in the back and didn't come out until he left. I should've had the bouncer throw his ass out, but I knew the drugs were making him act that way. I figured if he went home and slept it off, when I saw him again he'd be normal.I danced a little bit more that night, but I know I did a bad job because I wasn't into it, and it showed in my tips, which weren't much. Even though I was taking my clothes off and dancing, I was trying to conduct myself like a lady, but for the first time I felt dirty.

At the end of the night, I was looking for Dewey so that I could give him his cut because Roslyn, the house mother, had thrown up all over the damn place and gone home early. Nobody knew where he was. I went up to Sylvia, one of the older, broken-down looking girls. and she was damn near passed out at the bar. She picked her head up and said, "Girl, you know I don't keep tabs on him," and put her head back down.

My head was hurting so bad, I needed fresh air, so I went toward the back door. There I saw Dewey, smoking a cigarette and talking with Melanie, this stripper who was cute but dumber than a bag of rocks."Dewey, I need to go home. Here's your bread, baby," I said, trying to be sweet. He took out his money clip and put the money I gave him in it. He walked me out back because it was quicker to cut through the alley to get to my bus stop."What's wrong with you tonight?" Dewey asked, throwing his cigarette down to the ground and grinding it with his heel.

"It's late and I'm tired," I said.

"Aw, baby, you're too young to be tired. Do you want me to get a bouncer to give you a ride home?"

"No, I'll be all right. I'll just take the bus. The walk will be good for me. I need to clear my head."

"Anything I can help you with?"

"Nope."

"Okay, then. Have a good one, beautiful." Dewey kissed me on the cheek, took out his keys, and made his way to the door and went in.I looked around to see if anyone was lurking in the shadows because you never knew. As I proceeded toward the alley, a silver Corvette turned into it, blocking me. Alex got out of the car, looking a little bit normal, but still had an edge to him.

"Hello, Cheryl," Alex said.Who the fuck told him my name?

"It's Chocolate Drop to you, Alex. We all got names for a reason."

"What, it's all right for you girls to know our names but we can't know yours?"

I must have given him the dirtiest look because he said, "Sorry—Chocolate Drop. Can I talk to you?"

"I just wanna go home, Alex," I said, backing up toward the club.

"Just five minutes?"

I rolled my eyes. I was tired as hell and just wanted to get home to my son. I wasn't interested in anything he had to say. But, on the other hand, he did spend a lot of money on me—and me alone. I thought that I owed him that. What would five minutes hurt?

"I just wanted to apologize for before. You know that I don't usually act like that."

"You fucking scared me in there, Alex. I trusted you," I said as I stopped walking backward.

"And you still can. I love you, don't you know that? Why else do you think I spend all my time and money on you?"

"Look, Alex, I appreciate all of that and stuff, but I never asked you to do any of that. You did that of your own free will."

"Listen, you said you wanted to go to nursing school. I

meant what I said; you can quit dancing and you can move in with me and I'll help you out."

"Alex, you know, I'm really flattered, but I don't feel that way toward you."

Suddenly, Alex's eyes became narrow; there was a dangerous edge to his voice as he began to say, "You don't want me to go away feeling like a schmuck, do you?"

"I don't think you should feel like that. I don't think you're a schmuck," I said.

"Then don't you think it's only fair that I get something out of the deal, and we can call it even-Stephen," Alex said, sounding irritated.

"What do you want?"

"Just let me have one night. I promise that after that, I'll leave you alone."

"No, you won't, Alex. You know you wouldn't be satisfied with just one time."

"That wasn't a request," Alex said, grabbing my arm.

"Motherfucker, let go of me!"

"So where do you want to do this, huh?" Alex asked, looking around wildly, ignoring my fear.

"Do what?"

"Baby, I hear you colored girls know what you're doing in the sack."

"I'm black," I said with an attitude and still struggling, "I ain't 'colored'!"

"Well, baby, we're all the same color when the lights go down. You've got such beautiful hair," he said as he ran his fingers through my hair and tried to kiss me again.

"Alex, what is wrong with you? I'm not doing that with you. Let me go!"

"Bitch, I already paid for the pussy. Now let's go to the car," he said.Who in the hell was this fool all of a sudden? It was like I was seeing him for the first time. All that chatting me up for two months he did before was just a lure. He didn't give a shit a about me. He wanted what they all wanted, and at least with some of them, they made their intentions known upfront and I could say no. But Alex had been trying to reel me in.

With my heart pounding in my chest, I broke away from him and ran back to the door of the club only to find that Dewey had locked it from the inside. Alex grabbed me by my arm again and began dragging me deeper into the alley, looking for a dark corner. He pushed me face- first against a wall as he pulled at the back of my blouse and tried to hike up the skirt I had changed into. My fear and anger charged me up with such an adrenaline rush that I elbowed him, then pulled my shoe off and began beating him in the side of the head with it. He staggered a little bit as I saw a piece of board leaning against the wall. I picked it up and tried to hit him with it. He caught it as it came down, but we played tug of war with it. I wasn't about to let that motherfucker hit me with it. I brought my knee into his dick and he let go of the board. With every ounce of my soul, I beat him over and over again, and didn't give a shit where I hit him. I thought about my son, and how I knew I was going to see him again. Too many girls were getting raped in the streets or turning up missing altogether, and I sure as hell wasn't going to be next.

When he dropped to the ground, I spit on him as I put my shoe back on. It was hard for me to stand still to put it on because my body was still buzzing with anger. Once I had it on, I didn't wait around. I ran for my life; fuck Dewey, the money, and that raggedy-ass club.

After being nearly raped, my head was spinning. I didn't know where to go. There was a bunch of drag queens hanging outside this bar called Cloud Nine. I begged them to let me use a pay phone inside.

"All right, Miss girl! You *better* come over here lookin' perfected," one of them said.

"Please, I just need to use a pay phone," I said. I was crying and sweaty, so I don't know how "perfected" I could've looked at that moment.

"Darlene, let Miss Precious in to use the phone, Mama," another drag queen said.

I went in to call Diallo. It was so loud in there, I was afraid I wouldn't be able to hear him when he picked up, but the phone just rang and rang. Then I did the unthinkable, I called my mama. But Daddy answered the phone.

"Daddy," I wept into the phone.

"Yeah,"

"Please don't hang up. I need you to come and get me. Some man just tried to mess with me and I didn't know who else to call."

"Who the fuck tried to mess with you?" Daddy screamed.

"I don't know who he is, some drunk-ass white man. I was just waiting for the bus," I lied.

"Where're you at?"

"I'm on Hennepin Avenue, right outside the movie theater." I really wasn't, but my daddy wouldn't come if he knew I was standing next to a bunch of drag queens. I knew I'd have to get my ass over there before he arrived.

When Daddy showed up, he got out the car, looking like he wanted to kill somebody. He started yelling for somebody to call the police. I said that I didn't need the police. In truth, I didn't feel like telling the cops in front of Daddy that a regular customer of mine from the strip club went crazy.

If Alex had any sense, he would've limped himself back into his car and gotten the hell out of downtown before Daddy found him and did his best to knock Alex's head off.

After I convinced him that we didn't need to involve the cops, he grabbed and hugged me so tightly that I didn't think he would ever let me go. I guess he thought since he was my father it was all right for him to call me all kinds of names and kick my butt, but never a stranger. When he broke his embrace, I looked up to see that there were tears in his eyes. He looked the way he did when I used to stand on his feet on my tippy-toes and dance with him in the family room to Nat King Cole records. It was like my mama had said the afternoon of her Ladies Bible Study, that he did love me in his own crazy way. Maybe it was that Gemini in him. The two faces. Maybe the good side had won out this time.

"Where am I taking you?"

"Daddy, I wanna come home," I said.

"Yeah, I think that's a good idea."

"I need to go get my son, though, and some clothes."

When we got to the apartment, Rexanne was sitting on the sofa with her latest wench. I thought to myself, she's just as bad as a man—my dog number three. My daddy stood by the door and just gazed at the TV. I took a garbage bag and went through the closet and just threw everything my eyes saw into it. My daddy took the bag from me as I went to get Lawrence.

"Where are you goin'?" Rexanne asked me.

"I'm getting my son and a few things and then I'm gone. I wanna go home."

"So, Daddy's done let you back in?"

"Cheryl, go get the baby and let's go," Daddy said, ignoring Rexanne's attempt to start a fight. "What, you jealous? Baby, you best believe, I wait for no lady," Rexanne said, kissing her girlfriend on the lips.

"You know better than that. I told you I don't care what you do or who you do it to. It just ain't gonna be with me. I'll be back for the bigger stuff."

"Naw, you take that shit now or it'll wind up in the trash."

Rexanne was putting on a front. I guess she felt she needed to put on a show for her girl. I was too tired to argue. But for a brief moment, I couldn't help but think about the night she came in all beat up. As far as I was concerned, with all that had happened between her and me, she deserved what she got.

"You throw my son's playpen away, you're paying for it."

"Well, what do you expect me to do with it? I don't want that raggedy thing."

Daddy had come back from putting the bags in the car. The playpen was collapsible, so he just pushed it inward and carried that out, too.

"I sure hope you know who you're dealing with, because that bitch is crazy," I said to Rexanne's latest piece before leaving. Rexanne's girlfriend seemed more concerned with making sure her Lola Falana styled wig was on tight than with anything I had to say.

I got into the car and held my son tight. He was wet. That bitch had let him lay in his own piss while she was out there trying to bed that woman.

My daddy turned and smiled a tired smile before turning the ignition. He didn't say anything during the ride home and strangely, didn't ask me where I'd been coming from and I was just as glad. But when we pulled up to the house, he turned the car off and looked at me as though he'd been thinking something the entire drive home. As I turned to open my door, all the while keeping hold of my son, he grabbed my arm; his eyes were still wet from crying when he said, "Welcome home, Baby-love."

CHAPTER

6

I FEEL LIKE THIS: IF you have a child, then it's not about you anymore. That's why I didn't tell my parents that I'd been a stripper. I knew Daddy would put me out again, even though three years had passed and by 1978 it was old news, and Mama would probably just bury her head in the sand while he did it.

My son deserved some stability, and I knew that if worse came to worse, I wouldn't have any place else to go. Don't get me wrong; I wish I could've let my parents into my life. I wish I could've sat up late with Mama, eating popcorn and doing each other's hair, or help Daddy change a tire while sharing dark secrets like you see white people do on TV. But that wasn't my reality. I don't even think white people act like that in real life.I wanted Daddy to feel as though I called him first when I got into trouble; like there wouldn't have been a question in my mind. It would've done his heart proud to know that despite all the drama that had gone down between us, I still considered myself his little girl. Thank God his male ego ate that crap right up.

Daddy was spending more time at home. He still laid upstairs in the bed and drank his beer, but he wasn't out at the bars nearly as much. I guess he felt that he could make up for lost time; it seemed like he was trying to make himself a halfway decent father since he probably knew he'd been a horrible husband.

Through the beer, Daddy would try and kick knowledge at me. He'd tell me that my son and me deserved better than what Diallo was offering. I thought that was pretty damn true, since Diallo was back on the dumb shit; calling to say that he was coming for Lawrence, or had money to give me and then not showing up.

"That right there is an example of a no-good-nigga, Baby-love," Daddy said one night after a few beers. "Just remember, you can do bad all by yourself, you don't need anyone's help. You know that your mama and I will always be here if you need us, but you need to raise your son to be the kind of man you want him to be. Whatever little help that motherfucker calls himself giving you, consider that extra, but don't depend on it."

Daddy had a point.

I spent a lot of time trying to figure things out. I kept thinking about the night Alex tried to rape me, and how I was able to fight him off. I figured God deserved His credit for that, because I know that night could've gone another way altogether.

It was like what Mama used to tell us, "God won't give you more than you can handle."

Well, okay, that might be true for me, but what about those poor fools who kill themselves. Were their crosses too heavy? Why do people feel that giving up is an option? I don't care how dark things got with my family, or Rexanne, or even the stripping, I loved my life too damn much to end it. Not only that, I couldn't do that to my son. It's bad enough he didn't have a stable father figure in his life. I wouldn't rob him of his mother, too. And if I was gonna be his mother, I had to do what I had to do to better myself.I went back to get my GED. That was the easy part. They put me in a class with a bunch of folks who wanted to shuck and jive. I don't know why they even bothered coming to class. The boys were too busy trying to run lines on the girls and the girls' silly asses were falling for it. Some of those girls had kids like me. And I'm pretty sure that some of them who started the class without children, fast forward nine months and they had a baby, too. I learned that when you're trying to do something constructive with your life, you have to put blinders on, and don't take them off until you've reached your goal. I knew I needed to stay focused, or else I'd wind up in other people's messes. By the time Lawrence was four, I also had my nurse's aide certification.

~ * * * ~

Mama was still doing her Ladies Bible Studies; the strong women of faith series. I'd help cook and get everything ready. The ladies were like scavengers, acting like they hadn't eaten all day. Usually, I'd take Lawrence up to my room when they started their meeting, but this one time I shocked everyone by sitting down and listening as they talked about the Scriptures. Pretty soon the conversation turned to salvation. Mrs. Turner turned to me as I gave some food to Lawrence."Are you saved, young lady?"

"My mama told me I need to be baptized."

"You ain't been washed by the blood of the Lamb?"

"No, ma'am."

"Well, don't you think you best be gettin' a move on it? Time ain't forever."

I looked at her like she had two heads. She was just as bad as Mama. Don't get me wrong, if anybody deserved to go to Heaven, it was Mama. What she missed out on as a mother, she made up for as a Christian. After being attacked by Alex and feeling that God had blessed my life that night, I really had thought about becoming a Christian. That's all it took for me. Some people turn to the Lord when they bottom out, maybe that was my bottom, but the way my mama came at me with religion, telling me that it was the answer to everything, it made me want to run away. I figured if God really loved me, He could see that I was a good person doing the best that I could. Why would He want to throw me into a lake of fire?

"That's what's wrong with you young people today, you think that time is forever. The time is now to get your soul together. You ain't too young to burn, ya know."

I knew that I didn't want to burn forever. "Well, if I'm damned to hell forever, maybe I'll get used to the burning sensation," I reasoned.

"It doesn't work that way, baby. When you get cast into

the lake of fire, it's like the first moment the fire touches your flesh. Just think about all the agony you'll feel. You'll be begging somebody to give you a sip of water and there won't be any. You'll probably even beg to be spat upon, just for a second's relief."

I turned to look at Mama and all she did was nod her head in agreement as she gave Lawrence a cube of cheese. But then, sensing how uncomfortable I was, she changed the subject.

"Now, ya'll know that we're getting a new minister from Los Angeles this Sunday. His name is Markus Stone," Mama said.

"Girl, I was just talking to the Deacon about that. He told me you're gonna be playin' hostess to him and his wife until they can find a permanent place to stay. I hear he's a nice lookin' brotha, too."

Mama's eyes narrowed a little bit. Already this lady was trying to find out the juice. I thought God didn't like gossip. I thought He didn't like gluttony either. But I guess Mrs. Turner didn't know all that since she ran her mouth so much when she wasn't stuffing it with food. Tired-ass heifer.My sister, Marva, came swooping into the room with her drawings. Everyone could tell that she was proud of herself, and she should have been; she was a talented eleven-year-old. Her entrance seemed to break the tension. I could tell that Mama was relieved because she wasn't in the mood to answer questions. As quickly as she began talking about the new minister and his wife, she stopped.While everyone oohed and aahed over Marva's sketch of a little black girl clutching a doll, I just sat back, thinking about what Mrs. Turner had said about eternity. I didn't want to burn in hell, and if it was as painful as she'd made it out to be, I'd have my ass in church that following Sunday, and I'd jump head first into the baptismal pool myself if I had to.

That Sunday, Mama made us get up early because we had to pick up Pastor Stone and his wife from their hotel to bring them to church. She begged Daddy to be on his best behavior even though he wasn't really a Christian. Before I had my son, I used to laugh at how he would come to church service, perpetrating fraud, acting like he really loved the Lord when I knew he probably wished he was anywhere but at church. He always liked to poke his chest out; talking about things he knew nothing about, which was kind of funny since he had a stuttering problem. As much as I loved my daddy, I knew he was too dumb to realize people were laughing at him.Mama called ahead to tell the Stones to be ready at nine o'clock. And when she said nine o'clock, she meant it. We got there ten minutes early. She made me go inside the hotel and have the front desk call their room.

"Why didn't you wait for them?" Mama asked me as I got back into the car.

"They ain't ready yet," I said.

"Now how are they gonna know what car it is when they come out?"

"They're grown. They'll be all right," I said, adjusting Lawrence's little bow tie on his suit.

"Don't give me none of your sass!"

"Mama, I'll go wait for 'em," my sister Marva volunteered.

"No, you stay your ass right here," Mama snapped.

I stayed quiet. Daddy sat in the passenger seat and turned around and looked at us as if to say, "I guess she told ya'll!" And then he laughed one of those big laughs he usually laughed when he'd been drinking.

At 9:15 the pastor and his wife emerged from the hotel, looking like movie stars arriving on set to shoot a film. My mouth practically dropped to the floor of Mama's car, because the pastor was a disturbingly good looking man! I'm talking about Billy Dee Williams in *Lady Sings the Blues* fine. He wore a three-piece, dark gray suit with black sunglasses. His wife was very elegant, with hair as long as mine. I loved the black-and-white polka-dotted dress she wore. They both looked very expensively dressed. I guess being from Los Angeles, they could afford to look that way.

They marched across the street like they owned it. Pastor Stone had preached for a congregation of 1500 in Los Angeles. I was curious as to what he would think when he came to the Divine Souls of Christ Church and saw the pathetic eighty or so members we had. Mama said that part of the reason he was asked to come was to help build membership. The way that man walked toward the car made me think that he knew he would do just that.

"He looks like a faggot," Daddy said, smiling at them as

they approached the car.

"Joshua, you promised you wouldn't embarrass me. Don't start, please," Mama said.

"Clarice, I'm just callin' it as I see it. And don't *you* start."

Pastor Stone opened the door flashing a Hollywood smile. "Good morning, Christian soldiers."

"Amen," his wife said.

"Mornin' y'all," Mama said, trying to appear sophisticated through her southern drawl.

I put Lawrence in my lap as they got into the backseat with us. I looked at his wife, Dottie, and she was beautiful but I could tell right away that she had an air to her. Her nose was high in the air like she smelled something funky. She sat next to me, so, close up I could tell she wore too much makeup. She definitely didn't know how to put on her foundation. It was all slopped on, like she had put it on with a butter knife.

Pastor Stone delivered a sermon like one of those guys on television. He was so dramatic, strutting and carrying on. His wife looked on with a smirk on her face as the congregation screamed out, "Hallelujah" and "Amen."

"We're living in end times you all," the pastor said, taking out a white handkerchief and wiping the sweat from his face. "I don't think you all hear me. I said we're living in end times. Only the righteous shall go up to glory!" his voice thundered.

The congregation yipped and yelped, and even I was taken in. I looked to my left and Mama was clutching at the pew in front of her, rocking back and forth while muttering to herself, "Thank you, Jesus." Daddy was nodding off, but woke up to look at his pocket watch.

Another member of the church stood up, looking like she had cried her false eyelashes off. She had on a wig with a big ol' piece of hair falling over one eye. I called it one of her Diana Ross specials because it looked like something Diana Ross used to wear. She got up and began to speak in tongues. I had to wonder if she understood that gibberish she was saying or if she was even being sincere or if she had hypnotized herself into it because everyone else was acting as though they had lost their minds.

When the invitation to receive Jesus Christ and be

baptized was given, I froze. I wanted to go up there, but I was scared to have everyone looking at me. But then I thought about all those nasty men in the strip joint, watching me take my clothes off for them and licking their lips in that perverted way many of them did, I decided that if I could get through that, I could get through this. Slowly I rose to my feet. Mama nodded encouragingly and said, "You goin' up there?"

I nodded and she seemed pleased. As I inched myself from out of the pew and began walking down the center aisle, I noticed Pastor Stone standing up front, smiling broadly, with his hand outstretched as though he were receiving his bride.

The congregation began to sing "Just As I Am." When I got close enough, his eyes were hypnotic, beckoning me to come towards him, away from eternal damnation and into something better called salvation. As the song finished, he turned to me, beaming.

"We want to say praise God that this soul, this *sinner* has decided to walk with the Lord."

"Praise God!" the congregation yelled.

Then pastor turned to me and asked, "Do you accept Jesus Christ as your personal Savior?"

"Yes," I whispered, my body overcome by nervousness and emotion.

"Do you believe that Jesus Christ is the Son of God and that He died for the remission of your sins?"

"Yes."

"That confession brought death to our Father in heaven but will bring eternal life to you."

I went back into the little changing room to change into the baptism linens. Mrs. Bagley was happy to help me.

"Girl, this is the most important decision you're ever gonna make."I smiled at her as Pastor Stone came into the back; he had already changed into his baptism robe. He escorted me into the pool and we waited for the curtains to open. When they did, I tried my best not to look out into the audience. I just bowed my head and closed my eyes as he put his arm around me. Then, I was baptized; all that I was and all the foolishness of yesterday—gone.

Later, after all the congratulatory hugs and kisses, my family and I stood off to the side while the pastor strutted around like a peacock. He must have been full of himself since this was his first Sunday at Divine Souls of Christ church. His sermon was like nothing we'd heard before but probably needed to hear, and then he hit it out of the park with a baptism—my baptism.

Although I was scared, not knowing if I'd measure up, I was happy I did it. Mama was crying like crazy in the church but had collected herself by the time we got into the car. We had to take the Stones back to the hotel so they could get their things and then pile all of their stuff into my parents' station wagon. I sat with my son in my lap. My body shook from the adrenaline of becoming saved. "Brother Stone, I do declare, that was the sermon of sermons. And my baby is now a Christian! I am so happy this day," Mama said, looking through the rearview mirror.

"Thank you," he said. But he already knew how good he was. Dottie just stared out the window as though she had seen and heard it all before.

"Cheryl, I want you to know, I'm gonna do my best to be an example of Christian livin,' honey," Mama said.

"Me, too, baby-love," Daddy chimed in. I thought, here he goes pretending again. He knew good and well his ass wasn't a Christian. With the Stones staying with us for who knows how long, I wondered how long he could keep up appearances.

I smiled at Lawrence, who looked up at me. I wondered if he could see a difference in his mama. Then, my tears started up, flowing like water in the baptismal pool.

"Mommy, why you cryin'?" my son asked me, running his little finger down my tear-stained face.

"It's okay, baby. Mommy's happy."

CHAPTER

7

P EOPLE ARE A TRIP. I thought the point of moving back home with my parents was to give my son some stability. Instead, I got nothing but more craziness. Daddy's pretending to be something he wasn't had started to weigh on his shoulders. At first he tried to act like the best husband and father in the world. But then he started disappearing for hours at a time, usually after picking a fight with Mama. He came home one night from the bar, drunker than I'd seen him in awhile. Either he didn't realize Markus and Dottie were standing there looking at him or he didn't care. He started in on Mama about how she had us fooled; she wasn't as perfect as she made out to be. He stood in the middle of the dining room as we ate dinner, looking sweaty and swaying back and forth, telling us that my mother was a tramp."Yeah, don't be fooled. Just cuz' ya Mama goes to church don't take away from the fact that she was a real slut back in Mississippi. I bet y'all didn't know that!"

Mama didn't say anything; instead she just took a deep breath and stabbed at her cube steak with a fork. Dottie and Markus looked at each other, then at me, and all I could do was shake my head in disbelief.

"Brother Joshua, now, there's no need for all of that.

Come sit down. Your wife has fixed us such a fine dinner," Markus said.

"I already ate. She ain't even that good of a cook. I'm surprised y'all over there eatin' that slop!" And then he staggered his drunk self upstairs.

Mama looked at us with tears in her eyes. Her body shook as she threw her fork onto the plate. Then she got up and ran outside. And the madness didn't stop there.

The next thing to happen was Dottie Stone's birthday. She'd been dropping hints for weeks that her birthday was coming up. We had settled on a day out to lunch; just her husband, me, Marva and Mama. But when the day finally came, she acted bitchy because people had other things to do. Dottie's world revolved around her, so, I knew she'd act like that. She was the kind of person who'd find ways to make everything about her. If someone said they found a dead body, she'd one-up them and say she found three. Her time was very valuable and she'd act like ours wasn't. She'd wait right good until I went into the bathroom to put on my makeup, and then she'd decide she needed to get in there to put on hers. She'd stand at the door, holding her makeup bag, smiling sweetly, and start chatting me up as though she really gave a damn about what I thought about anything. Then, she'd move in closer and casually place her bag on the sink, like she's just resting it there for a second. While I'm engrossed in the conversation, she'd work her way around the mirror so that by the time I figured out what she was doing, she was front and center of the mirror and I'm the one off to the side holding an eye pencil. She took liberties because she knew that she and her husband were guests in our house, and that I wasn't going to fight her over it. After the third time, I started closing the bathroom door.

~ * * * ~

I had an important nursing test to take that would give me additional qualifications, so I couldn't go out to lunch with them. Then her husband decided he couldn't go because he was upset that his sermon didn't have the right effect when he did a rehearsal in front of us. We weren't jumping out of our seats. He decided that he wanted to stay at home and work on his sermon, but promised that he would take his wife out later that evening, which seemed reasonable to me.Daddy was at work that day, so Mama, Marva, Dottie and me piled into the car and they dropped me off at the bus stop so I could go to class, since it was in the other direction from where they were going. Mama said she'd look after Lawrence."Y'all have a good time," I said as I got out the car in time to see the bus pulling off.

"See, girl, you done messed around and missed the bus. Don't think I'm bringin' you, cuz it's out of the way."

"Mama, ya'll go ahead, I'll be fine."

Dottie started to grin and waved good-bye as they screeched off. I waited for about ten minutes until I realized that in my rush to get going I left my book bag at the house. It wasn't that far of a walk back to the house, and I figured I'd have plenty of time to catch the next bus.

When I got home, I started to go upstairs. That's when I heard this moaning and groaning coming from the guest bedroom the Stones were sleeping in. As I climbed the stairs, through the banister I saw Pastor Markus Stone with his back toward me, jerking off, wearing a pair of women's nylons pushed down to about mid-thigh. His ass was clenched tight as he thrust his pelvis. He was also wearing one of my mama's wigs that looked like a Shirley Temple curled mess on top of his head.I put my hand over my mouth, not knowing whether to ask him what the hell he was doing, or to burst out laughing. I didn't know what to do because I needed my book bag but I didn't want him to see me. I thought, "To hell with it," to myself and started to go back downstairs when I made a loud creak. As he turned around and screamed, "Sweet Jesus!" with cum dripping from his hand, I stood there like I was the one caught. For a moment I watched as he tore Mama's wig from his head and pulled the nylons up and found his robe to put on, all in a big motion.

"Sorry," I said as I started down the stairs.

"Cheryl, wait!" he yelled, running after me.

I glanced up and saw him wiping cum onto his gray-and-burgundy robe. I could see the streaks as he drew nearer.

"I can explain." He looked mortified.

"It ain't any of my business," I said, trying to turn my head from him, even though I had already seen the worst of it.

"What do you want?" he asked me, reaching out to touch me. Then he realized that he had just come on his hands and stopped himself.

"I don't want anything, I just need to get my book bag and get to class."

"Listen, my wife doesn't know. She'd *kill* me if she knew."

"What, that you're gay?"

"No, I'm not a homosexual. I just like to dress in women's clothes sometimes, that's all."

I didn't understand what he was saying, in fact, I didn't want to understand. All I could think about were the drag queens that let me in to use the phone at Cloud Nine after I was attacked by Alex. "Please don't tell anyone—*please!* I'd lose everything."

He looked so sad. It would have been funny if it wasn't so pathetic. I thought, "You should've thought about all that before you did it."

"Dottie and I have some money saved up. You know we're trying to find a place to live. You can't have it all, but I'll give you some of it."

My ears perked up. "How much?"

"I can give you a grand."

When he said that, I heard the cha-ching of a cash register. "How will you explain the money to your wife?"

"I'll think of something. Anyway, she doesn't handle the finances. I do." His chest was heaving and he was sweating.

I thought about it. It would have made my day to tell Dottie that I caught her husband jerking off, wearing a wig and pantyhose. Maybe then she'd wipe that smirk off her too-good-for-everybody face. Mama said that after I completed my course she could get me a job working at the Drake Patterson's Nursing Home, so, I would use the money for a nest egg. I didn't know how long the Stones were gonna stay, but I knew that he had just made things very uncomfortable.

"Okay," I said, trying not to appear like I was enjoying holding this over his head.

He let out a sigh of relief. "Okay, I'll have it to you by Friday." Then he turned around and went back upstairs, this time closing the bedroom door.

When that Friday came, I went into my room and found an envelope under my pillow. In it was my thousand dollar nest egg, along with a scrap of paper that read, "Thank you." Then a week later, the Stones announced that they had found a nice apartment. Two days after that, they were gone. And I kept my word; I didn't say anything to anybody. No one would've believed it anyway.

CHAPTER

8

NOBODY TOLD ME THAT LITTLE girls become grown women who model their relationships after their parents. And it would've been nice to know that those assholey traits I hated in my daddy would be what I ran toward in my men.

By September of 1979, I'd practically forgotten what sex was. I was so sexually frustrated that I went down the road of familiar territory. I slept with Diallo again. It was stupid of me, I know, but the man knew how to make me feel good.I saw him out one day with some heavyset chick and her two kids. I got pissed because he was making pitiful attempts at best to take care of his own son, and here he was running around with some other female and her children. And far be it from me to talk about another woman's children, but she needed her ass whipped for letting her kids come out the house looking any ol' kind of way. Their clothes were filthy and both of them looked like they hadn't seen a bath with all the dirt that was encrusted on their bodies. Plus, their hair wasn't even combed. The little girl had these plastic clips that hung off unraveling braids, and the boy had lint in his nappy hair. It was in that moment that I went into a dark place of desperation. I figured that if I gave him some cookie, I'd renew his interest in his son. Even though that decision was dumb, I was smart about it. I knew to keep it purely physical because I didn't want to scare him off with any emotional babble. None of that "I miss you, baby" type of crap.I'd been the primary caregiver to our son while Diallo did what he damn well pleased, ducking and hiding and only coming forward when he was good and ready. I figured this little game served him right.

Technically he was off the market; at least that was what the lady he was with thought. Ordinarily, I wouldn't think of trying to take another woman's man from her, but I wanted what was best for my son. My allowing him to dick me down gave me an advantage. If he wanted some of my cookie, he had to come correct and be a better father to Lawrence.I always knew what powers I had between my legs, and Diallo could never resist it. He didn't like eating me out; he thought it was nasty even though I was clean. But he loved humping a wet pussy, so, he slipped his fingers inside me and pumped until my juices were running down my thighs. The females he'd been with since me must have taught him a thing or two, because he was gentler than he had ever been before. The way he held my breasts as he sucked my nipples was different from when he used to grab at them and squeeze all hard and shit. He used to think that because I let out a gasp or sigh, I liked it, but it used to hurt so bad that my titties would be sore for days after.

I mounted him reverse cowgirl style. It was important that I faced away from him so that I didn't look into his green eyes. They were like kryptonite to me. If I let him use them in his seduction, it would've been all over. I got on top and he slid it into me, balls deep. It felt familiar to me as I bounced up and down on it when I wasn't swirling my hips. He was naked with the exception of some tube socks that went all the way up to his calves. I noticed his toes curl as he moaned in appreciation of the gift my cookie gave him.

When he announced that he was about to come, I gave his dick a couple more bounces before I leaped off of it, letting his juices fly up and hit me in my lower back. I hated the look and feel of semen, and was anxious to get it off me. I stood up, looking down at the twitching fool as his body shook in aftersex- convulsion.

"Damn, girl, your stuff is as amazing as ever," he said, trying to catch his breath.

"Yeah, I know this."

"I'm glad you finally got off that high horse and saw that we can still be friends."

"Diallo, that's all I've ever wanted, especially for the sake of our son. Speaking of which, my daddy and me got into it about you," I said, lying my ass off as I lay down next to him. I knew that if my plan was going to work I had to strike while the iron was hot. Diallo was never able to deny me anything after some good humping.

"Oh yeah? What about?"

"I told him that I'd seen you out with your new girl and her kids and that you seemed like a changed man."

"I looked like a changed man?"

"Yeah, you did. I mean, it takes a special kind of a man to be with a woman with kids that don't even belong to you. I told Daddy that you'd become the man I always knew you could be, and that if it took another woman to bring it out of you, then so be it."

Diallo got this goofy grin on his face. He put his arm around me and started rubbing my arm. "Well, you know, sometimes people need time to find themselves."

"Exactly," I said, trying to sound understanding. "I remember all the shit you went through. I'm glad you found someone who can help you become a better person. What's her name?"

"Jubilee."

"I tip my hat to her. I'm sure she's woman enough to let you do what's good for your child as well as hers, right?"

Diallo didn't say anything.

"I'm sure you told her that you have a son of your own, right?"

"You're right, I told her. Lawrence is my heart. I told her that if she wants me then she's gonna have to accept my son, too."

"See, that's the Diallo I knew you could be. My daddy said that I should go and file for child support. But you know what I told him?"

"What?"

"I said that we're grown and don't need anybody dictating to us how to do for our child. I told him that I was sure you and I could work out an arrangement we both were comfortable with, and if that didn't work, I would be filing for child support—and I would be sure to get my years worth of rears."

Diallo stopped rubbing my arm. I turned to look at him and smiled sweetly. He gave me a nervous smile back and turned away to stare up at the ceiling of his living room.

"I mean, if you play fair with me, I'll play fair with you, right?" I asked as I nuzzled closer into him and rubbed his chest.

"Yeah, that's fair," he said and then gulped.I looked into his eyes one last time and I could tell that he knew I meant business. Then I turned away from him and lay on my back on the floor, smiling a smile of victory. If I'd known it would be this easy getting him to step up, I would've thrown him some pussy a long time ago.

Why it had taken me all that time to broach the subject with him was beyond me. I knew Diallo wasn't shit, and after his mother died, even though he seemed to want to do right at first, he became harder and harder to locate. I was willing to do as my daddy had said and not rely on him for anything, especially since I had a family willing to help. But I'd be damned if I was gonna sit by and watch him lay up with some other woman and take care of her kids and not do squat for his one child he had with me. That just wasn't gonna happen.

CHAPTER

9

T HE GEMINI PENDULUM WAS STUCK on evil where my daddy was concerned. Nothing changed after Pastor Stone and his wife left. It seemed like he'd used them being at the house as an excuse to show the bad side of himself.

I had cooked steak and mashed potatoes while Mama worked. She said that she'd try to get me placed at the Drake Patterson's Nursing Home. I was hoping when she came home she'd say I had the job as a nursing assistant because I couldn't take any more of Daddy's drinking and nasty comments.

"Your slut for a mama ain't back yet?" he asked me as soon as he came staggering into the house.

"No, Daddy," I responded as I finished tossing the salad.

"Yeah, I wasn't playin' when I said she fucked every nigga down in Mississippi."

"Daddy, why do you have to come home starting. I don't know what she did to piss you off, but that's no reason to call her a slut."

"Were you there? Your ass wasn't even born yet, so how you gonna tell me any different?"

"Are you hungry?" I asked, trying to change the subject.

"I was worried about you for a minute. I was sure you

were goin' down the same path as your mammy."

"Here, Daddy," I said, taking a plate from the cabinet and spooning huge gobs of food onto it. The more food he had in his mouth the less he'd be able to talk mess.

"Smells good, Baby-love," he said and then gave me a sloppy kiss on the cheek. I could tell he was back on the hard stuff from the smell of booze on his breath.

Marva came into the house with her sketch pad. One look at my face and she knew what was going on. Without saying a word, she rolled her eyes and went right back outside. I wasn't letting her off that quickly, though. I'd be damned if she was gonna leave me with Daddy in his messy state. I watched him stuff his mouth with meat. I giggled so that he wouldn't catch on as to how disgusted I was with him. I checked to make sure the stove was off and went after Marva, who had speed walked down the block.

"Wait up!" I screamed.

"I'm getting tired of watching him act like that," my sister said, not even stopping to look at me.

"Well, I'm getting tired of babysitting his ass. Will you stop for a sec and let me catch up?"

Marva stopped and glanced back at me like she was annoyed that I had followed her.

"Why ain't you back at the house? Who's watching Lawrence?"

"Listen, little girl, Lawrence is with his daddy."

"Oh, you mean Diallo's finally making time for his son?"

"You don't need to be concerned with all of that. I just didn't want you thinking that you were gonna leave me with Daddy."

"Why not? You wanted to come home. You knew how he is."

My sister was twelve-years-old going on thirty-two. She had seen more stuff in that house than a kid her age ought to. I didn't say anything else. I was just glad to be out of the house. I followed silently as she led me toward the park. She sat on a bench and opened her sketch pad and told me to sit still.

"Am I gonna get a Marva original?"She just sketched away. Drawing was an escape for her. Once when she was at school, I went through her drawer which was filled with drawings she had done, going all the way back to the age of four. Some of the more recent ones were dark, probably reflecting the mood in the house.She had one of a blindfold over Mama's eyes, and another one of a scared, little girl lying in a bed with a shadowy figure standing in the doorway. That one disturbed me, because it made me wonder if Daddy was doing things he had no business doing to his daughter, but then I realized, even he wasn't that crazy.At the bottom of the stack there were some pictures that she had torn up, but then taped back together of evil clowns and stuff like that. I'd been so wrapped up in what I was going through that I never stopped to think about what was going on in my sister's head.

I sat still as she scribbled fiercely. Then, she tore the page from the pad and wadded it up.

"I'll do this later," she said.

"Let me see it."

"No, it's garbage!"

"Girl, nothing you do is garbage. I wish I had your talent."

My sister smiled slightly, and then she started in on Daddy again.

"Sometimes I feel like I just wanna run away. It ain't like he'd miss me, with all the drinkin' he be doin'!"

"I hear you. But, just remember that Mama would miss you. Think about how hurt she'd be if you left."

"Why won't she leave him?"

I took a deep breath. I knew that with my history with Diallo, I wasn't in any position to judge Mama's reasons for anything having to do with her marriage. Diallo was no prize his damn self.

"I know how you feel, but you know what? You need to concentrate on your art and let the grown folks take care of themselves. Just think, maybe when you're older, you can get an art scholarship to a college somewhere. Wouldn't that be nice?"

Marva didn't answer; instead she looked off toward the kids playing at the playground.

"Marva?"

"Yeah, my art teacher Mr. Pratt says I'm one of the most talented students he's had."

"Well, see?"

"I love to draw. I can draw when I'm happy or sad."

I bit my lip and then smiled. I was gonna tell her that I'd seen some of her drawings, but I remembered how pissed I was when I found out that Mama had read my diaries. I knew what it was like to have my privacy invaded, so I didn't say anything. Marva went back to looking at the playing children.Later, I took Marva to the convenient store and bought her a grape soda, her favorite. Then we walked around the neighborhood until I figured Daddy would be upstairs sleeping. As soon as we got back and opened the door, we could hear him snoring loud like a chainsaw. Marva ran to the stove where the food still sat, took a plate, and began to help herself to it like it was going out of style.

~ * * * ~

I was watching Carol Burnett when Mama finally came home. She looked tired but she still had energy to give me a big, warm hug.

"Young lady, I think I have some good news for you."

"I got the job?"

"Well, first, I'm gonna need to go with you so that you can talk to Evelyn. She's this white lady in charge over there."

"Okay."

Then Mama got stern with me, like when I was a little girl. "And another thing: assuming you do get this job, take your behind to work and you better do a good job. Don't embarrass me, ya hear?"

"Yes, ma'am," I replied. Mama needn't have worried. I was gonna take my ass to this interview or whatever it was and charm the pants off this Evelyn lady. Then I was gonna work my ass off. I was restless and needed to make a move soon. The thousand dollars Pastor Stone gave me was still in the envelope untouched, along with some of the stripping money I had left. With it, and the money I was gonna save from working this new gig, I could pay the rent on an apartment. The Clark family, our next-door neighbors, had a car for sale for pretty reasonable sitting out in front of their house. I wanted it. As Mama kept blabbing at the mouth about how I should be grateful she was doing what she was doing for me and how I better not embarrass her, I thought about who I could get to give me driving lessons, and where I could go to take the written exam, and where could I find a driving instructor. All of this went on in my head until I finally snapped out of it in time to see Mama smiling at me and saying, "Good-night."

Don't get me wrong, I loved Mama, and to some degree even Daddy. But I had to get out of there. Daddy wasn't going to change and I'd given up on that hope. I wanted to get out on my own and raise my son. I knew they would always be there if I needed them, but enough was enough. I figured that I'd give myself five to six more months to put some money away, then I was out....and hopefully for good this time.

CHAPTER

10

MAMA WENT WITH ME TO talk to Evelyn, the Director of Nurses. They'd worked together briefly at Mount Sinai Hospital, so they knew each other.Evelyn was a big woman. Her glasses rested on the bridge of her nose and she looked over them as though she suspected you of something. Actually, she looked like the type of woman who on her day off probably lay on the sofa in a housedress, ate a couple of tubs of ice cream, and watched her stories.I was excited to get started. Since I was the newbie on the totem pole I had to work the shifts the people with seniority didn't want. That meant working from eleven at night until seven in the morning.In the beginning, Drake Patterson's seemed like a fantastic place because I got the sense that 95% of the staff cared about the patients. There were a few who I thought only showed up to make a paycheck. Too many times when I'd come on duty, I'd go into the rooms and discover people like Mrs. Blanchett hadn't been repositioned all day and so her bed sores would get worse and I'd have to be the one to move her. To hear that woman scream out gave me chills. And to know that a couple of rotten apples in the staff were the cause of someone's suffering pissed me off.

It was ridiculous to see people like Mr. Freppart lying in

a bed saturated with piss and smeared with shit because people were too damn lazy to help him to the bathroom. It was also sad to see so many old people get tossed away by their families. I'd hear stories about patients who would wait for their families to visit. They would limp or wheel themselves out into the visiting room, usually dressed in their Sunday best, and their families wouldn't bother to show up. One evening when I came on duty, I was told that Mr. Herald had gone to bed hungry because he'd gotten up that morning, put on his suit, and waited for his son to bring the wife and grandchildren for a visit that never happened. He was so depressed that he refused to eat, and went back to his room.The one person that taught me the most was this nurse, a gay guy named Clayton Hall. He was a tall, light-skinned brotha with good hair. He was the one who got my head together when I thought I wouldn't last working there. He became my best friend and I was his ally because the straight guys that worked there didn't like him, and would try and show off in front of their buddies and girlfriends.

"Say, man, ain't you got some dicks to suck or somethin'?" Dwayne, another one of the male nurses, asked.

"Oh please, dear. You're just mad that I have the good sense not to suck yours."Dwayne stepped away from hislittle group and began grabbing himself. "Yeah, right. I guarantee that if I took my dick out right now, you'd get down on your knees and start suckin.'"

Clayton rolled his eyes and said, "And why do I think that you're only partially joking? If I were to offer to suck your ridiculous dick, I guarantee you'd accept it with ease."

That's the thing I liked about Clayton. He knew how to talk to people. A lot of the people working at the home, and I'm sure people Clayton came across in life, thought he was soft. But I never thought that about him. He had a regal bearing, like he was above anything petty. While those fools lollygagged, Clayton was about doing his work and making his money."Darling, I haven't the time to play with people's kids. When you deal with me, leave your inner child in the yard until it's full grown. Then, come to me like an adult," he explained to me one day.

Clayton had these sensitive, brown sloe eyes with long lashes that told you exactly what he thought, especially when he didn't feel like telling you with words. God blessed me when He sent Clayton to me. Besides my mother, he was the second person I knew who possessed a strong work ethic. If he asked you to do anything, you best believe it was something he'd either done himself, or was willing to do. He was a true gentleman that stood out from the pack of dogs I'd come to know there.

"Say, darling. My lover is down at the bar. Why don't we join him for an after work drink?"

"Who in the hell drinks booze at seven in the morning, Clayton?" I asked.

"People like us who work the late shifts. Working people keep all hours, you know?"

Clayton had told me about his lover, a white guy named Travis. To hear Clayton tell it, Travis was the cat's meow. He said Travis had lean muscle and a thick, bushy mustache. Clayton told me he loved Travis's head of curls, and loved running his fingers through it when Travis was inside him. I thought that last piece of personal information he could have kept to himself.

"I'll make a deal with you. Let's go to a 24- hour diner and get some breakfast, and if I'm feeling like it, I'll go with you to the bar to meet your man."

"I'm not really hungry. Most people drink first and then go to the diner for breakfast afterward."

I thought about it. I'd been nibbling on vending-machine food throughout the evening so breakfast could wait.

After waiting for Lorraine and Hannah to start their shift and take over, we left and went to Ty's Bar in downtown Minneapolis. I felt weird going to the bar because I didn't want people to think that I was a lush. I never thought that there were actually people who worked late shifts, so for them morning is party time.It was 8:30 am when Clayton led me through a side door which led to a narrow bar. The walls were painted black and Donna Summer's "Hot Stuff" blasted from the jukebox. The place was packed, and I was surprised to see so many people drinking that early in the morning.

There were a few people who looked like alcoholics sitting at the bar. Some were staring off into space and mumbling to themselves, while others were involved in lively conversation. Judging from the men bumping and grinding together, I assumed that Ty's was a gay bar Clayton had brought me to.

"Where's Travis?" I asked as I took the vodka and cranberry drink Clayton had bought me.

"He works security at the IDS building over on Nicollet Mall. Maybe he hasn't arrived yet."

I looked around the room and watched as a couple of guys started kissing each other as though they were going to eat each other's faces. I smiled. It was weird seeing two men kiss. I remember hearing sermons at church about homosexuality being an abomination, but I felt like this: I had my own problems and so if people of the same gender wanted to get together, so be it. There's only one true judge and that's God, so I have no heaven or hell to place anyone in. These people hadn't done anything to me, and if that's what they liked then I was glad there was a place they could go to handle their business. We were there for maybe fifteen minutes when Clayton said he wanted to use the bathroom. I sat by myself and bopped my head to the rhythm of the Trammp's "Disco Inferno." About two minutes later I heard a smashing of glass and a whole lot of yelling. It sounded like Clayton.

"What the hell is going on here?" Clayton yelled. As I got closer, I could see that he was talking to a man that fit Travis's description. Another man, dressed like one of the Village People in a cop's uniform, had his big arms wrapped around Travis.

"Clayton, calm down. It's not what it looks like," Travis said, pushing the "cop" away. "Yeah, that's right. You had better get your hands off my man!"

"Baby, can I talk to you in private?" Travis asked.

"No, you can't, Travis. Why do you always have to be out dicking somebody."

"This is just a friend, Clayton." Travis looked around the room with a nervous expression as the crowd looked on.

"Do you stuff your tongue down all your friends' throats, Travis? You know what? I ain't got shit else to say to you. Since you want to fuck other people, you can take your ass on home with them. Give me your key!"

Travis's expression seemed to ask, "Are you serious?"

"Baby...."

"Don't 'baby' me! Give me the fuckin' key!" The usually

eloquent Clayton was now sounding very street-like.

Slowly Travis handed over the key.

"Whoever you are, did he tell you he had a lover?" Clayton asked the "cop" guy.

"He mentioned it, yes."

"And yet you still were going home with him?"

"Listen, sir, I don't want any trouble."

"Well, it's too late for that. You should have thought of that before when he said he had a man."

"He told me that you two had an open relationship."

"Oh, really? Well, that's news to me. But I tell you what; he can have it as open as he wants now because I'm through. I hope you two are happy with each other." Then, Clayton turned, took me by the hand and said, "Let's go, girl," and led me out.

We went to a diner over in northeast Minneapolis. Clayton had been so upset that he insisted that I drive us. When I told him I didn't have a license he said he didn't care. When I said that I hadn't gotten behind the wheel since the age of sixteen, he said, "Darling, I just lost the love of my life. I feel like dying today. If that's true what you just said, and if it's God's will, you'll kill us both. But I have faith in you. Just drive slowly."

So I did, and did a pretty good job, too.

Clayton was quiet for a long time after we ordered our food. He just kept stirring the spoon in his coffee, staring at it like he was in a trance.

It wasn't until the waitress came back with our pancakes and bacon breakfast that he started to talk between bites.

"I gave that man four good years of my life," he said.

"Wow, that's a long time for anybody," I said, touching his hand.

"I even moved here from Chicago to be with his ass. That's where we met."

"You never know, maybe you two can work it out. My daddy fooled around on my mama for years and they're still together. Why, I don't know."

"Yeah, but did your father bring gifts back like crabs and gonorrhea to your mother?"

"Oh, hell no!"

"I didn't think so. Travis has been doing this shit to me

for years. Maybe I'm getting what I deserve because I keep taking his smug ass back."

"You don't deserve disease, Clayton. You need to leave him alone because you can do way better for yourself."

When I said that, he pushed his plate of food aside and folded his arms as his eyes spilled over with tears. I felt bad for him, and for a moment I forgot about the doggish men in my life because I saw that my friend had one of his own.

CHAPTER

11

"WHAT DO YOU WANT TO do for your birthday tomorrow, honey?" I asked Lawrence as I pulled the covers up to his chin.

"I want McDonald's."

"That's it? You don't want to do anything else?"

"Hmm. I dunno," he said, shrugging a little.

"You're getting to be a big boy, aren't you? How old are you gonna be?"

"This many," he said, holding up five fingers.

"Yes, and how many is that?"

Lawrence just smiled and pulled the covers over his head.

"Tomorrow, we're gonna see a movie and then go to McDonald's. Do you want to see a movie?"

"Yay!"

"And tomorrow night, you'll go over to your father's house, okay?"

"How come?"

"Because he'll have surprises for you."

Lawrence peeled the covers completely from his not-too-thrilled face.

"Don't you want to go to Daddy's house? He'll have presents for you," I said, picking lint out of his hair.

Suddenly he perked up. "Say, you know that Mommy is working really hard to save up more money so that we can have our own place and you'll have your own room, right?"

"Where will I put my toys?"

"In your room."

"I can take them out of the box?" My mama made Lawrence keep his toys in a box down in the family room.

"Well, you can keep the toys in the box when you're not using them, but we'll put the box in your room, how's that?"

"Yay!"

"All right, baby, time for nite-nite. I'll see you in the morning, okay?"

The next day, Lawrence seemed to take his time getting ready. It was as though he was testing me to see if I'd yell at him on his birthday. I stayed calm, though. In the end, he was only hurting himself because we were late to *The Muppet Movie*. We walked in on the part when Miss Piggy won the beauty pageant at the county fair and saw Kermit the Frog for the first time in the crowd. Of course after the movie ended we stayed to watch from the beginning, up to the point we came in on.

Afterward, I took him to the same McDonald's Rexanne worked at. It had been some years since I'd last seen her, especially since we hadn't parted on the best of terms. I was kind of hoping I'd run into her, just to see how she was doing.

The restaurant was packed. We waited in line, and I craned my neck looking for Rexanne. When we got to the counter, I ordered a Happy Meal for Lawrence, something he'd been bugging me about since it came out five months earlier in June. I ordered a Big Mac and a small fries for myself. I figured I'd share Lawrence's drink.

"Does Rexanne still work here?" I asked the employee.

"Who?"

"Rexanne."

Suddenly, the shift manager turned around with a look of acknowledgment toward the name.

"Rexanne ain't worked here in I don't know how long. She just stopped showing up. That's too bad, too, because she was one of our best employees. Is she a friend of yours?"

"You could say an old friend." I thanked them and took

my tray and found an open table that hadn't been cleaned yet, but was the only one available. Lawrence picked through the box to get to the toy; he hardly seemed interested in the food.

"Honey, eat your food before it gets cold. You can play with your toy later."

Out the corner of my eye I could see a man sitting next to us staring at me. I turned and looked at him and smiled half-heartedly. He wore one of those pimp suits, complete with the pimp hat. In the face he looked like Berry Gordy Jr.., the president of Motown.

"Lord, have mercy! Baby, has anyone ever told you that you're outta sight?"

"Are you for real?" I asked him.

"I ain't lyin' to ya, baby girl. You're fine, lil mama."

"First of all, I ain't your mama; second of all, I'm trying to enjoy my son's birthday with him."

He looked at me and laughed before saying, "You got a man? You can't have no man talkin' all that mess."

"Why don't you just turn around and eat your food, okay?"

He laughed again and said, "You know what? If you were one of my bitches, I'd slap the black off you."

"Then, it's a good thing I'm not one of your bitches, then, right?"

"Jive- broad," he mumbled under his breath.

"You're the one who's jivin,' *brotha*!"

"You raggedy bitch! I know where I seen you before. You used to work over there at that strip joint. Now you wanna act all high sa-diddy."

"Say, brotha, the lady asked you to leave her alone. Why don't you be a gentleman and do what she asked you to do?"

I looked up to see this gorgeous man who was the spitting image of Johnny Mathis, except with a fro.

"Who in the fuck are you, nigga?"

"Don't worry about all of that. The lady asked you nicely to leave her alone. I'm not as nice."

The man sized this brotha up, sucked his teeth, and said, "Yeah, all right," backing up slowly with his palms up like he was retreating."You all right?" the Johnny Mathis look-alike asked.

"We're fine. Thank you."

He looked down at my son and patted him on the head. Lawrence was nibbling slowly on a French fry as he gazed up at the man who'd become our hero.

"How you doin,' little man?"

Lawrence looked away shyly.

"Say hello to the nice man."

"Hi," my son said, and went back to playing with his Happy Meal toy.

"I'm Plez, by the way," the man said, extending a large hand to me.

"Oh, I get it. That's supposed to be short for pleasure, huh?" I asked, rolling my eyes.

"Actually, my mother named me Plez Darnell Jackson."

"Well, Mr. Jackson, again, thank you."

"Can I join you two?"

I nodded at an empty chair. His eyes were so darkly intense; I couldn't look into them for too long. He smiled at me, which warmed his face.

"You know who you look like, right?"

Plez laughed. "Yeah, but I don't have Mr. Mathis's money. I definitely can't sing like him either."

"I'm Cheryl Greene, and this is my son, Lawrence."

"Good to meet you both. What you all been up to today?"

"Well, today my son is five years old. I took him to see *The Muppet Movie.*"

"You don't say?" Plez said, gazing into my eyes and I into his. I don't think he was really interested in hearing about our day.

"And what were you doing all day?"

"After work, I went to play pool with some buddies of mine around the corner from here."

"Where do you work?"

"I work at the post office."

"Oh, are you a mailman?"

"No."

"Then what do you do over there?"

Plez smiled and said, "I do a little bit of everything."

I looked over at Lawrence and he didn't seem any closer to finishing his food, so I put the rest of it into his meal box and closed it up.

"You're getting ready to leave?"

"Yeah, I need to get him back so that he can visit with his father."

"Oh, you two aren't together?"

"If you must know, no we ain't."

"I'm sorry; I ain't tryin' to get all up in your business."

His eyes twinkled as he looked at me. I felt as though I was being hypnotized.

I helped Lawrence button his coat and gave him his meal box to carry. Plez stood up.

"How are you getting home?"

"The bus."

"I can give you a ride if you want."

"No, that's okay, but thanks."

Plez stood there looking like he wanted to say something.

"Can I see you again?"

"Excuse me?"

"I mean, I think you're beautiful. I'd love to, you know, get to know you better."

"Yeah, I bet."

"Listen, I ain't trying to get into your drawers. I just wanna get to know you better."

"I tell you what, if you want to see me again, come to the Little Light Church over on Lyndale Avenue in north Minneapolis. Do you know where that is?"

"Yes, I do."

"That's where I'll be. Bible class starts at nine."

"I guess I'll be seeing you Sunday morning. And I'll be seeing you too, little man."

Lawrence was so engrossed in his toy he didn't pay any attention as Plez waved good-bye to us.

That Sunday was an unusually warm day. It felt more like summer weather than the cold snap common for Minnesota in November.My family and I entered Little Light. As I sat through Bible study, I began to wonder if I'd done the wrong thing by asking Plez to come to worship. I was worried that he'd take one look at the pastor and know that he was a phony, and think that I was one too by association.Since the Stones had left my parents' house, I never knew where I stood with Pastor Stone. He'd either be overly friendly to me, or go out of his way to avoid eye contact. Sister Stone was her same uppity, fake self, so I knew she was none the wiser about the Pastor's and my little business transaction.I'd told Mama that I was expecting Plez no later than 11:00 am. When the main service started and he still hadn't shown, she leaned in and whispered, "He's not here, is he?"

I shook my head, no.

"Girl, he ain't comin.' I don't know why you waste your time with these trifling Negroes."

"I guess he really was trying to get into my pants."

"I could've told you that."

At a quarter to noon I turned one last time to see if I'd still been foolish. That's when I saw him, looking handsome in a blue suit, tiptoeing into the church and finding a seat in the back row. I smiled immediately when we made eye contact and he winked. I nudged Mama and whispered, "He's back there." Mama smiled back, rolling her eyes as though it wasn't anything special.

After service, I convinced my parents to meet Plez. I hoped that Plez could fill in a lot of the blanks since I didn't know much about him myself. When we approached him, Mama said he looked like "that singer." I told her that he got that a lot. Plez held his hand out to greet Daddy first, but Daddy seemed completely unimpressed.

"Good morning, sir," Plez said, respectfully.

"How old are you?"

"I'm 35, sir."

"Ain't you a little bit too old to be dating my daughter?"

"Joshua, please," Mama chimed in, trying to chuckle her way through the tension.

"No, ma'am, he's got a point. Actually, your daughter and I just met. But any woman who puts family and faith first is a woman I'd like to get to know better."

Mama was charmed from that moment on, and so was I. Lawrence ran up to him and pulled on his pant leg as though he'd known Plez since birth.

"Hey, there, little man," Plez said, scooping Lawrence up.

Daddy smiled a little bit and Mama beamed.

"I wanted to apologize for being late. I was thinking since it's such a beautiful day that maybe I could take you and your son to the park for a picnic."

"Now, that sounds nice," Mama said, not giving me a chance to respond for myself.

"It ain't much, just some egg-salad sandwiches, chips, and soda. I guess I should have asked first before packing lunch, that's why I was late. But, I was hoping you'd say yes. *Do you say yes?*"

"Girl, he ain't askin' for your hand in marriage, he just wants to get to know you," Mama said.

I smiled demurely. "Yes."

"Little man, do you like egg-salad sandwiches?" Plez asked as he put Lawrence down. Lawrence nodded and ran behind my daddy.

"Why don't we take Lawrence on home with us and you two can go ahead on. Lawrence can come along later when you both know each other a little better," Mama said.

I loved Mama for that because she said what I was thinking. In fact, I would never have introduced Plez to my son unless I knew there was something there. I didn't want to confuse Lawrence. But Plez had obviously met my son when he met me at McDonald's.

"You know what, Mrs. Greene, you're absolutely right."

Plez drove us to Loring Park in a brand-new, silver, 1979 Cadillac Elegante. I stood near him as he took off his suit jacket, vest and tie and put them in the trunk while he took out a cooler and blanket. Then we walked across the street toward the park. As we walked, catching a breeze, I could smell the Aramis cologne he wore. It was such a masculine scent that I couldn't help but imagine him on top of me; splashing me down with his scented sweat.

"I hope you weren't offended with my mama's suggestion that they take my son back with them," I said, helping him straighten the blanket out onto the grass.

"Naw, naw. She was right. I'll get to know Lawrence in good time."

He was so confident. He just knew things would go well and lead to that. I loved that quality.

"Sorry my daddy was on the chilly side. He can be like that sometimes."

"I'm not bothered by that. He's just being a father. Be glad you *have* a father."

"Well, we haven't always gotten along. But we're making it happen now, so I guess that's what's important, right?"

Plez didn't say anything. He opened the cooler and took out a plastic container that had sandwiches in them. You could tell that they'd moved around inside the container because egg salad was all smeared on the lid. It was a good effort, I gave him that. I took the paper plates and put one in front of each of us as he opened a bag of potato chips. As he sprinkled a few on my plate he never took his eyes off me.

"If you don't mind my saying, you look amazing. Your ex is stupid to let a lady like you get away," he said, closing the bag.

"Sometimes things just don't work out."

"I know it."

Plez looked off into the distance. Two men came from behind the bandstand, one zipping up his pants and buckling his belt, the other, licking his fingers. Plez's eyes narrowed and he shook his head in disgust.

"I forgot this was a breeding ground for faggotry."

"They're not bothering anyone," I said with a shrug. In truth, I didn't think it was cool that they were hiding behind a building scoring dick in broad daylight, especially when there could be children around.

"They're bothering me. I didn't come here to look at that shit."

"Do you want to leave?"

"No, we don't have to leave, but I got no use for people like them. Instead of going after the Jews, Hitler should have gone after their kind."

I thought that was a severe thing to say, and I hadn't expected it. Only a few hours before he'd been praising the Lord like someone filled with the Holy Spirit.

"Faggots, dykes, it don't matter. They should all be put to death. Ain't there a Scripture in the bible that talks about that?"

"I know there's a scripture that says, 'Judge not lest you be judged.'"

"That's a whole lot of bullshit. Those perverts count on people like you to say that, so we won't call them on their perversion."

I couldn't help but think of Clayton. To me, he was a good person, doing the best he could in a bad situation with a man who couldn't keep it zipped up. That was my mama's story, only topped off with a splash of alcoholism. And yet, she stayed with Daddy. I wondered what Plez would have thought of my daddy if he knew everything. Would he have been as quick to judge him, too?

I turned away and looked toward the park's giant daffodil fountain, its water shimmering in the sunlight. The next thing I heard was Plez yelling, "I got ya," as he sprinted toward a little boy who was on the swing set but couldn't get himself high enough. Plez grabbed hold of the chains and brought the boy to a stop, then drew him back as far as he could. The boy ascended upward with a *swoosh*. I heard the boy giggle as the boy's mother looked up from her reading to check on him before looking down into her book again. Just seconds before I saw hatred in Plez's eyes, but now as he pushed the boy, he smiled with the pride of a father. Maybe that was his attempt to show me he was good with children. When he finished playing with the boy, he carried him piggyback style to his mother, grunting like an ape all the way. The little boy continued to giggle, but his mother hardly seemed pleased that Plez had brought her son back to her to interrupt her reading.

"I think he likes you," I said when Plez found a seat next to me on the blanket.

"You think?"

"Yeah, I do."

"Do you think Lawrence will like me?"

"I know I like you."

Plez flashed the biggest smile. Here sat a man who, although I had known him only a short period, I felt could fit with me. As far as his dislike for gay people, that was his problem, not mine. He wouldn't have to meet Clayton. As long as he treated me and my son well, which I felt he had the potential to do, I could get past his prejudice.

We left Loring Park and he took me to Lake Calhoun. We got out and walked around the lake and that's when I think I fell into something. It wasn't love yet, but it was just as powerful.

He told me he had served in Vietnam until 1971 and that the post office job was the only gig he could get. Vietnam vets weren't looked at too nicely by a lot of people once they came back home. He was thirty-five years old, thirteen years older than me, the oldest man I ever had interest in dating.

"Do you need to get back anytime soon?"

"Mama should be all right with Lawrence and I'm sure Daddy's at the Spruce, drinking."

"Do you like music?"

"I love it."

He took my hand and led me back to his car. I thought he was going to take me to an outdoor concert or something. Instead, we pulled up in front of a house in north Minneapolis. No wonder he knew where the church was, he lived close by.

"What's in there?" I asked, playing coy.

"This is my house. I have one of the baddest music collections. I don't show it to too many people, but I really wanted to show it to you."

He leaped out of the car and had my door open before I had a chance to formulate a complete thought.

His house was small, white, and plain. When he opened the door, the house smelled of incense. We walked into a sunken living room with big pillows around a wooden coffee table in place of a sofa. He had mirrors with squiggly marks on them on the main wall. In a little nook were his record player and stacks and stacks of LPs. He pulled his shoes off and placed them by the entrance to the room and I did the same. Then he proceeded to flip through his record collection until he pulled out the Brothers Johnson's *Blam!!* album. I loved the song "Ain't We Funkin' Now." He took me by the hand and started to dance. I was so overcome by the driving music that I danced along with him.

"You want something to drink?"

"Yeah, you have some wine?"

"You know it, girl." And then he disappeared out of the room. He came back with a bottle of white wine and two glasses. He poured one for me and waited for my approval before pouring one for himself. We went through Sly and the Family Stone and Millie Jackson along with another bottle of wine.

I lay my head on one of those pillows and he came over and massaged me. His hands were so strong that I couldn't help but wonder how they'd feel on my breasts. I looked up at him and he stared down at me with mysterious eyes. I closed mine as I saw his face come toward me, and then he kissed me. His breath was warm from the wine; his cologne was faded, yet still present. His tongue danced in my mouth as I found his rhythm. He placed his hands on my face, lightly bringing me closer into him. The kiss started out soft but turned hungry. I pushed the pillows away and lay flat on my back and he got on top of me, running his warm tongue along my neck. He then stood up and looked down at me as he extended a hand to help me up. I knew where this was going, and there were so many reasons why I shouldn't have gone there with him: attending church service only hours before, my not knowing him very long, my being in a strange place. But his eyes spoke to me. They told me that everything would be all right if only I gave into their power.

He led me through a doorway of beads, which I was surprised anyone still had, into the bedroom. I could tell that he had been in the military because his queen-sized bed was made perfectly. He slowly unbuttoned my blouse while he continued kissing my neck. I got lost in those kisses as I fought to unbutton his shirt. He pulled his pants off and I pulled my skirt down and we both stood there admiring the other's body. His body had tone, but he wasn't ripped. I noticed a long scar running along his right pectoral muscle and he became nervous when he saw me staring at it. He guided me onto the bed and pulled my nylons and panties down to mid-thigh."Lord, have mercy," he whispered almost to himself, as though he was looking at the golden pussy of all pussies.

He ran his hand up and down my navel, up to my breasts. He leaned in and kissed right above them. I slid my bra straps down to give him better access. As I pushed my bra down to my waist, he took a handful of breast into his hand and began sucking like he was sucking for nourishment, rolling his tongue over my hardened nipple. He must have known that the other one felt neglected because he did the same to that one, too.

Then he jumped up and finished pulling his underwear down, his dick standing at ten and a half inches of attention. He smiled when he saw my eyes get big at the sight of that dick of death. He kept on his black nylon socks held up by sock garters. He put his index finger into his mouth and got it wet enough to rub over my clit. I flew onto my back instantly, my nipples pointing towards the heavens, sending me into orbit. I was waiting for him to go down on me, but by the way he played around it, I figured he didn't get into that.He pulled my panties and nylons completely off and then hopped around so that we were in sixty-nine formation. He had to be crazy if he thought I was going to suck his dick if he wasn't going to eat my cookie. After he got the hint that no dick sucking would happen, he kneeled on the bed and started stroking his meat, which had continued to grow. He slapped my clit with it and slowly slid inside of me. He was playing with me, putting only a little past the head in.

"Do you want it, baby?" he whispered.

"Give it to me," I moaned like a drug addict waiting on a fix.

Without warning, he slammed all ten and a half inches into me. I gasped for breath, as if not knowing where all that dick came from. I grabbed his back as he scooped his hands under my ass while he plopped in and out of me, our unified bodies bouncing up and down on the bed. My toes curled as sweet sensation shot through me, hot like fire. My wetness slicked his dick and ran down his balls as they thwapped against me.

"Damn this pussy is good," he moaned into my ear, tickling it with his warm breath. He clasped my hands in his as he tore my cookie up. Then he turned me on my stomach, pulled my ass so that it stuck up in the air, and mounted me again, holding me closely, like a lion pouncing on prey.

"I bet you never had dick this good, have you?" he asked me.

"Oh, Plez," I screamed out, "I ain't *never* had dick this good!" I sounded like I had been starving for it.

Only Diallo came close in that department. This was by far better. My tongue became dry as I gasped for incensed air, my vision becoming blurry. If he could've sexed me into another world, he probably would have.

Two hours later, he was nearing an end. I could feel the buzzing in his body like he wanted to come badly. He turned me back onto my back and held my numb, wobbly legs as far apart as they would go. All it took was three wet pumps and he jumped off me, his hot cum speckling my body like paint. I wasn't too thrilled with that, but before I could take the sheet and wipe his seed off me, he collapsed on top of me, breathing heavily. He kissed my glistening neck softly before erupting into laughter. He rolled off me and lay by my side.

"What's so funny?" I asked him.

"Damn, you're good!" His laughs became louder.

"Tell me what's funny."

"Naw, it's just that you church chicks are the first to scream 'Hallelujah' on Sunday morning, but by Sunday night, ya'll are screaming all kinds of shit that don't sound too Christian-like."

I was stuck for a response. It sounded as though he was calling me a hypocrite.

"I've done balled many a woman in my day, so don't feel badly when I tell you that you can't help but love it. When my dick is good, it's good. And I *know* my dick is good."

Suddenly, I felt like one more name from a sheet of many.

"Can I please use your shower?"

"Where are you going?"

"I need to get home."

"What, you're mad at something I said?"

"If you just wanted the pussy, you didn't have to whip out an egg-salad sandwich. Shit, nigga, all you had to do was ask for it!"

"What's wrong with you, woman?"

"You're making me feel cheap."

"I was joking," he said, jumping up from the bed to put his hands on my shoulders. His dick still felt hard as it poked the side of my ass. "Listen, I'm not gonna sit here and act humble about something I know I'm good at. I know how to fuck. The chicks dig me, and I dig the chicks. But I don't pull out a picnic basket for just anyone. I did that because I liked who I saw in that McDonald's the other day. I liked her so much that I'd like to get to know her even better."

I was stunned by what I heard. I thought for sure he was a hit-it-and-quit-it-type. Smiling, I said, "Well, she liked who she saw at the McDonald's, too."

"See, there? And here you were about to go upside my head because you thought I was only interested in the pussy."

"I really ought to get washed up."

"Yep, right through there, take a left at the end of the

hall. There's a closet that I keep my wash rags and towels in. Feel free."

As I washed myself, I tried hard to scrub the sex off me. But it was the state of mind that I couldn't get rid of. The thought of this handsome man wanting to get to know me made me keep on smiling. The sex was like none I'd ever experienced, and yet I hoped there was so much more to him. He seemed like the type who could keep me guessing and never bore me, and I was hip to that. Before we left his house, he wrote down his number.

When we arrived back at my parents' house, he turned the car off. I looked at him for only a moment because I didn't want him to know that his eyes were working strange powers on me like his dick had. "So, when do I get to see you again?"

"I keep some strange hours at the nursing home, and when I'm not there I'm with my son."

"I will get to see you again, right?"

"I'd like that."

He pulled me closer and kissed me on the lips. It was the perfect top off to a perfect day. As my eyes opened from the kiss I could see Daddy standing in the window, being nosy as usual. I'm sure when I got inside he'd try to act as though he'd been upstairs the entire time. "So, I'll call you and we'll take it from there, all right?" I said, trying to be noncommittal.

"I can dig it."

As soon as I closed the car door, Daddy disappeared from the window. As I walked to the front door, I knew that I'd met my Prince Charming. Finally, I could leave the dogs in the yard where they belonged, chasing their own tails.

CHAPTER

12

"SO, TELL ME, DARLING. WHO have *you* been screwing?" Clayton asked me on our lunch break.

"Oh, my God, is it that obvious?"

"Trust me, darling, I know the scent of someone who's recently had dick, be it man or woman."

"Well, let's just say that it was some of the best dick I ever had," I giggled to Clayton like we were two best girlfriends.

"And tell me, who is this man?"

"You're not gonna believe this, but I met him at McDonald's when I was with my son."

"Using your son as bait to catch trade? That's new."

"Will you be serious? No, this pimp was trying to rap to me and this man named Plez came by and scared the guy off."

"Really? He told you his name was Plez? How original."

"I thought the same thing. But, no, his name really is Plez. So anyway, I invited him to church Sunday and he came with a picnic planned for Lawrence and me."

"You brought this strange man around your child? Not a good move, darling."

"Well, first off, Lawrence was with me at the McDonald's when we met. Secondly, my mama took Lawrence back to the house with her. It was just Plez and me."

"I see. That sounds better. So, uh, what does he look like?"

"He looks exactly like Johnny Mathis."

"That pretty Negro? When do I get to meet him?"

I bit my lip and looked down. "I don't think that would be a good thing, to tell you the truth."

"Why?"

"Plez isn't hip to your type."

"My type? And what type is that, pray tell?"

"You know, the homosexual type."

"And how would you know that, darling?" There was an edge to how he said "darling" that time.

"Because we went to Loring Park and he saw two men doing what they had no business doing in broad daylight, especially when there were children around."

"It sounds to me like you agree with this guy."

"That's not fair, Clayton. You know I don't have anything against gays. But those guys shouldn't have been doing what they were doing with kids nearby. I don't care what you say."

"I'm sure there weren't any kids out there."

"As a matter of fact there was one. Plez pushed him on the swing because the boy's sorry mother was too busy reading a damn book to play with him."

"So, I guess he told you that you and I can't be friends, right?"

"He doesn't know about you."

"I don't even like the way that sounds, Cheryl. But hey, he's a man. Go get him."

I shook my head and walked away. Clayton was being ridiculous, and if he thought that I was going to allow someone to dictate who I could or couldn't be friends with, then he didn't know me very well. I pretty much stayed away from him the rest of my shift. Every once in a while I'd look up and catch him giving me sad glances, as though he'd lost his best friend. I took it as him just being dramatic.

At one point I was at the desk talking to a nurse and he walked past me in a huff. Dwayne was standing right there and couldn't resist making a dig.

"What, you and Eartha Kitt over there ain't speakin' today?"

"Dwayne, why don't you go sit down somewhere? Better yet, why don't you do some work?"

"T.C.B., mama. I'm always Takin' Care of Business."

"Well, T.C.B. your ass over there and leave me alone!"

"Excuse me, mama. I was just tryin' to crack a smile on that gorgeous face of yours."

"I don't need you to do anything for me. And like I told you before, I ain't your mama. Your mama is at home, who you still live with."

"You still livin' with your mama and daddy so what's the difference?" he snapped.

"Yeah, but not for too much longer."

"Jive-ass broad," he mumbled as he walked away.

At the end of our shift, Clayton came over to me with a hesitant smile.

"Are you going to need a ride home?"

"Is the silent treatment over?"

"Darling, please," he said, cracking a broader smile.

"Will you give me a ride home?"

"Of course."

"By the way, I need you to teach me how to drive."

"Girl, you already know how to drive. All you need is some confidence if anything."

"Yeah, but, I really need to get my license. I have a son to think about and I don't need to be on a bus schedule. What if there was an emergency?"

"You're right. Sure, I can teach you, just let me know when. It's not like I have shit else to do," he said, winking.

On the ride home, Clayton was silent, concentrating on the road. When we finally pulled up to the house, he turned and looked at me. He reminded me of how my father looked at me in the car the night he brought me home from my attack by Alex.

"I'm sorry, darling. It's not my place to give you the third degree about who you're seeing. You're a grown woman and I'm sure you're capable of making your own decisions."

"Thank you, Clayton. I am."

"Here I am, tragic as ever, because I can't keep my man from cheating and I've got the nerve to tell you what to do?"

"I didn't take it like that, Clayton. I know you care."

"Good. Just as long as you accept it in the spirit I intended. But do me one favor, darling?"

"What's that?"

"Don't ever let a man make you lose who you are, because in the end, you're all you've got."

"I won't, Clayton. That'll never happen."

CHAPTER

13

I HAD A HORRIBLE NIGHT at work. I blamed Dwayne McKinney for that. He called out sick, but I knew he really called out because he had two tickets to see Teddy Pendergrass. All week he'd been telling anyone who'd listen about how excited he was about the concert and that he knew he would get some pussy because the chick he was bringing loved Teddy Pendergrass. Because of his lie, I had to carry more than my fair share of the workload. I think Evelyn was scared of him, because I told her that he was lying, but she just shrugged and said, "Well, he sounded sick to me over the phone."

One of the cases I had to deal with was Mr. Thomas. I don't think that man was aware that the civil rights movement had even occurred, not by the way he talked to me.

"Ya know, back in my day, we had this colored maid who worked for us. Gwendolyn was her name. Yes sir, she had some of the sweetest colored pussy I'd ever had. I bet yours is just as sweet." Then he pushed the sheets away to reveal a hard dick. As he lay there, he looked at it and then up at me and then back at it as if to say, "You know what to do."

After I got over the initial shock of this old man showing

me his dick, I was amazed that he *had* such a huge dick. He was seventy-two years old.

"Mr. Thomas, put that away," I said, covering him again with the sheets.

"Oh, come on, gal. Don't you get tired of changing people's shitty sheets? I know that ain't all you're good for. I mean, that's mostly what you're good for, but that ain't all. A little nookie never hurt anyone," he said, pushing the sheets away again. "I can tell by looking at your lips that you can suck a mean peter."

So many thoughts raced through my mind. Should I just shake my head, smile politely, and say, "No, thank you?" Should I report him? Should I curse him out? Or should I do what I wanted: put a pillow over his white, KKK-loving face and suffocate the shit out of him? His family didn't come to see him anyway; they probably were waiting for him to die so there wouldn't be any nursing home expense. "Sir, with all due respect, that's inappropriate," I said, throwing the sheet back over his dick again.

"Boy, I tell ya. You niggers have forgotten your place. You think because LBJ signed all that Civil Rights Act nonsense into law you're equal to me? You people will *never* be equal to me!"

I felt my face becoming warm as anger filled me like a glass of water. I felt tears forming in my eyes. But I wasn't crying because of hurt feelings, I cried because I needed this job, and I knew had I been another type of person, Mr. Thomas would have lost his life. He didn't talk to Dwayne like that because of his fear of the black man. If he'd said something crazy like that to Dwayne, I guarantee there'd be a hole in Mr. Thomas's wall with his head hanging from it. But in the end, he was old, bitter, alone—and he wasn't worth it.

I went into Evelyn's office and told her what happened and that I never wanted to deal with him again. She told me she'd have a talk with him, but I knew she wouldn't. She was scared of confrontation; I just said that to get me out of her face.

With the exception of what Mr. Thomas said to me, it was usually easy for me to ignore much of what those people said. After all, they were old. Many of them had seen and done things that shaped how they saw the world. But the world was changing and many were scared of that change. I think some of them would rather die in that nursing home than accept or live through what the world was becoming.

"Darling, he said *that* to you?" Clayton asked me during a smoke break after I told him what happened. "The nerve of him, I would have slapped his face!"

Clayton lit a cigarette. He inhaled, then exhaled through his nose. "Did you know that the son of a bitch called me a faggot?"

"I'm not surprised. When did he call you that?"

"It was the day I had to go in to scrub his withered carcass of a body. He said, 'Listen, don't come up in here singing your show tunes. You and I both know what you're after.' And I said, really? I hardly think you're man enough to give it to me. There could never be enough alcohol in my system to get me to want you."

I laughed. I could totally envision Clayton telling off Mr. Thomas.

"You know that he probably reported you to Evelyn for that."

"I really don't give a shit."

"Please tell me that you really wouldn't go near that thing of his and you weren't just trying to save face."

"Darling, you needn't worry. Even I have my standards. Just like Dwayne, I truly believe that if nobody was around, he'd have me in a broom closet somewhere sucking his miserable dick. Which is unfortunate, because Dwayne is gorgeous; it's just too bad he's a pitiful human being."

When we came back from our smoke, I saw Plez standing there holding a bag. His smile disappeared when he saw that I was with Clayton.

"What are you doing here?" I asked as I jumped at the chance to hug him.

"I figured you'd be hungry. I brought you some egg foo yung I bought earlier tonight," Plez said, eyeing Clayton suspiciously.

"Plez, this is my friend, Clayton. Clay, this is Plez."

"A pleasure," Clayton said, extending a limp hand.

"Yeah, okay," Plez said, ignoring the hand and looking away.

Clayton gave me a pained expression before saying,

"Nice to meet you, too."

"Clayton is my best friend here," I said as I took the bag of food from Plez.

"Ain't you got any female friends? Well, I guess in his case it's the same thing."

"Ooooh, darling! That's voodoo; that's cold."

I looked into Plez's eyes. The expression on his face was the same as when he saw those two men together at Loring Park.

"Yeah, Clayton is going to teach me to drive."

"Is that right?" Plez said, shaking his head. He then turned his attention toward me. "Anyway, I brought this for you, but it seems like you must have already ate."

"No, I just went out with him for a cigarette."

"How about I come back later and give you a ride home?"I looked at Clayton, who put his hands up as if to say that he didn't want any trouble.

"Okay, I'm off at seven."

"I'll be back." And he left.

"Okay, I was *not* expecting all of that. Someone needs to tell your boyfriend that he is off the charts rude."

"I told you he has a problem with gays."

"Well, you weren't lying. I don't know why you bothered introducing us."

"Because you were standing right here and if I didn't, he would've been upset."

"So let him be upset."

"I don't know, I think he'd probably give me the third degree later if I hadn't introduced you."

"You haven't been seeing him long enough to entitle him to give you any kind of degree, my dear."

"Well, you know what I mean."

"No, I'm afraid I don't."

I didn't like where the conversation was going, so I said, "I have rounds to make." And I walked away.

At seven I got my purse and coat and darted outside, where it had begun to snow. Plez was waiting out front in the car.

"Since when do you smoke?" he asked, looking straight ahead.

"I don't, really. I just have one every once in a while when I'm at work."

"You can tell your friend that I'm sorry about before. I figure he's not after your cookie, so he's no threat to me."

I smiled slightly. I could tell that Plez was the jealous type, which I found kind of cute. I liked men to stake their claim, but Clayton was my friend, and I didn't want Plez or anyone else telling me that he couldn't be in my life.

"What time do you have to be at work?" I asked.

"I'm not working today. Why, do you wanna do something?" he asked, smiling a sly grin as he ran his hand along my thigh as he drove.

"I need to get home to my son. I have to get him up and off to preschool. But we can get together later if that's okay."

"Hey, that's fine. I was gonna go down to the pool hall and hustle a game or two."

By the time we got to the house, the snow had begun falling harder. I told him I would call him later. He kissed me on the lips, but it was different than the kisses he'd given me before. It was cold.

"Are you all right?"

"Yeah, I'm fine. But I'd rather be spending time with you than playin' pool with the brothas."

I put my hand against his chin and turned his face toward mine and then I kissed him again. That time I actually got some tongue from him. That time it felt right.

When I put my key into the door I could hear screaming coming from inside. I pushed open the door and the first thing I heard was, "Joshua, you better not hit me! I swear to Jehovah if you hit me, you'll pull back a bloody stump!"

I looked upstairs, beyond the wooden banister, to see my parents snarling at each other. Behind them, on the wall, was a portrait of them in happier times, sitting together on the sofa. Lawrence came running down the stairs as fast as he could. He ran up to me and clutched at my legs as though I had come to save him.

"What's going on?" I yelled to them as I picked up my son.

"Cheryl, your daddy has lost his damn mind, and for what? All because of some damn lunch meat!" Mama screamed down at me.

"All she had to do was get me my turkey meat for the week, and she couldn't even do that!" My daddy spat back.

"Both of you deserve each other. You have my son crying

because of some dumb shit!" I yelled up at them.

"Joshua, go to work," Mama said, turning to walk into her bedroom, slamming the door behind her. Daddy just stood there like a child with no one to bully.

"You hungry, baby? Let's go eat some cereal, okay?"Lawrence nodded his head as tears splashed down onto his little chest. He held on to my neck as we went into the kitchen, where I found Marva cleaning up lunch meat from off the floor.

"What in the hell happened?" I whispered to her.

"What do you think? He got pissed because there wasn't any turkey for his lunch sandwiches. He threw all this liverwurst and ham at Mama and it fell on the floor. It must be nice that you get to be gone for hours and come back like nothing happened."

"Marva, look, I work for a living. I'm trying to get my shit together so I can get me and my child out of here. Why am I even explaining myself to you?"

"You don't owe me any explanation. You asked me and I told you."

I put Lawrence down and helped her clean up. She and my son should've been in the bed sleeping, not witnessing yet another tirade."What if I get a place to stay and you can come over and visit after school and even stay on the weekends?"

"Can I bring my sketch pad?"

"You better bring your sketch pad," I said, smiling. I was suddenly faced with a renewed realization of what I needed to do, and not just for the sake of Lawrence and me, but for my sister Marva's peace of mind as well.

~ * * * ~

At six o'clock, Marva agreed to watch Lawrence while I went over to Plez's house. Although it was snowy and cold outside, Plez was burning up the bedroom with some of the best loving I'd had with him up to that point. I finally had to tell him to stop because even though I loved the sexing he was giving me, I was sure he was gonna make me sweat my perm out; that, and I had other things on my mind.

"Plez baby, come on, get off me, please," I said, tapping his sweaty back.

"What's wrong, you ain't feeling it tonight, baby?"

"No, I just can't concentrate."

"Do you want to talk about it?" he asked me while his dick was still inside me.

"Do you mind?"

"Not at all. Tell me what's on your mind. We can always finish later," he said, pulling out and lying next to me.

"I'm trying my damnedest to raise a child, and I can't do that with all of the craziness that's going on at home. Like today when you dropped me off, my parents were fighting over lunch meat, Plez."

He burst out laughing. Hearing it out loud made me giggle too, but I was the one who still had to go back home to the madness.

"Well, it sounds to me that you and your son need to get the hell out of there."

"The last time I came back home, things were better between my daddy and me. But now it's like the dark side of his personality is always out. I can't deal with it anymore."

"I repeat, get the hell out of there."

"Yeah, but who wants to move when there's snow on the ground?"

"If you're serious about leaving the nest then we'll just have to deal with that. You two can move in with me if you want."

As much as I appreciated the gesture, I knew it was too soon. I still felt guilty for screwing him so quickly that first time, and just hours after worship service at that. I also knew it would be us moving into his house—*his space*. I wanted Lawrence and me to have our own place, and after seeing the look on Marva's face, I wanted her to have a place to escape to.

"That's very sweet, but I think I need to go out on my own."

Plez's body shifted. He didn't like what I was telling him. "Listen, I love spending time with you. I know it's been a few weeks, but I can see myself being with you. Nobody else. You saw me in the park, I'm great with kids. I could be a father to Lawrence."

I drew some comfort from that. It was nice to have someone want me, especially with my being a single parent.

"I love spending time with you, too. It's been special,

Plez, it really has been. But I think for now it's best that I strike out on my own. I want to be able to do for myself. There's just one problem."

"What's that?"

"I don't know where to go."

Plez scratched his head as though he was thinking about something heavy.

"I know a man named Mr. Davis who has an apartment above a storefront over on Chicago Avenue. I haven't seen the place so we can go over there together and check it out this week if you want."

"I want, I want," I said, kissing his pec muscles. That's when I noticed the scar again along his pec. I ran my finger along the length of it and Plez grabbed my hand.

"What happened to you?" I asked.

Plez took a deep breath and said, "When I was in 'Nam, I was on patrol with a buddy of mine. It was late and we were having a cigarette. We weren't supposed to be smoking because the enemy can smell the smoke and see the cherry on the end of the cigarette."

"What happened, somebody saw you?"

"I heard some branches snap behind me. When I turned around, a Viet Cong stabbed me in my chest. My buddy blasted that motherfucker right between the eyes. I almost died that night. This scar is what's left from that."

"I'm sorry. I didn't know," I said, rubbing the scar again. This time he let me touch it.

"That's okay. Just do me a favor. Never ask me anything else about the war. We got treated like shit when we came back, and I don't like to think about it."

"I promise." Then I kissed the scar."Actually, we could check out the place before I take you home tonight, if you want," he said without missing a beat. It was as though the Vietnam topic had never come up.

I threw the sheets from my sweaty body and got up.

"Whoa, where do you think you're going?" Plez asked, pulling me back into his bed and embrace.

"I was gonna take a shower so we can go look at the apartment."

"And we will, but why don't we finish what we started first?"Plez lay on his back and his meat stood hard. I got on top of him and rode him into the most explosive orgasm I could give him. It was my way of saying, "Thank you."

CHAPTER

14

Pastor Stone's hush money and the money I'd saved up stripping was finally gonna be put to some use. Because for $125 a month I could have periwinkle blue walls with dark wood panels and crown molding. It was a two-bedroom with a living room, small kitchenette and medium- size bathroom. The old man said he'd throw in utilities since I was a single mother. There were three cans of beer someone had left in the refrigerator that he offered me to sweeten the deal.

"So, what do you think?" Plez asked, smiling.

"I like it. It smells kinda musty in here, though," I said.

"You can burn some incense. That ain't a problem."

"I'm guessing you won't be havin' any wild parties in here, seeing that you have a small child and all," the old man said, giving me a once-over.

"No, sir. I'm just looking for a place to call my own; a place to raise my son."

"I'm glad to hear that. There are too many of our folks walkin' around here not taking care of their responsibilities as it is."

I smiled to myself, knowing that I was moments away from calling this place my home. "So, when do I sign the lease?" I asked.

"Ain't no lease. Just pay the damn rent. I've known Plez since he was a little boy back in Alabama. I knew his parents real well, too. I figure if he brought you here then you ought to be all right."

"Well, thank you, Mr. Davis."

"Don't thank me. Like I said, pay your rent on time and everything will be fine. We'll do a month-to-month, is that okay?"

"That'll be fine," Plez blurted out. Then he turned to me and said, "You don't need to be bogged down with no lease anyway."

"Okay, I guess that's fine," I said.

"When do you wanna move in?" Mr. Davis asked me.

"Baby, how about this weekend? I think you should be in here before the New Year," Plez said.

"I think I can get off work."

Plez took out his wallet and paid Mr. Davis. I was surprised by the gesture. "Plez, you don't have to...," I began.

"Baby, I have to get something from Mr. Davis. Why don't you go wait in the car," he said, handing me his car keys.

It happened so quickly that I didn't feel as though I had much of a choice. I went out to the car. We were in the apartment for no more than fifteen minutes but the car was ice cold. I turned the car on and put on the heat as I waited. Moments later, Plez got into the car. I noticed he didn't have anything in his hands.

"Is everything okay?"

"Yeah, baby, everything is fine."

I didn't feel it was my place to ask what he was supposed to get from Mr. Davis. I just stared straight ahead as he hummed some tune I didn't know as he drove.

We pulled into a Sears parking lot and he told me he'd be right back. Once again I waited for him to do what he had to do. When he came back, he had a small bag of popcorn and he passed me a key.

"Good thing we got here when we did, they were about to close. Here's the key to your apartment."

"Is that what you had to get from Mr. Davis?" I asked, not knowing why he didn't let me get the key to my own apartment.

"Yeah."

"Plez, you know, I could've gotten the key. It's my apartment."

"Which I just laid down money for."

"Yeah, but sweetie, you didn't have to do that. I'm perfectly capable of paying my own rent."

Plez glared at me. "Is that how you say thank you? I paid your rent and you're gonna sit here and tell me what the fuck you're capable of doing?"

I blinked for a moment. Was he serious? I had saved up all that money myself, hoping the day would come when I could finally put some money down on a place for me and Lawrence. I'd been sitting on that money for months and it was finally burning a hole through my pocket. And anyway, it's not like I begged him to do it. "I am grateful, Plez. I'm just saying you didn't have to do it. I already had savings."

"Yeah, that's just like a woman to make a nigga feel guilty for trying to be helpful."

"Look, I can give you the money back."

"Did I ask you to pay me back?" he snapped.

"No."

"Well, all right then. The truth is, I won big time at the pool hall. Instead of being stingy, I thought I'd share what I won." Then, Plez's face softened. "Listen, baby, I don't want to be mad at you. Why don't you just tell me you're sorry and that'll be that."

He wanted me to say sorry for what? I hadn't done anything. Not wanting to argue, I swallowed, took a deep breath, and said, "I'm sorry."

When I got home, Lawrence was already asleep. Marva was at the kitchen table drinking chocolate milk, her trusty sketch pad right beside her.

"Where's Daddy?"

"He's asleep. Diallo called. He sounded funny. He said that he was gonna be leaving town and was going back to Chicago."

"What? Did he say when?"

"No."

I shook my head, knowing I'd have to call him to make sure he wasn't running out on our agreement. I was still in a decent enough of a mood to share my good news.

"I'm moving out this weekend."

Marva rolled her eyes at me. "Are you moving in with

that guy?"

"No, but he helped me find a place. I think you'll love it."

"You're lucky. I wish I was old enough to leave."

"You will be soon. Anyway, I told you that you can stay over on the weekends."

"When are you gonna tell Mama?"

"When she gets home."

"And Daddy?"

"I'm not telling him anything. He'll figure it out."

"How can you tell Mama but not Daddy?"

"Listen, don't ask a lot of questions. Everything will work out like it's supposed to, okay?"

Marva opened her sketch pad and said, "If you say so."

On December 15 Plez helped me put my last bag of clothes into his car. I was secretly glad that he'd paid the rent up-front, which helped free up some money to buy a couple of mattresses for Lawrence and me.At first Mama thought that I was moving in with Plez. She was better about the move when she realized that I wasn't, but she was concerned about Plez staying over nights since we weren't married. It wasn't a good example for Lawrence. But that didn't stop my intrigue about him. I was thrilled to see where things went.Of course Mama told Daddy, who surprisingly didn't say too much about it. He just hugged me and asked, "Now, you're leaving for good this time, right?" Later that night, I went through my boxes and pulled out some starter pans Mama had given me. She said they were on loan, but she had so many, I knew she wouldn't miss them.

As a "thank you" dinner for Plez, I made tacos. After that, we turned on the small black- and-white TV that he'd brought over. We were just in time to watch *Lady Sings the Blues* on channel nine. We sat in the dark on the hardwood floors and watched as Diana Ross smeared lipstick on a dressing-room mirror, sobbing hysterically. Lawrence looked confused and said, "She's crazy." I told him that the movie was too grown for him and that he should go to his room and play. He was excited to have his own space and didn't even protest having to leave the room.

Of course Plez tried to get frisky right there in the living room, but I stood firm.

"Baby, Lawrence is awake."

"So? He'll be asleep soon."

"Yeah, but he's awake now. He could come in here any minute."

Plez folded his arms, like he wanted to pout. Then he stopped talking, and we watched the rest of the movie in silence. When it was over I went to check on Lawrence, who was fast asleep. He had crawled up into a little ball on his mattress, clutching his teddy bear. I took a blanket from one of the boxes in his room and covered him with it. When I came back into the living room, Plez was putting on his boots and coat.

"Where are you going?"

"Am I picking you up tomorrow for church?" he asked, ignoring my question.

"Yeah, I was counting on it. What's wrong? Why are you leaving?"

"You know why," Plez said, looking as far away from me as he could.

"Do we have to have sex every time we're together? My little boy is in the other room. I don't want him to see us or hear us."

"He doesn't even know what he's looking at. Just like with the movie, he didn't understand that either."

"Maybe, but we're going to church tomorrow. I feel kinda weird doing it under all these circumstances."

"Why? You gave it up two days after meeting me, and hours after going to church. Now you wanna get all righteous?"

His words stung me like a slap in the face. Here he was, throwing my sleeping with him back at me, when I already felt guilty about it. Unfortunately, I wasn't guilty enough to stop doing it. Up to that point, his charms had worked on me, but this side of his personality I didn't find attractive at all.

"You know what? I think you should go. We'll take the bus tomorrow."

Plez shook his head and left me alone in the glare from the TV.

I was trying to stand up for what was right for my son. The church guilt, though I did feel it, wasn't as important to me, even though I knew it should've been. In that moment, I didn't care if I ever saw Plez again. But I soon realized that he was like a vampire. And like the myth tells it: once I invited him into my house, I could expect him to show up quite a bit.... and whenever he damn well felt like it.

CHAPTER

15

SOMETHING WOKE ME UP. IT was one of those urgent feelings pitted in my stomach, like when you're asleep and you feel someone is watching you. But in this case, I felt like someone had come into my space and taken my son from me.

I threw the sheets from my body and bolted up from the mattress. I went into Lawrence's room and saw the rumpled sheets and blanket and an indentation on his mattress where he'd slept. Panic shot through my body. The feeling had been too real to have been a dream. I walked into the living room where sunlight poured through the curtain-less windows.There I saw my son, squatting in the living room with a box of Captain Crunch at his side, pouring milk into an overflowing bowl of cereal. The scene was cute and I was relieved. But I startled him and he knocked the bowl over, milk and cereal covering the floor."Somebody's been trying to be a big boy, huh?" I said.

He smiled a cautious smile, not knowing if I was gonna give him a hug or a whipping. I didn't have any paper towels so I used a T-shirt to clean up the mess. He stood a safe distance, fearing punishment.

I poured him another bowl of cereal and let him eat while I took a shower to get ready for church. As I showered,

I couldn't help but think about Plez. I wondered if he had calmed down and if he'd surprise me and show up to take us to church, or if we were on our own.

After I washed Lawrence up, I helped him get dressed. I let him play with his toys as we sang "Jesus Loves Me" and "This Little Light of Mine." I waited for a knock or the ring of a doorbell until I realized Plez wasn't coming. I helped my son into his winter coat and boots and we went outside to wait at the bus stop, which thankfully was only down the block.

At church, I was prepared to give Plez a piece of my mind for being so petty. Then those feelings turned to concern when I realized a half hour into service he still wasn't there. As Pastor Stone preached, my mind ran thousands of miles away as my concern turned to fear. I couldn't help myself. I was so certain that I'd be fine without Plez and at the same time I felt a strange pull toward him.

Later, Mama and Daddy took my sister, me, and my son to Red Lobster. It was the first time in months we'd been able to sit down as a family. Everyone was on their best behavior, acting like the loving family we hadn't been in years. After lunch, as we waited for our doggie bags, Daddy gave Lawrence a miniature blue combination safe. It had a slit at the top that he could put his coins and cash through. Lawrence loved it and couldn't wait to put something in it. Daddy pulled out his little rubber, egg-shaped coin holder and gave Lawrence four quarters.

"What do you say, baby?" Mama said to Lawrence.

"Thank you, Granddaddy!"

"Go ahead, put them in," Daddy said.

Lawrence put each coin in, holding his ear to the safe so that he could hear the clank as the coins hit bottom. We all applauded.

When Lawrence and I returned to our new home, there was a sofa with two large potted plants, one on either side of it, a coffee table with children's books on it, and a TV stand with Plez's black-and-white TV on it.

We went into the kitchenette and there were rolls of paper towel on the counter, boxes of brand-new pots and pans, plus plates and cutlery. I even saw a broom and dust pan propped against the wall. I heard some movement in my bedroom and I went in and saw Plez lying on my mattress, fully clothed with a huge smile on his face. Lawrence was standing close by, the plastic bag of Red Lobster food swinging from his wrist while he clutched his little safe with both hands.

"Look what Granddaddy gave me!" Lawrence said, rushing into my bedroom toward Plez.

"Hey, there, little man! What do you got there?" Plez extended his hands to take the safe from Lawrence for closer inspection. "You're gonna need something to put in it, huh?"

Lawrence nodded his head.

"Oh, what do we have here?" Plez shook the bank and heard the loose clanking of the quarters Daddy had given my son. "Looks like you already got something in it. I bet you want some more, huh?"

"Yay!" Lawrence shouted.

Plez got up from the bed and fished through his pants pockets for change. He pulled out a fistfull of coins and began putting them into the bank one by one.

"I wanna do it!" Lawrence said.

"Oh, you wanna do it? Here ya go." Plez put most of the coins on the bed and a few in Lawrence's hand, holding the safe down at Lawrence's level. One by one, Lawrence put all the coins in his safe.

"Good job, little man! Gimme five!" Plez put out his hand palm up so that Lawrence could slap it. "Coins are great, but *cash* is better!" He took out three dollars from his wallet and gave that to Lawrence to put in the bank. Lawrence ran out of the room with the cash.

"Boy, get back here and put that money in your bank," I said.

Lawrence came back into the room, beaming. He put the dollar bills into the safe and applauded himself.

"Lawrence, baby, what do you say to Plez?"

"Thank you."

"Okay, why don't you take that food and put it into the refrigerator."

"Okay, Mommy!" And he ran from the room. I turned from my son and faced Plez, who winked at me."So, what do you think? Do you like the stuff I bought you?"

"Yeah, but what I want to know is, how did you get in here?"

"I have a key."

"Where did you get the key from, Plez?"

"Does it matter? How else was I supposed to get all this shit in here?"

Plez acted like a baby the night before because I wouldn't let him screw me, and now he was buying things and behaving as though none of that had happened. I found that to be a little weird.

"It seems to me that you can't appreciate the efforts of a good man."

"I just want to know how you got the key. Did Mr. Davis give you a spare?"

"No."

"He must've given you a spare because you gave me only one key."

Plez became increasingly agitated. "Why can't you just say, 'Hey, Plez, I really appreciate you getting me this stuff for me and my son.'?"

"Because I didn't ask you to; just like I didn't ask you to pay my rent. You took on all of that by yourself."

"Woman, let me tell you something, and you put this into your pack of smokes and smoke it; there are plenty of bitches out there who would kill to get a brotha like me!"

"Oh, so, now I'm a bitch?"

"No, but you're actin' like one! I said bitches, meaning any stray females I find at a supermarket, bus stop or at a..."

"McDonald's?" I asked, filling in his sentence.

Plez stopped talking, but I could tell in his eyes he'd meant it. Then his eyes shifted behind me. I turned around to see Lawrence standing in the doorway of my bedroom, holding his teddy bear, looking up at us like we were acting crazy. My son didn't sign on for any drama and I didn't want to expose him to any.

"Baby, grown folks are talking. Everything's all right, okay? Go on back to your room and play," I told him.

"I'm gonna leave," Plez said, starting for the door.

"Plez, you don't have to." I blocked him.

"I'm sorry if I'm moving a little fast. Maybe you can't handle that. I'm also sorry that you want to think that I'm out to dog you like whoever else you've been with. That's not me."

"I'm not saying that, Plez. I just wanted…"

"Sears," Plez interrupted.

"What?"

"I had the spare key made at Sears. Remember when we went after looking at the apartment? I wanted to surprise you with this stuff and I wasn't going to keep your original key, so when Mr. Davis gave me the key I brought you to Sears to have a copy made. I didn't go to church because I needed the time to get everything over here."

I felt like a fool. Here I thought he had some nefarious plan, and all he wanted to do was surprise me. A warm feeling washed over me and I smiled. But when I went in to give Plez a hug, he pushed me away.

"No. Don't touch me."

"Plez, I'm sorry. You were right. I should've just said thank you. Well, I'm telling you now, *thank you.*"

"I think I ought to give you some space. Whatever shit you got goin' on in your head ain't about me. When you're ready to let all of that go, give me a call."

And before I had the chance to respond, he walked out of my bedroom and apartment. In that quick motion, as I watched him leave, I realized something. Just like in a movie, I'd allowed myself to be swept up by the promise of romance. And when I settled, I realized I was falling in love with that man. He had taken the key to my heart just like he still had a key to my apartment. But I didn't mind. I knew he'd be back.

CHAPTER

16

"YOUR SON THINKS HE'S WONDER Woman," Vivian Frank, Lawrence's preschool teacher, told me when I went to get him. I searched her face for a smile, thinking that she was joking. But then she pulled two plastic links from behind her back to show me.

"We let the kids play with these. These are links used to make chains. Your son has been pretending they're Wonder Woman's bracelets. In fact, he's got the entire class doing it."

"What's the harm in that?"

"We don't like the children using toys for purposes other than what they're intended."

"These are just plastic. What could these things possibly do to a child?" I asked, taking one of them from her. "You know, Lawrence is very creative. He likes to organize little skits for himself and the other children. As a matter of fact, just the other day, I saw him reenacting a scene from *The Muppet Movie*. He gave out roles to all of the children and he gave himself the role of Miss Piggy."

I shrugged my shoulders at her.

"Doesn't that strike you as odd? A little boy pretending to be Wonder Woman and Miss Piggy?"

I handed her the plastic link and asked, "Is my son

bullying any of the other children?"

"No."

"Okay then. When he starts doing that, you let me know. As far as this foolishness, don't waste my time with it again." And then I turned to go get my son.

I may have wanted her to think that what she said hadn't fazed me, but it really had. I took a moment on the bus to explain some things to Lawrence.

"Mrs. Frank tells me you like to pretend to be Wonder Woman."

"Sometimes," Lawrence said, looking up at me innocently.

"Why do you want to pretend to be a girl? Don't you want to be someone strong like the Incredible Hulk?"

"But he's green. I'm not green."

I chuckled at his reason. "But Wonder Woman is a white woman. You're not white or a woman. Little boys should want to be boys and let the girls play act as girls."

Lawrence looked down and started to cry. That was another thing I'd noticed about him, he was very sensitive. You could blow on him and he'd cry. I didn't want him to grow into a sissy, or worse, be gay. I saw how Clayton was treated by Dwayne at work, never mind how bad he must get it outside of work by everyone else. Most people weren't accepting of that sort of thing, and it's not an experience I wanted for my child.

We got off the bus near the Dayton's department store because I wanted to show Lawrence their Christmas display windows and have him sit on Santa's lap. He smiled and pointed at the moving figurines in the display just like the rest of the kids gathered there. When we went to see Santa, there were tons of toys in their shiny boxes. Everything from board games to Tonka trucks and baby dolls, the room was filled with everything to make a child's Christmas special.

Lawrence whined the entire time, telling me that he wanted this and that, right then and there. I told him that Santa was going to fly right over and past our apartment and wouldn't leave him anything if he didn't stop acting like a brat.

When we got home, I realized the phone had finally been connected. I wanted to call Diallo. I'd been so wrapped up in moving and the newness of my relationship with Plez that I hadn't thought about Diallo since the night my sister told me he'd gone to Chicago.I called his sister, Roberta, to get some information. She sounded like she'd been having sex. She was all out of breath, giggling for some guy named Jermaine to "stop it," because she was on the phone. I could hear him in the background saying, "Bring that pussy back over here."

"You know how my brother is. He ain't shit and he ain't never gonna be shit. Plain and simple," she said.

"Did he say anything before he left?" I asked, ignoring the giggling. "No. I came home from work and he was gone. He called me when he got there to say he had taken a Greyhound bus, but he wouldn't tell me where he was staying. He probably got ran outta town by one of them no-good Negroes he'd been dealing with. I'm just glad to have him out my house. It's not like he was paying me any rent."

I knew then that Lawrence wouldn't be seeing his father for the holidays, and that his birthday was probably the last time he'd see Diallo for a while. Roberta didn't have an address for him so I wouldn't be able to sue for child support. My plan to get him to man up didn't work.

"Well, let me ask you this...," I began before I heard Roberta moaning like she was getting eaten out. I was gonna hang up when she said, "Girl, let me call you back," and the line went dead.

I called Plez. I was ready to tell him that I wanted to give us a shot, but he either wasn't home or wasn't answering his phone. As soon as I put the phone down, there was a knock at the door. I opened it to see Plez standing there with a bottle of wine in a paper bag and a puppy-dog look on his face.

"I guess it's true what they said in that song," he began, "What's that?"

"Everybody plays the fool sometimes."

I laughed at how corny that sounded, but he was right. We both had been pretty foolish. I rushed up to him, giving him the biggest kiss he'd received from me. Lawrence was happy to see him, too, and Plez swept him up in a big hug. Later, he and I sat on the sofa to watch TV and Lawrence sat between Plez's legs. He kept turning around to watch us steal kisses, even though I told him, "The TV is that way."After Lawrence went to bed, Plez poured us some wine in a couple of Dixie cups I had. We toasted to our future. Then he put his cup onto the coffee table and looked very meaningfully into my eyes.

"Nobody has made me feel the way you do. I think I'm falling in love with you. No, scratch that. I *am* in love with you."

Those words brought tears to my eyes because I felt the same way. I checked on Lawrence before we hurried toward the bedroom. I wanted Plez so bad, and by the way he held my waist, I knew he wanted me too.

"Are you sure you wanna make love?" he asked me as he took coins out of his pockets and placed them on my dresser.

"Lawrence is knocked out. He ain't waking up anytime soon."

We stood in the middle of my bedroom, looking at each other as though this was our first time. Then we got into bed and he made love to me. It was so beautiful, as his fingers found their way between mine, that I could feel the tears spilling from the corners of my eyes. The feeling of completeness with him was overwhelming; our bodies in perfect harmony. The bed shook so wildly that I could hear Mr. Davis beneath us, in his apartment behind the store he ran, hitting the ceiling with a broom to tell us to knock off the noise. But I didn't care. Plez peered into my eyes, his breath quickening as we enjoyed orgasm at the same time; the first time that had ever happened for me. I took it as a good sign.

The next day, in the morning light, Plez woke me up to say good-bye. He didn't want Lawrence to see him coming out of my bedroom. I was impressed that he'd thought of that. From then on, I felt like I'd found the one I could stand still with, and he was more than happy to stand with me. But Christmas Eve changed all of that.

CHAPTER

17

IT WAS HARD TRYING TO get presents wrapped when Lawrence kept coming into my bedroom to ask questions to things he already knew the answers to. He thought he was slick, but I knew that he wanted to sneak a peek at what I'd bought him. Finally, I told him that if he didn't go sit down somewhere, I would take all the gifts back to the store because Santa left receipts. That seemed to do the trick.It was Christmas Eve and Plez promised me he'd spend the night with Lawrence so I could work. It was a huge shift in my original plan to let my son get to know Plez gradually, but I couldn't fight my feelings for that man. Plus, Lawrence had taken a real liking to him too, so I knew he was in good hands.

The plan was to come home Christmas day, wake my little one up, and watch him tear open his presents. I even bought a few for Plez; an Aramis kit, complete with fragrance, soap on a rope, and talcum powder; a sweater, shirt and pair of pants; and a really nice green-and-black marble bowl that he could put his keys or coins in.

I took a break to make Lawrence grilled cheese and Campbell's chicken noodle soup. At one point I heard little feet pattering into my room. I'd put the gifts and wrapping paper in my closet so I knew he wouldn't see anything.

Suddenly, I heard coins dropping into his safe.

"Boy, what are you doing?" I asked as I marched into my bedroom to see that he'd climbed up onto my dresser to put all of the change Plez had left on it into his bank safe.

"My bank needs more money," he said unashamedly.

"Those coins don't belong to you. Leave them alone."

Then I remembered that Plez had given Lawrence coins to put into his safe. The coins on the dresser had just been accumulating, from every night Plez emptied his pockets. It amounted to about ten dollars in change, but I figured if Plez hadn't taken them with him, he wasn't missing them.

"All right, but next time, you need to ask someone before you just go taking things. You know better than that," I said as Lawrence finished putting the coins in his safe.

I heard the unlocking of my apartment door and Lawrence ran out of the bedroom to meet Plez in the living room. He had a duffel bag slung over his shoulder and a bag full of packages in his hands.

"Hey, baby!" I said, reaching in to give him a kiss.Plez put everything down on the sofa and picked up Lawrence into the air. "Are we gonna have fun, little man?"

"Yeah!"

"You ready for Christmas?"

"Yeah!"

"If you're good, maybe your mama and me will let you open one present, okay?"

"Yay!"

"Plez, I was hoping we could go to my parents' house for Christmas dinner," I said.

"Yeah, I'm hip to that."

Lawrence sat back down on the sofa and finished eating his cooled-off sandwich and soup. Plez pulled a piece from the sandwich and ate it. Lawrence slapped Plez's hand away.

"Hey, you don't do that!" Plez snapped.

"But it's mine."

"You can share with Plez, right?" I asked.

Lawrence shook his head.

"What the fuck is wrong with you?" Plez spat.

"Don't you think you're being hard on him? He's just a boy."

"You need to teach that little nigga some respect for his

elders or *I'll* do it."

Plez was so close to my face I could feel his breath. I blinked, not knowing what else to say. "Baby, go ahead and finish your food," I said to my son.

Plez took his bag and went into the bedroom. I followed.

"What was that all about?"

"That boy ain't got any respect."

"He didn't mean any harm, Plez."

"He keeps that shit up, and he'll see a different side of me."

Plez went into his bag and pulled out some sweatpants and a T-shirt with a Black Power fist salute on it. He began taking his change out of his pockets and went to put it on my dresser like he always did, noticing the change he'd left before was gone.

"What happened to the change I left on this dresser?"

"Oh, Lawrence put it in his bank."

"You gave that boy my money?"

"What's the big deal; it was just a little chump change."

"Lawrence! Bring your little ass in here!" Plez screamed.

Lawrence came into the room. Fright showed on his face.

"Did you take my money?"

Lawrence stood in the doorway, looking down, shifting his feet from side to side.

"Boy, look at me when I'm talkin' to you! Did you take my money?" He pulled Lawrence into the room, grabbing him by his arms. He threw Lawrence on my bed.

"Plez, are you crazy? Don't put your hands on my child! I told him he could have the money!" I said, pushing Plez away from my son.

"Oh, you've done lost your fucking mind. You don't put your hands on me, do you understand?" Plez grabbed me by my wrists and began backing me toward the wall. His eyes blazed like angry fire.

"Plez, let go of me!" I yelled."Leave my mommy alone!" My son yelled as he sat at the edge of my bed, tears streaming down his face. He swung his little clenched fists wildly in the air, then jumped off the bed and ran up to Plez, hitting him in the calves, still screaming, "Leave my mommy alone!" Plez turned around with a bewildered look on his face. He took off his belt, a black leather strap with metal holes in it, and grabbed Lawrence by his wrists and started beating him with it. Lawrence screamed as he thrashed around and away from Plez's belt."Don't you ever raise your hands to me again, nigga, do you understand?" Plez yelled. He seemed deeply lost in a zone I didn't know if I could bring him out of.

Lawrence caught the belt as it came down and held onto it.

"Let go of it!" Plez yelled.

"You're gonna beat me!" Lawrence yelled back.

"You damn right I am!"

I slumped to the floor, feeling light headed. The man in front of me, whipping the crap out of my son, wasn't the man who'd swung some stranger's child on a park swing back in November. I didn't know this man.

"You're gonna learn how to respect me," Plez said, yanking the belt from Lawrence with one big tug.

Lawrence began kicking at Plez, who grabbed his leg and brought the belt down. All of a sudden I heard a bloodcurdling scream. I looked over at my son, who was cupping his crotch. The screams were so loud, I became aware of Mr. Davis downstairs and I feared what he might've been thinking, assuming he was home. I leaped over to my son, trying to protect him like I should have in the first place. Whatever fear I had of Plez vanished and was replaced with anger when he hit my son in the crotch with the belt. Plez stood there for a moment; looking startled and out of breath, his belt swinging at his side.

"What are you, crazy?" I screamed.

"What's wrong with him?" Plez asked, his voice having lost its earlier heat.

I helped my son up and took him into the bathroom. I pulled down his pants and peeled down his underwear where I saw speckles of blood. His penis had been cut just below the urethra. Lawrence shook in pain as my blood boiled over. I jumped up and marched into the bedroom where Plez waited, like he was waiting for a doctor to come back with test results.

"Nigga, get the fuck out of my house!" I screamed.

"I ain't goin' anywhere! I paid the rent, remember?"

"Fine. You stay, we'll go." I went throughout the apartment like a woman on a mission, grabbing anything my eyes saw and put it in a bag. "Is he all right?" Plez asked, looking helpless in the middle of my swift movement.

"Hell no, he ain't all right! You hit him in his dick, and now he's bleeding. You don't do that to a five-year-old boy!"

"I didn't mean to hit him there. If he'd stayed still he wouldn't have gotten hit there. You saw him, he was kicking at me. I couldn't help where the belt got him."

"You had no business hitting him in the first place. He's *my* son, not yours!"

I looked over to my son, who looked like a small wounded animal. "Lawrence, baby, come on over and let me put your coat on."

Lawrence walked over with pain all over his face, careful not to look at Plez. He held his crotch and the tears continued to fall even though he'd stopped screaming. I knew it hurt, and I wished that I could've taken that belt to do the same thing to Plez to make him feel what my son was feeling.

"Hey, little man; you know that I didn't mean to do it, right? It's just that you can't take things that don't belong to you."

"You're gonna beat my child over ten lousy dollars, if that?"

Plez looked sorry, and a little bit scared. "Hey, little man. Look at what I bought you," he said, running over to the sofa and dug through the bag of packages he'd brought.

"Lawrence, let's go," I said, taking him by the hand.

I went into his room and took some pajamas and a change of clothes for him. He clutched his teddy bear as if it would help soothe the pain. I felt horrible. I'd brought this monster into my life and served him on a silver tray to my son. We left the apartment, not saying a single word to Plez.

We went out into the cold night. The fallen snow whirled around from the wind. As we got to the bus stop I could see the bus approaching.

"Where are we going, Mommy?"

"We're going to visit Grandma, okay. But baby, do me a favor; don't tell anyone what happened."

Lawrence nodded his head, which was hidden by the oversize hood of his coat. I felt bad enough that it had happened and I didn't want to hear what my parents had to say, especially Mama. Sitting on the bus, we watched as a real-life winter wonderland passed us by. Kids were running around on the white snow which glowed from the twinkling Christmas lights on the houses and trees. The children were running around a snowman, hitting one another with snowballs in the early evening. The joyful scene was a nice change from the earlier horror with Plez.

When we got to the house, I rang the doorbell. I was too nervous to look for the key that I still had. I was praying that nothing would appear strange to her. I wanted to just get inside, clean up Lawrence's wound, and get to work.

"Hey, Pumpkin-Doodle! What are ya'll doin' over here? I thought you weren't comin' over until tomorrow afternoon," Mama said, kneeling down to hug Lawrence.

"Well, it's the holidays and I felt Lawrence should be with Grandma, Granddaddy, and Auntie. Why wait, right?"

"Lawrence, I baked some Christmas cookies. Do you want some cookies?"

"Yeah!" Lawrence yelled, grinning. I was proud of him. He played his part well.

But my mama knew something was up when she said, "You look stressed."

"I just have a lot on my mind. I didn't want to have to work tonight."

"I know how you feel," she said, and left it alone.

After I managed to get Lawrence cleaned up and put Vaseline on his injury, I went to work. It was early, but I didn't want to be at Mama's house just in case she decided to ask more questions. I figured I could have Clayton take me back to my place and help me bring the gifts to my parents' house. That way Lawrence could at least have a happy Christmas day.

Thank God Clayton was there. I knew I could tell him what happened because he didn't like Plez anyway, and he'd lend a sympathetic ear. The moment I punched in and went onto the floor, I could see that Clayton was in a very good mood.

"Someone's getting into the holiday spirit," I said.

"Darling, I received the best Christmas gift ever. Travis came back."

"That's good news? Last I heard, you wanted nothing to do with him."

"Yes, but you did say that maybe we could work it out.

We're trying to do just that."

I had no idea that they were talking. Last he told me, Travis had been begging and pleading for Clayton to take him back, but Clayton enjoyed Travis's squirming. I was just surprised that after all the "I can't take this shit no more!" proclamations, he'd actually go back to him.

Still, it was nice to see him smiling. There had been a void in him before; despite all of the "darlings," I knew he held a lot of loneliness.Clayton said that the last time Travis came to the apartment he wasn't feeling well. "Maybe if he sees me taking care of his ass, he might appreciate what he gave up to go whoring around," Clayton told me.

"Has he been to a doctor?" I asked.

"He just has a nagging flu is all, darling. He'll be fine. His immune system is messed up from all that drinking he's been doing. That ought to teach him."

Clayton told me that when Travis was feeling better he'd like to have me and Lawrence over for dinner. Needless to say, Plez wasn't invited.

The night seemed to go by quickly, my stomach fluttering with butterflies. What was supposed to be a wonderful holiday had me running scared. I couldn't help but shake the feeling that Mama had tried to play as though nothing was wrong, but she knew. She probably waited until I left to start questioning Lawrence about what happened. I wouldn't have been surprised if she withheld cookies from him until he told the truth.

I could see it now, me opening the front door only to have her standing there, holding my son's hand while she shook her head like I was an awful parent. She was in no position to judge me after the years of hell she put up with from Daddy.

Evelyn decided she was in the Christmas spirit and let Clayton and me leave at six in the morning, an hour early. When it was time for us to punch out and leave I hee-hawed around. Just as I wasn't looking forward to Mama's twenty-one questions, I was afraid I'd go back home and find Plez still there. I was running on hours of paranoia and I was surprised that Clayton hadn't tried to slap the mess out of me to calm me down.As we waited for his car to warm up, I sat there shivering, exhaling streams of cold breath.

"Now, are you sure that you wanna do this? Please don't

have me come over to your place and have to go upside that Negro's head," Clayton said, gripping the steering wheel.

"He probably won't do anything if you're there," I said. The truth was, I didn't know. Clayton gave me the impression that despite his fey ways, he'd pick up a brick and knock someone out if he had to. I remembered how angry he was at the bar he took me to when we went to meet up with Travis.

"I'm just saying, darling. If he lays one hand on me, I will do my best to stomp him up in that place."

Although I knew Clayton wouldn't walk away from a fight with Plez, I knew he wouldn't win it. But I was sure that at the very least he'd leave Plez with something to think about.

~ * * * ~

When we pulled up to the apartment, I looked up to see the lights were out. I knew there had been lights on before I left with my son. Maybe Plez was asleep or he'd left. As soon as we got to the door, Clayton took my keys from me and opened the door so hard that the knob slammed into the wall. I don't know where he summoned it from, but he managed to put some bass in his voice to give it a menacing effect. He shouted, "Nigga, if you're in here, you better throw some clothes on and get your ass out of here quick-fast before I beat you like you stole something!"

We stood still, staring into the darkness of the apartment. I put my gloved hand to my mouth to keep from breaking into laughter at Clayton's fake thug voice.

"Girl, ain't nobody here," he said, throwing on the light switch. "Hurry up and get whatever you came here for so we can go."

I noticed that Plez's stuff was gone. Even the packages he'd brought were gone. It all felt oddly permanent.

We loaded up all of the gifts, plus my overnight bag into Clayton's car and headed toward my parents' house. I prayed they were still asleep. "Are you working tomorrow night?" Clayton asked me.

"No, thank God."

"Well, merry Christmas. You have a wonderful time with your family, and don't get caught up in any mess."

"I won't," I said, giving Clayton a kiss on the cheek. "You and Travis have a merry Christmas, too."

I got out of the car and ran to the house, my feet sliding over freshly fallen snow. I went around to the back and went in through the kitchen. The smell of cornbread dressing tapped my nose, reminding me of past Christmases. I saw that Mama had made two sweet potato pies, both held up on a couple of canned goods. I knew she had been cooking well into the early morning because the kitchen was a mess.

I went upstairs and took a shower. I tried to get a little sleep even though I knew that Lawrence would be around shortly, waking us all up to tear into his gifts.

~ * * * ~

At eight o'clock, I'd just started to reach a deep sleep when I felt a pushing against my shoulder. It was my son with a big Kool-Aid grin on his face.

"Mommy, can we open presents now?"

I'd have plenty of time to nap later after we all ate Christmas dinner. "Sure, baby. Go wake up Grandma and Granddaddy."

I went into Marva's room. She was already coming out of a deep sleep. I think she knew Santa had brought her new sketch pads.

We all sat and watched as Lawrence tore open the carefully wrapped presents. I smiled as his smile got bigger and bigger after each toy package he opened. The clothes he got were tossed to the side; even though we had him try things on just to make sure they fit. Mama showed me a fifty-dollar savings bond she'd bought him and said that she would start buying one for him every Christmas so he'd have money put away for college. That meant more to me than the toys.

Daddy went back upstairs to watch TV and drink beer. He was very low-key. Marva put her sketch books and colored pencils away and sat on the floor with Lawrence, building stuff out of his Legos. Mama was working hard in the kitchen trying to finish dinner so we could eat by 1:00 pm. And that's when the doorbell rang.

"Well, don't you look handsome," Mama said to the unannounced guest. I walked to the door to see Plez standing there with bags and bags full of gifts. He was wearing the clothes that I'd bought him for Christmas and his Aramis scent entered the house before he did.

"If you croon me a tune, Mr. Mathis, I'll help you with these bags," Mama joked.

"Merry Christmas to you" Plez sang in his pitiful voice. What made it worse was that he was actually serious with it, too. Mama looked disappointed but took the bags from him anyway. Just because Plez looked like Johnny Mathis didn't mean he could sing like him.Plez took off his boots, giving me a quick glance. "I had to run home and get all this stuff for you all. I hope ya'll like them." Then he dug through the bag like he was Santa Claus himself, passing out gifts for everyone.He gave Mama a pearl necklace and earrings. I wondered if they were even real pearls because they looked cheap. He gave Daddy a red silk tie and matching handkerchief. Marva got a book of world-famous artists, and Lawrence made out really well. Plez had bought him a toy rifle and bunny rabbit that when shot at, would run in different directions. He bought him Candy Land, Connect Four and a whole bunch of other games. At first Lawrence just stood near me, holding onto my leg, afraid to go anywhere near Plez. But Plez was determined, and he playfully tackled Lawrence to the ground, lifting up his shirt and began blowing farting sounds into his stomach, which made Lawrence crack up with laughter.

Mama stood off to the side admiring her jewelry. "Isn't that beautiful?" she kept asking as though she didn't own a single piece of jewelry and this was her first. Daddy simply said, "Thank you" and shook Plez's hand and went to go sit down in the family room.

"Come here, baby, I wanna show you something," he said, grabbing my hand and leading me to the window in the living room. Outside, near the curb, was a 1977 champagne-colored Cadillac Eldorado. I crossed my arms, trying to act unimpressed.

Mama poked her head around the corner to see what Plez was so excited about. "You mean to tell me he bought you a car? Honey, you need to hold on to this one!" Mama said, patting Plez on the back before going back into the kitchen.

"Why are you here?" I asked.

"You like the car? I know it's used, but it'll get you through once you get your license. I'll even teach you how to drive it," he said, ignoring my question.

"Clayton's teaching me how to drive, remember?" I said sharply.

Plez made sure no one could hear us. "Listen, don't think I don't know what this is about, okay?" Plez said in a hushed tone, "I fucked up. I know that."

"You're damned right you fucked up," I said, fighting to keep my voice down. "You put your hands on my child. How am I supposed to forgive you for that?"

"Baby, I'm not perfect. I'm sorry that I hurt him like that. I'm sorry I hurt *you* like that."

I looked up into his sensuous eyes. I was spellbound, though that didn't change my feelings about what he did to my child. He stood silent for two beats, knowing that no words would help make this better.

"You're pissed. I get that. I'd be pissed too if I were you. Just know that I love you and I'd like another chance with you." Then he looked over at Lawrence, who was off in the distance playing and said, "With the both of you."

Christmas dinner was both delicious and confusing. I sat across from a man who'd done something I wasn't sure I'd be able to forgive or forget. But as our family's fellowship went on, Plez charmed the room. Everyone laughed at his jokes, or nodded at his observations about stuff. In between all of that, I'd catch him looking at me, his lower lip twitching in a vulnerable way, his eyes telling me that he was sorry for what he'd done.

Later, me and Marva helped Mama put all the food into plastic containers, or covered plated food with aluminum foil. Daddy had gone upstairs for what seemed like the millionth time that day, only this time to sleep. The rest of the house was quiet despite our women chatter. I went to the window to see Plez outside with Lawrence, playing in the snow. My eyes welled up with tears, seeing them laying side by side, making snow angels. Then they ran around the yard throwing snowballs at each other. They both seemed so full of life. They also looked the way I'd hoped they would: like father and son.Plez kneeled down at Lawrence's level and whispered something to him. Lawrence smiled broadly and gave Plez a big hug. Plez turned and looked up at me through the window and smiled. I smiled back half-heartedly. That's when I asked myself, if my son could forgive Plez, why couldn't I?

CHAPTER

18

S OMETHING TOLD ME THAT EMMA Pruitt wouldn't make it past the first of the New Year.

Clayton warned me that people were going to die. It was just a fact of life. He'd been working at the home for so long that he was almost numb to it. But she was the first patient whose body I saw the life leave from, and it hurt me to know I couldn't stop it.

I saw how some of those nurses "cared" for her in her last days, which meant they hardly cared at all. Sure, they did what was necessary, but you could tell they were just waiting to dump her stuff and change the bed sheets for a new patient.She was a sweet black lady who always had family visiting, unlike some of the other patients. She loved to talk and as I helped her bathe and dress, she'd tell me how she loved being a nurse and my bedside manner was like hers, and that I was much too valuable playing the background to the nurses' foreground.When I saw them come to take her body away, I realized that I wanted to go back to school to further my education. I'd finally recognized my calling.I still enjoyed patient care, but I wanted more. I knew that I could be a better nurse than Dwayne, who spent more time trying to catch phone numbers from women than taking care of his patients. But I watched

Clayton very closely and knew that he was the kind of nurse I wanted to be.I used to watch my mother come home tired, but she never regretted her life as a surgical technician because she did her part in helping people. I longed to come home tired from doing my part to help people too.

I knew that 1980 was the beginning of something, but I didn't know what. Maybe it was in the air, or just one of those feelings I had in my gut. I still wasn't sure what I wanted to do with my relationship with Plez. After seeing him beat my son like that, I wasn't sure I wanted to be bothered. But the image of him hugging Lawrence outside in the snow warmed my heart.

"Do you love him?" Clayton asked me.

"What do you think?"

"Darling, if you think he's worth it, you need to move past all of that other stuff. Do you think he meant to hit Lawrence like that?"

"No, I don't. I saw the whole thing, and Lawrence *was* moving around a lot, kicking and stuff."

"Maybe Plez was raised to believe in spanking as a form of discipline," Clayton said with a shrug.

I didn't know one way or the other. Plez hadn't really spoken about his family.

"Listen, you know I can't stand the guy."

"I know," I said.We were quiet for a moment when something else hit me. I was two weeks late with my period. I suddenly thought about all the sex we had, and it wasn't protected. Most times Plez pulled out, but there were the times when he was in me so deep that I didn't care where he came. I looked at Clayton. I could feel the tears coming, and even though I tilted my head back and took a deep breath to stop them, they fell.

"Cheryl, what is going on with you, girl? He's just a man. You shouldn't let any man rent that much space in your head."

"I'm two weeks late," I said, turning my face in shame.

"You mean..."

I nodded my head, tears falling all over the place. "I can't be pregnant, Clayton. I got one child and that's hard enough."

"Well, you need to go get that checked out."

"Did you take Travis to the doctor?"

"No, but this ain't the same thing, darling. The flu goes away; a pregnancy doesn't, unless you...well, you know."

Yeah, I knew what he was saying, and *that* was out of the question, just as it was when I became pregnant with Lawrence. But maybe I was getting ahead of myself. There may have been other reasons why I hadn't had my period. I hoped so, anyway.

~ * * * ~

February was the month of fear. It took that long for me to swallow whatever it was that made me afraid of the possibility of carrying Plez's child; that and the fact that my breasts were so sore.Clayton agreed to take me to the free clinic. I needed his support, and even his advice on how I would break the news to Plez and my family. I was most concerned with how my family would take it. Being on my own had given us enough space to come together out of love, but I was afraid of taking steps back, because I knew they'd think I hadn't learned anything.

When Clayton came to pick me up, I was surprised to see Travis sitting in the front seat. As I got closer to the car, he turned and looked at me. He looked like a living skeleton with death in his eyes. His hair was thin and wispy, nothing like the lush curls he had on his head the first time I saw him at the bar.

When I got into the backseat, kicking snow off my heels before closing the car door, I could tell Clayton was in a bad mood. I said hello to them, but I was so horrified by Travis's appearance that I couldn't bring myself to say much else.

"Anybody ever tell you that you look like those black girls from Sister Sledge?" Travis asked me in a vacant tone.

"Travis, she doesn't look anything like those women. What, you think because she's black that we all look alike?" Clayton snapped.

"Clayton, it's all right. I'm flattered, actually," I said, trying to improve the mood in the car. But Clayton was right; I didn't look anything like those women.

"He's been uttering nonsense for the past three weeks and I'm getting sick of it," Clayton said, looking at me through the rearview window.

"I'm sure he doesn't mean any harm."

"No, darling, something is very wrong with him."

When we got to the clinic, the look on people's faces was close to what I'm sure my face looked like when I saw Travis. But I had tried to hide my expression. After signing in, we found three seats together. People stared as Travis sat down. The truth was he looked horrible. His face was sunken in and his clothes looked like they were way too big for him. Whatever Travis had, wasn't the flu.

When the nurse called me, I felt like a rock had hit the bottom of my stomach. This was the moment that would decide my fate. Clayton grabbed my hand and kissed it, telling me, "Girl, go on ahead. Everything is going to be fine."

The nurse had me pee in a cup and told me to hang on tight. There were so many people in that clinic that I knew I'd be waiting a long time. In my mind, I played over and over again different responses Plez and then my family would have if I was pregnant. In between those random thoughts I couldn't help but wonder what Clayton was going through, worrying about Travis.

The nurse finally came back into the consult room. I tried to search her face for some indication of the results. I should have known better, because she had the best poker face I'd ever seen in my life. She looked at me, put her hand on my shoulder, and told me what I'd already figured out in the last 45 minutes: I was pregnant.

When she told me, it was as if someone had punched me in the stomach. All the color drained from the room. Her touch was supposed to be comforting, but I got no comfort from it. I just said "Thank you" and then I forgot everything else that she said. I watched her lips move, and I shook or nodded my head, but I didn't hear anything she was saying to me.

I walked back into the waiting room, my legs feeling as though they were covered in concrete. Travis and Clayton weren't back yet, so I sat down and tried to let my news sink in.

Would it be so bad? After Christmas, Plez pursued me with a vengeance, his charms more powerful than ever. He was over at my apartment practically every day. And those days had been good ones, so good that I began to forget why I was upset with him in the first place. Then, I'd look at my son and remember. But I watched Plez very closely with Lawrence, and he knew I was watching him, and he was once again like the man I'd seen in the park, pushing that boy on the swing. As Travis and Clayton came back into the waiting room, I asked myself again, would it be so bad?

Travis appeared shaky and tears fell down his face. Clayton had tears dripping down his face too, but he couldn't wipe them away because he was helping Travis walk. When I saw them, it made me press pause on my own dilemma and brought me back into the present moment.

`I got up and rushed over to them as they made their way to the door. For a second I thought they were going to leave me.

"What did they say?" I asked.But Clayton didn't say anything until he helped Travis into the car and closed the passenger door. He turned to me and for the first time was able to wipe away those tears that continued to fall.

"Clayton, you're scaring me. What did they say?" I asked again.

Clayton leaned against that passenger door as I saw Travis's head slump down, putting his face into his boney hands. Clayton tilted his head toward the gray sky and exhaled, then he looked at me and said, "They said two things. They said that Travis has something called GRID."

"What in the hell is that?"

"It stands for Gay-Related Immune Deficiency."

"What else did they say?"

"They said that the Center for Disease Control had a few reported cases in San Francisco, Los Angeles, and New York and that most of those men haven't survived. There's a good chance that Travis is going to die."

I reached over and hugged Clayton tightly, which he allowed me to do. He sobbed loudly. Standing in the snow drift, I rocked him, patted his head, and told him that I'd be there for both of them.

When I got home, I felt as though I'd been up for days. My emotions were heavy; my own future was changing, andClayton was losing his boyfriend. All he had ever wanted was someone to love, so I knew he didn't deserve this. I opened the apartment door to see Plez sitting with Lawrence, sharing a box of animal crackers while Lawrence colored in his coloring books. It was a welcome sight that offered me some comfort in telling Plez what I had to tell him.

Plez looked up and knew immediately something was up.

"What's the matter?"

"We need to talk," I said, letting my coat fall onto the floor.

"What happened?"

I turned to look at Lawrence. I had a split second to figure out if I wanted him in the room when I told Plez I was carrying his child. That was the easy part. Talking about Clayton's boyfriend dying was harder.

"I'm pregnant."

"You mean, I'm gonna be a daddy?"

"Yes," I stuttered out. Plez leaped up and hugged me so tightly I couldn't breathe. Lawrence looked up and smiled.

"You don't seem too happy about it," Plez said.

"I was worried about how you'd respond."

"That's outta sight!"

I smiled, avoiding eye contact.

"What, you don't want to have my baby?"

"It's not that. I got some bad news today. It's Clayton. His lover is dying."

Plez's face tensed up at the sound of Clayton's name. Then it softened as he looked into my eyes.

"Look, I'm sorry about your friend. How's he holding up?"

"He's devastated. How do you think he's holding up?"

"He's got cancer or something?"

"No. It's some gay-related something or other."

"Figures," Plez mumbled.

"You could be a little more compassionate."

"Well, what do you want me to say? If it's some gay thing, he probably got it from doing some of that nasty shit those people do."

"Okay, fine. I get it. You don't like gay people. I guess it doesn't matter that my best friend is losing someone very close to him."

"I'm sorry, Cheryl. Just don't expect me to understand that shit because I don't."

There was a silence. Lawrence had his eyes so far down our mouths that I knew I should get him away from the conversation.

"Lawrence, take your coloring books and those crackers and go into your room. You can come back out when we're done, okay?"

Lawrence slowly did as he was told, turning back one last time as if to say, "Are you sure?" Since Plez was uncomfortable with the news about Clayton, I didn't know what else to say.

"So I guess we should get married then, right?" Plez asked, changing the subject.

I shook my head, rolling my eyes. "Plez, you don't have to marry me. Just help me raise your child."

"It doesn't matter if this happened now or later. I want to marry you. I love you."

"How can I marry you when there are still things I don't know about you?"

"But ain't that part of what makes this so great? Every day is a revelation. You don't have to know everything all at once."

"But marriage is a huge commitment. Not only that, but it will also affect that little boy in there. He already has one man in his life that doesn't give a shit; I wouldn't want you to run from him if this doesn't work."

"It will work. I promise that."

"I don't know."

"Okay, what do you wanna know about me?"

"You ain't talked about your family."

Plez's face tensed up again. He closed his eyes and gulped softly. "My father was killed by the Klan in Alabama. They beat him in front of me, my brother, and sister. While he lay on the ground bleeding to death, they took my mother into another room and raped her."

"Oh my God!"

"When I heard the screams, I ran to the room and found one of those men with his Klan robe hiked up to his waist and his pants down around his ankles, ramming into my mother while those other sons of bitches stood there laughing."

Plez said that his mother tried to fight back and as she scratched at the man on top of her, she managed to pull his hood off. The man on top of her was a man named Mr. Bentley, who owned the local Five-and-Dime. Plez had been there earlier that day to buy some cornmeal so that his mother could fry some catfish. Mr. Bentley had sold him the cornmeal. The Klansman nearest the door turned to look at Plez, who had his hand in the doorway. He slammed the door on his fingers.

When the Klansmen were through, they took Plez's father out back, dragging his body down splintered, wooden steps and shot him in the head.

"Mama wasn't the same for a couple years after that. She shut down. She turned into a real whore, bringing all kinds of strange men into the house. My aunt Maybelle came and took us kids to Eatonton, Georgia, with her. Then one night, we got a call that our mother had cut her wrists, trying to kill herself. She survived it, though. My aunt had to bring her back to Georgia."When Plez finished the story, I was sorry I'd even asked. I looked at him, searching his face, trying to get a sense of how he felt. But he told the story very matter-of-factly, like it was about someone else's life.

We were engaged although I had my reservations. I knew it was the right thing to do and at least this way Plez would be around.When I told Mama the news, I left out the fact that I was pregnant. I figured I could wait a little while longer to work the pregnancy into a conversation. Plez was with me. I needed his strength to make up for my fear. Mama was surprised, and I could tell she wasn't happy. All she said was, "That was quick."Plez stood behind me and kept rubbing my belly. That's when it sank in for my mother what the real deal was. She started crying and her body shook. I was sure she was gonna hit me. She raised her hand up, palm out, like she was about to testify to something and said, "Cheryl, am I gonna live long enough for you to make me proud? Why are you such a disappointment?"

I didn't have the chance to respond. She went upstairs to her bedroom and slammed the door. I stood there, feeling as though Mama *had* hit me. With those words she tore up my heart because I knew she was right. Then it occurred to me that Daddy would find out and I was thankful he wasn't there when I told her.

"Watch, she's gonna run and tell it," I said as we made our way to the car.

"They'll come around."

"And what if they don't?"

Plez put the key into the passenger door and opened it for me before saying with a shrug, "Well, if they don't, then fuck 'em."

~ * * ~

By the end of March, Travis, Clayton's boyfriend, had died. It was hard to see a once confident, put-together man like Clayton fall apart from this death. He was unable to go to the funeral because Travis's family didn't want him there. After that, he took a whole month off from work but when he came back, we all noticed the physical change in him. He'd lost some weight and had these dark spots on his temples and a few on his neck. I broke down in tears before he had the opportunity to tell me what I had been fearful of back at the clinic. Whatever Travis had, this GRID thing, or as Clayton said, the *gay plague*, he had given it to Clayton.Clayton didn't even work when he came back, but marched himself into Evelyn's office and said that he had this thing and didn't want to be a danger to the patients and quit.

It would be another two years before the CDC changed the name GRID to AIDS-Acquired Immune Deficiency Syndrome, but it didn't matter because nobody knew anything about either word back then. I think Clayton wanted to quit before anyone had the chance to be uncomfortable with him and plot to get rid of him. Dwayne, like so many others on the floor that day, tried to stay as far away from Clayton as they could. But I didn't care. He was my friend, and before he left, I joked that he wasn't going anywhere because he still had to take me to get my license.

"Darling, so long as the good Lord gives me the strength, you got it. But let's get a move on it," he said with a forced laugh.

But he wouldn't be taking me to get my license. And when things became worse for him, I'd remember hugging him the day he quit— in a way I never hugged my own parents. And as our bodies parted, and before he walked out into the sunlight, I thought that here I had someone special growing inside of me, soon to start a life, while my best friend was losing his.

CHAPTER

19

I THINK GOD HAD A sadistic sense of humor with Clayton.
In those early days of AIDS, most who got it were here
today and gone tomorrow. What God allowed to happen
to my friend made me wonder if God and the Devil were
placing bets on him.

I went to his house with some chicken noodle soup
because he hadn't been eating. When I got there, he opened
the door, holding a lit cigarette in his hand. He looked like
he'd lost a few more pounds by the way his turtleneck hung
loosely around his neck. "I look like shit. I already know this,
darling."

"I wasn't gonna say that."

"You didn't have to. It's all over that pretty little face of
yours." We went inside his apartment. All of the shades were
pulled down, and except for the little sunlight that came
through the cracks at the bottom, the place was dark. It
stunk in there, too. It smelled like sweat, cigarettes, and
stale beer. I noticed that he had empty cans all over the
floor near his sofa. There was a pillow, and a white sheet
rumpled on the sofa. It seemed he had been sleeping in the
living room. Clayton sat down on the sofa and continued
puffing on his cigarette.

"God, Clayton, they make bedrooms for a reason," I said.

"I can't even go into that room. Travis died in there," Clayton said as he put out his cigarette.

"I'm sorry."

"What is that you brought me, some soup?"

"Yeah, it's chicken noodle. I can tell you ain't been eating."

"You can put it in the kitchen. I'll do something with it later."

"You know, a little sunlight never hurt anybody," I said, pulling at the shades to open them.

"No! Keep them closed."

"I'm sorry."

"Put that soup in the kitchen."

I went into the kitchen which looked a wreck. Odors rose from the dish-filled sink. I was shocked that Clayton, despite his hurt, was living like this. I went back into his living room and found a spot next to him on the sofa. He looked at me and shook his head. "You know what kind of fool I am?" he said.

"What are you talking about?"

"I don't know how to feel. Travis ran the streets, fucking every man that would let him, and he brought sickness back here. This plague I have, he gave it to me. But my stupid ass still loves him."

"You two had some good times together. It's normal to feel like that."

Clayton looked at me and chuckled. "So what's it like being pregnant again?"

"It's all right. Plez is doing right by me. He asked me to marry him."

"And what did you say?"

"I said yes."

"Then you're a fool too."

"What?"

"You let yourself get knocked up by somebody you've only known for a couple of months and have the nerve to come up in here and explain feelings to me?"

"Clayton, you're not feeling well, okay? So I'm gonna pretend you didn't say that."

Clayton looked at me for two beats and sucked his teeth as though what I said didn't matter. He reached for his pack of cigarettes and lit up another one. His face wasn't sad, but his eyes were angry. I knew that he wasn't angry with me, but about dying.

"Why me, huh?"

I put my hand on his leg. "Baby, I don't know."

"All I wanted was someone to love me. And look what I got from loving the wrong man."

Clayton pulled his shirt up to reveal more spots covering his chest. I tried not to seem grossed out, like lesions were the most common thing for me to look at.

"Darling, I wish I had something to wear to go with these spots. Polka dots are in this season, you know?"

I laughed nervously. "Don't you think you ought to get those checked out?"

"What makes you think that I haven't already? I'm tired, Cheryl. I'm tired of people coming into the room with space suits on as though I'm some bio hazard. I'm tired of answering the same questions over and over again like, 'Are you homosexual?' or 'Do you or have you ever engaged in the act of sodomy?' They act like they're too grossed out to even say it. And I see these doctors get this 'That's what you get' look on their faces when I answer that yes, I'm a homosexual."

"You gotta keep fighting, Clayton. I mean, there's gotta be someone out there with enough compassion that…"

"Fuck compassion! Anyway, I don't want to talk about me. We're supposed to be talking about you right now. I just want you to make sure you found the right man. *Is* Plez the right man?" he asked, pulling his shirt back down.

"I had my doubts, but he's been much better."

"Just remember, when a person shows you who they really are, you need to believe them."

"Well, I don't want to talk about Plez. I'm here for you," I said, changing the subject. "Are you hungry right now?"

Clayton nodded his head. "I don't know why I lit this cigarette up. I don't want this," he said, putting it out.

I went into the kitchen and found a clean pot to pour the soup in. I heated it up and found a couple of bowls and spoons. We ate the soup in silence. At one point he asked me if I made it or if it was store-bought and I told him that I didn't know how to make soup.

"Well, you better learn fast, darling. You got a family to feed. Kids like their soup almost as much as grown folks."

After we ate, I tried to keep him talking, but I could see he just wanted to sleep. I was tempted to let him lie there on the sofa so I could just watch him; freeze every line and curve of his face into my memory. But then I thought that was weird, so I left.Afterward I went to the community college; which had brochures of different nursing school programs. I wanted to go to school as soon as the next session started. I was determined to be as good a nurse as Clayton. I owed myself that much. I couldn't shake my sadness at seeing Clayton laying up the way he was. He had been a nice-looking man, but to see him whittled down to what I saw in his apartment stayed with me long after I'd left.

When I got home, I let Lawrence watch TV while I sat on the sofa and cried softly. Every time he turned back to look at me, I would pretend I had something in my eyes. He was too young to understand what was going on anyway.Plez finally came over. I was hoping I would've stopped crying by the time he got there, because I knew he wouldn't understand. I could tell by the expression on his face that he had something heavy he wanted to talk about.

"We gotta discuss this arrangement," he said, walking into the apartment without even saying hello first.

"What arrangement?"

"This living arrangement; it don't make no sense that we're together and you're gonna have my child, and we keep jumping back and forth between places."

"I don't want to move into your house, Plez."

"Why? I got more space over there. And at least that way, y'all won't be sleeping on some raggedy mattresses, but actual beds."

"Those mattresses aren't raggedy. Anyway, like I said, I don't want to live in your house. It's *your* house. Plus, I'm closer to work on the south side."

"Why do you think I insisted that you be on a month-to-month? You didn't think I was gonna let you stay here forever, did you?"

I couldn't help but blink when he said that. I didn't realize that he was "letting" me do anything.

"But it's too far from work, Plez."

"I bought you a car, use it."

"I will, once I get my license. Clayton was supposed to..."

I couldn't even continue.

"What's the matter with you?"

"I went to see Clayton today. He's not doing well."

"I know that's your friend, but maybe you shouldn't go over there. You're carrying my child, and I don't want you doing anything that'll put stress on you."

"But he's my friend."

"There ain't anything you can do for him. Ain't he got a family?"

"He doesn't talk about his family."

"Baby, that's their problem. You need to worry about what's going on right here, right now, with your family."

I knew in my heart that I was all that Clayton had, and I planned to be there for him even if Plez didn't approve. I decided then that I wouldn't say anything else to him about the subject. What he didn't know wouldn't hurt him.

CHAPTER

20

MY PREGNANCY WAS NINE MONTHS of hell. Plez saw to that, whether he realized it or not. Instead of Plez worrying about Clayton's illness stressing me out, he should've been worried that *he* was stressing me out.Every hour on the hour, for months, he was on me about giving up my apartment, to move me, Lawrence, and our unborn into his house. My reasons for not wanting to didn't matter, and the more he brought it up, the more it sounded less like a suggestion and more like a command.

He dropped the ball on getting married, too. We'd gone to get all the necessary stuff folks needed when they get their marriage license, and then, nothing happened. I was already pissed that things hadn't gone as I would've hoped. I'd gotten pregnant again outside of wedlock; that in and of itself probably made me look trampy to my parents. Plus, I wasn't even going to get the wedding of my dreams. No beautiful white gown, no church, no crowd of well-wishers or champagne toasts.Plez said that so long as we were together and determined to make everything work, then it didn't matter if we had that piece of paper sooner or later as long as we got it eventually. To me, sooner was better than later.But then, out of the blue, he surprised me with an announcement that made me wonder if he'd always been thinking about things, or if he was just shrewd.

"I hope you don't have any plans Friday. I made an appointment for us to go down to the courthouse."

I'd just started on an eighteen month nursing program to become an LPN. "When on Friday?"

"We're booked at 2:00 pm."

"How long ago did you make that appointment?"

"What difference does it make? You've been bitching about us getting this shit over and done with. Do you wanna get married or not?" he snapped.

I didn't answer right away because I wasn't sure. He was always doing things without asking my opinion. I was still holding onto the hope that Clayton would get better and go with me to take my driver's test. Maybe it was my denial of how serious things were with him, but Plez came over with a driver's manual and insisted that *he* prep me and take me to take my driver's test. I didn't want to start a life with someone who didn't care if I had an objection to something. But all I needed to do was look over at Lawrence and I knew: I couldn't risk having another baby and not having the relationship work out. I had to admit, even though Plez made decisions alone for us, things usually worked out for the best. Maybe things wouldn't be so bad.

"Cheryl, I'm talking to you," he said, drawing me back into the conversation.

"Of course, I do. I'm just surprised you didn't ask me when a good time was. This is such short notice. I wanted to ask my family to be there."

"I don't know why you'd even bother with that. You heard what your mama said. She thinks you're a disappointment, remember? I know I wouldn't want somebody at my wedding who thought that about me."

His truthful words popped me in the face. But I had faith that my parents would eventually get over it."You're right. I guess I should give them more time."

"Yeah, baby. It's not like we're having a big ol' ceremony and they got left out. We're just going down to the courthouse."

"Maybe when we get settled we can have a bunch of people over to celebrate," I said with hopefulness.

There was a knock on the door. I was surprised to see Mr. Davis from downstairs standing there.

"Hi, Cheryl," he said, then looked past me to Plez. "Hey, Plez, I'm glad you're here. Listen, I talked to my nephew, and he said he can bring the truck by. When are you two moving Cheryl's stuff out?"

I was hearing this for the first time. I looked over at Plez. He tossed me a quick glance.

"You know, I was thinking that maybe we could leave everything here and you could get a little extra money from your next tenant for a furnished apartment," Plez said, rubbing his chin.

"Naw. Take this stuff with you," Mr. Davis said, "Do you want the truck or not?"

"Let me get back to you," Plez said, gently pushing Mr. Davis toward the door.

"My nephew is busy, so he's gonna need to know right away."

"Yep, okay." Plez closed the door and looked at me like a little boy caught doing something he had no business doing.

"What was all that about?"

"I figured since we're getting married, we'd have to move you and Lawrence. I sure as hell ain't living here. I told Mr. Davis that you're gonna be out by the end of the month."

"Seems like what I think ain't important. You just do what you want to do anyway."

"Listen, chick. I did what was best for our family. If I left it up to you, I'd be driving back and forth between places."

"You know that's not what I want."

"This is why I didn't want you to sign a lease. Do you know how much he would have charged you to break a lease? It's done, and I don't wanna hear anything else about it."

Nothing I wanted to say would have made a difference.That Friday, we went down to the courthouse and were married. At first I was embarrassed about showing up a full nine months pregnant, but when we got there, there were other couples waiting in the hallway to be married, and at least two of the women were pregnant.

Lawrence looked happy as me and Plez took our vows. Finally, he'd have a father figure and I'd have a husband. We went to Rudolph's Barbeque afterward to celebrate. Plez was in a fantastic mood, and it was infectious. Despite how he did it, I was happy he'd finally made an honest woman out of me.Mr. Davis's nephew came by at the end of the month. The apartment was ready for its new tenant. My boxes were piled high into the nephew's truck. I realized this would be the beginning of my life with Plez. I did love him, and if moving in with him would make him happy, and keep him with me, it was a small sacrifice to make. I was fairly confident that I would pass my driver's test, so that car Plez bought me would finally get some use.

~ * * * ~

September 30, 1980, I gave birth to another son; an early arrival we named Plez Darnell Jackson Jr.. His father was thrilled that I'd suggested it. Not only did he have a son, but one whobore his name.My family came by the hospital. Plez acted like he didn't want anyone to hold the baby except for him. My mama was overwhelmed with joy and didn't care what Plez wanted and excitedly held her newest grandbaby. Plez took that moment to slip a gold band on my finger to make our union official. Again, it seemed more calculated than anything else. On the one hand he seemed annoyed that my family showed up, yet he wanted them around when he declared that I was his wife and he was now the head of our family. The ring wasn't what I expected, nothing like the dazzling diamond I had dreamed I'd one day wear. But I shouldn't have been surprised; I hadn't gotten the wedding I wanted either.

A few days after I was released from the hospital, I called Clayton to tell him the news. He was happy to hear from me, since I hadn't talked to him in a while, but he sounded funny. I asked if he wanted me to bring the baby over so that he could meet his godson, and Clayton began coughing over the phone.

"I'm flattered, darling, but I don't think that's a good idea," he said.

"You sound strange. I'm coming over there," I said.

"Cheryl, please don't. I've been doing a lot of thinking and there's something I need to do."

"What are you gonna do, Clayton?"

"I just want to go to sleep. I'm just getting worse. I can't take this anymore. My body is doing all kinds of crazy things to me. I can barely breathe half the time and I got some kind of yeast infection in my mouth."

"You still haven't been back to the doctor?"

"I told you, they can't do anything for me. They couldn't do anything for Travis, either."

"Did a doctor tell you that? Let me come over and see you," I begged.

"I'm just so tired."

"Have you talked to your family?"

"They want nothing to do with me. Maybe they're right; maybe I brought this on myself." Clayton started to sob.

"I don't wanna hear you talk like that. It's not your fault. Please, let me come over."

"If you want to, but I wouldn't if I were you." Then the line went dead.

I went to work to tell Evelyn that I'd talked to Clayton and that he sounded like he was gonna do something desperate. She took out Clayton's employment file. We looked to see if there were any emergency contact numbers. I found two numbers: one was Travis's work number and the other was for Elizabeth and Eddie Hall, Clayton's parents in Chicago. Travis's number was useless, so I wrote Clayton's parents' number on a piece of paper and put it in my purse.

~ * * * ~

Plez was at work and I'd just put the baby down for a nap when I decided to call Clayton again. He didn't answer his phone. I called the number on that scrap of paper.

"Hello," an older female voice said.

"Yes, am I speaking with Elizabeth Hall?"

"This is she."

"Mrs. Hall, my name is Cheryl Jackson. I'm calling from Minneapolis. Do you have a son named Clayton?"

There was silence on the other end.

"Mrs. Hall?"

"My son is dead," she said.

"Mrs. Hall, Clayton isn't dead, but he's very ill. He doesn't have anyone here in Minneapolis to see about him except for me. I was wondering if there was any way you could come here and…"

"Clayton is dead to me. He made his choice."

"What choice?"

"To live like *that*."

"To live like what? Are you talking about him being gay?"

"First of all, Miss, I don't know you. And, I don't feel I need to explain myself to you. But I will tell you this: You can't win against the wrath of God. I know all about that gay plague Clayton's got. He called over here to tell me about it. Since he wanted to depart from God's plan, then he got what he got. Good day to you." And she hung up on me.

I knew that I had to go over to Clayton's apartment right away. His life was at stake, and I didn't want my last memories of him to be some vague conversation. I waited until Plez came home from work and told him that I wanted to go to the grocery store. He offered to drive me.

"But baby, how am I ever gonna learn to be confident in my driving if I don't do it myself?"

"That's true. Just don't get pulled over by the police, because I ain't got the money to spring your ass out of jail," he said.

"Don't worry, I'll be careful."

I jumped my ass into my car like *my* life depended on it. I stayed off the freeway and took the side streets. When I got to Clayton's place, it felt chilly all of a sudden, even though the day was beautiful. I went to his door and banged on it. I didn't get a response. Luckily there was a woman who was coming out of her unit and she told me where I could find the landlord, who lived on the premises. I knocked on his door just as loudly until he opened it. He looked at me as though I had interrupted something.

"Yeah?" he said.

"Hi. My name is Cheryl Jackson and my friend is one of your tenants."

"Who's your friend?" he asked me, smacking his bubble gum.

"Clayton Hall."

"Okay."

I was pissed at this man because he acted like he just didn't give a good fuck.

"I spoke to him earlier and he sounded funny. I tried calling him back and he isn't answering his phone."

"Maybe he doesn't wanna be bothered. Did you ever

think of that?"

"You didn't hear our conversation."

"So what do you want me to do?"

"You have keys to all the units, don't you?"

"Maybe."

He was being so smart-ass about it that I wanted to slap the taste out of his mouth. "Do you think we could go up to his apartment and see if he's all right?"

"Lady, people around here tend to keep to themselves. Like I said, maybe he just doesn't wanna be bothered."

In the background I could see some woman moving around with a white sheet covering her naked body. I noticed he had on a navy terry cloth robe, his belly poking out. I guess I had been interrupting their sex.

"Wilber, tell whoever that is to go away before my kitty cat gets cold."

I know I made a face when I heard that because I couldn't imagine any woman letting this greasy fat man bounce up and down on top of them unless there was some money involved, or unless she looked worse than he did.

"As you can see I'm kinda busy so if there's nothing else," he said, attempting to close the door, but I blocked it with my elbow.

"Look, sir. I'm not trying to waste your time. I didn't mean to get you out the bed but I'm worried about my friend."

This Wilber guy sized me up and suddenly started to smile. I guess he thought I was going to throw him some of my cookie in exchange for him letting me into Clayton's place."Gimme a minute," he said, and shut the door. I stood outside his door, preparing to beat on it some more if he didn't come out. Thank God he finally threw some clothes on and came out. We went up two flights of stairs to Clayton's apartment.Wilber took out a large key chain that seemed to have every key to every house and apartment complex in Minneapolis. He took his time going through them.

"Now let's see what we have here. Brewster, Carlson, Dodd, Thompson—oh wait, I've gone too far. Baxter, Brewster, Carlson, Dodd, Hall—here it is."

"Would you hurry up, please?" I said. I didn't care how bitchy I sounded.

"Now watch. We'll go in here and he'll be in the bathroom showering or something. I'm sure there's nothing to worry about, pretty lady."

As he put the key into the lock, it seemed like an eternity. When he opened the door the air felt both cold and still. My feeling that something was wrong only increased.

"Mr. Hall?" Wilber shouted.

"Clayton?" I shouted even louder.

We went into the living room, the last room I'd seen Clayton in. There on the sofa he lay with a quilt covering him up to his neck. His face was even more sunken in since I last saw him. One eye stared upward toward the sky while the other one was closed. His mouth was open. Wilber went over to him and pulled the quilt away to reveal Clayton laying there naked, with the exception of a towel he had folded around his privates and butt into a soiled, diaper-like thing. He looked like a skeleton with skin. He was covered with more lesions since the last time I saw him.

I felt as though my breath was being pulled from me, followed by a numbing. Wilber stood there, not knowing what to say or do. I'm sure he'd never seen anything like it either. On the floor was two empty bottles of insulin and a syringe. Clayton wasn't diabetic, so I bet he had stolen them from the nursing home, because someone had said that they had come up short two bottles when they went to do inventory. I didn't think anything about it then, but Clayton must've taken them the day he went to resign. He must've known then he was going to do this.

Wilber went to the phone and called 911. I leaned over Clayton and covered him up again. "I knew it, I knew it, I knew it," was all I could say.

Everything that happened after that was a blur to me. I didn't care to talk to the police and paramedics. I looked around, hoping Wilber could've spoken for me, but he was gone.

After what seemed like hours of pacing Clayton's apartment, I finally went home. I drove the entire way back on mental auto pilot. As I got out of the car, I realized that I didn't have any groceries to show for being gone for so long. But I didn't care. I had just lost my best friend. Plez was gonna have to understand that.

Before I could even get my key out, Plez opened the

door. His eyes hit every part of my being as though he were looking for something.

"Where's the groceries?" was the first thing out of his mouth.

I just looked at him stupidly. I knew my face was a wreck from crying the whole ride home.

"Did you fall and bump your fucking head? I asked you a question."

"Clayton killed himself," I blurted out, walking into the kitchen.

"Didn't I tell you to leave that shit to his family to deal with?"

"I'm all he had, Plez."

"So you lied to me? That's cool."

At that moment I heard Plez Jr.. crying. As I turned my face in the direction of where his crying came from, I felt a sharp stinging on my face. The surprise element was only part of the force that sent me falling into the counter and then to the floor. Plez grabbed my hair, which sent my memory back to when my daddy had pulled my hair, stomping me for being pregnant that first time.

"Plez, what are you doing?" I screamed.

"That's for lying to me," he said, pushing my head forward as he released his grip on my hair. My mind raced. I thought, "Why didn't I go by the store and pick something up real quick? Why did I lie in the first place? Did he just put his hands on me again for the second time?"

I could hear our son crying in the distance and it was like we were crying in duet.

"Shut that shit up before I give you something to cry about!" Plez commanded.

The sun shined through the kitchen window and while I looked up at him, he was surrounded by light. His body was like a muscled shadow. I tried telling myself to shut the hell up before I got anything worse, but my body trembled and the tears kept coming. I prayed to God to help me collect myself. That's when I noticed the shift in Plez. He had grabbed my wrists and pushed me against the wall the day he beat Lawrence and now he was slapping the mess out of me.

I knew I'd brought it on myself. I should've just told the truth. At least then all he would've done was yell at me. And then he would've calmed down, just like I knew he'd calm down after slapping me. And in that calm, I'd work my ass off to keep him happy. While Plez went to pick up his son, my thoughts became like clouds, drifting by slowly. One of my thoughts was that Clayton was dead. Then I thought about who would clean out Clayton's apartment and what would happen to his stuff since his parents wouldn't want it? And then, a smile creased my lips. Because I realized in the long run a slap was nothing. If I could just keep Plez happy, and I was determined to do that, I knew I'd avoid much worse—a full fledged beating.

CHAPTER

21

T HE 1980s WERE A BLUR of pastels and neon lights; teased hair, frosted lip colors, and blue eyeliner. And through the fashions and the fads, Plez either sent me into orbit with his love, or kept me pelted to the ground with his temper.Plez wasn't a make-love type of man; he was a fucker. He'd get a shit-kicking grin on his face whenever I came because he loved to use sex as a way of keeping me in line. And it was so good, that he'd call me a bitch in one angry second, and then screw me to the point I was speaking in tongues the next.

It was important for him to always feel in control. He was a god in his own mind because the real God could no longer do anything for him. I should've known that after; we moved in with him he lost all interest in worship service. At first he pretended to be sick, but finally he came clean and said that our worship service was boring because we didn't believe in using musical instruments. He said he wanted to hear a bass, drum, or tambourine underneath our voices as we sang. Plain and simple, he wanted to be entertained. As far as he was concerned, he didn't need to go to church, but could stay home and read his Bible and be just as saved, if not more than us folk who professed to be Christians and had our butts in the pews on Sunday mornings. Maybe that was true, or maybe it wasn't. All I know is that he loved anything that helped me surrender to him as the head of our household, and he knew book, chapter and verse of the bible to remind me. In case that didn't work, he used the back of his hand or a punch to my eyes. But it didn't matter, because I knew that with heavier eye makeup, wearing a look that was better suited for the nighttime in the daytime, no one would dare ask any questions, right?

The first time he really hit me was on a school night. I'd finally gotten my license, but my car was acting up; probably God's punishment from before, when I sometimes drove without a license. I called Plez over and over to come pick me up and he never answered the phone. I finally accepted a ride from one of my male teachers, Mr. Wald. Something in my spirit told me I'd pay for it. I got home and sure enough, Plez was wide awake, sitting at the kitchen table. He had his coat on.

"How'd you get home?" he asked me, as though he had the whole scenario pieced together. No "Hello" or "How was class?" I didn't even get a chance to ask him where *he'd* been half the night.

"I tried calling you but you weren't home."

"So who gave you a ride home?"

"I tried calling eleven times, Plez," I said, trying to sound like I'd done all I could do.

"You know, I had a funny feeling you weren't doing what you were supposed to be doing. I took the kids over to your mammy's house, and I sat in the parking lot of your school. Why did I see your black ass get into the car with some white dude?"

Before I could even respond, Plez knocked me upside my head and then right in my face. I dropped to my knees and as my head was bowed from the shock of being hit, I noticed blood speckle the floor. Then a rush of pain came from my nose and I realized he had hit me there.

"Bitch, I'm always one step ahead of you," he said, "If you think you can do better than me, stay your ass over there with the motherfuckers you be fuckin'!"

The shock of being hit froze me. I kept my head bowed as though I had something to be ashamed of. Tears hit the floor, mixing with the fallen blood. Then he turned the light off and walked out of the kitchen, leaving me sitting on the floor in the dark.

The next day he came home like nothing had happened. But he brought something home with him. A black velvet box with a diamond ring in it, sized to perfection. It looked like one of the rings I'd dreamed about but gave up hope of ever getting. It was beautiful, and his way of saying, "I'm sorry," without actually having to open his mouth to say it. And he'd do shit like that: slap me, beat me, and curse me, and the gifts would keep coming and be just as fabulous as the ones before them. And as long as I kept accepting them, he knew he could charm his way out of acknowledging what he did to me; from having to say those two words that I would have traded all of those gifts back to hear. And in between the beatings and the gifts, there were the mind fucks.

We took Lawrence and Plez Jr.. to the Minnesota State Fair. We looked at farm animals, went on rides, and ate funnel cakes and hot dogs, washing it all down with strawberry shakes. The good food and fun came to an end when we walked past the haunted house.

"Hey, little man. Why don't you and your mama go into the haunted house?" Plez asked.

"I don't wanna," Lawrence said.

"Why not?"

"Because it's scary."

"Aw, hell, it ain't scary. It's just some white folks dressed up in costumes. They'll jump out at you. There's nothing to it."

Lawrence shook his head no and Plez got that look in his eye that let me know his mood was about to change. "What if I go in there with you?"

Still, Lawrence shook his head.

"Honey, if Lawrence doesn't want to go, he doesn't have to go," I said.

"Shut up, Cheryl. That's what's wrong with him now. You're turning that boy into a sissy. When we go back home, remind me to stop by JCPenny's so I can get him some little girl panties and a dress!"

I looked at Plez, whose eyes had turned dark like coal. I knew he wouldn't let up, so I gave Plez Jr. to Plez Sr. and took Lawrence by the hand and said, "Come on, baby. I'll go in there with you." Then I took my firstborn, kicking and screaming into the haunted house, just to keep the peace. As we stepped in, both of us turned back to see Plez holding his son in his arms, smiling. The sun lit up the entryway and we went in. The further into the haunted house we went, the dark became so thick we couldn't see our hands in front of us. There was the old-fashioned scary music, and taped sounds of monsters growling and wolves baying at the moon. I thought the whole thing was silly, but I could see how it would be scary to a small child. Suddenly, a mummy jumped out at us. Lawrence screamed. Then a wolf man jumped out, then a vampire, followed by loud witch cackling in the distance. When we finally made it out the exit, Lawrence was hysterical. He ran out so fast that his feet got away from him and he fell to the ground, making a cloud of dust from the dirt and gravel. Plez was nowhere to be found. We looked everywhere for both him and my baby. I even had the people working the fair get on a loudspeaker and call out to them to meet us at the front of the park.

After three hours of waiting, searching, and hoping, Lawrence and me took a bus home. That's when I finally figured that Plez had been pissed with the haunted house foolishness and wanted to teach Lawrence and me a lesson. When we got home, both Plez Jr. and Sr. were laying in the bed asleep. I shook with anger, knowing that son of a bitch had did it all on purpose, but of course I couldn't do squat about it. And that was just the beginning...

CHAPTER

22

AFTER HAVING PLEZ JR., GOING out on the town was the furthest thing from my mind. Sure, Plez and me got together for a lunch here and there, or we'd pile the boys into the car and go out to eat as a family. There was even the occasional concert. The last night out we'd enjoyed had been a traveling tour of the Broadway hit *Dreamgirls* in 1984. It was humid as hell that summer night. Even though I thought the show was fantastic, we'd sweated through it in a hot-ass theater. Plez said that was the end of going out because he hadn't wanted to see the show in the first place and would've rather sat home, watching TV. Plus, with two working parents in the household, who had the time to go out?

I stood in the bathroom, checking my makeup for the millionth time. Marva busied herself, reading a history book and jotting down notes in between glancing up to see what the boys were doing.

"Are you sure he's gonna show up this time?" she yelled from the living room.

She had every reason to ask. The previous Friday, Plez had called to tell me to get dressed in my best. Marva had come over to watch the kids so that Plez and me could go out.By 11:00pm I knew he wasn't coming home. I put the kids into the car and drove Marva home. The kids went to sleep when we got back and Plez still wasn't home. I woke up at 2:30am when Plez stumbled through the door. He yelled at me for not meeting him. He never told me to meet him or even where to meet him, but insisted that I be ready when he came home because he was gonna wear what he had on.

"Plez, you told me you were gonna pick me up," I said, careful not to sound too angry.

"Bullshit! I called you at four to tell you to meet me at seven. I know what I told you, woman," he slurred.

"Whatever," I mumbled under my breath.

"What did you say?" Plez asked me, which made me stop in my tracks. I knew that look in his eyes, and I knew that it meant I'd better think quickly.

"I said that you're probably right."

"Bitch, that ain't what you said," Plez said, before popping me in my mouth. He hit me so hard that he smeared my lipstick onto my cheek. "Say something else smart," he said. Then he left me standing there with smeared lipstick and eyeliner and mascara running down my eyes, looking like Bozo the Clown.

~ * * * ~

"Cheryl, do you hear me talkin' to you? I asked you if you were sure he was comin' tonight?" Marva asked again, this time standing in the bathroom doorway, bringing me out of my memory.

"Yeah, he's coming tonight," I said."Are you sure? Don't be wasting my time with this because I could've gone to Donna's house to study."

"On a weekend?"

"We have a history test come Monday."

"I see. Well, don't let me stop you."I looked at Marva who stood there, looking very serious at the age of seventeen. It seemed like only a blink ago she was seven years old, sketching in art pads. I liked that she took her studies seriously. She knew it was her ticket away from our father, who she seemed to hate more and more. She wanted her grades to be flawless so that she could attend a university— preferably out of state.

Lawrence was happily eating the Ramen noodles Marva cooked for him, and Plez Jr.. was asleep when Plez pulled up. I grabbed my bag and took one last look. I was gorgeous, as gorgeous as a mother of two could look, anyway.

"You look nice," Plez said, taking one look at me before driving off.

"Thank you."

"How's Plez Jr.? Did he cry when you left?"

"He was asleep. Anyway, he's almost five now. He doesn't cry like he used to." I was curious as to why he didn't ask about Lawrence. "Lawrence was eating noodles."

"Oh, okay," Plez said, acting like he didn't know who I was talking about.

He took me to Sunny's Bar on Chicago Avenue. As soon as we pulled up, I knew that I was overdressed for that kind of place. My body hadn't really recovered since Plez Jr. was born. My little tight— yet conservative— black dress was one of the only outfits I had left that at least created the illusion I had a halfway decent-looking body.When we went inside it was packed. "Let's Go Crazy" by Prince boomed from the speakers. There were three tables of people off to the side playing pull tabs and drinking, spending their Friday paychecks and probably hoping for the big win. At the bar, I could see clouds of cigarette smoke rising to the ceiling. We made our way toward a booth. I tried to look straight ahead, even though I could see some of the men checking me out through the corner of my eye.

We were seated for about five minutes before a waitress fought her way over to us. She was a skinny chick with bad teeth and big eyes who acted like I wasn't there. She noticed Plez right away, and what woman wouldn't have? He was fine looking that night. Plez ordered rum and Coke and me a vodka and cranberry. Plez looked around the room, bopping his head to the music.

"Plez, baby! I ain't seen you in the longest,"said, a pretty, light-skinned woman in a turquoise blouse that hung off the shoulder and tight white pants that exposed her camel toe.

"Hey, Roslyn. What's goin' on with ya?"

"Not much, baby. Stayin' beautiful."

"Yes you are, girl," Plez said, standing and reaching in to hug the bitch. She made sure to push her titties up against his chest, too.

"Cheryl, this is Roslyn. We go way back."

"Yeah, hi," she said, hardly even looking at me. She was more interested in batting her lashes at Plez than in meeting me.

I sat there with a frozen grin on my face. I knew better than to show my true feelings. Plez took my jealousy as childishness. He told me one time that I should be flattered to have such a nice-looking specimen of man on my arm, especially since I'd gotten a little pudgy and out of shape. But it was perfectly all right for him to be jealous of what little attention I got.It was more of the same for two straight hours. It seemed like every woman Plez had messed with, or who was still waiting in line to get screwed, had come to the table. And all the bitches acted like I was competition, when they should've recognized that I'd already won the prize. A few times Plez glanced over at me to check my face to see if I was mad, but I kept it together. He squeezed my leg under the table and winked at me after each one of those whores got through talking to him, but he never put his arm around me or showed any affection when they were standing there.

The hours passed and I counted the empty glasses on the table. There were five in front of Plez and two in front of me. I didn't understand why the waitress didn't bother to take the empty glasses away when she brought over fresh drinks. There was only one other server on and she managed to keep her tables clean.I'd decided that Plez was intent on getting tore up, so I switched over to Sprite. Partly because I knew how mad I got when I drank when I wasn't enjoying myself, and partly because I had to drive us home.

Suddenly, the tide changed and the men started coming around our table, eye balling me. Some would act like they were trying to talk to the other ladies but they would throw a look my way.

It started when Plez went to the restroom and the first guy came over trying to sweet talk me. He wasn't even cute. He was tall and skinny and had a kitty cat jheri curl, rocking clothes from three years earlier. Under the lights I could see the curl juice drippings on his polyestered shoulders. He knew Plez had been there because as he spoke his weak game to me, he kept looking over in the direction of the restroom like he was expecting Plez to come back at any minute. I guess he figured he needed to hurry it up if he was going to do his dirt. He gave me a kiss on the cheek and scurried off after I told him that I wouldn't give him my phone number, nor would I take his.

As the night wore on, those liquored-up brothas became outright brazen with their moves, and Plez became quieter the more I got hit on.

This nice-looking man who called himself Aubrey came over and said, "Brotha, I know this here is your woman. As a gentleman, I come to ask if I can have just one dance with your young lady."

Plez folded his arms and sucked his teeth at the guy, then turned to me and nodded his head at me, indicating that he wanted me to go dance with the man. I was shocked, feeling like he was pimping me out like a prostitute. Neither one of them asked me what *I* wanted to do.

"Baby, I want to dance with you," I said, leaning in close to Plez and kissing his lips.

"This brotha was gentleman enough to come over and ask me to dance with you. Most brothas in this room wouldn't do that."

"Yeah, but you and me haven't danced yet."

"It's just one dance. Aubrey, is it?"

"Yeah, man. The name's Aubrey."

"You two go on over there and tear that dance floor up. Just keep your hands where I can see them," Plez said, laughing.

He got up and pulled me out of the booth and pushed me into Aubrey, who smiled and took my hand and led me to the already packed dance floor.

Earth Wind and Fire's "Fantasy" was playing. I loved that song. While I danced with Aubrey, I made sure to keep a safe distance between us, but because there were so many people out there dancing, we kept getting pushed together. I turned and tried to keep Plez in my view, making sure I didn't appear to be enjoying it too much. Aubrey could dance his ass off and for a brief second, I thought if he could move that good on the dance floor, how well could he move in the bedroom.

"Boy, I tell ya, your man is one lucky dude. If you were *my* lady, ain't no way I'd let another dude ask me to dance with you," Aubrey hollered into my ear over the music.

"But, yet, you came over and asked *my* man," I hollered back.

"Hey, I took a chance."

I looked over to Plez, who was watching every move we made. He wasn't smiling. I don't know why he was acting this way. He was the one who literally threw me into the arms of another, and now he just sat there, arms folded, looking pissed.

"Shining Star" came on next. I could see they were playing the oldies but goodies, and had the situation been different, I would've liked to have danced with Aubrey again for that song too. But something in my gut told me that I needed to go back to the table and do some damage control.

I walked back over to Plez, being bumped from all over by drunken people who were having so much fun they didn't even know what they were doing. Plez looked up at me and offered a smile.

"See, now that wasn't so hard, was it? But I bet Aubrey's dick got hard after dancing so close to you, looking the way you do."

"I wouldn't know. I wasn't looking at all of that. Plez, baby, let's go dance," I said, trying not to give him much time to sulk, or question me.

"I don't feel like dancing."

"Please."

"I wanna go. Are you ready?"

"Okay."

We got into the car and the silence bothered me. I had no idea what was running through Plez's mind, but I knew it wasn't anything good.

As he drove, he turned off in a direction that took us farther away from the house. I figured that maybe he wanted to go to another bar. But we wound up in some industrial area of town that was barely lit. He found a dark area and turned off the car.

"You know, Cheryl, you made me very unhappy tonight," Plez said, looking at me for the first time since we got into the car.

"What did I do now?"

"You failed the test."

I felt my stomach drop. Plez sounded almost happy that

I had "failed" this test.

"What did I do now?" I repeated.

"You let some pretty-ass nigga talk me into letting him dance with you."

"Plez, baby, I told you that I didn't want to dance with him."

"No, you didn't. You said that you wanted to dance with me. You didn't say shit about not dancing with that man."

That's when I figured that Plez had tested me to see what I'd do. If I had jumped up quick and went to dance with Aubrey, he would've thought I wanted to have sex with him. If I hadn't gone, Plez would've thought that I wanted to and wished I had. I was damned and slutty either way. "And on top of that, you let some nasty-ass looking motherfucker kiss all up on you," Plez said as he turned to me and folded his arms again. He leaned back against his door as though he couldn't believe what he had seen or heard. "Plez, nobody was kissing all up on me."

"Cheryl, are you calling me a liar?"

"No, of course not, baby. But I don't understand who it is you said was kissing on me."

"That jheri-curled fool."

That's when I realized Plez hadn't gone to the bathroom. He was off watching me to see how I would handle the men at Sunny's. Or maybe he'd gone to the bathroom and on his way back, he saw that man kiss me on the cheek. That wasn't what I would call kissing all up on me.

With disgust in his eyes he said, "Get your ass out this car."

I sat for a moment, not knowing what he was going to do next. He went around to the trunk and opened it. I sat in my seat, my heartbeat pounding through my chest.

"Bitch, did you hear what I said? Don't make me ask you again."

I slowly got out and stood by my open door. A breeze blew through as Plez came from behind the car holding a crowbar.

"Let me explain something to you. I am not the kind of nigga you wanna fuck with."

"Plez, what are you gonna do with that?" I asked, keeping my eyes on that crowbar.

"Bitch, do you realize that I could bust you in your

motherfuckin' head right now and nobody would know anything about it?"

I started crying. All of a sudden I started getting these flashes of my life up to that point. I wasn't sure what Plez had in store for me. But I knew that I had to get home to my children. I couldn't have them at ages ten and four being raised without me.

"Plez, baby, you're right. I should've done a better job in telling that nigga to fuck the hell off! You're my man, not him!"

"Now see, how come you couldn't have said all of that back at the bar?"

"Well, you know how stupid I can be sometimes," I said.

I watched as he lowered the crowbar. He seemed satisfied with my answer as he nodded and said, "Yep. Stupid, but beautiful." I wanted to breathe a sigh of relief, but I didn't want him to think I felt safe. If it would spare my life, I wanted him to see my fear.

"You know, truth be told, seeing you dance with that guy was kinda sexy. It got my dick hard."

I looked at him with a confused look on my face. One minute he wanted to bash my head in and the next he was telling me he had a hard-on.

"You feel that, girl?" he said, taking my hand and putting it on his thickened dick. I think the power he had and the fact he'd scared the shit out of me made him hard.

"I feel it, baby. And when we get home, I'm gonna ride you real good."

"Naw, naw. Take care of this shit now."

"What?"

"I said, take care of me right now," Plez said, unbuckling his pants.

I stood there shocked at what he was asking me to do. My makeup was running off my face from sweating and crying and I had snot hanging down from my nose. Yet he was serious. I looked around as though I expected someone to walk by.

"Cheryl, ain't nobody out here this time of night. Get on them knees and start sucking this." He had taken it out and started waving it.

I took a deep breath and got down on the cold concrete. I tried to put my mind in a different place so that I could pretend to enjoy it. I was scared of what would happen if he didn't think I was doing a good job.

As I sucked him, he closed his eyes, becoming lost in the sensation of pleasure. "That's a good bitch," he whispered to me over and over again. I finally heard the crowbar drop to the ground.

When he was ready to come, he pulled out and let his milk fly into my face. To be on my knees on cold pavement while he came in my face was low. I stayed on the ground as he put his dick away, zipped up, and buckled his belt. Then he picked up the crowbar so quick, he must've thought I was gonna snatch it up and beat him with it. Then he went toward the car as I waited for permission to get up. "Well, come on if you're coming," he said, throwing the crowbar into the backseat before getting into the car. I got up and began fixing my dress as I wobbled over and got in the car.

"Damn, girl, you can suck some dick," he said, turning on the car and proceeding out of the darkness of that area. "I should say 'fuck the pussy' and let you get me off like this more often."

I dug into my purse and pulled out a tissue and began wiping his semen off my face. I was thankful I didn't have to speak to him because he was quiet after that. As he drove, I let the night air hit me in my face as though the breeze would rid me of the stickiness of his cum. That night wasn't even my bottoming out, because I knew I had deserved what I'd gotten. I should've told Aubrey to get lost, and I should've never let the guy with the jheri curl put his nasty, big lips on me. Plez had called me a bitch and I deserved the title. I felt like I was a dog and he was my master, and his grip on me had tightened. When we got home Plez gave Marva a ride back home. After a long hot shower, I put on my pajamas and went into my sons' room where I kissed them on their foreheads as they slept, thankful to have gotten home to them. It would be a new day soon and a new beginning. Plez had taught me how I needed to be treated. We never talked about what happened that night. Instead, I left it where it happened—on that abandoned street where Plez spilled his lousy seed.

CHAPTER

23

"**P**LEZ JR., STOP EATING ALL those donuts before you get sick. Here, have some eggs and sausage," I said, spooning scrambled eggs from an overflowing bowl onto his plate.

We were at Paul Bunyan's Cook Shanty restaurant in Wisconsin Dells. It was our last stop before we got on the road headed back to Minnesota. I had to beg Plez to take me and the kids somewhere special as an end-of-summer treat, so that the boys would have somewhere nice to say they'd been when they started school in the fall. Lawrence was entering the fifth grade, but the only thing he was getting excited about was getting to wear his new school clothes. Plez Jr. was starting kindergarten, and I was hoping he wouldn't cry on the first day of school when I left him alone like Lawrence did on his first day.

~ * * * ~

We got on the road as soon as everyone had gone or at least tried to go to the bathroom at the restaurant. Just as I'd hoped, my full belly made for nap time once we got in the car and were on our way. I awoke to Plez poking me in the thigh. I thought we had just pulled into our driveway, but

153

then I realized that we were still in Wisconsin and would be for awhile. I had only been asleep for half an hour.

"Cheryl, do you know what your son had the audacity to ask me just now?"

"Who?"

"Lawrence. I said *your son*."

"What did he ask you?" I asked, trying to ignore the jab.

"He asked me if there'd ever been a black president."

Even I had to chuckle at that. Lawrence's worldview was only of a soon-to-be eleven-year-old. He didn't know any better. Or did he?

"Black folks are having a bad enough time as it is just trying to make it, and you have the nerve to ask if there's been a black president?" Plez looked into the rearview mirror as he asked Lawrence a second time. "No, honey. There's never been a black president, and even in 1985, there probably ain't gonna be one either," I said. "Why don't you try and take a nap?"

"Naw. Naw. Since he wants to ask questions, I got some questions for him."

I heard Lawrence gulp in the backseat. I'm sure he wished he hadn't asked the question in the first place. Plez started asking all of these random-ass questions; questions even *I* didn't know the answers to. Like, could he name three of the Minneapolis City Council members? Did he know who the vice president was, and who would become President if both the President and vice president died, or can't do the job? Could he name all of the Branches of Government? I knew Lawrence didn't know those answers, and maybe he should've. But I knew that people learned things differently. And anyway, how did we know they were even teaching that kind of stuff up at his school? I just shook my head and hoped that when a pause came in the 21 questions, Lawrence would doze back off to sleep and fast.

"How much is 75 times 82?" Plez asked, still glancing back at Lawrence to let him know that he was serious. I was getting nervous because I thought Plez should've been concentrating on the road.

"I can't do that in my head," Lawrence said, thinking on it for what *seemed* like forty minutes.

Plez turned to me and hit my leg and asked me the same

thing. "I don't know," I said. But in my mind I continued with, "And I don't care, either."

"Man, Cheryl. You're really raising a dummy back there. I can't have you raising Plez Jr. like that."

I tried to slide my arm in back of my passenger seat and touch Lawrence's leg, because I knew he would be upset. Sure enough, my hand felt his leg shaking. I knew he was crying.

"What are you two doing?" Plez asked, trying to see where my arm closest to the door was."You upset him, Plez."

"Look, that's why he acts so funny, you baby him too goddamn much! Just like when he was younger and used to come hollering like a little girl into our bedroom during thunderstorms. You thought I was doing him wrong by sending him back to his room. I've been trying to teach him to be a boy and not some little girl."

"He's not like all the other boys, Plez. Ain't nothin' wrong with that," I said, trying to keep any anger out of my voice.

"Yeah, I *know* he's not like other boys. That's the motherfucking problem! Next thing he'll be doing is asking for baby dolls for Christmas."

"But I know a boy who has a Cabbage Patch doll," Lawrence cried from behind me.

"See what I'm talkin' about?" Plez looked at me quickly before shooting a pissed look through the rearview mirror at Lawrence. By that point I just sank lower in my seat and prayed to see a "Welcome to Minnesota: Land of Ten Thousand Lakes" sign.

"Little boys don't play with dolls, honey," I said.

"That's all right, Cheryl. Just remember, that's *your* son. You keep on babying him like you're doing. Just don't be surprised when you come home one day and catch him wearing your clothes and high heels, playing in your makeup!"

"Lawrence ain't like that. Don't say that!" Suddenly I thought of Clayton.

"Yeah, okay. I'm telling you, he's a sissy in the making, and I'll be damned if I'm gonna let you fuck my son up like that. Ain't happening!"

As soon as it quieted down, I guess Plez wanted to keep the topic hot because he made one last remark to Lawrence. "Come Christmas time, don't even think about asking for no doll. Was the boy you saw with a doll at your school black or white?"

"White," Lawrence replied in a defeated, small voice.

"See? That ought to tell you something right there. Black people don't buy our boys dolls. Next thing you'll be telling me is that you wanna go play jump rope and hopscotch with the girls. This Christmas, you better be praying for a football or one of them remote-controlled trucks, cuz' that's what your ass is getting."

Then, Plez shut the hell up.

Thank the Lord.

CHAPTER

24

I WAS AT THE KITCHEN table, looking through recipes. Plez came up to me and slid a business card onto the table toward me.

"I need you to give that lady a call," he said, walking away with a smile on his face.

I looked at the card. It read, "Paulette Dobson—Your Realty Specialist: Serving our community proudly for over five years!"

I could feel a smile of my own forming. Finally, Plez realized I wasn't happy in his house and wouldn't be happy until we all lived together in something called *our* house. Every weekend since Plez forced us into his place, I'd taken the housing section of the newspaper after he finished with it. I circled homes in yellow I dreamed we could live in, and homes in red that we could actually afford. But as time went on, all those houses went off the market because they were sold. All I had left were my dream homes that I knew we'd only get if someone dumped a large bag of cash at the front door. Still, I kept my eyes open for something simple and inexpensive, but worlds apart from the riff raff neighborhood Plez had us living in.

I went into the living room where he sat on a sofa I had begged him to go out and buy because those bean bag like-pillows he had before just weren't getting it. His feet were up as he watched TV. I stood in the doorway, hoping he'd catch the smile on my face. He looked up at me and winked.

"So why now?" I asked. I hoped he didn't think I was being mouthy.

"I ain't stupid, Cheryl. I know you ain't happy here. But I needed time to get some money saved."Just the fact that he was aware that I hadn't been happy made me happy, and made me remember why I'd fallen in love with him. I went and sat on the floor near his feet and wrapped my arms around his leg. He smiled down at me and ran his fingers through my hair.

It would be the last happy moment in this whole house thing.

~ * * * ~

Paulette Dobson was a mess. We had just seen our third home with her. Either she didn't get what we were trying to tell her we wanted or she was just plain stupid.

When we went to her office that first day, I brought newspapers red with circled properties I was interested in seeing at or at the very least to give her ideas of what style of home I wanted and where Plez and I wanted to raise the boys.

Paulette had her own catalogue of listings to share with us. Although many of those houses were out of our price range, she had an idea. Me and Plez sat on the other side of her desk, holding each other's hands. I felt like she was the gatekeeper who held the power to make us homeowners, even though Plez had already been one; this was more about my getting a piece of that American dream. To have a stable job, family, and home was what it was all about to me. Maybe then my mama would come to my side and stop looking at me like I was capable of so much more but missing the mark. Maybe she'd stop looking at me with that tear hanging in her eye like it wanted to fall but wouldn't because she swore she was done crying over me.

I was so excited about Paulette. I was hoping she'd show us the dream house on Monday and by Wednesday at the very latest we'd be putting in an offer. I blame my lack of experience for that foolishness. I should've known better.

The first house Paulette showed us was a fixer-upper. I knew that with two kids and two incomes, Plez and me didn't have the time to break down walls, retile floors and caulk bathtubs. Maybe we could manage a coat or two of paint on a Saturday at the very most.The second place she showed us was *deep* in the hood. All you heard about on the news was the gunfire and drug dealing going down on both bordering main streets. That was the last thing I wanted for my two young boys. They were my heart and it would break if they ever got jumped into some gang, or wound up selling or using drugs. Some of the women from church were losing their sons to the streets; I wanted to keep my boys away from all of that.

The third house was a couple of miles out of Crack Central, in a slightly better neighborhood. But it had one problem that to me was unpardonable: Roaches.

Paulette seemed to get pissed off that we weren't settling with the first thing she showed us. She acted like we should've been grateful with what she threw at us. The best we could come up with was $63,000. She told us, and I was shocked at how straight she was with it, "If ya'll want to live in one of *these* houses then ya'll need to cough up some more money," she said, tapping her long, red fingernail against one of the newspapers I'd brought in. "I mean, do you even have the ten-percent to put down when the average home today in 1985 is $89,000? I mean, this isn't 1975, folks. Those days are long gone."

I looked over to Plez who squeezed my hand while I watched my dream go up in smoke.

"I was gonna sell my house and use that to put down on another one," Plez said meekly. Considering how he had roughed me up from time to time, I was surprised he was so soft-spoken in front of this lady.

"Have you been to the bank? Maybe you qualify for a loan."

My ears perked up. I hadn't even thought of that. Maybe after the meeting in Paulette's office we could take our selves down to the bank. But I didn't have any credit, so it was all up to Plez to be the man and get us what we needed.

Plez turned and looked at me, shaking his head sadly. I knew what that look meant.

"Paulette, I went to the bank already. I was gonna put

my house up as collateral, but they said I don't have enough equity in it," he said.

"So what do you people expect me to do? You don't qualify for a loan, and you don't have enough money to buy anything half-way decent."

"Oh, I'm sorry, lady. I'm just supposed to have you dump me and my kids into some ghetto where we're running from bullets every damn day? Or that last house, nasty roaches? Are you kidding me?" I said, trying to keep my voice down.

Plez jumped on it with me. "And what makes it so bad, is that we'd expect this kind of treatment from white folks, but you're *black*. I thought you'd be about helping a brotha and a sistah out," he said.

"Well, if you had come into my office, bringing me something to work with, then maybe I'd be about helping ya'll out."I noticed how all of a sudden her street voice came in through the same door her professional voice had left. Then she said, "Ya'll think these white folks are gonna treat you any better?" She reached for the Yellow Pages. "Here, go ahead. Open it. The Yellow Pages is filled with tons of white folks in this industry who don't give a damn about you. And they definitely don't want any of us living next to them. But if you think they'll treat you any better, be my guest."

Paulette Dobson was a sistah who was about business. And she made it clear that Plez and me had no business in her office.

"See, with bitches like that, acting like she's better than everybody else, how are we supposed to get ahead?" Plez asked me once we made it back to the car.

"I have no idea. She did seem kinda uppity, though, didn't she?"

"She ain't nothing but a female Uncle Tom."

"I wouldn't say all that."

"Why wouldn't you? She ain't no better than white folks. Just because she's got hers, she's pulling the ladder up and we're supposed to get ours the best way we can."

I let Plez continue his rant, even though I was counting down the minutes until he was through in my head and we were home. The truth was we should've had our shit together. It wasn't her fault we didn't have enough money. Yeah, she was bitchy, but she was out trying to make a living like everyone else. I probably would've said the same thing too.

"She probably ain't got no man. That's why she was talking to us like that."

"You don't know that."

"And you do?"

"There's gotta be another way for us to get this going." I was desperate. Plez should've known better than to get my hopes up like this. Now that I knew he was willing to go the distance, I was gonna make sure that he did.

"I got an idea," he said, with a sudden burst of spirit.

"What?"

"We can go by my mother's apartment. She lives in those low-income high-rises just off the freeway."

"What's over there?"

"She's taking care of my aunt Maybelle. I guess she felt guilty after what she put my aunt through back in the day. Anyway, she always has money."

"How do you figure she has any money if she's living in one of those high-rises?"

"She knows how to play the system. She doesn't even keep bank accounts. Mama probably got all kind of money stashed under a mattress."

"Even so, I'm sure she ain't got the kind of money we need."

"Yeah, but something is better than nothing."

I didn't know that Plez even spoke to his family. He never spoke about them except for when he told me about what happened to his dad and mother down in Alabama.

We pulled into the parking lot. Plez shut the car off. His eyes followed a car that sped by as if he recognized the driver. "Okay," he said, turning to look at me like he was strategizing. "Let me do all the talking. Just smile and look pretty if anybody asks you anything."

"Plez, baby, I don't feel right asking your mama for money. I'm looking at this place and it seems like she can barely keep herself afloat."

"Do you have any other ideas? Don't worry about it. She owes me anyway."

"Owes you for what?"

"One time when my father was alive, he was away trying to find work; I caught her behind the shed getting felt up by the preacher and she was liking it. I never told Dad."

"What good does that do you now? Your dad's dead."

"Yeah, but she blames herself that she never told him. Her becoming slutty wasn't an accident after he died. She must've figured that with him out of the way she was free to tramp around as she pleased. Yeah, he's dead, but my aunt doesn't know."

I still didn't like the idea. I thought it was wrong for him to try and blackmail his mama into giving him anything. A new house wasn't worth this, but I was scared to speak out any further. When Plez's mind was made up to do something, it was made up.

The inside of the building stank like piss. We walked down the hallway, in between puke-green brick walls. There were half-naked toddlers running around with no parents to be found. Plez seemed to hate the building, filled with Section 8 welfare recipients, many of whom were probably second-and-third generation. I wasn't in any position to judge because I used to be one myself before I became a nursing assistant. When we got into the elevator that took forever to get to the lobby, he closed his eyes, avoiding the dull lighting and McDonald's trash thrown on the floor. "Why do black folk gotta live like animals?" he asked.

When we got to her floor, Plez put his finger to my lips, whispering again for me to be quiet and look pretty. After knocking on the door, his mother opened it, looking skinnier than he had remembered. I could tell just by how he looked at her. A Newport cigarette dangled from her mouth, ash dropping to the floor as she breathed from her nose.

"Peanut, how you doin', boy?" she said. I smiled when I heard his nickname.

"Hey, Ma," he replied, giving her a hug while trying not to get burned by her cigarette.

"You know your sister was just here."

"Yeah, I thought I saw her car driving past."

"And you know she's pregnant."

"Again?" Plez said in disgust.

"Joveeta's my daughter, and God knows I love my child, but she's a tramp. She act like she can't stand bein' without a man. Every time she gets one that can put up with her ass, here comes another baby. She's fixin' to have number four. With what she gets from the state, she ain't even gotta work."

"The apple didn't fall far from the tree," Plez muttered under his breath as he looked around the room. I figured that his aunt was sitting in the chair near a window that looked out toward the dumpsters and just beyond to the highway. We approached her. I noticed both the faraway look in her eyes and her Sunday wig resting in her lap.

"What you doin' over here, Maybelle?" he asked, leaning in to hug her nonresponsive body.

"Waiting to die," she said, looking up at him as though he were a stranger. The sunlight that shone through made her face look greasy. The few, sparse gray hairs she had were braided into little snakes so she could pin the wig to her head. Plez noticed a smell of urine and underarm must coming from her.

"Maybelle, you ain't gonna die any time soon," Plez said, laughing.

"Who are you?" she asked suspiciously.

"That's Peanut, Maybelle," Plez's mother said from across the room as cigarette smoke escaped from her mouth.

"I don't know nobody named Peanut," Maybelle said, turning back toward the window.

I looked around the small apartment. It smelled almost as bad as his aunt; like stale cigarette butts and liquor.

"Ma, when's the last time you bathed Auntie?"

"Boy, you see this?" Eve asked, running a finger underneath a scratch on the side of her face. "Auntie did that?"

"Yeah, and I'm tired of the scrapes and bruises I get tryin' to help her wash her ass. I figure, when she gets sick of the funk, she'll jump her old ass in the tub."

Plez's mother looked at me for the first time and smiled crookedly. "Who's this you brought to my house?"

"This is my wife, Ma. This is Cheryl. Cheryl, this is my mother, Eve."

"Your wife?"

"Don't act like you don't remember me telling you that I got married. I got a son, too. Remember?"

"Peanut, don't play with me. Now, I ain't like my sister over there. I do believe that I would remember if you told me that you was gettin' married and that I had a grandchild. Whoop-de-damn-do. *Another grandchild.*"

"It must've been when you were stressing over Auntie's operation. We just went down to the courthouse. You didn't miss anything."

I looked at Plez. I couldn't believe that he wouldn't have told his mother of all people that he had a wife, and that as his wife I'd given him a son. I could tell that Plez was trying not to look at me. Just like he tried not to look at me when I heard for the first time that Mr. Davis's nephew was coming by with a truck to help pack my stuff and move me out of my apartment. It didn't make any sense.

"How you gonna come by and tell me some shit like this? I know good and well you never told me nothin' about gettin' married. Where's the grandbaby?"

"Oh, Cheryl's mama is watching him. And he's not really a baby anymore; he's gettin' ready to be five years old."

Plez's mother's eyes practically jumped out of her head. "Five years old? You mean to tell me ya'll been married five years and ain't said boo to me about it?"

"Ma, you were having all those back problems too, before Auntie came to stay with you."

"See how he does me? He only comes around here when he wants somethin.' I hope you didn't drag this wife of yours over here to ask me for some money cuz' I ain't got any."

I knew she was talking to me. But I couldn't focus. I felt tears coming to my eyes, but I didn't know if they were from sadness or because the apartment stank so bad.

"Your junkie brother, Lamont, stole what little money I had. He came in here actin' like he was tryin' to get clean. He asked me to find the number for that place he could go to get help. When I left out the room, his ass reached under the sofa and stole $2,500."

That's what we came over here for, $2,500? I thought to myself. His mother became so angry that she started puffing on the cigarette and blowing the smoke out without inhaling it. She butted the cigarette and immediately lit a new one, while sitting down on the same sofa that had given up her money.

"That nigga better not come around here no more," she said, leaning back.

"Ma, you gotta have something," Plez begged.

"Boy, what do you need money for anyway? Ain't you workin'?"

"Never mind all of that. I just need it." Plez walked over to his aunt and gave her a quick kiss on the cheek. She started wiping her cheek away as though he'd given her germs. Then he turned back to his mother and shook his head. "I'll be by next week to show you your grandson. I'll see ya'll later. Come on, Cheryl."

"It was nice meeting you both," was all I had time to say.

We were silent in the elevator on the way downstairs. I snuck a look at Plez and he stared straight ahead with a really pissed look on his face. His jaw was clenched and his fists were balled up. I wanted to know why he had neglected to tell me about his family—who were in town—and why he hadn't bothered to tell them about me. Was he ashamed? All I knew was that I wanted to cuss him for filth, but of course I knew better than that.

When we got into the car, he didn't start the car right away. Without looking at me he said, "Look, I know it looks bad, but it's just as well that you don't get too comfortable with my people."

"Yeah, Plez, but five years?"

"I know them better than you do. My aunt is a wackjob and my mother is a slut. I'm surprised she ain't got some nigga living up in there with her right now."

"And what did she mean by, 'another grandchild'?"

"She was talking about my sister, because she keeps farting babies out. That's all she's good for. You heard my ma say she's about to have a fourth. That don't make no damn sense."

"Oh."

Plez banged his fists against the steering wheel and muttered, "I can't believe she didn't have any money."

"I could've told you she wasn't going to have any money."

"Yeah, I know. Do me a favor, will you? Let's not talk about them anymore, okay?"

I nodded okay. It's not like I had a choice.

~ * * * ~

When we picked up the kids, Plez's mood changed. He

was suddenly Mr. Nice Guy. He talked with my mama like they were old friends. He was more pleasant with her than he'd been since Plez Jr. was born. He was acting almost like he was trying to get in good with her to ask for something, though he didn't. When we got home, the phone was ringing.

"Hello," I said, pulling Plez Jr.'s shoes off.

"Yeah, I didn't want to tell you this while Plez was standing there, but Diallo's been callin' round here." It was Mama.

"What did he want?"

"He said he wants to see his son."

I laughed into the phone. I had given Diallo only a passing thought since he moved to Chicago. In fact, after Plez and I got married, I hardly thought about his stupid ass.

"Are you gonna let him? He *is* Lawrence's father, you know."

"No, he's Lawrence's daddy, not his father. There's a difference."

"Well, just so you know, this ain't the first time he's called askin' to see his son. He's called a few times over the years, either when he's drunk or high or both."

"Mama, I need to get dinner ready. Let's talk about this later, okay?"

"Hold on, girl. You ain't told me what you're fixin' to do about letting him see his boy. What should I tell him if he calls again?"

"Hang up."

"Girl, that ain't Christian. If the man is willing to see his child, then you better let him."

"I tell you what; you show me a man and I'll show him a child. Diallo ain't no man. Anyway, Mama, I gotta get dinner going. We'll talk later."

Then I hung up.

CHAPTER

25

I BROUGHT THE CHEESEBURGER HAMBURGER Helper down to a low simmer, then I cut up vegetables to put in the salad. I knew the kids were going to tear up the Hamburger Helper, but I couldn't even remember the last time they'd put a vegetable in their mouths. I was working the three to eleven shifts, so I could only hope they were eating what I cooked. Instead, I usually came home to find broccoli, spinach, squash, and green beans at the bottom of the trash can hidden under piles of papers and garbage. They thought they were slick, but they didn't realize I used to be a kid too. I knew all the tricks. Plez could've seen to it that they ate their vegetables, but he never ate with the boys. Not even when I was home. He'd just take a plate of food into the living room or, if he was in a really bad mood, the bedroom and watch TV.

My shift change came a few weeks after our new boss arrived. His name was Robert Evangelist and he was taking over as Evelyn was forced to step down. The Drake Patterson's Nursing Home was being ranked last, partly because the powers-that-be took forever to realize that Evelyn wasn't fit to do the job. She was one of those white ladies who were scared of black folks. All you had to do was say "Boo!" and she looked like she was gonna jump out of her skin. The bottom line was that she didn't run her nurses; she let the nurses run her and run a once-promising nursing home into the ground.

Our last survey with her had been one of the worst. Someone had filed a complaint, and the powers-that-be came in to investigate. Since they found that paperwork and charts weren't in order (though my paperwork was always legit), they had probable cause to check everything else. We had a month to get everything in order before the higher-ups came back to check up on us. Evelyn complained she had shitty people to work with. Even though that was partially true, it dawned on them that she was the problem for running a leaky ship, and told her she could either quit or risk being fired.

Robert, on the other hand, was a breath of fresh air. You got the sense that he actually cared about the patients first and foremost, and let it be known right off the bat that if people weren't gonna step up, more permanent changes would be made. I could tell he had an ego because he said, "The scores this facility has been getting are abysmal. That ain't happening on my watch. Playtime is over with."

The truth was, I hated my shift change, but he said the change was necessary because the shift I was starting was a problem area. He felt that if he moved some of us around, that would solve part of the problem. Split some of the good nurses off and put them where they could be the most useful, that way he could see who wasn't performing. The way it stood with Evelyn, all the good nurses worked the morning shifts, while all of the bullshitting-do-nothings worked at night, so it wasn't balanced. He came right out and said that if people didn't like these changes then they knew where the door was.

Robert liked that I wasn't afraid to say what was on my mind. Maybe because I had to watch what I said to Plez, I had all of this pent-up frustration that I gladly let out at work.I already knew they were looking to get rid of this one male nurse, an African guy named Ben. I didn't know him, but I knew of him. The nurses talked about him all the time. Apparently he was sexually harassing some of the female nurses even though he had beaucoup kids back in Africa by two wives. They also said he had really bad underarm smell, but everyone was too afraid to say something to him about it because they didn't want to offend him. Forget that noise; I'm not the one to let someone offend my nose like that. I would've pulled his ass aside and said, "Listen, I'm not trying to be nasty or anything, but you stink! Do you know what soap and water is?"

I missed being home when the kids got home from school, but my sister, Marva, was an angel to come by the house after she got out of school to watch the boys until Plez came home. Marva had studied her ass off and took the SAT and ACT tests. She'd been looking at different liberal arts colleges, but was waiting to hear from Parson's School of Design in New York City. I doubted my parents would let her go all the way to New York just so she could draw. They were more practical than that. I'm sure they felt if they were gonna spend their hard earned money sending her to school, then she'd better come home with a degree she could use. Sure, drawing was a cute talent to have, but could it pay bills?

~ * * * ~

I had taken out the ironing board from the broom closet when the phone rang.

"Hello,"

"Mrs. Jackson?"

"Speaking."

"Good afternoon. This is Mrs. Shively, I'm Lawrence's teacher."

"Okay."

"We had an incident today involving your son pulling a girl's hair. Another of my students named Sarah Johns."

I looked at the clock above the refrigerator. I hoped this woman wasn't gonna tell me that I'd have to go up to the school and get my child. If so, I wished I could've inched the clock back a few hours so that I wouldn't be late for work.

"Mrs. Jackson, are you still there?" Mrs. Shively asked, bringing me back to the present moment, exactly a half hour before I needed to leave the house for work.

"What happened? That doesn't even sound like something he'd do."

"Well, apparently Sarah called Lawrence a sissy because he was holding another student's Cabbage Patch doll. I made them both apologize for their parts in the incident and I don't think it will go any further."

Something about her using my son in the same sentence as the word "sissy" made the hairs on my neck stand up. "Did you see him playing with the doll?"

"Yes, I did."

"And you didn't think to tell him to give the doll back to whoever it belonged to?"

"Mrs. Jackson, I didn't want to embarrass him in front of the other students. But I don't advocate violence, either. Lawrence could have been suspended for that. But I didn't feel the situation warranted it. My concern is that he is being taught in the home that it's all right to put his hands on girls."

Who in the hell did this bitch think she was talking to? I didn't teach either of my sons that it was okay to hit a female or pull her hair. I didn't know where she would have gotten that to ask it.

"I don't teach my children that, and how dare you even ask me that. What, you think that because we're black that we can't teach our children how to behave themselves?"

"No, that's not it at all."

"Is my son able to come to school tomorrow?"

"Yes. Like I said, I don't feel there was any need to send him to the principal's office. After the apology, they seemed fine. But again, I thought that you should know."

"Well, thank you for calling. It won't happen again," I said, before hanging up.

I was getting tired of hearing from people that my child was soft just because he had different interests. As I ironed my uniform, I remembered when Lawrence was in preschool and the teacher got mad because he used those damn plastic links as bracelets, pretending he was Wonder Woman. So what? He was using his imagination. Ain't that what kids are supposed to do?I had just unplugged the iron when the phone rang again. I still needed to jump in the shower and I was tempted not to answer, until I heard my mama's voice come in on the answering machine.

"Mama, make it quick. I'm gonna be late for work," I said, picking up the phone in the middle of her talking.

"I was just callin' to see what you were up to."

"That's it?"

"Well, that and to see if you thought more about what we talked about before."

"What, Diallo?"

"Yes."

"Mama, look. I ain't got time to think about that. We're busy trying to figure out how we're gonna pay for a new house."

"Ya'll movin'?"

"We're trying to."

"Ya'll saved up enough money?"

That's when I knew I needed to end the conversation. Mama was too damn nosy. "Gotta run, Mama. We'll talk soon. Love you. Bye." And I hung up.I didn't even have the chance to hang up the phone good enough when the phone rang again. At this rate, I was gonna be far beyond late for work.

"Hello," I said. Attitude was in my voice and I didn't care.

"Yes, this is Mike Andrews. I'm Lawrence's homeroom teacher. I'm calling because Lawrence hasn't been turning in his homework, and I was wondering if he's been coming come with it."

I felt like a bad mother who didn't know whether her child was coming or going. It seemed that after I started the new shift, I never saw a single textbook or notebook paper. All I knew was as of Lawrence's last report card, he was doing okay.

"To be honest with you, the last I remembered, Lawrence was doing just fine. I'm talking about our last parent/teacher conference."

"I recall that. But his grades seem to have sunk this time around. I know it may not be my place to ask this, but is everything all right in the home? I know that for a lot of children who are experiencing some substantial changes, or if the home environment isn't a good one, their grades are the first to suffer."

"No, there isn't anything going on at home," I said. I felt like Mr. Andrews was judging me. I could hear it in his voice; like he had his shit together in his household to be telling me what I ought to be doing in mine. But he didn't know what was going on in his own house. That's why I heard that his wife had been cheating on him with a gym teacher from another school. We mothers talked, it was some of the fastest traveling gossip in the school district.

"I know that he's been acting out lately. He's been disrespectful to me, and I hear that he pulled a young girl's hair today. That sounds to me like there are some things going on that perhaps you're not privy to."

"Listen, I already got a call about that. What *you* need to be worrying about is who's coming in and out of *your* house, and that's all I'm gonna say about the subject. I'll talk to Lawrence, since you seem to think that I don't know what's going on with my own child."

"Ma'am, that was uncalled for," he snapped.

"If you'll excuse me, I have to go to work." And I hung up. It seemed like I was hanging up on people all day.I jumped into the shower with more stress on my shoulders than I could handle. I didn't want to give Plez the satisfaction of getting in Lawrence's ass about his schoolwork, so I'd have a talk with him myself. Plus, Plez was leaving it to me to call a newly widowed woman about the selling of her house. She was in a hurry to sell the house because she was moving to Florida to be closer to her family, and decided to sell the house herself rather than risk it sitting on the market forever. We were hoping we could talk her down to the $63,000 range.

It was in a fantastic neighborhood; a cute, blue, ranch-style home that sat on a cul-de-sac, with a big yard and close to the elementary and junior high schools. It would have been the ideal home in south Minneapolis, because it was closer to work, and I wouldn't have to worry about the boys getting into any trouble with other people's bad-ass kids.We were still worried about where we were going to cough up the rest of the money to pay for it. Plez had gone back to playing pool with those lowlifes; trying to win thousands of dollars, but instead he was losing just as much. At the rate he owed people money, we weren't ever gonna move. He tried to keep his gambling debts a secret, but when we started getting last notices for bills that were owed, he finally leveled with me.

~ * * * ~

I was surprised that I managed to be only ten minutes late for work. Robert didn't chew me out for it since he knew

I was usually on time. He had a man with him, someone I figured was new.

"Cheryl, I'd like you to meet our new nurse. This is Dino Taraborrelli, he just moved here from Mankato."

Dino was a tall, slightly pudgy Italian with warm brown eyes and a beautiful tan. His hair was buzz-cut and he had amazingly white teeth. He extended his hand to me.

"Hi. Nice to meet you," I said, allowing his huge hand to envelope mine.

"You're going to be Cheryl's shadow for the next few days, so whenever I see her, you make sure you're right behind her, okay?" Robert said, patting him on the back."Absolutely, Robert. Thank you," Dino said, flashing his smile.

We watched the boss walk away and when I turned back I saw Dino staring at me. His smile was adorable."Where did you work in Mankato?" I asked.

Dino shook his head, "Aw, man. I worked at the hospital. But my real focus has always been in geriatrics. There weren't enough opportunities there, so I got the hell out and moved here to the good ol' Twin Cities."

"How could you stand living in Mankato?" I asked. I'd been there with my mama and the kids to attend Bible Bowl trivia contests. But after our congregation lost for three years straight, and badly, I stopped going.

"It's a nice town, kinda slow paced. My wife and I moved there from Detroit. We wanted to settle somewhere safe to start a family."

"Oh. So you and your wife have children?" I was being nosy, but I couldn't help it. For a white guy he was pretty cute, even with the bump in the bridge of his nose."No, we never got around to that. Gia left me."

"I'm sorry."

"Don't be, I'm not."

For the rest of the shift, Dino Taraborrelli did as Robert told him; he was my shadow, and a damned good one at that.

At 4:30pm I called the house. Marva picked up right away.

"Hello," she said.

"Hey, girl. Do me a favor, put Lawrence on the phone."

Lawrence took his sweet time getting to the phone. I'm

sure he knew what I was calling about.

"Hello," he said cautiously.

"Let me ask you something," I said, trying to keep my voice down. "Do you like school?"

"Yeah."

"Then why did I get calls from two of your teachers today?"

Lawrence didn't answer right away. He probably was trying to figure out where I was going with the question.

"Boy, I asked you a question."

"The kids are always picking on me. I got tired of it."

"So you thought it was a good idea to pull some girl's hair? Who told you it was all right to put your hands on a girl?"

"Plez puts his hands on you all the time."

I was stumped for something to say. I immediately thought back to the teachers asking if something was going on in the home, or if Lawrence picked up bad habits from the home. I knew Lawrence was right. He'd watched Plez cuss me out a million times, and I'd try to fight back tears so the kids wouldn't think anything was wrong. But they knew. They'd never seen Plez hit me, but I knew they heard it behind the closed doors when the screams started. And they saw the damage afterward; a busted lip or a swollen eye. But they never asked about it.

"Lawrence, look. You and your brother are too young to understand what goes on between your daddy and me."

"He ain't *my* daddy," Lawrence snapped.

"Okay fine, your stepdaddy. And you had better watch the tone, mister. I'm the parent and you'd better remember that."

"I'm sorry."

"And why haven't you been doing your homework?"

"I have been doing my homework."

"You know what? I'm not going to go round and round with you about this, Lawrence. Teachers don't call parents when the children are doing what they're supposed to be doing. No TV, no phone, and no playing outside. When you're done eating, you take your ass into your room and you hit those books. Do you understand me?"

"Yes, Ma."

"And I will be checking."

"Okay, Ma."

I hung up without even saying good-bye.

I called home a couple more times. Marva assured me that Lawrence was doing his homework. I told her to make sure it was on the kitchen table so I could check it when I got home. I was surprised that Plez still wasn't home by 7:30, and Marva had been getting anxious.The shift had been a long one, but Dino had at least kept a smile on my face. I knew he'd make a terrific addition to our staff. I left work, exhausted. I knew how my mama must've felt working long hours and being too tired to even say, "Hey, ya'll!"When I opened the door and went into the kitchen, Plez stood there panting, all out of breath. I could tell from his sweating that he'd been drinking.

"You weren't gonna tell me that Lawrence pulled some little girl's hair today?" he said. In his hands he had an extension cord.

I wondered how he knew about that. "Plez, baby, you got enough on your plate. I didn't want to bother you with that. I already put him on punishment."

"Your son's teacher, somebody named Mrs. Shively called, wanting to apologize to you in case you took offense to something she said earlier. She said you thought she was implying some racial shit."

You mean to tell me that lady called back? I thought the issue was squashed once I put Lawrence on punishment. "How long have you been home? Marva said you were out when I called at 7:30."

"I got home at 7:45. Anyway, I had to beat his ass because I don't wanna hear that he's fighting girls. He needs to be fighting other boys, to toughen his ass up!"

I just nodded at Plez's nonsense. My child shouldn't have been fighting anybody, male or female. Plez threw the extension cord down on the kitchen table and left the room.

When I got downstairs, I saw Lawrence lying in a fetal position, his back to me. Plez Jr. was stroking his back, saying quietly, "Don't cry," over and over again, trying to comfort Lawrence, who sounded like he was dying.

"Plez Jr., go on to bed now." Plez Jr. jumped up and left the room like he was afraid he was gonna get beaten too.

"Why can't you just take your ass to school and do what you're supposed to damn do?" I hissed at Lawrence.

175

Lawrence turned around; his face was puffy, like he'd been crying for days. "Everybody teases me," he sobbed.

"Can't you ignore them?"

"Plez does it, too. You don't know how he looks at me sometimes. He doesn't love me."

"Of course he loves you. That's why he disciplines you. I discipline because I love you."

"But you don't tell me you only have one son. He acts like he doesn't want me here. One day I was coming upstairs and he wanted to come downstairs, as soon as he saw me, he shook his head and closed the basement door in my face."

I didn't realize Plez was doing that to him. This all must have started when I started working the three to eleven shifts.

"Baby, he loves you, okay. He just doesn't know how to show it. His father passed away when he was young so he didn't have anyone to teach him how to show love."

"But what did I do? He doesn't treat Plez Jr. like that."

"He's just stressed. You know we're trying to buy a new house. But just wait. When we move, everything is going to be fine. You'll see."

Lawrence didn't look convinced.

The next day was Saturday and thankfully I didn't have to work. Plez woke up in a fantastic mood and helped me cook breakfast. When the boys came up to eat, you'd never know that Plez had spanked Lawrence the night before.

"How are my little guys doing this morning?" Plez asked them as we sat down at the table. I was shocked, because Plez never sat down with us.

"Fine," they both said. Lawrence blinked as though he was seeing Plez for the first time in his life.

"When you get done cleaning your rooms, we're going shopping," Plez announced.

The boys smiled smiles as big as the sun. During breakfast, Plez farted and made jokes that the boys had done it. We all laughed and I looked at Lawrence and winked.

After we ate, Plez said he was going out to buy his morning paper. My stomach dropped. I knew there was a good chance that the happy man who left was gonna return as someone different. But when he did return, he had not only his paper but a box of popsicles. He gave them to Lawrence, who looked like he had just been given a million bucks.

Plez took them shopping. They came back with clothes and Plez Jr. had a few new toys, while Lawrence had a stack of comic books. That night we went out to eat at Red Dragon, this Chinese restaurant in the Wedge neighborhood of south Minneapolis. Plez even let Lawrence stay up way past his bedtime and watched TV with him. Finally, Plez was connecting with Lawrence just as I knew he would.

Lawrence fell asleep on the couch and Plez picked him up and took him to his bedroom. Then he came upstairs and crawled into bed with me.

"You know we haven't screwed in a while," he said, nuzzling up close to me from behind.

I'd thought Plez had lost interest. One of the last times we had sex, he told me my ass was huge when he was hitting it from behind. He kept smacking it and making horsey sounds. He even joked that he was gonna have to hurry up and finish so he could go see his girlfriend, who knew how to keep her figure together. From that point on when we screwed, it was quick, anywhere between two to ten minutes. He was more about getting off than becoming one with me. Sure, Plez never really made love to me, but he at least made sure to put some decent dick down to keep me satisfied. Now, it seemed like his attitude was, if I couldn't get any thrill out of it while he was inside me, oh-the-fuck-well, he got his.

But that night, he was different. Plez gave it to me like he'd just read the Kama Sutra. He put me in all these different positions I didn't even know existed. I was happy I was still limber enough. We ended with him on top of me, and at that point, it was the closest thing to love making we'd ever done. He locked his fingers in between mine and looked me in my eyes. His pelvis swirled deeply, his dick stuffed so deep within me that I felt a sweaty build to climax. I knew for sure that my roots were nappy from sweating my perm out, but I didn't care. It was some of the best sex we'd had in a good while. We came together, which hadn't happened in a long time and he even snuggled with me afterward, which *never* happened.

"I think I owe you an apology," he said, his breath

warming the back of my neck.

"For what?"

"I love you. I guess I don't say it enough."

"I love you, too," I said. Tears ran from the corners of my eyes. I pushed back into his embrace and held his arms around me. I held on to him, wanting to live in that moment forever. Again, he was the Plez I'd fallen in love with. I felt a new hope come over me that I could keep this version of the man lying next to me present.

"Oh, before I forget, when you took the boys this afternoon, my mama called. She wants us to come over after church for dinner. Marva got a full scholarship to that school she applied to."

"The one in New York? She told me about it last night when I came home," Plez said, still breathing hard.

"She told you she got the scholarship?"

"No, just that she wanted to go to school there."

"She must've found out today. Anyway, did you want to just meet us over at my mama's house after we get out of church?"

"No. We can go to church tomorrow as a family."

That made my night. Plez hadn't stepped foot in a church in the longest time. It would be good for him, for all of us. As Plez ran his fingertips gently on my back, I began to fall asleep. I slept well that night.

CHAPTER
26

MAMA TOLD US THAT SHE hadn't started cooking yet, so we should come over that evening. We went home from church. The boys went downstairs and played while Plez put on some music by Loose Ends. After turning up the volume he closed our bedroom door. I knew then what he had in store for me.

After an hour of sex pounding me into the mattress, we got up, took a shower together and got ready to go to my mama's house for dinner. I had barely recovered from Saturday night's sex and with the Sunday screwing he'd just given me I was sure I'd be walking funny for the next week.

We got to the house, and went into the dining room. The room was lit by candles. Daddy sat at the head of the table with his hands together, which made it feel like the Godfather was gonna make us an offer we couldn't refuse. Finally, dinner was brought in and we proceeded to enjoy one of Mama's best meals: catfish with hush puppies, potato salad and for dessert, peach cobbler.

Daddy, drunk as usual, was blubbering about how he hadn't done right by us and that while he knew he'd done us dirty in the past, he was ready to go the distance with us now. He told us that he was proud of his children. I think with Marva graduating soon, that really got to him. I'd never seen my daddy cry, but it was moving to see him show that side of himself. Even Mama seemed touched. Eventually he got himself together and the tears stopped. I thought to myself, "Damn, we've been enjoying such a nice dinner, was the other side of his Gemini gonna come out?"We finished eating and Mama got up and began clearing the table. When I offered to help she told me to stay put. Plez and I gave each other a glance as I shrugged."You know that with your sister getting that college scholarship, it frees up a lot of money," Daddy said, business-like.

"I'm sure it does," I said.

"Your mama told me ya'll are trying to buy another house." Daddy had pushed his beer away and seemed very in control of the conversation.

"Yeah, we met with a black real estate agent, but she wasn't any kinda help," Plez said.

"But we found a house that's for sale by the owner over on the Minneapolis/Richfield border near the Cross town Freeway. It's just what we need," I jumped in.

"How much is it?" Daddy asked.

"$80,000," Plez said.

That was a bald-faced lie. The lady said she'd sell it to us for $65,000, and only because she was tired of dealing with it and wanted to get out of town fast. The woman had been shocked when we came to look at it. Apparently there weren't too many black families living over there. But she was nice. Both Plez and me put on our professional, white-sounding voices so she wouldn't think we were riffraff.

"Let's say I was to give ya'll a loan, and I do mean a loan, how much do you need, and when could you pay it back?" Daddy asked.

"How much interest are we talking?" Plez asked.

"Since you're married to my daughter, I won't charge you interest."

I looked at Plez, since it was his house we'd have to sell. Plez did better when I let him act as the man of the house anyway. He scratched his goatee like it was itching and said, "Once we sell my house, I can give you the money. We need $20,000."

I turned and looked at Plez like, "Where in the hell did *that* figure come from?" but he ignored me and looked my daddy dead in his eyes. He was probably back to his old tricks again, owing people money. Daddy blinked for a second and started chewing on his tongue. To watch them, you would've thought they were playing a high-stakes poker game.

"I'm gonna tell you right now, if I loan you this money, you better pay it back when you say you're going to. When the time comes to pay up, I don't wanna hear any excuses about how come you ain't got it."

"That's understandable," Plez said.

"Daddy, I'm not trying to appear ungrateful, but how on earth do you have that kind of money?"

"Girl, you askin' too many questions," Daddy said, smiling to let me know he was just teasing. Then he turned back to Plez. "Gimme until next week. I'll get the money. And you'll pay it back when you get what you get for your house, right?"

"That's the plan," Plez said, smiling from ear to ear.

Mama came back into the room just in time to see Plez and Daddy shake on it. My relationship with my family was finally on track. Plez was acting like the dream man I'd dreamed about as a little girl, and everything was perfect.But nothing ever stayed perfect. The evil Plez was biding his time, just waiting to show up.

CHAPTER

27

W E BOUGHT THE HOUSE FROM the woman moving to
Florida. I thought it would be smooth sailings, but
her son, an attorney, had to come up from Florida
and draw up the papers for us to sign. That was a mess. He
came up for a visit and his mother told us we should all get
together and discuss things like inspections and whatnot.
He struck me as one of those types of people who didn't
want to take us seriously, all the while smiling a fake-ass
smile. We made plans to get together the next time he was
in town, but he hee-hawed around with that. We found out
that he thought we were trying to take advantage of his
mother, even though she was the one who suggested the
amount she'd settle for. Finally, after she had the lamppost,
a cracked window on the garage door, and the electrical
wiring fixed, we were ready to sign our lives away.

Plez had put his house up for sale and took forever and
a day to get someone to buy. He had a lot of renovations to
do, but he wanted to sell as is. We took our precious time
moving into the new place, and not because I wanted to. It
was hard on him to move, to leave those memories
behind.Through the grace of God, by February 1986, we
were in. We were well on our way to saying what was mine
or his was ours.

When Plez got his money, I made sure to tell him that Daddy was waiting for the $20,000, but he acted like he wanted to take his time paying it. That's when the phone calls started.

"See, I knew ya'll were going to be trifling about this. Your daddy had to take out a loan for that money. And he was trying to be decent to ya'll by paying down the loan himself and letting ya'll pay him back and not the bank."

"Mama, I've tried to get Plez to pay Daddy. But what do you expect me to do? That's between them."

"I mean, this is ridiculous. Ya'll can't pay fifty dollars a month, something, to show you intend to pay it?"

"Like I said, that's between them."

"You mean to tell me ya'll can't cough up five dollars a month, even? And that's pushin' it!"

"You try talking to Plez."

"You're putting me in a really hard place. Your daddy ain't got the you-know-what to tell you himself, but every damn day I got to hear about it. Well, I'm tired of hearing about it."

I'd go to church and Daddy would act like it was no big deal. He knew we were doing the best we could, and he seemed to accept my excuses, even though he had told Plez he didn't want to hear any. But it was just like his two-faced ass to yell in Mama's ear that we hadn't done right by him, and then on Sundays act like the money didn't matter.

More than a year had gone by and I'd had enough. I avoided telephone calls because of that crap. Plez didn't seem to care about what he was doing to my relationship with my family. The day Daddy agreed to loan us the money was the first time I'd ever been proud to call him my father. His helping us was all on account of Marva getting that scholarship. That blessing put us in God's favor. But Daddy should've told us that he was gonna take out a loan. Maybe then Plez would have understood what was happening.In July of 1987, I thought a family gathering would help close the wounds. But Plez had decided to rip the goddamn bandage right off.

It was the first time in a long time that we'd spent any time as a family. Marva was home for the summer, and we all decided to go to Phelps Park for the fourth of July to have a picnic. Things were already tense between me and

183

my family before that. Plez made sure to make it worse.

Daddy was drinking, as if that was anything new. All of a sudden he had the liquid courage to ask Plez about the money.

"Say, Plez. It's been more than a year. Don't you think it's time that you run me my money, man?" Daddy asked.

"Man, don't you think I'd pay you your money if I had it?"

"I already know you have it. I wanna know when you plan on payin' me. Didn't I tell you I wasn't gonna hunt you down for it? You didn't have to hunt me down for me to give it to you, did you?"

"Man, we're trying to have a family day. Why you wanna start this shit right now, as beautiful a day as it is?" Plez asked.

"I ain't tryin' to start shit. I just want my motherfuckin' money! Is that too much to ask? Ain't you thought of the predicament you placed my daughter in?"

"Mr. Greene, Cheryl already told you that we've been struggling. I'll give your money to you when I get it. Matter of fact, I'll give it to you when I feel like it!"

When I heard that, I wanted to run away. Plez knew I'd been stressed. But like always, he didn't care. They weren't his parents. Every time I asked him to talk with Mama when she'd call, wanting to know when we could make a payment, he'd just walk away.

Daddy walked away from the grill. He'd been grilling some chicken wings and hamburgers and they were gonna burn. Mama came over from the bench she shared with Marva and the boys and stepped close by just in case it got nasty.

I hadn't seen Daddy so riled up in years. Then it occurred to me, Plez had no intention of paying back the money. He didn't think he had to.

"What kind of example are you setting for your boys? Don't you want them to learn to pay their debts?"

"Man, you better sit your old ass down, drink that low-grade moonshine of yours and shut the fuck up!"

"Plez, please, the children!" Mama said.

"Clarice, you better tell your drunk-ass husband to back the fuck off!"

"Daddy, we'll pay. I promise we'll pay!" I threw in, trying

to smooth things over.

"I always knew he wasn't any good. Lord knows I've made my mistakes, but at least I pay people what I owe 'em!" Daddy said.

"You better get him, Clarice!" Plez said, looking like a bull seeing a red cape.

"Ya'll need to remember where you are. Do you want these white folks to call the police on ya'll?" Mama said, trying to reason with them.

"No, you're right, Clarice," Daddy said, trying to lower his voice.

"You ain't nothing but a house nigger anyway. You better act right; you don't want Mr. Whitey over there seeing you act niggerish. You got a lot of nerve talking to me about anything, you ol' drunk!" Plez yelled.

Daddy took a swing at Plez, but he tripped over his own feet and fell to the ground. I looked around and saw the white families off in the distance looking at us and shaking their heads.

"You see how your husband is, Clarice? I was more than willing to put things aside and come out for some barbeque, but this fool here's gotta fuck up the vibe."

"What, you ain't gonna hit a man? I know you probably beatin' on my daughter. Try beatin' on me, you bitch-ass nigga!" Daddy screamed.

Plez shot me a look of death. I turned away and started calling out for Lawrence and Plez Jr. to gather their things so we could go. Plez started laughing. We all knew that Daddy was no match for Plez. Daddy probably knew it too, which is why he was so angry.

"Okay, nigga, I tell you what. You ain't got to pay the money. But don't think your black ass is gettin' away with ruining my credit because I've been payin' on the loan. But you know you owe me this money. You better never come by my house ever again, do you hear me? I will cut you too short to shit if you do!"

Plez rolled his eyes, a huge smirk on his face and said, "Whatever, Mr. Greene. Go to AA. They're looking for you!"

"And Cheryl, since you picked him, you ain't welcome at my house neither!" Daddy said, turning to me.

My eyes burned with tears. Mama turned away and started throwing meat from the grill into the garbage. Marva started putting paper plates and cups and stuff back into huge, empty Avon boxes. I was speechless. I went to hug Mama and she stood limp in my embrace. Marva hugged me and whispered, "I don't know why you had to marry him."I didn't know either.

Plez grabbed me by my arm as we made our way back to the car. When we got in, Plez pulled away from the parking spot and got to the parking lot entrance. Then he turned to me, his eyes fiery, and he slapped me.

"There. Run and tell that!"

"Why'd you hit me?" I cried.

Plez started laughing. "Bitch, you're mine. Go and tell your mammy and pappy that. Oh, I forgot, they want nothing to do with you! You've probably been putting all of our business in the street. You just wait until we get home."

I spent the rest of the car ride hoping he'd change his mind. I knew that Daddy had played into Plez's hands. Plez wasn't gonna pay back the money, so he did what he did best when he knew he owed people, he either disappeared, like he did when he owed those guys down at the pool hall, or he started arguments, like he did with Daddy.When we got out of the car, I took my time getting to the front door. I tried to hold Plez Jr. back and Lawrence started asking me all kinds of questions to slow us down because even he knew what was in store for me once we got in the house and the door closed behind us.

"Ya'll go to your rooms and close the door." Plez said, pointing in the direction of their bedrooms.

"They already saw you slap me; why not let them see you put your foot in my ass, too?"

"I'm getting tired of playing games with your monkey-ass," Plez said, pulling me by my shirt. He had bunches of my neckline in his hand.

"Let go of me!"

"Or what? What's your funky ass gonna do? Nothing. You ain't gonna do a goddamn thing!"

The next thing I saw was Plez's fist coming toward me. I was knocked senseless, hearing my own thud as I fell to the floor, covering my eye.

"Plez, please! Don't hit me!"

"Bitch, shut up!" he said, kicking me in my stomach like I was a wore-out dog. I felt the wind get knocked out of me. I positioned myself in the fetal position, hoping to guard myself from his punches and kicks. He reached down and tore my shirt completely down the middle so that my bra was exposed. I put my arms up, scratching at the air, so that he would get away from me. He stood there, sweating like he had just put in a full day's work. I felt my face swelling up, my lips stinging from being cut open. I knew I wouldn't recognize myself when he was through.

But like a child growing tired of playing with a toy, he left me there to cry. I cried so hard that I got a headache. I hated him and I hated my life. I knew I had nowhere to turn.

I fell asleep crying. I woke up later when Plez decided to go out. I was thankful. When the boys heard the door close and Plez's car speed off, they came out of their rooms. Lawrence had tears in his eyes, his nose flaring in anger. Plez Jr. just stared at me with no emotion in his face. He was too young to understand anyway.

"I wish I could kill that motherfucker!" Lawrence said.

I propped myself up, leaning against the back of the sofa. I held my ripped shirt closed with one hand, wiping away tears with the other. My face was too sore to touch. "Don't say that."

"He treats you so bad, Ma. Why do you put up with it? We ought to just leave. I'll get a job after school. I'll help you pay bills, whatever we have to do."

I was touched by the thought, even though he didn't realize that he was too young, nobody was gonna hire him. But in what Lawrence said, I heard myself and my sister asking Mama that same question. Why couldn't we just leave? If Mama had gathered us up Daddy wouldn't have fought that hard to keep us. He probably would've been just as glad to drink and screw his women in peace. But Plez couldn't give up that kind of control. He made it so that anyone who stood to question him was out of my life. It happened with Clayton, and now with my parents. Daddy talked all that shit when he was drunk about how he would fuck somebody up, but we knew he couldn't bust a grape. "Lawrence, he's under a lot of pressure right now. Things will get better. We'll all be happy again, just you wait." I said, addressing my child, and once again taking responsibility for Plez's shit.

I made my way to the bathroom, dreading what I'd find when I looked into the mirror. Just as I thought, Plez had jacked up my face pretty badly. I looked like the Elephant Man. Tears forced their way through the tiny slits I had for swollen eyes. I don't know why I was surprised. Plez's actions had been leading up to it. It was his reward for finally having me where he wanted me.

I felt like the years that had passed was wasted life, and I wished I'd never met Plez Darnell Jackson. His Aramis scent lingered behind after he walked out the door. I knew he was coming home late. He was probably going out to find brand-new pussy to charm while I lay in bed, tossing and turning in pain.As bad as I felt, both emotionally and physically, looking pitiful in a mirror, not being able to look my boys in the eyes and offer them anything better, I was glad Plez left. He left me a broken woman, crying out to be fixed, and he wanted to keep me that way, and I wanted him to love me, because when the love was there, it was good. But it was showing up less and less; he was too busy spreading it around to some other bitches.

I stood in front of that mirror, goddamning myself while I tried to clean myself up the best way I could. But the stinging was too much. My eyes pulsated in pain; my face felt raw and busted. I would've given anything to have somebody rip my eyes from their sockets just so the pain would stop. Hell, I would've done it myself if I had the nerve.I turned out the light and told Lawrence that if he made peanut butter and jelly sandwiches for his and his brother's dinner, I'd give them money to order a pizza the next day. Anything they wanted to put on it, too. I went into my bedroom and closed the door. I looked at the phone and started to practice my cough.

"Drake Patterson's Nursing Home, this is Tammy speaking, how may I help you?"

She was one of those new nurses sent to replace the bullshit ones. I didn't know her.

Cough. Cough. Cough.

"Yeah, this is Cheryl Jackson. I'm calling out. I'm not feeling too well," I said, trying to make my nose sound stuffed up.

"Let me transfer you to Robert's office."

Damn, I didn't want to talk to him. I started practicing

my coughs again.

"This is Robert."

Cough. Cough. Cough. "Hey, Robert, this is Cheryl."

"You sound horrible," he said.

"I feel worse than that."

"Say no more. We've got enough coverage. Keep me posted, but we should be fine. Some of the morning nurses who were after me about some overtime can pull doubles."

This was easier than I thought it would be. "I'm sorry to put you out like this," I said. Cough. Cough. Cough.

"Just feel better soon, okay. Drink lots of OJ. It works for me every time."

"That sounds like a good plan," I said. I hated lying to Robert.

"Okay, get some rest."

"Thank you." I hung up.

I looked into the mirror that was attached to my dresser. I inspected my face again. I needed to get some ice on that bad boy to bring the swelling down. Yeah, it should only take about a week to be like new again, I thought to myself. At least, that's how long it took the last time.

CHAPTER

28

I TURNED MY RADIO DIAL to KMOJ. It was Minneapolis' only black radio station. Levert's "Casanova" was playing. I thought of Plez, who I knew thought of himself as a real-life Casanova. And he was living it, too. Since that last beating, I found a whole bunch of cocktail napkins with women's numbers; some written in eye pencil, one written in lipstick, most written in pen. He was acting just like my father used to; laying up with whorish women who didn't care about that wedding band on his left hand, assuming he wore it. Bitches had started calling the house all hours of the day and night, and had the audacity to get mad that I was upset that they were disrespecting my house by calling a married man.

Eventually the tears stopped when I saw the phone numbers, or when the phone rang at 2:30 in the morning with some heifer calling, looking for dick. I was glad Plez had his extracurricular activities. My love for him was drying out like some old-ass flowers. To me, he was becoming more like the dirt, but just because you grow pretty flowers in that dirt doesn't make the dirt pretty.

I pulled up to the job, which had become my sanctuary. As much as I loved my children, I fought for any and every piece of overtime I could get at work. I figured the less time I was at home, the less opportunity Plez had to jump on me. I checked my rearview mirror for the last time to see if the makeup job I'd done covered the bruises, which took a bit longer to fade than the last time. I didn't even care that people knew I didn't ordinarily wear that much makeup, so long as the bruises didn't show through. The good news was that no one could see the faint remainder of bruises on the rest of my body.

Dino did a double take when he saw me. I prayed that he wouldn't ask me any questions. When we took our break together, he sat down across from me. My face was open for full inspection. His eyes, which were as large as saucers, darted from my forehead down to my chin. Finally, I got tired of it. "Is there something you'd like to ask me?"

"You don't normally wear makeup."

"Sure I do."

"Well, it's different today. You look like you're planning on going to a club after work."

Suddenly I became self-conscious. "Does it look bad?"

"No. It's just a bit much. I'm sure I'll get used to it. Sure is a shame though."

"What is?"

"You're naturally beautiful. It's a shame to hide that beauty under all that stuff."

I blushed, and was relieved. "I was just trying something different."

"That's fair. I'm just giving you one man's opinion."

"Are you the type to just offer opinions whether somebody asked for them or not?"

"It's a flaw. My ex-wife hated it."

"See, that's what I don't understand. You seem like a really nice guy. I can't see somebody not wanting to give you her heart."

"I gave her *my* heart. She didn't want it anymore." Dino smiled and then shrugged it off, trying to pretend that it didn't still hurt. But I knew it did. I knew because I felt the same way toward Plez. But Plez went a step further and threw my heart in the trash can, put the lid over it, and some bricks on top of the lid so that no one else could have it. I felt a connection to Dino. He'd been hurt and so had I. I was glad to have him as a friend.

"It's funny; my family insisted I marry Italian. I did all

the 'right' things and still this happened. I wanted it to be forever, just like my folks. They've been married forty years."

"Yeah, but forever is a long time. I look at my parents and they can't stand each other. I think they stay together because they're too damn lazy to find someone else; well, at least my mama is."

Dino laughed. Suddenly he shivered, shaking off those bad memories. He opened his brown paper bag and pulled out a sandwich. He pulled it apart and looked at me and winked. "Here, take some."

"What is it?"

"Tuna fish."

"I hate tuna fish."

"I make the best tuna fish. I guarantee it."

I looked at it, and then took it from him. After that one bite, I fell in love with tuna fish. With him looking at me with those young, Al Pacino-like eyes, I could've fallen in love with Dino, too.

We ate in silence, and the silence felt good. If I'm comfortable, I don't like needless chit chat. With Plez, if we weren't talking, I felt like he was thinking up something crazy and it was always my duty to figure out what was going on in his head, otherwise, he'd start playing his games.

"You haven't given up, though, have you?" I asked Dino.

"What, on love?"

"Yeah."

"I'm hopeless when it comes to love."

"That's good. You'll find the right woman. Does she have to be Italian?"

Dino started to laugh. "You know, it's funny you ask that. Ever since Gia divorced me, my buddies tell me that I've developed a Robert De Niro complex."

"What is that?"

"Robert De Niro only dates black women. You never knew that?"

"No. So, you're attracted to black women?"

"Well, yeah. I ain't gonna lie; I've seen a few recently who've turned my head," he said, his eyes burning into me, "But my buddies say you have flings with black women, you don't marry them."

"That's a crappy thing to say. Maybe you need

new buddies."

"Maybe." His eyes were fixed onto me.I quickly looked at my watch. "Well, I guess we should get back on the floor. Thanks for the tuna."

He stood up, towering over me. "Anytime."

~ * * * ~

When I left work, I was nervous. I had this attraction to Dino and I didn't want it. Unlike Plez, I took my vows seriously. I guess he thought he could hump someone new, but come home to me, his familiar wench.I wasn't happy, and I hadn't been in a while. Our lives had become like a cycle. Things would be good for a while, and then he'd change. And you could see it in his eyes when the switch happened. Or you felt it in the air when he came home. His energy was like that, and I was tired of it.I had a decision to make: either I would try and get him to work on our marriage with me, or I had to get out.

After work, I drove around to find a 24-hour drugstore. I had a craving for gummi bears. They were the one comfort food I allowed myself since I'd been trying to lose a little weight. I wasn't big as a house, but sometimes Plez made me feel that way. Maybe if I took better care of myself, he'd take better care of me too.

My intent was to buy just the gummi bears, but I picked up a few more items: hair relaxer, curling iron. I even bought my *Ebony, Jet and Essence* magazines.When I got to the checkout counter, there was no one there. That's what I hated about shopping late at night, because I always had to go searching for the cashier. Finally, I saw someone coming from one of the aisles. It looked like a big man from a distance, but as the figure got closer it looked like a mannish woman. I almost dropped my basket of items when the person got so close, I couldn't mistake who she was."Rexanne?" I said.

"Cheryl?"

"Oh my goodness, girl, how have you been?" I said, placing my basket on the counter as she gave me a big hug.

When we parted, I had the chance to get a really good look at her. Time hadn't been good to her, physically. She had gained a lot of weight and she looked like someone who'd been drinking and drugging it for years. Her hair was different too; she was sporting dreadlocks. "Girl, you're working here?" I asked, not wanting to appear too taken aback.

"Eh, I'm just tryin' to make that money, you know?"

"I hear you. How have you been?" I asked.

"I've been doin' all right. I'm a little tired, though. This is my second job." She shrugged.

"Well, you're doing what you have to do, right?"

"Sure am. You look good. I bet somebody done swept you up, huh? Lucky bastard," she said, looking me up and down.

"Yeah, I'm married now. I have two sons. Different daddies unfortunately, but they're my world." I fished through my purse for my wallet so that I could show her a family photo of me, Plez, and the boys. I found one and gave it to her. Rexanne took one look at the photo and her face changed."Good for you," she said, handing the photo back to me without looking at me. She started taking things out of my basket and scanning them quickly.

"Are you okay?" I asked.

"Yeah, I'm fine. My boss is gonna come around here so I gotta finish this," she said, looking around in a panic.

"Well, maybe we could get together for lunch. I feel kind of bad that we didn't part on the best of terms."

"Yeah, okay. Your total is $42.98." She still avoided my eyes.

I paid her and took out a pen. When she put the receipt in the bag, I fished it out and wrote my number down on it. I handed her the paper. "Call me, will you?"

Rexanne looked at the paper for a moment and finally looked up at me. "It was really good seeing you. You look well." Then she came from behind the counter and scampered back down the same aisle she first appeared from.

Time had healed the bitterness I had toward Rexanne; after all, we were just kids, fumbling our way through life. We thought we knew every damn thing. I was ready to let bygones be bygones. Even though she'd gone a little crazy, she still helped me when my daddy threw me out. And while he had tried to be a better father, I could forgive Rexanne's nonsense faster than I could forgive his.I'd been giving my daddy money. I gave him whatever I could afford since Plez had thrown it in our faces that he had no intention of paying up. Sometimes it was fifty dollars, sometimes a couple hundred. Things were still shaky with Daddy and me, but I knew I was doing the right thing. But at the rate I was going, I'd be paying him back until I took my last breath or he took his, whichever came first. The good news was that I was allowed back in his house to visit, even though Plez still wasn't, which I don't think made Plez a bit of difference.

I took the kids over to my parents' house after church one Sunday, and we just hung out over there. Me and Plez had been arguing over foolishness and he was getting that look in his eyes again, like it was time for another beating. I figured if I wasn't there, he'd have nobody to hit.

Mama made us some tea. She sat down and poured hot water into my cup and slid a tea bag over to me.

"You know, Diallo's been callin' again."

I rolled my eyes. What else was new? "So?"

"He's back in town. He gave me something to give to you."

Mama got up and went upstairs. When she came back, she handed me a white envelope and sat back down to enjoy her tea. She had already opened it, probably even read it. She was so nosy, just like my daddy. There was a piece of paper inside with a check for $500.00. The letter said:

Dear Lawrence,

You may not have anything to say to me. I understand that. I was a chump when you were born. I wasn't ready for that kind of responsibility. But I want to try and do right by you now. I'd like to have a chance to explain things. Maybe you'll be able to understand where my head was at. I know if I was you I'd probably tell me to go on about my business. I'm sending you some money. It doesn't cover all the years you probably wondered where I was, or the heartache of watching your mama struggle to care for you, but it's a start. I've cleaned up my life, so there's more where this money came from. In a weird way, going to Chicago was the best thing that could happen to me.

Son, all I'm asking is for a chance to be in your life now. For real this time.

I love you, Son. I never stopped.
Pops

When I finished reading the letter I didn't know what to think, besides wanting to wad it up and throw it in the trash. Lawrence had long ago stopped asking for his daddy. Plez had been his father, or the closest thing to one, anyway. Why was Diallo trying to come around and upset our peace now? I knew Plez would have a fit if he knew Diallo was trying to be in the picture now because it would diminish Plez's role. For all of his faults, Plez was the one who helped me keep a roof over the boys' head, food in their stomachs, and clothes on their backs. Not Diallo, not even close.

"I'm not tryin' to sound like a broken record, but you need to let the man see his son."

"Look, Mama. When Lawrence turns 18, he can do whatever the hell he wants to do. Until then, how do you expect me to explain this to Plez? You know how he is."

"I don't know, baby. When I read the letter, I thought that Diallo must have a good reason for bailin' out like he did. Just give him a chance, girl. You know he's tryin'."

"But what about before he left? He barely did anything. Yeah, sure, he gave Lawrence some toys and a couple of outfits. Big deal."

"All I'm sayin' is, right is right."

"How long ago did he bring this to you?"

"Yesterday. Cheryl, he looked pitiful. He was cryin' and carryin' on."

"I'll think about it. All I know is that Plez can't know about this."

"What if you bring Lawrence over here so that they can meet?"

"Like I said, Mama, I'll think about it."

Mama didn't say anything else. This was just what I needed, more stress to add to my life. That Negro thought he could just waltz back into our lives all easy-breezy, but he didn't know what I had to deal with.None of them had a clue.

CHAPTER

29

I'D BEEN PULLING A WEEK of working doubles and I was so tired that I didn't know whether I was coming or going. Dino made it easy to get through. He was always bringing in dishes he prepared for us to eat together; treating me to my very own taste of Italy. I'd enjoyed his homemade lasagna; sausage and peppers; ziti; linguini with olive oil, garlic, parsley, and blacked chicken; or his eggplant or chicken parmigiana. Plez had never made me anything more than a couple of egg salad sandwiches when we had that picnic in the park nine years before; that and maybe a frozen pizza here and there.

There was an undeniable attraction between Dino and me, but I felt dirty about it. I'd never really been attracted to a white guy before, and the only one that ever approached me was that crazy-ass Alex, when I danced at the Land-O-Ladies strip joint. That kind of attraction I wanted to feel for the man who had put a ring on my finger.

But it seemed the only time Plez and me saw each other was when I came home from work and was ready to go to sleep, and he'd already be asleep most of the time. Or on my days off— and on those days he was barely at home.

The phone calls from his whore of many, kept me up when I was trying to get some much needed sleep. I guess he'd found his regular chick on the side. Sometimes he'd get up out the bed and take her call in the kitchen, or, if he was feeling real brazen, he'd lay right there in the bed and talk to the scamp. What killed me about it was that she was so casual about calling. She had no respect for my marriage. Sometimes when she'd call, the bitch would have the audacity to try and crack jokes and shit, like we were best girlfriends. Then she'd ask to speak to Plez. They both acted like they wanted to rub that mess in my face.Sometimes I'd wonder if the effort I put into our marriage were even worth it, since Plez seemed like he couldn't care less. Here I had a husband who hardly looked twice at me, who only wanted me to give him some of my kitty cat when he'd come home drunk and couldn't get it where he came from, and only interacted with me to start an argument or play one of his head games so that I wouldn't forget who was running things. And despite all of that, I was the one still tied to the *till death do us part*. For my children, and myself, I stayed put, hoping the old Plez, who was buried somewhere inside of my husband would remember why he fell in love with me.

Dino was the perfect distraction from all of that. He was kind and he noticed me. He actually *listened* to me. When Plez and me talked, or should I say, argued, I could tell that he never listened to what I had to say. I knew that as I spoke, he was formulating a rebuttal in his mind to shoot back at me.

Dino had started fixing himself up better. He'd come in smelling good, and looked like he was trying to shed a few pounds. I wondered if he was doing that for himself or for me. We were professional, don't get me wrong. We knew better than to flirt so openly, especially with all the gossipy folks we had to work with. Usually our stolen moments came when we took our breaks together, or in a back corridor where no one else was.

I tried not to lead him on in any way. At first he would make little sexual innuendos. I'd just walk away when he said stuff, even though I secretly liked it and wanted to hear more. He stopped for a while because he thought I was uncomfortable. But then it got to the point that I would match him pound for pound with some filth. One day I could see through his pants that he had a hard-on. I said, "Is that for me later?" and he'd say, "It's ready when you are."

My pussy would just about melt when he'd stand next to me, or brush past me, smelling all good and shit. He knew how to do it and make it look accidental, but I knew he was deliberately brushing his dick against my booty, because as soon as he walked away, he'd turn back and look, with that glint in his eye and sexy-ass smirk of his.

We talked about his ex-wife, and had just started talking about my life with Plez. I'd complain about how unhappy I was, but I never told Dino that Plez beat me. I didn't want Dino to feel like he had to rescue me from a bad situation. I already lived that before with Plez, and what I got with him was ten times worse than what I had living with my family. I knew I wanted out, I just didn't know how I was gonna get out, and with as little complication as possible.

Dino listened, and I could tell he wished he could come in like a knight in shining armor and get me out of my marriage. But I had two kids who I'd be taking with me; especially Plez Jr., who adored his father and who I felt thought his father could do no wrong.

"I just know that if you and I were together, there's no way in hell I'd put you through the shit your husband does. I'd treat you like the queen you are."

His saying that brought tears to my eyes. I got pissed because I allowed myself to say too much, and feel things that I shouldn't. Our attraction was professionally dangerous, too. There wasn't supposed to be any dating between staff. Since we weren't dating, we were in the clear, but if we were perceived to be, it would mean trouble.

"Damn, I could use a drink," Dino said, one night after our shift. "You wanna go grab a quick one before you go home?"

"I'd love to, but I can't."

"He's that jealous, huh?"

"And more."

"So, what's a guy gotta do to spend some quality time with you? I hate that the only time I can talk to you is when we're working."

"Dino, look, I think you're a great man. If things were different..."

"I know," he said, the disappointment obvious in his eyes.

I thought for a moment. I took a scrap of paper and handed it to him. "Here, write your number down. I can call you."

Dino's face lit up as though I had kissed it. He snatched the paper from me and scribbled down that number quicker than I could tell you what my name was. I'd just have to make sure Plez never saw it.

When I got home, I was happy. I felt like Dino and me were moving safely into another realm of our relationship, and I wasn't even screwing him. I hadn't had a male friend that I could really talk to since Clayton. The temptation to find myself in Dino's bed was definitely there. That's what made me human. But I also had a good enough reason not to even go there with Dino...it was called the back side of Plez's hand.

By the summer, Plez's whore had stopped calling the house, but I wasn't sure if he was still screwing her or not. I hoped that he was, because I wasn't trying to give him sex. When he came to me at night, rubbing against me, trying to get cozy, I'd tell him I had a headache, or that I had the runs; anything to avoid him hopping on top of me. And that was sad, because there was a time in our lives together that I looked forward to intimacy. But that time was over with. I knew it was just a matter of time before Plez's alter-ego would emerge.

Later that summer, we planned a family day of fishing at Lake Minnetonka. I had packed Plez's beer in the cooler and some turkey sandwiches and soda for the boys. I still had a little time to make sure my hair was decent and while in the bathroom, I overheard Plez talking to Lawrence.

"Say, man, you don't even like fishing, do you?"

"Not really," Lawrence said.

"Well, then, you don't have to go if you don't want to. I bet you'd rather hang out with your friends than put some nasty worms on a hook, huh?"

"My friend Zach asked me to come over, but I told him I couldn't because we were going fishing."

"There you go. Call your boyfriend up and see if he still wants to get together."

"My boyfriend?" Lawrence asked.

"Yeah. He's your friend, right?"

"Yeah."

"And he's a boy, right?"

"Yeah."

"So that makes him your boyfriend. What did you think I was saying?"

"I don't know."

Plez laughed. "You're all right in my book, little man. I'm gonna put the poles in the trunk. Call your friend." Then I heard the back screen door open and close.

"Lawrence, can you come here for a second," I called from the bathroom.

Lawrence appeared in the doorway. I grabbed him by his shirt and pulled him in, closing the bathroom door behind us.

"What the hell is your problem?" I snapped.

"Nothing."

"Then why aren't you coming fishing with us?"

"Plez said I don't have to."

"Why are you gonna let him play with your head like that?"

Lawrence looked at me and shrugged stupidly.

"Don't you know he's poking fun at you? Don't you know that he thinks you're a sissy?"

"He told me I could call my friend," Lawrence said, shaking. His eyes were brimming with tears.

"You should have said, 'No, I wanna go fishing with my family!' That's what your stupid ass should have done!"

I was pissed. Lawrence should've known better. If he wanted to be a part of this damn family then he should've been willing to fight for his place. Plez was playing games. Lawrence knew how Plez could be, why did he give him what he wanted?

"Look, you're the one who told me he doesn't give a fuck about you. You're messing everything up for me! I'm working my ass off to keep this family together! The next time he tries to discourage you from going somewhere with us, you tell him you wanna go. Do I make myself clear?" Lawrence had a look of fear on his face as he nodded yes. I pushed him away and he fell into the tub.

"What did I do?" he cried from the tub. He was trying to pull himself out, but the tub was still wet from whoever last used it. Tears were streaming down his face. He looked pitiful and defeated. I suddenly realized what I'd done and reached in to help him out of the tub.

"Oh, baby, I'm sorry," I said, hugging him as he sobbed into my shoulder. "Don't cry. I'm sorry."

We parted, and Lawrence's shirt was all bunched up from where I grabbed it. I tried to help him smooth it out.

"Go on and call your friend," I said, rubbing his head as he walked slowly out of the bathroom. I straightened myself up and went out to join Plez and Plez Jr.

CHAPTER

30

*G*OOD *EVENING, LADIES AND GENTLEMEN, and welcome to the "Let's see how we can mess with Cheryl next show."*

That's what I called the last few months of 1988. I was still working my doubles because Robert was firing every-damn-body. He needed the coverage and I was beyond exhausted.

I came home one night, my eyes barely able to stay open. I was surprised I didn't crash my car on the way home from nodding off. As soon as my head hit the pillow I was out.

Deep in sleep, I started feeling a tapping against my legs. Even in my drowsiness, I knew it was Plez, and I knew he wasn't up to any good. Then, the tapping stopped. But, I could feel his eyes on me. I knew that if I opened them, he'd try and start in on me. I shifted my position, moaning like I was deep in sleep and rolled over.

"Wake your ass up, you ain't sleep!"

"What, Plez?"

"You've been coming through here the last few months all glowing and shit. The last time you glowed like that was after my dick was up in you. I know you ain't been getting it from me lately so, who've you been fucking?"

I could tell instantly he'd been drinking. He was reminding me more and more of my father. "Nobody, Plez. I've been working so many doubles; I can't even remember what day it is. When do I have the time to be out messing around? Can I please go back to sleep?"

"Bullshit. You better turn your ass around and look at me when I'm talking to you."

Apparently I didn't do it fast enough, because Plez grabbed me by my throat and pulled my body so that I was facing him.

"I can't breathe!" I croaked.

"Shut that shit up! You couldn't talk if you couldn't breathe! Now, tell me who've you been fucking!"

My initial fear turned to anger. I knew he was trying to trip me up by getting me to confess to something while I was half-asleep. I started to beat on his chest. Years of emotions roared to the surface: the pain of his abuse, the embarrassment that I'd become one of *those girls* that let their man put their hands on them. And the anger of feeling robbed of support, be it from my family or the few friends I had to sneak around to have. I hadn't realized how much I was carrying inside of myself. It was an awful burden.Plez grabbed me and threw me onto the bed so hard that my neck snapped back. "Are you out of your fucking mind?" he roared.

"I ain't been messing around! Do I say anything when your bitch calls here?"

"I ain't been fucking anybody!"

The anger in me was still in charge. "You mean to tell me you ain't been screwing that heifer?"

"I don't need to explain myself to you!"

"Oh, so since you've narrowed it down to one, I'm not allowed to ask any questions, right?" I asked, tears streaming down my face.

"Bitch, I will kill you, do you hear me?"

I could feel my lower lip tremble while my heart beat so fast I thought I was gonna go into cardiac arrest.

"Yeah, I don't hear all of that mouth now," he said, seeing the anger melt and the fear return in my face.

And he would do this, night after night; without any warning or just cause. I hadn't done anything, and Plez knew I hadn't. But he wanted to tighten the emotional leash around my neck. He wanted me to know that like he said, he was always one step ahead. He was always watching.

Plez sat me down one night and asked me a question. "Are you happy?"

"Happy like how?"

"Pick a topic."

"Work's been hell."

"Now you know that ain't what I'm talking about. I'm talking about us."

"Every marriage has its ups and downs."

"I want out," Plez said bluntly.

I blinked a couple of times; not knowing if he was serious or if this was another one of his tests. "You do?"

"Yeah, this has been shitty for a long while now, and you know that."

I made every effort to make sure my face was appropriately surprised and sad, but in my mind, I was doing somersaults and kicking him and his couple of raggedy suitcases with the clothes hanging out the sides, out the front door.

"How would you feel if I signed everything over to you? You can have the house, I just wanna be free."

"Is there someone else?"

"Yeah."

Ain't that about a bitch? And I meant that literally, too. I thought it was funny that a guy I'm not even attracted to can kiss me on the cheek, or I can dance with a guy Plez practically forces me ton, and *I* get threatened with a crowbar.

I got popped in the face for visiting a dying friend and accepting a ride home from my nursing instructor. I even got beat like I stole something because he thought I was putting our business in the streets. But yet, he could waltz in, say that our life together sucked and that was supposed to be the end of it? In my heart I knew it needed to be over. Love didn't live here anymore as far as I was concerned, but I wanted to be the one to end it. I hated that he'd come into my life, messed it all up to be damned, and then had the luxury of walking away, fresh and spotless into the sunset while I was left behind to pick up the shattered pieces of my life.

His little announcement made me feel as though he'd

dropped a great big block of cement on my chest. My breathing slowed and my chest tightened as I tried to really take in what he said. Yeah, I had heard what he said, but it hadn't sunk in. "I'll take Plez Jr. on the weekends," he said, his mind apparently made up.

I felt my lungs open up, allowing air to fill them. "That ain't happening. I won't have one of your whores anywhere near my child," I said, finding strength to say it if not for myself, then for my child. "One of my what?" Plez's body twitched in the chair.

"If you wanna leave, fine. But don't bring my child around that."

"Bitch, who do you think you're talking to?" Plez was standing up and over me, the chair he had sat on pushed back against the wall in no time flat. He pulled me up by my throat.

In a flash I saw red. All the years of abuse flashed before me in a red lens, like someone's life is supposed to flash before them before they die.

I used my closed fists and swung wildly, hoping a few punches would land on him. As soon as my neck was released I ran from the kitchen toward the bedroom, catching my breath. I went into his dresser, trying to find his gun he bought for protection of the household. After opening the dresser, I flung his raggedy-ass drawers, pants, socks and whatever else my hands grabbed as I went on to find the gun.

Plez stood in the doorway just in time to see me aiming it at him. I didn't care what the make of the gun was, just that I'd blow his motherfucking head off with it.

The half-second look of panic on his face turned into delight. He leaned back against one side of the door frame, folded his arms and crossed one leg in front of the other.

"Oh, I get it. You're big and bad now, right?"

"Plez, you better stay your ass right there!"

"Nah, go ahead, squeeze that shit. I dare you."

"You ain't taking my son!"

"First of all, bitch, I was just taking him for the weekends, but you've done pissed me off. I'm taking him for good now."

My legs felt like jelly with all of my strength put into holding the gun. "I mean it, Plez, I'll do it!"

Plez began walking toward me very slowly as if he was giving me a chance to rethink what I was doing. He kept taking those god-awful steps, his eyes telling me that he wasn't afraid.

"You've got heart, I like that. But there's one reason why you won't shoot me."

Oh, so he wanted to test me? I closed my eyes, preparing for the recoil. I squeezed the trigger. Nothing happened. I squeezed again, still nothing. As I opened my eyes, I saw Plez taking faster paces toward me.

"It's called a safety, dummy," Plez said, snatching the gun from me. I cowered in the corner, seeing him hold the gun by its barrel, looking like he was going to pistol-whip me with the handle. But then he stopped, his own adrenaline pumping. "I ought to knock your stupid ass into the middle of next week for this shit. Better yet, I should shoot you on principle alone. But your blood ain't even worth the cleanup."

I could feel my legs give way from beneath me. I slid down the wall in that corner he had me.

"And anyway, you dumb bitch, I was only joking with you." Then he looked around the room at the clothes thrown all over the place and said, "Clean this shit up!"

Plez went out that night, probably to the Spruce, to make me a joke among his so-called friends, the pack of losers they were.

I refolded the clothes, making sure to put everything back where I found it. Afterward I went into the living room and fell asleep on the sofa. I didn't want to be awakened by Mr. Personality in the middle of the night, demanding drunken sex. That is, if he came home at all.

The next morning I woke up, feeling too defeated to even get up to start my day. I told Lawrence to go into my purse and take ten dollars for lunch if he would pack something for Plez Jr.'s lunch. I laid back on the sofa for much of the afternoon. My clothes stuck to me from sweating all night. Plez had come home for just enough time to change, shower, and leave for work. He left his skid-marked drawers on the bathroom floor and that's where they stayed because I wasn't about to pick those nasty things up.I called out of work that day. I just couldn't face anybody. I needed a "me day" just to get my head together.

After taking my shower, I was glad I had fogged up the bathroom mirror because I didn't want to look into it and see my mother staring back at me. To think, I'd worked hard, found a husband, had my boys, but had done nothing else to set myself apart from her. At that point, we'd basically lived the same life.

Plez called at 2:00, right around the time he knew I got ready to go to work, if I'd gone.

"Hey, Shooter," he said, his voice cheerful.

"Hey," I said.

"My boys at the Spruce told me that I'm terrible for pulling a stunt like that on you. I'm sorry."

"Yeah, I know."

"No, I mean it, Cheryl. That was completely uncalled for."

"Plez, I know."

"But, seeing you come alive like that, goddamn it, girl, that shit got my dick hard. You know what I want when you come home tonight, right?"

"Didn't you get that last night," I said with a laugh. I couldn't believe his nerve.

"No, baby, I slept at my boy Terrance's house after the bar closed. I wasn't in any condition to drive."

So instead of waking me up from a sound sleep to fuck, he wants to do it tonight? I just can't catch a break, I thought to myself. "Well, I'm not working today."

"What happened?"

"My boss called and asked if I wanted to take the day off since I pulled all those doubles to help him out before," I lied.

"Even better. You better get ready, baby, because I'm gonna give you something real good tonight."

"Can't wait," I said, trying to sound thrilled. When I hung up, I felt that drop in my stomach again. I couldn't believe Plez's crazy ass. I had just pulled a gun on him and he was acting like everything was cool. Now he wanted some pussy, which is how he measured that everything was hunky-dory. Whenever we had sex after a fight that told him he could move on, that all was forgiven—until the next time.

That night, The Isley Brothers covered the noises of our squeaking bed and Plez's moans. I threw in a few moans just so that I could appear involved, but if I could've been real about it, I would've just laid there and let him do what he had to do so he'd hurry up and finish.

He was predictable; the same swirling of hips, thrashing around with no kind of decent rhythm. But then, I thought, had Plez always been this lousy in bed and I just didn't realize it because things were better between us at one point? No, he'd been great in that department. Now, it was emotionally empty. More like he had to bust one off and I was the receptacle.

Through the manic friction, I closed my eyes, creating a fantasy world that night. In my mind I imagined Dino doing everything right to my body that Plez was failing miserably at. With that imagery in my head I started rocking my pelvis to meet Plez's thrusts. That's when it started to feel good. I laughed out loud at the mental infidelity. I opened my eyes to see Plez with a puzzled look on his face, sweaty as ever from putting in work that would never please me. "I'm sorry, baby, but it's feeling so good tonight, I didn't know what else to do. It was either start laughing or singing," I said.Then Plez laughed, wiping some of his sweat off of my face with the bed sheet in his hand, with his, I'm in-the-moment-right-now-loving way. And while he had his chuckle, and his ego stretched all out of shape for something he wasn't even doing right, I closed my eyes again, wishing what Plez was attempting to do to me, Dino was doing perfectly.

CHAPTER

31

T HE BOYS WENT BACK TO school. Lawrence was a freshman in high school, and Plez Jr. was starting fourth grade. I was happy to have the boys back on a schedule. They pretty much lazed around the house that summer, though Lawrence had found himself a job working at Wendy's to put some spending money in his pocket. I don't know who the hell he was talking to over there, but they must have put some thoughts into his head for him to pull the shit he pulled.

Plez met me at the door one night when I came home from work. He was clenching a piece of paper in his hands, looking at me like he was ready to beat my ass again. But he said, "Read this shit," and walked away.

I didn't know what he handed me, and I hardly had a chance to put my things down when he did. I went and sat down on the sofa and read:

Dear Martin,
You were right. I know a guy where I work who's been telling me it's all right to be the way we are. I'm glad I have him to talk to because I know my ma and stepdad would flip the fuck out. You're lucky, though. You told both of your parents a long time ago and they accept you. But my ma

keeps bringing me to church and I know that just by what they talk about there that she'd never accept me. Plez would probably kill me if he knew.

I can't wait until I move out the house so I can find a nice guy to fall in love with. I'm happy for you and Rick; that you two can go on about your lives and not give two shits about what anyone at that school thinks of you. But while I'm happy, I fear for you, too. I know that some of those thuggish dudes and those jocks hate our kind, and want to not just kick our asses, but put us into the ground.But, you two are lucky because you're going away to college soon. I'll be stuck in that school with people who don't understand me. I don't know what I'll do then. I'm glad that you both aren't afraid to be seen with a lowly underclassman, like me. (Smile)

I guess I'll just go back to reading my GQ magazines and wishing that I could be as gorgeous as some of those male models. Martin, you know you have it made because you're light-skinned. That's why your ass can pull a white guy as cute as Rick.

Okay, I know, I promised I wouldn't throw you shade. I'll shut up.

Do me a favor though. When you're done reading this, throw this into the garbage. I don't want the wrong people seeing this. I can't imagine the embarrassment.

Lawrence.

When I finished reading that letter, I was heated. In it, Lawrence pretty much copped to what Plez had been saying about him for years; what I'd secretly prayed wasn't true.

Between the two of us, I don't know who was angrier, me or Plez. Don't get me wrong, I didn't have a problem with gay people as long as it involved other people. It was a totally different feeling when that sort of thing moved to my doorstep. I remembered Clayton, and what happened to him. I didn't want my son to have that kind of life; people giving him such a hard way to go because he was different. I didn't want to get news that he had AIDS or some crazy person had bashed his head in for a thrill. I had normal dreams for who I thought was my normal son. The boy speaking in the letter wasn't who I dreamed him to be.

Plez came back in. I quickly tried to wipe the tears from my eyes as I folded the letter up. For a moment I didn't know what to think or say. Plez looked like he was ready for me to give him the go-ahead to beat the hell out of Lawrence. But I doubted a beating would change anything.

"Where did you find this?" I asked Plez.

"I went into his room to get my 2 Live Crew tape back from him, and I saw the letter lying on the bed. I sent him out to the garage to find something that I knew wasn't even out there so I'd have enough time to read this shit and put it back."

"I'm gonna go talk to him."

"Yeah, you do that, Cheryl. You do that before I break his goddamn neck!"

Lawrence's door was closed and I didn't bother to knock. I went in and saw that he had his earphones on, with an endlessly long cord hooked into his stereo. I pulled the plug from the cord out, which blasted music at full volume. Lawrence bolted up from his bed as though his room had been invaded.

"What, what," he shouted, looking around his room.

"You need to explain this shit to me," I said, holding the letter in my hand. Lawrence took one look at the paper and he knew.

"You mean to tell me you like boys now?"

"Okay, okay. If we talk about this, we need to talk like rational human beings."

"Lawrence, I'm not gonna go through this with you, okay? Ain't nothin' you can say that's gonna make me accept this."

Lawrence started to cry. "I knew you wouldn't understand," he said.

"You're damn right I wouldn't understand. Why are you writing letters to some sissy?"

"He's my friend."

"You ain't got any better friends than this? And who is this person at your job encouraging you into this?"

"Ma, no one is encouraging me into anything!"

"You don't have any idea how much shit you just caused. Plez wanted to come down here and stomp you up in here."

"I can't help how I feel, Ma. I've tried. You don't know what it's like being me."

"Listen, my best friend was like that. And you know

where he is? He's dead. He had AIDS. Is that how you want to end up?"

"I don't have AIDS, Ma."

"What's this crap you're talking about hoping to meet some guy and fall in love? Have you ever had a relationship?"

"No, Ma, honest, I haven't. I haven't even had sex yet."

"What makes you think that you're even really like that?"

Lawrence took a deep breath. I could tell he was trying to go to some source of power within himself to tell me what was on his mind. I don't know why I even asked, because it wasn't like he could make me feel any better about it. As he talked, I went in and out of my head. He was my child and I loved him. That wasn't the issue. Maybe I was acting like this because I saw what happened to Clayton only a few years earlier. I'd die if that happened to my child. And maybe I was acting like this because I knew how hateful Plez was. Maybe I was playing the part of disgusted parent, when I should have been trying to come into the conversation with an honest intent to understand.I was being forced to look something in the eye that I'd gone to bed many nights asking God to fix. But I knew. I knew from the time Lawrence was a little boy that this day would come. From the comments Plez made, to the times Lawrence's teachers would tell me things; even his infatuation with Michael Jackson during the *Thriller* days. While we sat and watched "*Motown 25*," dazzled by Michael's moonwalk, I turned to look at Lawrence and I knew something was different.

Suddenly, Lawrence changed his tune. He decided to give me the best gift he could."I don't know, Ma. Maybe I'm not gay. Maybe I'm just being what people have said that I am. I get called faggot so often that after a while I started to answer to it. It's a whole lot easier than trying to explain to people for the thousandth time that I ain't that way."

And then he looked me in the eyes, and I knew he wanted to believe what he was telling me, probably more than I wanted to believe it. By that time, I'd stopped trying to play the hardcore mother and let my tears fall where they did. But I still had that nut I called a husband in the other room. My show had to go on.

"I don't know, Lawrence. You better start doing a better job of convincing people, because I can't have that in my house." I said.

When I left Lawrence's room, Plez was standing in the hallway. He'd heard every damn word. My heart jumped because maybe he was pissed at what I'd said about him. He motioned me over with his index finger.

"I'm glad you said what you said to him at the end. I don't want that in my house. I have a son to think about and I don't want him around any of that faggotry. Get him out of here."

I felt like Plez had punched me in the mouth. Here he was, going to that low-blow place again; this my son vs. your son shit.

"I don't care where he winds up, but you make the shit happen. Do we understand each other?"

I could've taken a stand right there. I could've said, "No, nigga, we don't understand each other. That's still my child you're talking about!" But I didn't say that. I just nodded my head, like the obedient dog I'd become. "I'll call my mama tomorrow," I said, looking past Plez.Maybe it was for the best. Plez was pushing me to a point, past hatred. I knew something dramatic was gonna happen. If having Lawrence out of the house so he wouldn't have to bear witness to any of it was necessary, then so be it.

CHAPTER

32

As soon as I stopped thinking about Rexanne, she called.

I should've been like, "Whatever," but she acted so strangely at Walgreen's. I remembered she seemed happy to see me at first, but after she saw that photo, she changed. I think she held on to the hope we would be together. The reality of seeing me with a husband and two children made her realize that wasn't gonna happen.

I barely recognized her voice when she called. She sounded timid; nothing like the fear-no-one person I'd known when we were teenagers.

"Cheryl? Sorry it took me so long to call you. To be honest with you, I wasn't sure I was gonna."

"I'm glad you did."

After she finally calmed down, we had one of the nicest conversations we'd had in years. She even apologized for getting weird after she ate me out. I never hated her for that. At that time, I was a kid going through a dark spot in my life and I was open to the experimentation. When things got funky between us, I just knew it was time for me to go. We were both young and thought we knew what the world was all about.I was feeling close to her, the flow of the conversation was comfortable. We put some things into perspective and to rest. Neither one of us had any regrets.

The conversation was going along so well, that I almost felt guilty about changing the mood of it. I had to know what happened to her the night she came home looking a wreck. At the time, she'd said she had gotten into a fight with some dudes, and received the worst end of it.

"Well, since we're being all open and honest, girl, I gotta ask you something."

"What?"

"It's kind of personal."

"What?" she asked again, this time cautiously.

"Remember the night you came home all beat up? What really happened?"

"I don't wanna talk about that."

"Rexanne, come on. We've been open and honest with each other this entire conversation. Don't stop now."

"I gotta go."

"No, you don't. You just don't want to answer the question."

"Well, since you know all that, you need to take the hint."

"Look, when that happened, we were in a bad place. You put me through hell, but I still felt sorry for you."

"I didn't ask you to get involved in it. It's done, Cheryl. It's water under the bridge, and if you don't mind, I'd like to keep it that way."

"You obviously haven't moved on, Rexanne. Listen to yourself. You're not the same person I knew then. That's good on some levels, but in order to truly heal, you should come clean. Just put it all out there."

"You had this in mind all along, didn't you?"

"No. I was just..."

"That's why you slipped me your number. You've been chatting me up just so you can find out what happened."

"I was in your life when it happened. I deserve to know."

"And here I thought you'd changed. You're still a fake-ass bitch!" Then she hung up.

I spent the next few minutes wondering if I'd come on too strong. We would never be friends like we'd been in the past. But I did care for her. No matter what she said, I could tell that whatever happened that night was still eating at her.

Three hours later, I sat down to watch a rerun of *The*

Oprah Winfrey Show. Oprah was looking fantastic, having lost all that weight. She had on a black turtleneck, some blue jeans she was excited to fit into again, and black boots, dragging out a red wagon with a bagful of fat in it. For the perfect dramatic effect, she said that fat in the bag represented the fat she once carried in her body.

I just sat on the couch. Plez hadn't gone to work that day because he didn't feel like it. He went to take a shower before going out to take care of some business. I didn't have to work, either. Suddenly, the phone rang.

"Hello."

"It's me," Rexanne said. She sounded like she'd been crying.

"What's the matter?"

"You don't know what these years have been like."

I sat up in my seat. Suddenly, I felt like I was back in her apartment, pushing her bedroom door open, finding her looking beat-down the way she was. "Rexanne, I'm here for you, girl, just tell me what happened."

"Remember when I worked at that McDonald's that used to be on Hennepin Avenue?"

"Yeah." I was scared. All I wanted was to know what happened. Now that the time had finally come, I wasn't sure I wanted to know anymore.

"I had the closing shift that night. It was late. When I left, I started walking down the street. A group of dudes, about three of 'em, were coming from around the corner."

"Okay," I said, deciding that I did want to know.

"They started talking all kinds of shit to me. The usual shit niggas say to a chick like me. Like, 'Eh, baby, all you need is the right dude. I guarantee you'll never look at a pussy again.'"

I started to shake my head. I could picture it.

"I told them they could take what they called dicks and fuck each other with them. They kept talkin' shit, following me to the parking lot at the public library, where I'd parked." Rexanne started to cry uncontrollably like it just happened the day before. Then she tried to calm herself and continued, "They cornered me over by a dumpster. Cheryl, your ex, the one who came over to the apartment that day you went to the grocery store, the one that I hit in the side of the head and kicked him out, he was with them."

"Oh, my God, Rexanne! Did Diallo rape you?"

"No, he tried to stop him. The one guy just stood there, looking stupid and Diallo told the other one that they'd scared me enough and that he was going too far, but he pushed Diallo back."

"Diallo tried to stop who?"

Rexanne paused for what seemed like an eternity. Then she said they just kept taunting her. But the one guy wasn't finished. The third guy started looking around to see if anyone was coming then he said, "Man, to hell with this," and ran away leaving Diallo and the guy."I was just trying to get home," Rexanne said, sobbing again."Rexanne, please. You have to tell me. Who did Diallo try to stop?"

"Why'd they have to do that to me? I wasn't lookin' for no trouble." She was barely understandable.

"Rexanne, honey, I'm going to help you through this, but you have to tell me who did this to you."

Plez had gotten out of the shower and came into the living room with a towel wrapped around him, his body dripping wet.

"Rexanne, hold on, girl."

"Cheryl, do we have any more deodorant?" he asked me.Hearing her story made the air thin as I looked at Plez, who looked at me like I was wasting his time.

"Didn't you buy any more deodorant?" he asked.

I nodded yes.

"Then where is it?" he snapped.

"Look in the closet in the bedroom. There's a white plastic bag on the top shelf. There's a whole pack of your Right Guard in it."

"What's the matter with you? Who are you talking to?"

"Just a girl from work," I lied.

I must have looked pale, because Plez asked, "What are you two talking about?"

"One of the patients died. She was a real nice lady. We liked her a lot."

He seemed satisfied with my answer and left. Rexanne cleared her throat. When she spoke again she sounded like a lost, little girl, the first time I ever heard her sound feminine at all."It was that man in the picture. It was your husband."

CHAPTER

33

REXANNE'S REVELATION MADE ME GO into a dark place mentally. I believed her as soon as she said it. I didn't even have to ask Plez. It's not like he would've bust out with the truth anyway. After years of living with his aggressiveness, I knew he was the type.

I finally realized that any chance of us fixing things was over. I wanted out. But I knew that he wouldn't let me go that easily. That's when I started having thoughts I had no business having.

It started with me cooking stew. As I stirred it, I wondered, what if the only way I could get away from Plez was to kill him. What if I ordered takeout from somewhere and I put arsenic in the food? But it would be suspicious if only he got sick, so what if I put in enough to get us all sick, saving the lethal dose for him? If the police asked any questions, I wouldn't look so guilty because me and the boys would be sick too. That's if it played out like that. But cops weren't fools, and I bet I wouldn't be the first battered wife to try something like that. Plus, that idea scared me because I didn't want to hurt my kids. And it would be just my luck that I accidentally gave the wrong plate of food to one of the boys and they died from the poisoning.

I'd started having really bad dreams about doing him in.

I dreamed that I put glass in his food and blood came pouring out of his eyes and mouth before he dropped to the floor. But in the dream, I was scared because the blood saturated the carpet and I couldn't get the stains out no matter how hard I tried.

Hearing Rexanne tell me what happened made me reflect on what I put myself and the boys through. They were growing up, and their eyes were open to what was going on. I couldn't shield them from that truth.I felt like I was holding on to a secret too big for me. I wanted to tell someone, anyone at that point. Rexanne hadn't gone to the cops when it happened, and I wasn't sure if there was a statute of limitations on rape. I just knew the more I looked at Plez, the more I hated him. I had to bide my time, doing my best to not act as though anything was wrong.When I went to work, I decided to confide in Dino. But I made sure to speak in generic terms. I didn't want him to know I was married to a rapist.

"Can I ask you something?"

"Shoot."

"I have this friend. She was raped a long time ago."

"How long is a long time?"

"I wanna say, 1975 or '76. Anyway, she hasn't come forward to talk to the cops about what happened to her. But she's thinking about talking to them now."

"Man, if it was that long ago, I wonder if there's a statute of limitations on rape. One of my brothers practices criminal law. I'll ask him."

"We used to be tight around that time, but we lost touch. I asked her if she wanted me to call the cops and she said no. I just reconnected with her not too long ago."

"Yeah, I'm pretty sure there's something on the books about that. I think with murder there's no statute of limitations, but rape's a whole other ball game."

"Even if she knows who did it?"

"Again, let me ask my brother."Then Dino winked at me and went off to do his rounds.

About an hour later, he came back to me.

"I just got off the phone with my brother. He said that in the state of Minnesota, after nine years you can forget about it, unless, of course, there's DNA. But basically it'll be her word against his."

I didn't want to hear that. I wanted him to tell me that Plez could wind up behind bars where he belonged. And since he liked raping people so much, I hoped Plez's cellmate picked him to be his bitch and raped him day and night with his donkey dick.I never told Rexanne that I was asking around, weighing options. As far as she knew, the issue was done the moment we finished the conversation. Truth be told, I had to step back, because my wanting to see Plez brought to justice wasn't entirely a selfless act. It was easier to call the cops for a third party than to call the cops for something Plez did to me. I don't know why. Maybe it was easier because I could call anonymously for Rexanne, but with me, I'd have to face Plez, and there would be a bunch of questions, and he'd know that I was telling people what he was putting me through. But either way, having Plez put away would give me and the boys our freedom and that was worth the price.Weeks went by and Plez got weirder and weirder. I didn't think it could get any worse. He went back to coming by my job, pretending that he just wanted to bring me food or see how I was doing, when really he was spying on me. Sometimes after he'd given me the food or came by for one of his "visits," I'd sneak out the back entrance and find his car sitting out there. One time he caught me watching him and he sped off. It even got to the point where he started creeping around when I was on the phone. I could be talking on the phone with my mama or with Lawrence and he'd be hanging around outside the room listening in.

~ * * * ~

I was painting my toenails when Plez Jr. came into my bedroom to ask me if he could spend the night over at some boy's house. I told him not on a school night."Is it because I got a faggot for a brother?" he said.

"Boy, who in the hell is teaching you that word?"

"Daddy said that Lawrence is a faggot like the ones who hang out at Loring Park and do nasty things to each other."

"First of all, I don't like that word, and secondly, that's not true."

"Then why ain't he here? You think I'm gonna be doing nasty things with my friend? He's just my friend."

"I'm saying no, because it's a school night, like I told you before."

"I bet Daddy would let me go."

"You didn't ask him, you asked me."

"I'll ask him when he gets home then."

"Boy, go in your room and do your homework!"

Plez Jr. sucked his teeth and left. It seemed his father was telling him things to undermine my authority. He was never disrespectful to his father, because he knew his father would get in that ass. But with me, everything was a contest of wills. I think it was Plez Jr. seeing his father disrespect me, and he decided that he could too.

As I waited for my toenails to dry, Dino called. I was surprised because I never gave him my number, and I wasn't brave enough to call him. My desire for him had reached an all time high, and I wanted to make sure our dealings with each other was back to strictly professional. It really was a "yes, yes, no, no," kind of a thing, because while I played that I didn't want to be bothered, I secretly loved the attention he gave me. And it added to the fantasies that I had about him and me getting together. I didn't need Plez inside of me to fantasize. I knew how to take care of my own business.

"How did you get my number?" I asked.

"I told Robert I needed to call you to see if you'd be willing to change shifts with me, since I've been working mornings."

All of a sudden I heard a click and a distant beep. I didn't know where the sound came from since it sounded so far away.

"Is that really why you called?"

"No, I hate not seeing you."

"Dino, come on, I'm a married woman."

"Correction, you're an *unhappily* married woman."

"What difference does it make? My husband wouldn't be happy to know you're calling here."

"You two rarely see each other."

"That's not the point."

"You don't miss me?"

The truth was, I missed him like crazy, just like that Natalie Cole song said. But I made a vow, which was practically empty now. I wasn't that kind of person to do dirt just because Plez had been finding his loving elsewhere. And where he was concerned, what was good for the goose wasn't good for the gander.

"Cheryl?" he said, bringing me back into the conversation.

"What?"

"You heard what I asked you."

"So?"

"So, tell me you don't miss me and I'll leave it alone."

"You already know."

"I wanna hear you say it."

He sounded so sexy. If I had the nerve, and if it were possible, I would've jumped his bones through the phone. "I miss you, too."

"See there? Now was that so hard?"

"No," I said, giggling like some ridiculous school girl. I'd been staring at the floor, swirling my now dried big toe into the thick, beige carpet, when I heard a creaking sound. I looked up and saw a brief glimpse of Plez Jr.'s back as he walked away. "Plez Jr., what do you want?"

"I had to ask you a question," he said, out of view.

"What?"

"Never mind." And then I heard him close his bedroom door.

"Fuck," I said, quietly into the phone.

"What's wrong?" Dino asked.

"I think my son was standing at the door this whole time. I think he heard me say I missed you. I gotta go."

"Wait," then he paused for a second and said, "All right, I guess that's a good idea. I'm actually working with you this Friday so, we'll talk then, okay?"

"Yeah, okay." I hung up.

I left my bedroom and went over to Plez Jr.'s and knocked at the door. I went in and he was playing his Mario Bros on Nintendo. His book bag was lying on the floor with a few books in it. His math book and notebook were with him on his bed. He threw me a quick glance before looking back at his TV.

"What did you want to ask me?"

"That wasn't Daddy you were talking to, was it?" he said. He gave me the oddest look; a mixture of catching me red-handed doing something I shouldn't have been doing, and disgust.

"How long were you standing there?"

He smiled at me saying, "Long enough."

I wanted to say, "Look, you little brat! I pay the bills around here, don't forget who the parent is!" But I didn't. Instead I asked, "Do you even understand what you thought you heard?"

"I understand that you told someone who wasn't my daddy that you missed him." He put his game controller down into his lap and gave me a look that said, "Yeah, I said it."

"You need to not talk about things you know nothing about. Didn't I tell you to do your homework?"

"Yeah," he tossed off.

"*Yeah?* Boy, I ain't one of your friends. You answer me with *yes*."

Plez Jr. threw the game controller to the side of him and said with attitude, "Yes."

"Those games will still be there when you get through with your homework, so let's get it done."

Plez Jr. squinted his eyes at me, shaking his head. And I left him alone to keep doing it.

CHAPTER

34

I WAS EATING LASAGNA FROM a Tupperware bowl when another nurse named Meeka told me I had a phone call. "Bitch, you better not come home tonight," said the angry voice on the other line. I knew it was Plez. His voice was dipped in an evil I hadn't heard before.

"I ought to come up there and stomp your ass right now. In fact, that's what I'm gonna do."

"What are you talking about?" I asked, feeling as though the little lasagna I had eaten was going to come right back up.

"You must think I'm a fool. I know you've been fuckin' some other man!"

"Plez, will you calm down. Who told you that?"

"Never mind all of that, bitch. Just remember, I'm always one step ahead of you." Then he hung up.

The room began to spin as I tried to put the phone back in its cradle. I put my other hand on the desk to catch myself before I fell.

"Girl, what was that all about?" Meeka asked me.

"Tell Robert I gotta go. Plez is gonna kill me if he finds me here." I reached under the desk to grab my purse.

"Honey, you've got to calm down," Meeka said, putting both hands on my shoulders and shaking me gently. But she didn't know what I knew. Plez would do exactly what he said. I rummaged through my purse, trying to find my keys.

My boss Robert came from down the hall and saw my panic. I looked over at him and he looked at Meeka as though she had done something wrong to me.

"What's happening? Where are you going?"

"Robert, I'm sorry, but I have to go. My husband is coming up here and he'll kill me if I'm here."

"Why don't you come into my office and relax. He's not going to kill you."

I looked at Robert, not finding his optimism refreshing. It was just like a man to tell a woman who'd been abused that everything was going to be okay. *Everything would not be okay.*

"Robert, trust me, I gotta get the hell out of here. I'll explain later. Just give me a couple days, please!" I stood there waiting for him to respond. He seemed so flustered; I could tell he'd never dealt with a situation like this before. He slowly nodded his head as I pushed past both of them, still determined to find my keys inside my purse. Once I found them, I ran like a slave running toward freedom. Yet I knew it wasn't really freedom as long as Plez could pop up at any moment.

I drove in any direction that wasn't toward home. I didn't care where I was going. But knew I needed to be close in case my children needed me, which was the one chance I was willing to take.I weighed my options of where to hide out. Mama's house wasn't an option; that would be one of the first places he'd look. I drove for hours, going around in circles, seeing the same buildings and houses three or four times.I finally pulled into a gas station to get gas before I went to a restaurant to eat something. I wasn't even hungry, but my nerves left me in search of something to do. I had a grilled chicken caesar salad and a cup of tomato soup, pretty harmless, because I didn't want to throw up.Sitting in the restaurant, I saw an elderly couple who still had that look of love in their eyes, even while they ate silently. At least they put in the work to get to that point. As I ate, making every bite and gulp count, I realized it was a point that Plez and me would never see. I should've left him when he brought me to that isolated part of town to tell me he could've done anything to me he wanted to. But the woulda-shoulda-couldas of life didn't mean shit.Women were always standing on the outside watching other women act stupid with their lives, talking about what they wouldn't put up with. But the truth is, they'd never understand, because they hadn't experienced the fear of not being worthy of a man loving them, or the fear of believing that a single woman with a kid or kids didn't make them anything a good man would want. Maybe they'd never have to wake up one day after years of getting their butts kicked by their men to find their self-esteem shot down so low that they'd think they couldn't get anything better because they didn't deserve anything better.

Those same sistahs out there, still skinny and beautiful enough to have men looking and catcalling them on a regular basis didn't know that abuse doesn't start with a punch in the mouth. It starts off with one big mind fuck. Plez met me when I was alone and vulnerable. He saw me struggling to do better as a single parent and swooped in to become my idea of what I *thought* better was. He became everything the people in my life up to that point hadn't been. But worse than the deception that he could be those things for me was that I'd allowed him into my head in the first place.

~ * * * ~

My thoughts silenced when I noticed it had become busy in the restaurant and the waitress kept walking back and forth to see if I was ready to pay the check she put on my table. My stomach began fluttering again, the way it did those Saturday mornings I woke up, not knowing which Plez would be laying next to me. He'd start off so loving; the picture-perfect husband and father, and then, he'd go out to get his Saturday newspaper and the Plez that stepped back through the door would be one filled with suspicion and anger, ready to bully.

I paid the tab and got back on the road. With every block I passed, I missed my children more and more, and I wondered, since Plez was so ballsy to threaten my life, would he be as ballsy to tell them he had murdered their mother?My eyes began to tear as I thought about them; two sons who hadn't asked for any of this. Even though it was for the best, at least in the short term, it hurt me to have Lawrence living with my parents, and I knew that Plez was just as happy because it meant he'd only have to be a father to one child, *his* child, Plez Jr.

I clenched the steering wheel, remembering the ways Plez made Lawrence feel inferior. Everything changed when he told me that Lawrence loved Michael Jackson. I thought he was just being a kid, looking up to an idol. But in my heart, when Plez told me, "Cheryl, your son loves Michael Jackson," I knew what he was getting at. But I wasn't ready to own it.

Plez Jr.. on the other hand, was the rough-n-tumble-kind; happy to help his father work under the hood of the car, to go fishing and not shriek like a girl when he put a worm on a hook.I thought back to the summer Plez suggested that Lawrence not go with us on our day of fishing out in Minnetonka; he had hatched his plan.I was so upset that I pulled over and let traffic pass me. If Plez was involved in the equation, it seemed like all I ever did lately was cry. I kept thinking about the day I got angry at Lawrence for deciding not to go fishing with us and pushed him into the bathtub. I remembered looking down on him as he cried out, "What did I do?" He shifted and strained to try and get out of the tub. I knew then that my anger was with Plez. He was the adult who knew what he was doing. He played on the fact that Lawrence was sensitive, and not into most guy things, and Lawrence went along with it, not knowing he was being left out, but, thinking he'd been given the freedom to do something else. It was easier for me to strike my own child than to stand up to Plez and demand that Lawrence be allowed to take his place in our family.

I wound up in front of Greta's House, a women's shelter. It was the last place I wanted to be, but at least I knew Plez wouldn't come looking for me there. I sat in the car for a moment, watching a couple of women talking out front, laughing about something while they took long drags from their cigarettes. I knew I didn't look like them. Who knows how long they had those clothes on by the looks of it? And I sure as hell didn't have anything to be standing outside laughing about.I pulled the car around to the back of the building. I got out with my mind made up; I just needed a place to crash for the night and get my head together and figure out what was next. I wasn't interested in anybody else's problems. Hell, I had my own problems. I didn't want to play any games to see who won first prize for America's favorite sob story, or sit in a circle, holding hands and hear what drugs people used, or guess whose man had beat them the worst or who'd hit rock bottom the hardest.

I didn't feel like answering anybody's questions; all I wanted to do was find a bed or cot or whatever they had, in a corner and hope I didn't catch a case of crabs or bedbugs. I wanted to wake up the next morning and find everything in my purse the way I had left it. Better yet, I wanted to wake up and find this whole thing had just been a bad dream.

The next day I still had all my stuff, thank the Lord. I barely slept. Part of me was worried Plez would bust his way through, snatch me up by my hair and drag me home like the caveman he was, and part of me was scared somebody would try and take my purse. Either way, I spent most of the night sleeping with one eye open.

I know I should've been grateful, because there were folks who didn't know where their next meal was coming from, but they had some of the nastiest food at that shelter. Everything tasted like it was made with old, powdered milk. I picked at my food, dissecting it in search of anything edible. I finally gave up and just ate my bacon, but even that was gross. The woman who ran the joint told me they were going to have a group session for us to talk about what we felt had brought us there. That was the last thing I wanted to do and I said so. But she told me that if I had any intention of staying another night, which it looked like I might have to do, I needed to go along with the program.

"Well, can I at least make a few phone calls first?" I asked her with more attitude than she needed.

"Look, you're the one who came here. *I* got a place to stay. And my ol' man doesn't go upside my head either." Then she stopped herself, like she knew she had just thrown professionalism out the window. Her eyes became soft, then her voice. "I'm sorry. I don't normally talk to the ladies like this. Lord knows they've been through enough. But you're trying my patience. If you feel you can't get something out of this, then you need to get off the bus and stop wasting time. There are plenty of other women who can use the bed."

She had me there. I felt bad for giving her attitude, but this was way out of my comfort zone. I was used to coming and going when I pleased and having my own bed to sleep in at the end of the night. This wasn't me.She looked at me like she was waiting for me to say something else smart-ass, but I decided to keep my mouth shut. "I'm sorry. I'm just not used to this."

"Honey, you think any of these women *want* to be here?" She looked at me for two beats and said, "There's a pay phone in the back." Then she walked away. I'm pretty sure I wasn't the only one she had to have that talk with.

I dug through my purse, hoping I had enough quarters to use the phone. I did. I called my mama first.

"Mama?"

"Girl, where in the hell have you been? Plez has been over here looking for you!"

"I figured that."

"Where are you?"

"I can't say, but I'm safe."

"Has he been putting his hands on you, as if I even have to ask?"

"Mama, how's Lawrence doing?" I asked, ignoring her question. I didn't have the guts to admit to her that I was a battered wife. I had even less to admit it to myself.

"He's doing fine. He's been driving me crazy, blasting that loud music. All he ever plays is that theater stuff. But he's behaving himself."

"What theatre stuff?"

"You know, that show-tune mess. Like, 'One...singular sensation...every little step she takes', oh Lord, now he's got *me* singin' it."

My country mama, singing a song from *A Chorus Line*; I had to laugh at that. It was the first time I had laughed since Plez called me on my job. "That was cute, Mama. Tell him I love him, will you?"

"Cheryl, where are you?"

"Mama, I gotta go. I'll call you later. I love you." Then I hung up.

Mama could never go with the program. She would keep pushing until she got out of you what she wanted. I wasn't in the mood to tell her everything. I still had a few more calls to make and I didn't want to start crying.

I called my job and asked to talk to Robert. He picked up the extension almost immediately.

"Cheryl, how are you? *Where are you?*"

"I'm safe. I just wanted to know if my husband has been there."

"Aw, man! I almost had to call the police on him. He came barging through here, demanding to know where you were. He was looking through patients' rooms, the cafeteria, everywhere. I told him you had run out of here muttering something about going down south."

"That's good. Thank you for that. I have a lot of kin folk down in Mississippi. So that sounds possible, right?"

"What?"

"I mean, did he look like he believed you?"

"I think he bought it. He left right afterward."

"I'm trying to figure something out, but I promise that when I do, I'll be back to work."

"Cheryl, don't worry. Look, you're an excellent nurse. Your job isn't in jeopardy. We'll be here when you return." Then his voice became a whisper. "Do you need me to do anything? Do you want me to call the police?"

"No! I have to handle this on my own."

"I know it's none of my business, but I'm scared for you, Cheryl. You didn't see the look on his face; the look in his eyes."

"I already know that look, Robert. Thank you. I'll talk to you soon."

There was one more call I had to make and I felt weird about making it. My hands shook as I dialed the number. I just prayed he was home.

CHAPTER
35

I ARRIVED AT THE CAFÉ a little early. I needed some time to get myself together. I barricaded myself in the bathroom and used the hand soap to try and wash myself the best I could. It wasn't the same as a nice hot shower but it would have to do. I looked at my hair. It was a mess. The new growth that had sprouted up was practically screaming at me, "Perm me! Touch me up!" But that would have to wait. I had worse problems on my hands.

When I went back out into the café, my nerves started acting up. I didn't know how this meeting would go. I noticed him sitting there right away, looking toward the door as though he expected me to come through it at any moment. He looked so handsome. His hair freshly cut and his eyeglasses shining from the sunlight, which was a surprise because I didn't know he wore glasses.

"Thank you for meeting me," I said, sliding into the booth across from him.

"Cheryl, you're shaking. Will you tell me what the hell is going on, please?"

I looked into Dino's eyes. It was the first time I *really* noticed them, which were deep with concern. His hands clutched his coffee mug, like he was afraid someone was going to pry it out of his hands.

"It's Plez. I think he's gonna try and kill me."

Dino's eyes got big and practically jumped out of his sockets. "Did he say that to you?" he asked.

"No. But it was the way he said what he said."

"What'd he say?"

"He accused me of fucking another man. He said he was coming up to the job. That's when I left."

"Where'd you go?"

"A women's shelter," I said, dropping my eyes in shame.

"Good God, Cheryl, why didn't you come to me sooner?"

"I panicked. My head was all over the place. Anyway, it ain't your problem."

"What do you mean it ain't my problem? I care about you."

My body shivered when he said that. I cared about him, too. But I wasn't going to say it. Telling him that I missed him had gotten me into trouble. Putting my heart out there for a man to step on wasn't what I called him for anyway. I'd already had my heart mashed into the ground more often than I could wish upon my worst enemy."I dunno. I keep racking my brain, trying to figure out what it is about you that keeps me up at night; that makes me want to know how you're doing. When we met, I had no idea that you'd be my lifeline away from this cruel, shit pool we call a world," Dino said, trying to make sense of things.

"Dino, please..."

"No. You brought me out here. I want to say what I'm feeling. After Gia left me, I thought my life was over. When you put in time with someone, you think you'll get something back besides heartbreak. And then you came into my life. Meeting you and talking with you for hours during our times at work made me realize that the beat does go on."

I turned my face toward the sunlight because if I looked into his eyes anymore while he spoke, I would've busted out crying. I wasn't ready for what I thought he was trying to tell me. "You don't wanna get involved up in this, Dino, trust me."

"See? There you go again, trying to go off on a different subject. I dunno. Maybe you aren't ready for anything different. Maybe you like how Plez treats you."

"Bullshit!"

"Is it really bullshit? Or are you afraid to face that I'm right?"

"You *think* you're right."

Dino leaned back into the booth and extended his hands, palms out, like he had all the warmth in the world to give. I wanted to wrap myself up in that warmth, like a coat shielding me from the cold. But I couldn't because I was scared. Scared to make myself that vulnerable again, and scared because I had a crazy-ass husband looking to bring me into harm's way.Then, Dino leaned in. He stopped for a moment and looked around. I followed his gaze. All eyes were on us. We had an audience. I didn't give a shit. I hope they enjoyed the show.

"We haven't done anything to be ashamed of," Dino said, bringing his voice down.

"He doesn't care. Plez is the mad-jealous type. He knocked me once in the face when an instructor of mine gave me a ride home from my nursing class. And we hadn't done anything, either."

Dino shook his head as he stared into his coffee. I was just as confused as he was. We weren't fucking, but I'm sure our conversations and flirting would've led to that. I couldn't believe his wife left him. In front of me sat a man who I knew in my gut knew how to do right by a woman, and she up and left his ass. I wanted to know who she left him for. This Gia bitch left behind a man who was trying hard not to be broken.

I would've turned back time if I could. I would love to have found someone like Dino, instead of the trash I'd been messing around with. But if I'd done that, I wouldn't have had my beautiful boys.

"What do you want to do now?" he asked me, back on point.

"I need to get some things from the house. Plus I need to take a shower. I stink."

"You're not serious. I know you're not going back over there. Come to my place. You can shower over there. We can always buy you new clothes."

"But my son has things I need to get for him."

"Then I'm coming with you."

"Plez is at work. I'll be fine."

"Are you sure?"

"Yeah."

"Okay. But as soon as you get whatever it is you need, call me."

"I can do that."

We left together and I noticed that he parked next to my car. "So, I'll call you in a little bit, all right?" I said, putting my key into my car door. I had been walking in front of him and I assumed he had gone over to his car. That's when I felt his hands on my shoulders. I turned around slowly to see Dino standing there looking at me; an unsure look on his face, like he had something else he wanted to say. He leaned in and kissed me; his lips fit mine perfectly. He backed away, checking my face for approval.

"What was that for?" I asked.

"I dunno. It felt right." Then he got into his car and drove away, leaving me to feel like a princess who'd finally found her prince charming.

CHAPTER

36

I DROVE SLOWLY DOWN THE street our house sat on. Even though I knew he was at work, I was still scared. I needed to figure out how I was gonna explain Plez Jr. not coming home and how he was better off with me than with his mentally ill daddy.

I put the key into the door and turned. The house was quiet and smelled like nothingness.

I went into the closet closest to the door and pulled out two duffel bags. I made my way to the bedroom and got a good week's worth of bras and panties, a couple pairs of jeans and assorted blouses I could match with them. That took care of the first duffel bag. I went downstairs to look for clothes for Plez Jr. But before I did, I went into Lawrence's room. It was exactly the way he had left it. His bed was half-ass made like usual. I could've remade it myself, but that would make his being gone feel more real. It got me thinking about that letter. Goddamn Lawrence for writing that letter.

I shook myself from the memory, smelling the funk that came from my body. I needed a shower badly. I quickly went into Plez Jr.'s bedroom and threw some things into the second duffel bag and went back upstairs.

In the bathroom, I practically ripped my uniform off. I really wanted to burn it, that's how funky it was. Splashing water under my underarms at the cafe didn't get it. If I had the time I'd love to have thrown some bubble bath into the tub and soak the shelter grime off myself, but a shower to pelt the nastiness off would do just fine.

I must have been in that bathroom for at least a half hour, trying to scrub clean. A new tampon topped off my freshness. The air was so humid from the heat of the shower that I towel blotted myself dry three times. I wrapped the towel around my body and opened the door.My heart nearly jumped out of my chest. Plez stood there with an evil grin on his face. His arms were behind his back.

"Boo," he said.

"What are you doing here?" I asked, waiting for my heart rate to return to normal.

"Can't a man come home early if he wants to? You look like you're in a hurry to get somewhere."

"What?"

"What?" he said mockingly. "I said, you look like you're in a hurry to get somewhere." He brought one of his arms forward. He was holding a bottle of Budweiser and brought it to his lips and took a swig. I sighed in relief that it wasn't a gun or something.

"I was just grabbing a few things."

"Where have you been?" he asked, taking a deeper swig of the beer.

"Excuse me," I said. I pushed past him and headed toward the bedroom to get dressed.

"Bitch, don't act dumb. So now you're wearing your big girl panties, right? That motherfucker you've been fuckin' put it in your head that you're a *real* woman now?"

"Plez, you need to get out of my face," I said, my voice rising. "I'm not fucking anybody, Plez. *You*'re probably the one fucking somebody, though."

Plez laughed at me like I was telling jokes. "I know you were probably over at your boyfriend's house getting dicked down. Then you had the audacity to tell your job you were going down south; like I really believed that shit."

"I want to know who told you I was messing around because they're a damn lie!"

"You need to be more careful about what you talk about with your boyfriend. Jr. told me you were talking all hushed when he walked in on your conversation. You even told the motherfucker you missed him."

Plez Jr.! I knew it was him. He was pissed with me for not letting him go stay overnight at his friend's house, that's why he told. Never in his little fourth-grade mind would he have thought of the consequences of what he started. I came back from that thought to see Plez chugging the rest of the beer.

"Yeah, I already figured something was going on so I fixed the phone so that it would record all of your conversations. That motherfucker doesn't even sound black. You mean to tell me you're sucking white dick now?"

"Plez, I haven't done anyth..."

"Don't lie to me, bitch!" That was the last thing I heard him say. I saw Plez's arm swing up suddenly and I felt the heaviness of the beer bottle hit my head. I heard an explosion of shattering glass. Then I felt the warmth of blood tricking down my face. After that, everything went black.

~ * * * ~

I awoke to Plez nudging me. I heard him say, "Bitch, you ain't dead. Get your ass up."

Finally, as I opened my eyes, his panicked face looked relieved.

"I guess I gotta take you to the hospital. They're gonna have to stitch you up. And you better let me do all the talking, too."

The look on his face told me he was serious. I knew if I didn't do what he said, the next time it wouldn't be a bottle, but much worse. And the next time I wouldn't wake up.

When we got to the hospital, he played the part of the loving, concerned husband to the hilt.

"My wife and I were trying to put up cabinets. She bent down to pick up some nuts and bolts that had fallen. But I guess one of the cabinet doors wasn't hinged good enough and it came off and hit her in the head."

"Looks like you got knocked pretty good there," the doctor said.

Nodding to him, I acted my part of dazed and confused.

"I told her to let me do it on my own. But you know these women these day, they gotta prove they can do anything a man can do," Plez chuckled, rubbing my shoulder.

"I hear you," the doctor said, laughing. But while he laughed, he shot me a few glances, like he was trying to read my face. I don't think he believed a word Plez was saying. I became self-conscious so I threw in a few chuckles for good measure.

As I sat through getting my head stitched up, Plez held my hand. If he hadn't just busted me upside the head, I would've believed it myself. It made me think back to November 1979, the Plez I met at the McDonald's and how much he changed. And I, blinded by incredible orgasms and the need to feel complete, didn't see it coming.

After I was stitched up, Plez thanked the good doctor and bolted out of the examining room, heading toward the bathroom. The doctor held the door open for me, but as I tried to pass through he blocked me.

"Do you mind telling me what *really* happened?" He asked me, now that we were alone.

That was my moment of rescue. I had a split second to tell the doctor that cabinets had nothing to do with it. Plez had gone upside my head with a beer bottle, and he'd been kicking my butt for years. I didn't even have to tell him, he could look into my eyes and he knew. But I'd have to confirm it if I wanted help.

"Just say the word," he said in a soothing voice.

I felt like I was living that scene from *The Color Purple*, when Celie wanted to leave with Shug Avery, but when the moment came, she was terrified of Mister and so beat down that she buckled. She had the perfect opportunity to leave and didn't, and that's what happened to me, I buckled.

"It happened just like he said. I had no business trying to do a man's job anyway," I said, chuckling. "Okay, if you say so. Just know that if he is responsible, the next time you might not be as fortunate."

I shook the doctor's hand and walked quickly to join Plez who'd just come out of the bathroom. The doctor didn't tell me anything I didn't already know.

I'd given Plez what he wanted; immunity from any consequence for what he'd done to me, from what he did to Rexanne, even. I knew that once we left the hospital it would be the same as before. Plez would continue to play his games and smack me around, and I'd continue to do what I did best in front of strangers after he did it, stand there and smile.

CHAPTER

37

PLEZ JR. WAS ALL SMILES when his father brought me back home. He was home from school, sitting at the kitchen table, eating his Captain Crunch. He paused for a moment to look at me. I had a bandage on my head from where I'd been hit and stitched up. This really weird smirk crossed his lips then he looked at his dad, shrugged, and went back to eating. I knew then that Plez brought our son to his side of public opinion. As far as they were concerned, I'd gotten what I deserved.

Plez didn't go out that night. I felt like I was under lock and key. He probably thought I was gonna call the police on him. I should have.I kept thinking about that scripture in the Bible that said, *Vengeance is mine, sayeth the Lord.* Even though my blood boiled inside, I knew I had to let the Lord do His job. But He seemed to be on a totally different time table, and I needed to get out before Plez put me six feet under.

~ * * * ~

I went back to work earlier than I had planned. I needed to get out of the house and away from Plez's insisting that I was up to no good. Plez Jr. always happened to be around when Plez would start up with me, and he'd just stand off in a corner, watching like he was watching a basketball game. Not once did Plez Sr. tell his son to leave the room. I figured it was only a matter of time before Plez Jr. started kicking women's butts; after all, his daddy was his example.

I kept up the lie that the cabinets fell on me when people at work asked what happened to my head. I should've known that after I ran out of work, telling my boss and Meeka that my husband was gonna kill me, people wouldn't believe me.Dino was back to the three to eleven shifts. That gave me strength. He was the only person at the nursing home that I trusted. There was Meeka, who was nice, but she'd run and tell your business as soon as you got it out your mouth.

I had no fear when I was with Dino. He was a manly type, but I knew if the day ever dawned where Plez and he came to blows, he might not win, but he'd at least give Plez something to think about.

When our shift was over, I didn't want to go home. I don't know what came over me. All night while I tended to my patients, I kept thinking about what had happened to me and who I had become. I didn't want to go home after a long night and face whatever new accusations Plez had dreamed up. I felt separated from what mattered to me most, my children. Plez worked his magic in turning Jr. against me, and Lawrence wasn't allowed anywhere near our house because of Plez. Everything was because of Plez and I had given him everything he wanted. But I was the one left empty-handed.

"So I'll see you tomorrow, same time, same station?" Dino joked as we put our coats on.

I just stood there, staring at the floor. I was so agitated I couldn't even button my coat.

"Cheryl, what's wrong?"

"Earlier I said that some cabinets fell and hit me in the head. That didn't happen."

"Do you want to tell me what really happened?" Dino asked, reminding me of the doctor who'd said the same thing.

"Plez beats me. If he's not beating me, he's playing mind games. I don't wanna go home to that."

Dino stared at me, not knowing where to go from there.

"My youngest son told Plez that me and you were talking. Plez had been recording my conversations I'm guessing way before that. He hit me over the head with a beer bottle when I went home to shower," I said, feeling tears in my eyes. I couldn't bear to look up at Dino.

"Oh, honey, come here," Dino said, snatching me into his arms. That's when I lost it. I sobbed into his chest, feeling so alone in the world.

"I don't feel like I have anybody."

"That's not true, Cheryl, and you know that. I'm here for you."

"I can't go back there. I don't care, I'll take my medicine from him later. I just can't go back there tonight."

Dino looked up suddenly to make sure no one was around. He lifted my chin up and wiped my tears with his thumb. "Don't let that sorry son-of-a bitch keep you from being who you're meant to be in this life. You deserve to be happy."

"I know, it's just..."

"You're more than welcome to stay with me tonight. You have my word as a gentleman that I won't do anything inappropriate."

I couldn't speak, I just nodded.

"All right, are you okay to drive?"

"I think so."

"I live in Bloomington. I have an underground garage at the condo. You can park your car there, just in case, you know?"

"Okay."

When we got to his condo, it was like a maze. Dino parked on the street and got in my car with me and showed me where the underground garage was. As soon as we got out of my car, I looked around, making sure Plez wasn't lurking anywhere.

"He's not gonna hurt you, Cheryl," Dino said, taking my hand in his and leading me to the elevator. I was jumpy, but I decided to trust him.

When we arrived to his condo, it wasn't what I expected. I thought there'd be mixed-matched furniture; cardboard boxes holding up the TV and card tables in place of coffee and dining room tables. Instead, his apartment was decked out by someone who actually had some taste. His walls were neutral beige and he had those masculine, brown, wing-backed chairs and matching sofa with the gold studs in the armrests. There was a fabulous glass coffee table that I would've killed for with art books on top. I never would've taken Dino for the artsy-type. The main wall had a life-size mural of Sophia Loren and there was a huge framed poster of the Rat Pack hanging on the wall behind the sofa. All around the living room were smaller framed posters of different Italians: Joe DiMaggio, Robert De Niro and Al Pacino.

I dropped my purse to the floor and just gazed at the cleanliness of the place. If I didn't clean every day before work, my house would be in a constant mess. Plez never helped keep anything tidy, and the boys were just as bad.

"Make yourself comfortable," Dino said, picking up my purse and placing it on an end table.

"You have a nice apartment. It wasn't what I was expecting."

"And what were you expecting?" he asked me with a grin.

"I don't know. Maybe a few beat-up old couches and a card table."

"No. Actually, when I married Gia, I had to help *her* find her decorating way. Her taste was lousy."

"See, I would've thought it was the other way around."

"Most people would. Can I take your coat?"

"Oh, yeah. Thank you."

Dino took my coat and hung it up on a dark wooden coat rack. "Can I get you something to drink?"

"Do you have any wine?"

"Do I have any wine," he said with a chuckle. "Am I Italian?"

I giggled.

"I have wonderful Chianti I've been dying to open. I'll be right back." Dino winked at me as he placed his hand on the small of my back. I took a seat in one of his wing-backed chairs.

As I waited, I heard the shower go on. Dino was in that shower for what seemed like an hour. When he finished, he came out, holding two glasses of the wine in his hands. He looked fresh in his T-shirt and sweat pants. He sat down on the sofa, his eyes beckoning me to follow. He placed both glasses down on a couple of coasters on the table and patted the space next to him just in case his eyes alone hadn't told me that he wanted to be next to me.

"Can I use your shower, too?" I asked. I was nervous as hell. I felt like a girl on her first date.

"Sure, right through that hallway. I have a linen closet in the bathroom. There's everything you'll need in there."

I went into the bathroom which smelled like Irish Spring soap. As I showered, letting the suds slide down my body, I imagined Dino coming in there with me, or that when I wiped the water away and opened my eyes, he'd be standing there naked, ready to take me. I envisioned feeling his entire masculinity pressing against me; not just his dick but his whole being. I wanted to be washed away by his kisses. I imagined him to be a full, hungry type of a kisser, none of that thin-lipped-pursed together stuff. His tongue was so soft the first time he kissed me in the parking lot of that cafe; I could only imagine what else he could do with it. His being in the other room only heightened the fantasy. My kitty cat was practically dripping on its own that I wanted to stick my finger in it and handle business, but I remembered where I was and that I was an invited guest in his home.

When I finished and opened the door, I saw a Minnesota Vikings jersey and a pair of his too-small-for-him sweat pants neatly folded on the floor. Silly me, I hadn't even thought about what I was gonna wear to bed. Once I was changed, feeling fresh my damn self, I went back into the living room where he was right where I left him. I looked down at the two glasses of Chianti and noticed they had the same amount in them.

"I thought you would've taken a sip or something while I was away."

"No. I wanted to wait until you came back."

"That was sweet. I really don't need to be drinking too much because wine makes me do naughty things."

Dino's eyebrows raised when he said, "I should be so lucky."

Sitting down next to him felt right. It felt like it would if I were sitting down with my man to watch TV, discuss our day, or just sitting in the quiet of our being together. It felt perfectly natural. He put his feet up onto the table and I noticed that he had beautiful feet. Plez had ugly feet; his toenails, discolored and ingrown, looked like talons. I could tell Dino took care of his, unlike the hooves Plez called feet.

"So, what's on your mind?" he asked, putting his own glass of wine back down.

"Well, for starters, I know that I want a divorce."

"When was the first time he hit you?"

"Oh God, I don't even remember. I just know that it wasn't a right away thing. He worked up to that."

"I could never hit a woman. I'd rather walk away, go outside and have a cigarette, walk around the block a few times if I had to, anything but that."

"I don't know, it sounds like Gia needs some sense slapped into her for leaving you. I still can't understand that."

"Trust me, I was tempted, but I have a mother and three sisters. My parents have been together for forty years. In that time, not once have I ever seen my father lay a hand to my mother. I wouldn't want some asshole hitting any of my sisters, either."

"See, I saw beatings in my family. Until I was about 16 or so, then it was just my daddy not keeping it zipped up."

"Oh there was plenty of fooling around in my family; uncles, cousins, and what have you. But I can honestly say my pops never went behind my mother's back with another woman. Both Gia's parents fooled around on each other. I say, why get married?"

"True."

"So, um, how are your sons taking all of this?"

Just the mention of them made me sad. "Well, Plez turned my youngest against me. Do you know that the little ingrate started grinning when I came home from the hospital bandaged up?"

"That's ridiculous."

"I know. I'm still not sure how I feel about it. That's my child and everything but, and I hate to say this, for a moment, I felt hatred toward him. Because he knew what he was doing."

"Just remember that Plez is the puppet master, your son is the puppet who thought he was getting by with something."

"And Lawrence," my voice began to shake. "Oh, Lawrence." I shook my head.

Dino moved closer and put his arm around me. I felt like I could tell him anything even if it hurt. I leaned my head against his shoulder.

"I think Lawrence is gay."

"How do you know that?"

"I read a letter he wrote to some friend of his."

"*Friend-friend* or euphemism friend?"

"Friend friend."

"Well, what do you think about that?"

"Honestly, I have nothing against gay people. But I lost the best friend I ever had to AIDS. That's my fear."

"Yeah, but Lawrence isn't your best friend, he's your son."

"I know, but it scares the hell out of me that I have a gay son who might get AIDS."

"He's his own person, Cheryl. Whatever happened to your friend doesn't mean your son would have that same fate."

"Plez made me throw him out."

Dino began shaking his head. "How can you throw your son out? Listen, to be frank, I don't get the whole guy-guy thing. But, one of my four brothers is gay. He's my older brother, *my family.* And I love him and wish him all the happiness in this world with his companion. I know they're gonna have a hard way to go because of what a lot of idiots out there think, but they've been together for sixteen years. That's saying something. I don't have that and I'm straight!"

I felt encouraged, but questioned if I was a bad mother for allowing Plez to tear my family apart. The list was as long as a roll of toilet paper of what I could've stood up to Plez about. I wondered if Lawrence knew that it wasn't me who wanted him out. He had been telling me all along that Plez didn't care about him and I kept insisting that he did. Then, I put him out. I couldn't make sense of my own madness.

"I think once you settle down in what you want to do, you need to do everything in your power to get your sons back. The little one may not understand it now, but he's gonna rue the day he ever took his father's side over yours, especially when all you tried to do was what you thought was right."

"I feel like a bad mother."

"You're not a bad mother. Sounds to me you were just trying to do the best you could in an awful situation. That would be hard for anybody."

I didn't fight the tears. Letting them fall into my wine made me feel lighter, like I was getting a load off my shoulders. I had to know if there was a light at the end of my tunnel.

"Why do the men get to walk away? Why do the women always have to sacrifice?"

"Don't let him walk away. Make him man up for what he's done. Make him pay."

Looking at Dino was like looking into the eyes of an angel. His intent seemed pure. He didn't want anything from me that I couldn't give him. I looked up at him; he continued to wipe my tears away. I leaned up and kissed him. His lips were wet from the wine and his tongue felt and tasted as good as it did before. He seemed taken aback at first, but eased into my desire with his own, grabbing a fist full of my wet hair.The next thing I knew, he was on top of me, feeling me like forbidden fruit. As his body writhed against mine, my body buzzed like a live wire, waiting in blissful anticipation for what was to come next. It was the first time in a long time I felt wanted, needed, *desired.* Those feelings rushed over me like an avalanche and I wanted more.Then he stopped.

"Cheryl, what are we doing?"

"Kissing," I said, bringing his face back to mine.

"We gotta stop this," he said, pulling away.

"But I want to."

"So do I, but that's not the point. Remember your vows."

I bolted up. "Fuck my vows. Plez never thought of his vows when he was out there doing his dirt."

"Yeah, but you're better than him. This would only put you in the gutter with him. I don't want to be party to that."

I fixed my disheveled jersey and ran my fingers through my hair. I scooted to the far side of the sofa. "Happy now?" I asked, pissed off.

"Listen; you don't know how long I've waited for this moment, or how many nights I've dreamed about it. Trust me; it'll happen when the time is right."

"Now is as good a time as any in my book," I said, folding my arms like a bratty child.

"No, it's not. I don't want to be some form of therapy for you. I want you to be here when there's no fear of a Plez, or anybody else for that matter. I want you to be with me and not have to look at your watch to see if it's time to get back to him."

"I'm not going back to him."

"I know. But I want our first time to be special. I don't want either of us waking up tomorrow regretting what we did."

"I'll never regret it."

Dino scooted over to me and put his arm around me again. Then he put my hand into his free hand and brought it up to his lips and kissed it.

"I never thought I'd be the one to even say all of this. But, it's the right thing to do."

I nodded slowly in agreement, even though my hormones felt differently.

"But I promise you, when all of this is over, I'll make it worth the wait."

I smiled. It was a promise I was gonna make sure he kept.

CHAPTER

38

D INO AND ME HAD A plan. We decided he'd follow me to
my house the next morning and wait outside for me
to give him the signal that everything was all right. I
didn't want to take the chance of Plez going upside my head
with another bottle. Once was enough.

My back was sore and I had a crook in my neck when I
got into my car. It was his damn couch. He offered me his
bed, like a real gentleman. But I didn't want to be in his bed
if he wasn't in it.

When I got home, Dino parked across the street. Once
inside, I was gonna act like I was opening the curtains and
wave at him if things were okay. I turned my key into the
door and Plez opened it from inside.

"You know, the next time you wanna stay overnight at
your mama's house, you could give a nigga some notice. I
mean, goddamn," he said, buttoning his shirt.

I had a half second to get the *I don't know what the hell
you're talking about* expression off my face.

"I'm sorry, Plez, but Lawrence needed me. I couldn't go
before work because he was in school," I said, shocked at
how easily I could lie.

"That ain't new. What's his problem now?"

"He's just been having a hard time in high school. Same

stuff we went through as kids."

"Yeah, but I wasn't running after my mammy to kiss me and make it better. Anyway, I'm late. I've been craving some of that Rice-a-Roni and ground beef skillet shit you make. I want that for dinner," he said, kissing me on the cheek. His kiss was like acid on my skin. I couldn't wait to wash it off after he left.

I went to the window and opened the curtains. Plez was like a vampire. He didn't take to sunlight. He liked to walk around a dark-ass house. He said it was because he didn't want anyone to be able to look into our house and see what we had.

"Fine," I said as Plez turned away. I gave a quick wave to Dino so he knew I was all right.Plez went off whistling that little blip of a song he always whistled when he was happy, "Grazin' in the Grass." He left for work, just as happy as he could be without a care in the world, or a thought of the fact that he had probably ruined everybody's life he was in. I was more than happy to make his dinner, and I wished that after he filled his belly, I could take that skillet and knock him upside his head with it.

~ * * * ~

"Hi, Mama," I said, after she picked up.

"So I guess I'm supposed to lie for you, huh?"

"I never asked you to tell Plez I was staying over there with you."

"But you knew that I would, didn't you?"

I was silent.

"Where were you anyway?"

"I was at a friend's house."

"Yeah, okay. This friend better have the same business between their legs that you have between yours."

"That's none of your business."

"Listen, missy, as long as I'm lying to keep your butt safe, it is my business!"

"Even if I was messing around on Plez, it ain't anymore than he deserves with all the dirt he's done to me."

"Then you'll burn in hell right along with him."

"Why is everything a moral dilemma with you?"

"You need to give your life to the Lord," she said,

ignoring my question, "I mean really give it to Him."

She was right in a way. I'd become an empty shell, showing up to church just to listen to a pastor I didn't respect. I was there in body, but my mind and spirit were someplace else.

"Mama, the Lord ain't kept Plez from cheating on me; ain't kept him from beating me, either."

"Well, look. I don't profess to know what's goin' on in you all's household."

"That's why you need to mind your business. But since you asked, no, I ain't sleeping with another man."

I could hear Mama sucking her teeth through the phone. I didn't know why she'd become so high and mighty. This life of mine, as pathetic as it was, she'd lived. I knew she thought God was trying to tell me something, and I'd heard a thousand times at church that every saint had a past and every sinner had a future. Mama was big on the belief that you had to have a test before you could praise God with a testimony.

I wasn't feeling her sermons, no matter how true the words. To me, at that point in my life, God was sitting on a big, white cloud, playing with us like we were broken-down puppets.

"If you'd pay attention, Pastor Stone could tell you about yourself," Mama said.

"That man ain't got nothing to tell me. He's a phony. As a matter of fact, I'm thinking about leaving that church."

"What has he done to you? I'll tell you what; he's been trying to give you spiritual food. But you don't want to eat it. Now, whose fault is that?"

Before I shot off at the mouth, I remembered Mama didn't know about Pastor Stone's hobby of jacking off, wearing church lady wigs and nylons.

"I know you've been goin' through a rough time. Life ain't easy. That's when you need to turn to God. Stop thinking you can do every damn thing on your own. Let God help you. Let Him love you."

"Mama, I'm sorry, okay? Tell Lawrence I'll be over tomorrow for his birthday."

"When, Cheryl? Because Lawrence asked me to have his..."

"I don't know yet. I gotta go, Mama. Bye."

I never meant to drag Mama into this. Things between us were better, so long as the money Plez owed Daddy kept coming in. She said that she had no interest in telling me or Marva how to live our lives; that she'd raised us with the best morals, and she hoped that we'd take what she taught us and go into the world with it. But it always seemed that if she didn't agree with something she'd let us know it.

When I came home from work, Plez was sitting in the TV room but the TV was off. He had a sad look on his face. I was so tired that I would've rather just went to bed. But he was sitting where I slept. I hoped he wouldn't be in there too long.

"Hey," I said, putting my purse down on the table and pulling my coat off.

"Hey." Plez seemed far away. He didn't even look up at me when I walked in. I could tell that whatever it was that was bothering him didn't concern me for once.

"You seem upset. What's wrong?"

"I just found out that my buddy Terrance was killed at the pool hall."

I wasn't surprised. I'd only been in there a couple of times years ago when things were still fresh and new between Plez and me. I knew nothing good ever came of that place. As far as Terrance was concerned, I only remembered his name because Plez had supposedly slept at his place when he stayed out all night once.

"What happened?"

"He owed Tom-Tom some money. Tom-Tom and two of his boys beat Terrance up with a pillowcase full of pop cans. Then they took him out back and ran over him with the car."

"Are you serious? Did the police arrest them?"

Plez looked up at me for the first time. His expression was like I said something ridiculous. "Cheryl, nobody calls the police in a place like that. It's the rules of the street in there. Terrance was my boy and everything, but if he owed money he should've paid it. Hell, I owe the motherfucker and at least I have the sense to stay out of there when I know Tom-Tom is around. Terrance should've disappeared if he knew he wasn't gonna pay it."

I couldn't believe what I was hearing; this from a man who owed my father money and had decided to create strife rather than pay what he owed. Plez owed a bunch of guys money from hustling pool, and I wonder how many he actually paid. Whatever was going on in that place, it seemed like a lot of illegal mess.

"Yeah, ain't nobody gonna call the police because they don't wanna wind up like Terrance. You don't rat on those cats down there. You might as well put a gun to your head."

"Well, I'm sorry about your friend," I said, leaving the room.

I went into the kitchen and saw more than half of that Rice-O-Roni gone. Between Plez Jr. and his father, neither one had the decency to cover the pan up and put it into the refrigerator, leaving it to sit out all night. I guess they figured I had nothing else to do after a hard shift at work but to come home and play the role of the maid. I put it away and ate a glazed donut and had a glass of milk. Then, I went to take a shower.

After the shower, I went into the bedroom and Plez was pulling off his clothes to go to bed. He didn't say anything, which I was grateful for. I put another donut on a small plate and poured another glass of milk and went into the TV room to watch a little TV. *The Arsenio Hall Show* was just going off when I turned it on. I flipped through the TV channels, finding nothing of interest to watch. I turned off the TV and went to sleep, hoping to dream about the day I'd be rid of the thug in the other room.

~ * * * ~

"Just to let you know, I'm going into work for a little bit and then I'm gonna be with Lawrence for his birthday," I said, standing in the doorway of the bathroom while Plez showered before work.

"You should just stay overnight. You said yourself that he needs his mama," Plez yelled out from the shower.

"I might do that. Have a good day," I said before going back into the TV room to lay back down. I didn't wake up again until it was time for Plez Jr. to get ready to go to school. When I saw him, he looked wore out.

"What's the matter with you?"

"Dad whupped me last night."

"Why?"

"Because he told me to stop playing video games and do my homework and I didn't do it."

"See? So all I have to do is whip you to get you to do your homework?"

Plez Jr. just shifted from foot to foot."What do you want for lunch?"

"I dunno. We got any lunch meat?"

"If you two haven't gone through it, we should."

I got up and went into the refrigerator, pulling out bread, mayo, cheese slices, and pastrami. Plez Jr. went into the little pantry closet next to the broom closet and pulled out a bag of chips and a snack cake.

My son backed away and let me get his lunch together. I turned to see him staring at me, looking like he wanted to ask me something.

"Is there something you want to say to me?"

"Are you and my dad gonna get a divorce?"

I stopped spreading mayo on his sandwich and turned to face him. I didn't trust him enough to tell him anything. For all I knew his daddy could've sent him in there to spy on me some more. But I couldn't leave my son hanging. I had to give him something. "I don't know Jr.. If your dad wants to divorce me then I'll have to go with it." Maybe with that I said too much, but at least I put it on his father as opposed to him thinking I was trying to break out. He'd probably run and tell that to his daddy too, but I really didn't care.

Plez Jr. seemed satisfied with my answer and went into the refrigerator to get a drink box.

"Do you want me to pick you up for Lawrence's birthday party tonight?" I asked.

His face dropped. "Aw, man. Do I have to?"

"You know what? Never mind, you don't have to go. Just remember, no matter what, he's your brother and the day may come when you'll need him for a kidney or something."

"Fine, I'll come."

"No, it's too late," I said, putting the finishing touches on his lunch and bagged it. "Have a nice day."

CHAPTER

39

I PULLED UP AT MAMA'S house at 7:30. I had a birthday card for Lawrence with $100 in it. Since he was a teenager turning 15, I didn't know what to get him. But I knew he still loved his German chocolate cake, which I brought.

I went into the house to the sound of "Ease On Down the Road" from *The Wiz*. Walking into the family room, I saw Lawrence sitting on the couch, wearing an off-white, billowing poet's shirt, black slacks, and a black beret. He was sitting cross-legged, grinning widely as though he were in his element holding court. On the floor were dozens and dozens of presents: designer clothes, books and cassette tapes of music. Mama was leaning over to wad up the wrapping paper and stuffed it into a trash bag. Standing by the heater was Diallo.

"What are you doing here?" I asked Diallo.

"He wanted me to come by," Diallo said. He was older looking, wearing jeans and a black and white printed, button-down shirt. His hair was nicely faded and he looked sexier than the last time I saw him.

"I thought I made it clear that Lawrence could make that decision when he turned 18."

"Cheryl, don't come in here with none of that! I tried to tell you yesterday that he was comin', but you couldn't get off the phone fast enough," Mama said.

"It ain't his fault, you know," Lawrence said, repositioning himself on the couch, "He called here one day and I answered the phone. We got to talking and I asked him to be here."

"I told him the truth, Cheryl. I was a punk for leaving you the way I did and not stepping up to the plate. But I can't undo all of that. All I can do now is go forward."

"Yeah, right. Just like you told me you were gonna do right by him? Don't come over here making more of your empty promises."

"Lawrence is a young man now. Why don't you let him decide for himself?" Diallo spat.

"Ma, listen. I know you're angry, but I needed to see him. It's my birthday, and if I wanted to give a present to myself then that's my right. I don't see Plez over here making any effort!" Lawrence snapped.

"Yeah, I like how you let your husband kick my son out of the house the way he did," Diallo said.

I turned to look at Lawrence, who had a smug look on his face. He should've been glad it was his birthday because I wanted to slap him silly. "You told him Plez kicked you out? That's none of his concern."

"He was upset, Cheryl. You can't tell people how to act when they're upset," Mama said. I felt like I was being ganged up on.

It was all out in the open. Diallo had copped to being a lousy father, but I didn't want anybody walking away thinking I was just as lousy a mother. They didn't understand what I had to go through. Lawrence being with my parents was a much better option. I hoped that in time he'd understand that. I just didn't want my son to be disappointed in case Diallo decided to revert back to type."Did you give Lawrence the letter I sent?" Diallo asked my mama.

"I gave it to Cheryl. I don't know what she did with it."

"What letter?" Lawrence asked.

Diallo smiled at his son and then shot me the nastiest look. "I sent you a letter trying to explain some things to you about what went down. I sent you some money too. I suppose you didn't get that either."I knew that the day would come when I'd have to give it to Lawrence, but I was hoping that day would come later rather than sooner. My intention was to give it to him when he came to me asking to see his father. Standing in the family room of my parents' house, I felt put on the spot. I wanted to tell Lawrence myself and have him understand from my point of view. I hardly said a bad word to him about his daddy when he was younger, and after a while, he stopped asking about him. So getting that letter didn't seem like a big deal to me.Lawrence stood up and faced Diallo. He had tears waiting to fall from his eyes. "I just want to say that I don't care what went down between the two of you, when I asked for my father he came. That's all that matters to me right now. We can work all that other stuff out later." Then he extended his arms out and hugged his father. "Thank you for coming. Now can we please get on with my birthday celebration?"

For the next hour, we ate cake and watched Lawrence try on the clothes his father bought him like he was in a fashion show. Diallo must've spent a fortune. Later,Diallo followed me into the kitchen when I was trying to find more dip for the potato chips.

"How have you been, Cheryl?" Diallo asked me.

"So, what did the two of you talk about?" I asked, ignoring the pleasantries.

"I didn't plan this, Cheryl. I was surprised when he picked up the phone."

"As far as Plez kicking him out, don't think that was easy to watch. I don't want you walking away thinking I picked my man over my child."

"How long have you been with that cat?"

"Why?"

"Stop trying to be so fucking mysterious. That motherfucker made my son's life a living hell."

"You've made *my* life a living hell, so what's the difference? I figured you were due to pop up at some point. Now you're pumping Lawrence for information because you can't stand the fact that I've made a life for myself that doesn't include your trifling ass."

"Woman, don't flatter yourself."

"I'm not gonna go around and round with you about that. Let me ask you something else since you're here. A long time ago you were with some people who did something to someone I care about. I want you to tell me what happened."

"I've done a lot of bad shit, can you narrow it..."

"Rexanne. Her name is Rexanne and you put her in a situation where she was raped," I interrupted.

I knew from his face that he knew exactly what I was talking about.

"All right, I ain't gonna lie. That day your friend hit me when she threw me out, I was pissed. One night, me, Plez and Charley were coming from the pool hall. I saw her and all that shit came back to me."

"How do *you* know Plez?"

"I met him back in the late 70s. He was always down at the pool hall. It was after you and me were done. I know he never mentioned you. He always had some female of the week. I got tired of keeping track."

"Anyway, about Rexanne!"

"What about her?"

"I guess you thought you'd kick her butt real good, huh?" I snapped.

"Cheryl, it wasn't like that. I was just talking mess. Plez was the one who took it too far, and Charley just ran off. I just wanted to scare her."

"Did you rape her?"

"Hell, no, I didn't rape anybody! Plez took that shit to a whole new level. And I tried to stop him, but he took a swing at me and shit. Finally, I said, to hell with it and I booked."

"I saw Rexanne not too long ago. She hasn't been doing too well."

"Because of that?"

"She was raped! What, you thought she'd get over that in a day?"

"No! Listen, I'm sorry about your friend. If I had it to do over I would, but I can't. Just like I can't take back not being there for you and my child."

"Save it."

"No, you brought the shit up. Anyway, I'd like to get my hands on that motherfucker, Plez! There's more to the story of why I left town in such a hurry."

I made Diallo come outside with me. The conversation was getting loud and I didn't want anyone else to hear what we were talking about. Diallo reached into his pocket and pulled out a cigarette. I asked for one too.

"I didn't know you smoked," he said, lighting the one in his mouth and handing it to me before lighting another.

"Trust me, there's a lot of shit you don't know. Anyway, as you were saying."

I stood there while Diallo told me that Plez beat him within an inch of his life down at the pool hall because he had beat Plez in a game and Plez didn't want to pay up. Before he hobbled out into the night, he turned around and in front of everyone told Plez that he made a big mistake putting his hands on him and that Plez forgot that Diallo knew what he did to Rexanne. He threatened to go to the police.

"Cheryl, Plez followed me out to my car and pulled a 9mm out on me and told me to repeat what I'd said to him. I was coughing up blood and I just wanted to get the fuck out of there. I told him never mind."

"What happened after that?"

"He pulled the trigger. Thank God the fucking thing jammed." Diallo's jaws tightened as he spoke.

"What would you do if you could see Plez now?"

"What do you think?"

"Would you kill him?"

Diallo didn't answer, looking away while exhaling a long stream of smoke.

"Diallo, I'm serious. Would you kill him?"

"You want me to answer you so you can run back and warn the nigga?"

I shook my head, threw my cigarette to the ground and crushed it with my heel. "Come back inside when you're finished with your cigarette."Diallo finished and followed me inside. I found my purse and took out my wallet. I pulled out the picture of Plez and me with the boys; the same picture I showed Rexanne. Diallo took the picture from me and looked at it. His eyes became fixed on it and I could see his jaw muscles tighten again.

"I don't know the man in that picture," I said.

"What do you mean you don't know the motherfucker? You married him."

"You know what I mean. It was the worst mistake of my life. I'm not gonna go into our issues because frankly it ain't any of your business. But I'll tell you this: I know that the man in that picture is gonna get what's coming to him. I have to believe that or else I can't believe there's any justice in this world."

"You're still in love with the nigga."I shook my head.

"Yeah, you are."

"No, I'm not. But you're not going after him."

"Right is right, and payback is a bitch."

"You're right. But, you need to let God handle it."

"You sound just like your mama."

He was right. I couldn't believe that came out of my mouth. I really was my mother's daughter.

"Listen, I've had some evil thoughts, too, about what I'd do to him if I had the nerve. But, in the end, I have to trust that God will find the appropriate punishment for Plez in due time."

"God's time doesn't move fast enough for me," he said, trying to avoid my eyes.

"You just reconnected with your son. Why do you want to throw that all away and wind up in prison?"

Diallo stared at me, his eyes spooky. Before he answered, Lawrence came over to us. "Are the two of you coming back or not?"

It was all smiles the remaining time I was at Lawrence's party. I made a point to tell him that I'd stop by more often, even if it was just to go out to lunch or dinner. More importantly, I wanted him to know that I missed him and we'd be together soon. Diallo's hinting around made me nervous that his days were numbered. I decided to let Diallo have the rest of the evening with his son, alone. I hoped he'd value the time he spent with him, and think differently.There was confusion with me during the ride home. If Diallo got his way, finally, Plez was gonna pay. His debt to me, my father and Rexanne would be paid in full.But, knowing Diallo like I did, I knew that whatever he planned to do was gonna be something grimy. I didn't know if I could stand by it. He seemed a little disappointed when I showed him the picture of Plez, me and the boys. It probably shocked his system to know that I had married the man who'd run him out of town. How was I supposed to know that? Diallo never told me why he left Minneapolis before. If he'd done like he was supposed to, he would've been in Lawrence's life and we would've never had to feel like we needed to sneak around in the dark about Diallo being

Lawrence's father. But he wasn't the only one learning new things. How did he think I felt learning that my husband was a rapist?Plez wasn't my favorite person and I wanted to find a way out of my marriage to him. But I didn't think it was right for me, or anyone else to wreck revenge on him. I knew he'd get his in the end, and hopefully I'd be long gone when he got it.

I wasn't sure if Diallo was really gonna do anything. While he had cleaned himself up nicely, I could tell that he still had some thuggish ways about him. And if he really was going after Plez, should I warn him about what was coming, if anything at all, or should I do like my mama always did and turn a blind eye? All of that filled my head as I drove home.

I pulled up to the house, which was pitch-black with the exception of the glare coming from the TV in our bedroom. Opening the door, I heard banging coming from the bedroom and a lot of wet smacking sounds.

"Oh, Daddy, you're making me dizzy," a female voice moaned.

"Let your pussy talk to me, baby," Plez said, sounding out of breath.

I stood in the doorway of the bedroom, watching as the headboard kept banging the wall while Plez screwed his whore. I flipped on the bedroom light. They scampered around, trying to find the sheets to cover themselves. I continued staring, feeling like my spirit had left my body. I stood by, watching the ultimate betrayal of Plez bringing his bitch into our bed. I wasn't necessarily mad, either. But it was still a shock. I never thought he'd be so bold as to bring women back to the house, especially where Plez Jr. could see them.I felt my spirit rejoin my body. A smile crept across my face because Plez had given me the perfect gift—a reason to divorce his ass.

"Don't let me stop you," I said, folding my arms, my smile turning into a grin.

"I thought you said she was going to be gone all night," the lady said, whose voice I recognized as the female that had been calling. If I didn't want the divorce so bad I would've sprinted over to her and tore every stringy hair out of her head. She was a white chick with a rose tattooed over her right breast.

"Cheryl, what are you doing back here? I thought I told you to stay the night over your mama's place."

"I didn't feel like it."

The air stunk like rotten fish. It was a shame that he was screwing her, and didn't have the decency or self-respect to tell the bitch to wash her stuff before he jumped in her hole. It would serve him right if she had every venereal disease known to man stuffed inside her and he caught them.

Plez got up; his body tense from the little workout I'd walked in on. He tried to put his hands on my shoulders.

"Plez, don't even start," I said, flicking his hands away. "Catching you in the act was perfect. I want a divorce. And you're gonna give it to me, too."

"Cheryl, I'm sorry. You and me haven't messed around in God knows how long, I just needed a little something to get me through."

"That's okay, and from now on you can have your *little something* as much as you want. I'm done."

He looked ridiculous, standing there, butt-naked, with a bunched-up condom hanging off the tip of his dick. Suddenly, with whatever Diallo was planning, I felt empowered. The fear I'd owned for years, reduced. I figured there was nothing he could do to me that Diallo wasn't going to pay him back for. But Plez was on his best behavior. He didn't want the blonde chick, lying in my bed behind him, to know that he was a punk who liked to beat or rape women. I didn't want my newfound strength to go out like a candle, so I took it where it would hurt.

"Listen, whore, you can have him. Just as long as you know, when he's pissed, he'll go upside your head. But you're a brave whore. I see that because you're the type who'll call the house at all times of the night and not care that you're fucking a married man."

"He's never gone upside *my* head. Unlike you, I know how to keep a man happy," she said, throwing the sheet away from herself, probably looking for an excuse to air her pussy out.

"Give it some time."

Plez grabbed me by my arm and I yanked it away from him. He wasn't dealing with the old Cheryl. The old Cheryl would've just cried and ran out the room, hoping he wouldn't beat me for catching him doing something he had no business doing. I'd be damned if I was gonna waste any more tears or fear on him. That bitch was in for a reality check once she met the real Plez Darnell Jackson.

"Oh, and just so you know, you've been laying up here with a rapist. Did he tell you that he raped a chick a while back?"

The bitch tried to swing her hair to the side like what I was saying wasn't anything to worry about. But she got what I was saying because her face said it all. Plez looked like he wanted to start kicking my ass right then, but knew he had an audience. Hearing me put his shit out there, talking about something he didn't even know I knew about, made the blood drain from his face.

"I didn't rape anybody!" he snapped, grabbing my arm again. I had crossed the line, but I didn't care. I knew that I wouldn't be able to let my head fall on a pillow that night if I didn't let this woman, no matter how slutty she was, know what kind of a person he was.

"I ain't even mad at you, Plez, because I've prayed on it, and I've asked God to show me a way out of this foolishness and misery and He's delivered it to me."

"Okay, bitch," Plez said, showing his true colors, "You want a fucking divorce, fine! I'm *glad* you know. She sucks a better dick than your stupid ass, anyway!"

"You hear that, whore? Plez thinks you suck a better dick than me. And you should, since you wanna go running after married men."

"Fuck you," she said, getting out of the bed to find her panties. The air smelled so gross from her pussy, I could only imagine what the inside of her panties looked like.

"Don't leave now. You can have him. And Plez, if you even think about putting your hands on me again, I *will* be calling the police. Let your bitch be a witness to what I'm saying! You may have gotten away with all that other stuff you've done to me, but that stops today," I said, turning to walk away. As I made my way to the door, I could hear him in the background begging the white chick not to go, telling her that he loved her and only put up with my worthless ass because I bore him a son. I got in my car and turned the radio on. Babyface's *Whip Appeal* was on KMOJ. I didn't care that it was cold outside; I rolled my window down and blasted the volume like the song was the sweetest of symphonies, wearing that same big grin all the way back to my folks' house.

When I got back there, I went in. Diallo was getting his keys and was ready to go. Lawrence was all smiles and Mama was putting the rest of the food away. Daddy was home, completely drunk and had forgotten my son's birthday. I saw him go into his wallet and pull out a measly $5 to give to his grandchild like that was big money. He probably had spent everything else at the bar and the $5 was all he had left."I thought you were going home," Mama said, following me into the living room where Diallo and Lawrence were.

"I changed my mind," I said, feeling at peace and still wearing my smile. "Diallo, can I walk you out?" I asked, ignoring Mama.

"Cool," he said, giving Lawrence a hug before turning back to me. "Why are you so smiley all of a sudden?" he asked.

"I caught Plez fucking some white bitch in my bed."

"Are you serious?"

"Yep. Anyway, about what we were talking about earlier."

"Yeah?"

"You've got my blessing. Do what you gotta do."

CHAPTER

40

“WELL, IT'S DONE.”

“WHAT'S DONE?” Dino asked as he pulled a Totino's party pizza from the oven in the nurses' cafeteria.

“I told Plez that I want a divorce.”

“Yeah, right. Just like that?”

“I caught him in bed with someone else.”

Dino's eyes widened.

“He had it all planned out, too. It was my son, Lawrence's birthday. He told me to stay the night at my parents' house. He let Plez Jr. stay the night at his friend's house.”

“I'm sorry,” Dino said, putting two slices of the pizza onto my paper plate.

“I'm not. I asked God to give me an out and He did.”

“But do you really believe Plez will give you the divorce?”

“He ain't got a choice in the matter.”

Dino began nodding his head. Then he smiled. “Well, then I guess this is a good thing, right?”

“Yep,” I said, blowing on the hot pizza.

“Do your sons know?”

“I bet Lawrence will be thrilled. He hates Plez. But Plez Jr., I'm not so sure about.”

"Do you think Plez will fight you for custody?"

"That won't happen."

"How can you be so sure?"

"Let's just say that I have it on good authority."

~ * * * ~

Dino was nice enough to go to the house with me. Since I had caught Plez in the act of screwing another woman in our bed, I didn't care what he made of Dino. When I called him to tell him I'd have someone with me because I was coming for some of my things, Plez said, "It didn't take you long, did it?" Then I had to wait for him to stop cussing me out to tell him that I meant what I said about calling the police if he ever tried to lay a hand on me again. That shut him right up. Thankfully he wasn't there when Dino came with me. Staying at my parents' house was good because I got to be with Lawrence and he was happy I was there. But it meant leaving Plez Jr. with his father, for the time being. That weekend Lawrence and me were in the basement doing laundry. We finally had the opportunity to talk openly about things. We had watched *Do the Right Thing* on videotape and talked about race relations in America. I could tell he didn't just watch the world go by, but actually had opinions about things. He was telling me that high school wasn't what he thought it would be, and wished he could fast-forward to graduation to get the hell out of there. I was proud of his progress. He was off to a great start, pulling in better grades than he had when he lived at home. The dryer buzzed and Lawrence paused before picking up the laundry basket. He had a funny look on his face.

"Can I ask you something completely off the subject?" he said.

"Sure."

"Are you sure you're going to divorce Plez?" Lawrence asked, taking a load of clothes out of the dryer.

"Baby, I have to do what's best for me now. I can't say that all the years were bad, but I don't like who I've become."

"I think you should, Ma. That's what I'm learning to do. If people don't like it, then screw 'em."

I put down the shirt I was folding, choosing my words

carefully. "But maybe the way you want to live your life isn't really gonna bring you true happiness. In fact, I'm gonna be nosy for a second. You're only 15, what do you really think you know about the world? I mean, how do you plan to live your life?"

Lawrence raised an eyebrow. "You know what? I don't want to talk about this anymore. You do what makes you happy, okay?"

"Wait a minute. I've had to do a lot of soul-searching to get to this point to talk about this with you. I wasn't sure I even wanted to have this conversation."

"Ma, look, we're having a great day. Please don't ruin it, all right? I actually enjoy you being..."

"Are you gay?" I blurted out.

"You read that letter, what do you think?"

"How long have you felt like this?"

Lawrence began digging nervously through the laundry basket of dry clothes. Then he stopped, looked at me suddenly, like he was searching my face to know if he could trust me.

"I didn't know I was gay. I just felt different."

I let out a deep sigh. "Okay, how long have you felt *different?*"

"I don't know; it feels like forever. I remember having a crush on one of my preschool teachers, Mr. Weinblatt. He wore his hair pulled back into a ponytail. He had these really freaky, icy eyes. I don't know if they were blue or gray. I remember him always wearing these clogs. Anyway, on Halloween, he dressed up like a wizard, and I remember staring at him all day and I didn't think there was anything wrong with staring at him. I made excuses to be near him."

"Oh my God, he didn't molest you, did he?"

"What? No, Ma. I'm just saying he was probably my first crush."

"So you don't find girls attractive at all?"

"I mean, I can look at a pretty woman and say, 'that's a nice-looking woman.' But that doesn't mean I want to go down on her."

"But you could sit there and go down on a man?"

"Well, when you say it like that, you make it sound gross. Anyway, like I said, I don't want to talk about this."

"Wait a minute, Lawrence. Just relax, okay. I'm gonna

be honest. I knew about you, Lawrence. Ever since you were a little boy, I knew. But I also prayed. I prayed long and hard, hoping you wouldn't be this way. I'm not gonna lie and say I understand it, because I don't. I may never understand it. All I know is that you're my child, and I love you."

Lawrence eyes were wet. Then he started nodding his head and the tears began falling from his face. "Thank you," he began softly, looking at me eye to eye, "I really needed to hear that. I needed to *know* that."

With a laundry basket between us, we hugged. It wasn't gonna be easy for him, or me, but we knew that. And I had to shake all of those fears of what happened to Clayton happening to Lawrence. I didn't want my child to feel he had no one to talk to, even if I didn't understand and had questions of my own. I wanted to do my part to make sure Lawrence grew up with enough self-worth so that he wouldn't rush out into the world and do anything crazy that would put him at risk for AIDS or anything else tragic. Like Dino had said, they were different people, and I wanted to give my child something that Clayton's parents' were either unable or unwilling to give him: love and support. "Just promise me something," I said as we parted.

"What?"

"Just make sure that your grandparents don't find out. They're old school. They'd never understand."

"Grandma was kinda snooping."

"Well, don't take the bait. She's just too religious a woman to understand."

"All right."

"Good."

"And as far as that sorry excuse for a man, Plez, don't worry about him. You'll get divorced from that zero and get yourself a hero," he said.

"I think you're right. I think my hero is closer than I thought."

CHAPTER

41

I WAITED OUTSIDE FIELD ELEMENTARY school for Plez Jr. to come out. The day had been cold and cloudy. My mood wasn't the best, and I didn't know what I was gonna say, but I knew that we needed to have a conversation that was long overdue.

When the bell rang, the children flooded the sidewalks on their way to the school buses. I finally saw Plez Jr., with a friend emerge from inside. They walked a few paces and then Plez Jr. paused for a moment to pull the hood of his coat up. Then he saw me. He shot me the nastiest look and motioned to his friend to walk faster. I rolled the window down.

"Plez Jr., I know you see me. Come on and get in the car."

His friend stopped and looked at the both of us with a confused expression. "Dude, your mama's calling you."

"I don't care, let's go."

I beeped the horn for what seemed like a thousand times, startling Plez Jr. and his friend and causing everyone to stop and look at me.

"I'm takin' the bus!" he yelled.

"Boy, you better get your little ass into this car before I get out and make a fool out of both of us!"

"Man, call me later," Plez told his friend and he looked both ways before crossing over to get to the car.

"You know what, mister? I'm getting real sick and tired of your attitude."

"Why are you picking me up?"

"I need to talk to you about some things."

"What things?"

"Let's get something to eat first," I said. I still needed time to piece together what I wanted to say. And, I didn't want to have the conversation in the car.

"I ain't hungry," he said, folding his arms.

"You know what? Eat, don't eat, I really don't care, Plez Jr.. You're trying my patience."

He sat there in the passenger seat the whole way to Wendy's. The silence was uncomfortable, but I knew he was just being a kid, mixed with nonsense his daddy had taught him.

We went inside and I ordered something for myself first. When I asked him what he wanted he just stood there in silence. I ordered the same for him as I was having for myself: a chicken club sandwich meal with a frosty. When the food came and we found a seat, Plez Jr. said, "I didn't want chicken."

"You had the opportunity to get what you wanted. Times up. You'll eat what I bought you."

Plez refolded his arms and looked out the window.

I took a few bites of my sandwich before starting the talk. "You're dad and me are getting a divorce."

"Yeah, he told me."

"Do you know why?"

"Yeah, because you wanna run off and be with your boyfriend," Plez Jr. said with a smirk.

I dropped the fries I had in my hand and said, "Did your daddy tell you that?"

"Yeah."

"Try *yes*."

"Yesssssss," he said exaggeratedly.

"Let me explain something to you. I'm the parent. Do you talk to your daddy like this?"

He sat there, saying nothing. I looked down at his untouched food. "There's kids starving in Ethiopia and you're gonna just waste that food?"

Plez Jr. unwrapped his sandwich and took a bite out of it and threw it back on the table, as if to say, "Satisfied?"

"I'm not divorcing your father because of some boyfriend. I'm divorcing your father because he doesn't know how to treat people. There are two sides to a story, Plez Jr., and I'm tired of you always taking up for him. He's not as innocent as you think he is."

"Well, I'm telling you right now that I wanna live with my dad."

"That's out of the question."

"I wanna live with my dad," he repeated, this time louder.

"Hollering and screaming won't make it happen, so lower your voice."

"Fine, I'll just run away."

I had to laugh at that. Where was his ass gonna go? I didn't have the heart to tell him that his father was humping some nasty broad in our bed. He was too young to understand, and he wouldn't have believed me. But I saw in his young eyes that his father was his hero, good or bad. He wouldn't be happy living with me and Lawrence. I knew then that I couldn't let Diallo take his father from him. Unlike Plez, who could threaten to kill me and rob his son and Lawrence of a mother, I had a conscience. The whole thought of Diallo possibly ending someone's life was becoming more of a turn-off, even if that life belonged to someone as low-down as Plez. Just as I couldn't live with something happening to my children, I couldn't call myself a Christian; no matter how imperfect a one I was, and know that I had the opportunity to save Plez from being killed, but didn't. Plez Jr. practically hated me already; I didn't want to seal it in if he were to find out. But by the same token, I could live with Diallo roughing Plez up a bit. He deserved that much if not worse.

I brought Plez Jr. home, realizing that I wasn't getting anywhere with him. His brain was so far rotten by what his father had put in it that I knew I was wasting my time. Plez may have won that battle, but he wasn't gonna win the war.When I got back to my parents' house, Lawrence was home."Is anybody else home?" I asked.

"Granddaddy gave me some money to order a pizza. He said he was going out. Grandma is still at work, but she called."

"What did she want?"

"Nothing important. She just asked me if you were home and if I had a good day at school."

"Did you order the pizza yet?"

"No. I was waiting for you to get home to see if you wanted anything special on it."

"Get whatever you want."

"How did it go with Plez Jr.?"

"It was a total waste of time. I couldn't get through to him."

"I figured that."

"But I can't give up. I'm the one who gave birth to that boy, not Plez!"

"Don't give up."

I didn't want any tears. I had cried enough over it. "Listen, do you have your father's number?"

"Yeah, why?"

"I have to talk to him about some things."

"What kind of things?"

I should've known that Lawrence would ask questions. I had to think of something to say other than *I want to make sure your father doesn't kill Plez.*

"I'm glad you two met. But we have some unfinished business. There are some things that still hurt," I said.

Lawrence nodded his head. "I wrote it down on the back of one of Grandma's Avon catalogues. I haven't called him, though, because he always calls me."

Lawrence went upstairs to find the catalogue but came back empty-handed. Then he found it under a stack of mail on the kitchen table. I snatched the catalogue from him like it was crack waiting to ease my fix. Lawrence went to find the number for the pizza joint. I recognized the number as belonging to his sister, Roberta. I hadn't talked to her since Diallo left the first time. I called it and she answered immediately.

"Hey, Roberta, this is Cheryl. Is your brother there?"

"Now why would he be here? I haven't talked to him since he left for Chicago."

"But he came back. He's been visiting his son and everything."

"Well, he knows good and well he ain't welcomed here.

He should have thrown my number away than give it to you, no offense."

"Then why would he give my child this number to reach him?"

"Girl, I don't know. But like I told you the last time, my brother is trifling. He obviously doesn't want ya'll to know where he's at. But tell the nigga when you do see him that he still owes me for rent!"

"Oh, I'll do better than that. Sorry to bother you."

I hung up the phone and let out a loud, "Damn!" I wasn't sure what game Diallo was playing, but he had involved his son in it by giving him a bum phone number. Time wasn't on my side. I had to get in touch with him before he did something that I'd regret for the rest of my life.

CHAPTER

42

I WASTED A WHOLE MORNING down at the office of Ronald Colby's, my divorce attorney. I started the meeting with a bad attitude. On his desk was picture after picture of his smiling, picture-perfect family. There was one of him and his wife, dressed like they were at some formal dinner. She had that, "I have it all" snooty smile on her face. Then there were the ones of his children standing with their trophies they'd won with their track and football teams. Made me totally feel like crap. Here I was, coming to him to dissolve my marriage and he was throwing it up in my face how grand his family life was.After that tone was set, he proceeded to tell me that after filing the paperwork, there was gonna be a 90-day wait, just in case we changed our minds. I told him he could forget that noise because I had no intention of changing my mind. But he said, "The law is the law." Then there was the breakup of property, and custody of Plez Jr. So, assuming Plez wouldn't go back on his word and contest the divorce, we still had a lot of things to work through.

That afternoon, I called Dino and told him I'd gotten the ball rolling on my divorce. He was happy to hear it and invited me over for lunch to celebrate me having done that much.

When I arrived at his place, the smell of freshly made spaghetti sauce hit my nose. He told me that in the colder months he liked to make huge batches of sauce and then freeze them to use later.

Dino was looking good. He had on jeans and a matching denim button-down shirt. His eyes smiled at me as I walked into his condo. Once the door was closed he hugged me as though he hadn't seen me in years."What's all that for?" I asked when we parted.

"I'm just glad you're here."

"It smells really good."

"Thank you. I think you'll like it."

"When haven't I liked your cooking?"

I moved into the kitchen. I had never seen it before. It was a decent size with medium-brown cabinets and black appliances. The aroma of garlic bread baking in the oven added to the already delicious scents in the air.

"Can I help you with anything?"

"No. I invited you here. I wanted to do this for you," Dino said, easing a glass of red wine into my hand. He lifted the lid on one of the pots he had going on the stove. After a quick stir he turned the heat down and re-covered the pot. Taking my hand, he led me to a small table that he used as his dining table.

"Lunch is about ready. Here, sit down."

He went into his living room and reached into his stereo which was hidden behind glass cabinets. He took a cassette out of a case, put it in the player and pressed play. Nat King Cole came on. Hearing it took me back to when I was a little girl and Daddy played those records.Lunch was great. We had spaghetti Bolognese, garlic bread, and a mixed green salad with balsamic vinaigrette. It was my first time ever having a salad that wasn't made with just plain ol' iceberg lettuce. He topped a perfect meal off with a tiramisu for dessert.

"Damn, you cook *and* bake? I'm impressed," I said, wiping my mouth with the napkin.

"I can't take credit for the tiramisu. It's store bought."

Dino held his glass of wine in one hand and stared at me. His eyes were romantic.

"Why are you looking at me like that?"

"I don't know if I should say."

"Say what you feel."

"Okay," he began slowly, like he was unsure of himself. "I want to make love to you."

My heart skipped when he said that. I wasn't sure what to expect or if things would be weird, especially after the last time I was at his place. "You do? What changed?"

"Nothing really changed. I've known for a long time now that I've wanted to share my bed with you. It's just important that the time is right."

"When will the time be right?" I asked, trying to give him my best sexiness.

Dino looked over towards his stereo as Nat King Cole sang "The Very Thought of You."

"I just about did a cartwheel today when you called to tell me that you'd been to see a divorce attorney."

"You did?"

"Yeah, I did. I also thought about you finding your husband in bed with that other woman. I was thinking that maybe we should even the score."

My heart started beating faster. I'd fantasized about us getting together for a long time. But he had told me he wanted to wait. Now I was just confused.

"When I told you that Plez didn't honor our vows, I wasn't saying it just to get you into bed, I meant it. He planned his infidelity when he told me to stay over my mama's house."

"Cheryl, there are so many things going on inside me right now. I don't know if we should go that far. I mean, on the one hand it would serve the bastard right. But, is that who we really are?"

My heart sank. Honestly, Plez's feelings weren't a consideration anymore. I was a grown woman with needs. Dino was the one I'd hoped would take care of those needs. But I also didn't want him to feel obligated to do something that went against who he was as a person.

"I'm gonna wash the dishes," I said, bolting up from my seat. "Cheryl, leave the dishes."

"No. You cooked, I can wash."

I looked under the sink for the dish detergent and sponges. The pots needed a good soaking before I could wash them. I ran water to cover the sound of Dino's voice insisting I come back into the room to finish talking. But I was through talking. He wasn't ready, and that was sort of fine by me. I just didn't want to hear the list of reasons why not.

I started scrubbing the pots with all the elbow grease I had, just so that I wouldn't have to go back into that room and face him. Then all I could hear was the water beating down on the pots. I put the plug in the sink to let the water collect, pouring detergent into the sink as the water rose. Suds began covering the dishes as I felt Dino behind me. He leaned his body into mine, his hands on my shoulders. I shut the water off.

His hands fell to my waist. I could feel the warmth of his breath on the nape of my neck. He didn't say anything. I let the sponge I was holding drop into the water as we stood in the middle of his kitchen, his grip tightening around me. I could feel his nose resting on my neck, then his face rubbing against me as though he were trying to take in my scent.

"Look, Dino, if you don't want to do this, it's fine. No hard feelings."

"Cheryl?" he said, my name caught in his deep breath.

"What?" I said. My body weakened as he began turning me around to face him.

"Shut up."

Then he put his hands on both sides of my face and kissed me like he was starving for me. His kiss was hot enough to melt a whole gallon of ice cream. He pushed me against the sink and I could feel some of the water splash on the small of my back, but I didn't care. I was losing myself to this man.

He picked me up and I straddled myself around his waist. The kissing continued, fiercer than ever, as he brought us to his bedroom. We fell onto the bed as he pulled up for air. We were centered perfectly on his king-size bed. He kneeled over me, with a look in his eyes that told me what he wanted to do to me. He smiled a closed smile, as his hands explored my body from head to toe. Even through my clothes, his touch was soft as feathers without the tickle. He took his time caressing me. His eyes had a mix of joy and sadness in them, drawing me into his world.

"Are you sure you want this?" he asked suddenly.

I nodded slowly, never breaking eye contact.

"Good, because you have no idea how long I've waited for this," he said, laughing nervously.

I laughed too. Then the laughing stopped.

I heard the thud of his shoes hitting the floor as he kicked them off before he got on top of me, clasping his hands in mine and expanded my arms up over my head. His kisses were still hungry, our tongues finding perfect rhythm. I felt like I was floating as he gently sucked on my neck and held my breasts in his hands. But he didn't yank on them, but held them delicately, like they were fine crystal. And while I was lost in the passion, I felt helpless as more clothes were pulled from my body. Soon I was naked, and he got off the bed and took his clothes off. He had lost some weight since we had started working together, but I could tell that Dino would never be a thin man. He was soft like a teddy bear with a spread of shiny, dark hair on his chest. He stood there almost ashamed of himself, but I didn't care. He was perfect to me. His dick, nestled in a bed of bushy pubic hair, stood at full attention, dripping a thin stream of pre-cum. I loved that I had him so excited.

He slowly inched back on the bed, sliding his piece over my throbbing opening. He was more thick than long. He began kissing me again, working himself downward. He licked and sucked my nipples, which were rock hard. My body quivered with good feeling. Then he got down to my pussy and ate it like it was gonna get up and walk out of the room. He paid close attention to my love button, and while I thrashed around like a fool with pleasure, I could tell he liked eating the kitty cat. He wasn't afraid of it. And he let his tongue send me into sexual orbit, rather than use his fingers. The only other person who did a good job in that department had been Rexanne, but it was better with Dino because he was the object of my desire.

Finally, he lifted his face from my pussy, my juices all over the sheets. I was dripping wet and I could tell he was proud of the job he'd done. He got on his back, his dick pointing toward the heavens. I wiped the pre-cum from it with my hand and went to town on him.

"Oh my God! Aw, man!" he shouted, twitching like he hadn't been sucked in who knows how long. I let the head rub back and forth against the roof of my mouth as my tongue took care of the shaft. I noticed his eyes were closed tightly, like he was lost in a dream, while his hands clenched the bed spread. His dick was good and stiff by the time I was through with him and he reached for me and had me straddle him, sucking my titties again and rubbing my back. Then he laid me flat against him for a moment and I could hear his heart beating fast. He reached for his night stand and I got up to give him space to move. He reached into the small drawer and took out a condom. I laid on my back as he rolled it on, awaiting insertion.

When he was ready, he gave me one last look, smiling a shy smile.

"Hi," he said softly.

I wanted to laugh. I never had anyone say that to me before. "Hi," I said, trying to match his soft tone.

He got on top of me and I spread my legs. He tried to let his dick find its way on its own, but he finally had to guide it in with his hand.

"Oooh," he said, with a goofy smile on his face as he entered me. He just lay there for a moment, wiggling his ass a little, taking in the sensations of my warm place.

He pressed himself over me so much that I felt I couldn't breathe. I started to think, *Is this what it's gonna be like? The fantasy was better.* But then, he leaned back from me, grabbed my legs and put them on his shoulders and went to work. Those first, soft thrusts he had done previously couldn't have warned me of the pounding I was to receive. The sex reminded me of the song "Proud Mary"; when Tina Turner said that they were gonna do the beginning nice and easy and then the finish rough. That was Dino come to life.His body was so slick from sweating that it felt like a Slip-n-Slide. He wasn't like Plez, who was pretty even when he came. Dino didn't care how he looked during sex. His face was usually very handsome, but that handsome stuff went out the window when his dick was inside some pussy.He wasn't a dirty talker, but his moans were lusty. He took his time, wanting me to feel what he was feeling. He did a lot of kissing, sucking and touching of my body while he was in me, unlike Plez, whose bedroom bag of tricks were just a lot of practiced flim-flam he'd probably done to all the women he'd been with. Dino was natural.

Dino's breathing began to change as he started up that mountain to orgasm. He was humping me lightly, watching as his own wet dick went in and out, but then, he leaned in close, wrapped his arms around me and started pounding me so hard, I thought he was trying to bang me into the bed.

"Oh God! Oh my God!" he shouted as he finally found the release he was after. My hands were on his back and I could feel his wild convulsions as he came. When he was done, he rolled over and took the condom off and went into the bathroom and flushed it down the toilet. When he came back, he got back on the bed, spread my legs and went back to munching my kitty cat."No, don't!" I said, pushing his head away and closing my legs.

"Why not?"

"Because I'm all sweaty down there?"

"But I want you to come."

"I don't have to."

"Listen, I got mine, you're gonna get yours too."

I laid back helplessly as he threw my legs open and started eating me out again. This time he used tongue, fingers, whatever was necessary to make me climax. He lapped at my pussy like a cat lapping up milk.

Suddenly, I felt a rush in my thighs so intense, I thought I was gonna have a heart attack. I had never had an orgasm that powerful before. My legs felt numb as he rolled over with a big grin on his face. He knew he did a good job.

He rolled over to me and kissed my lips as I tried to catch my breath. "How was that?" he asked.

"Why did Gia's stupid-ass leave you again?" I asked, panting. Dino laughed.

"You're doing all right? Everything okay?" he asked, still laughing as he put his arm around me.

"I think I'm in love," I said, finally breathing normally.

Dino stopped laughing and turned to look at me and said, "Well, I *know* that I'm in love."

"What?"

"Yeah, it's true. I'm in love with you, Cheryl."

I turned away from him and stared up at the ceiling. My eyes spilled over with tears.

"I'm sorry. I shouldn't have said that. Don't be mad, okay? I was just being honest," he rambled.

"No. It's not any of that." I smiled at the realization that I'd finally found a good man. And it didn't matter that he was white. It mattered that he cared about me and encouraged me to care about myself.

We laid in that bed for what seemed like an eternity. I turned onto my side and he held me from behind, kissing my shoulder blades every once in a while. We didn't have to talk, just being that close to him made up for the silence.

After we showered, I saw that it was getting dark outside. "I better get going," I said, buttoning my last button of my shirt.

"Are you working tomorrow?" he asked me, tumbling back onto the bed.

"Yeah, Meeka asked me to work her shift in the morning."

"Aw, then it's too bad you can't stay longer," Dino said, stroking himself.

I would've loved the second go round, but I really needed to get home.

"I'll call you when I get home," I said, leaning in to give him a kiss. He reached for me and pulled me onto the bed. I had to playfully claw myself away from him because he wanted to make up for lost time with the sex. "Will you relax? There's plenty more where that came from."

I finally escaped Dino's endless kisses. Bless his heart for trying to keep me there, but I had to get going if I was gonna beat the rush hour traffic. As I waited for my car to warm up, I kept thinking about the way Dino smelled. I held on to his scent in my mind, afraid that if I didn't, the whole experience would fade like a dream.

I felt like a freed woman who was starting her life all over again. But before I could go too far down the road of the future, I knew I had to put a period at the past.

A piece of it was waiting for me when I pulled up in front of my parents' house. I noticed Plez Jr.'s bike laying on the ground like he had thrown it there in a hurry. I had been trying to wipe the *I've just been screwing* look off my face, trying to concentrate on more serious things like if Diallo killed Plez then he wouldn't be able to sign any divorce papers, but I'd be a widow. Or it would be just my luck that nothing happened to Plez and he was nice and healthy enough to renege on his promise to sign the papers.

I walked in the house and I could hear a lot of carrying on. Plez Jr. was crying and Mama was asking Daddy to try getting a hold of me again at work.

"What's going on?" I asked, trying to suppress the afterglow I was still feeling.

"Girl, where in the hell have you been?" Mama demanded.

"I was at a friend's house. I needed some me-time."

"Yeah, well, while you were having your *me-time*, Plez was sent to the hospital!" Mama said.

"Oh God! Is he..."

"No, he ain't dead," Daddy said, suddenly speaking up. "But I wish the motherfucker was!"

"Joshua, you ain't helpin' none! And you're talkin' about this boy's father!" Mama said, patting Plez Jr. on the back.

Plez Jr. continued sobbing, "Yeah, that's my dad you're talkin' about!"

"Plez Jr. rode his bike over here after he got a call at you all's house. We've been callin' all over tryin' to find your butt," Mama said.

"Does anybody know what happened?"

"I guess somebody jumped his ass," Lawrence said, coming out of the kitchen eating an apple. He didn't seem too worried, and wasn't trying to pretend that he was.

"Lawrence, don't you start," Mama commanded.

"Oh, I'm sorry. You expect me to feel bad for a man that beat my mother? Ya'll are trippin'!"

"Lawrence, all that's not necessary," I chimed in, trying to appear part of the conversation. I wanted to wink at him to let him know that I agreed with what he said.

"Can we get going to see my Dad, please?" Plez Jr. said, in a way that wasn't really a request but more like a demand. Lawrence rolled his eyes and went back into the kitchen, chewing his apple.

"Yeah, baby, let's get going." I said.

The ride down to Hennepin County Medical was difficult. Plez Jr. sat with his arms folded, staring out into the blackness of the evening. It wasn't like he could really see anything, but he wanted to avoid talking to me. Any good feelings I had enjoyed the last few hours were gone and they'd been replaced by the very real fact that my youngest child's father was hurt, and I had to pretend to feel sad about the whole thing. I started smiling to myself. A couple of times I started to laugh and tried to cover it by pretending

I had sneezed instead. I fantasized about what Plez was gonna look like when I saw him; if he'd have a busted lip and black eyes. Then I could ask him how *he* liked it.

But then, my conscience kicked in. I wasn't sure if I'd ever make peace with what I allowed to happen. On one hand, I knew better than to seek vengeance because Plez wasn't worth it. But on the other hand, I didn't give a good hoot. Clenching the wheel, I remembered all the games, lies, and physical hurt Plez had inflicted on me and it inspired more hatred.

Nothing prepared me for what I saw when we got to his hospital room. The cocky smile I thought would be on my face never came. Plez's whole right side, from his arm down to his kneecap and leg, had been broken. Even the right side of his face was smashed in from what I could tell through his bandages. He looked cross-eyed, as one eye stared straight ahead and the other eye looked inward toward the bridge of his nose. I could tell he was in pain. Plez Jr. burst into tears and ran to his daddy's left side, while I stood frozen in the doorway.

Plez patted his son's back the best he could with his left hand, his one good eye looking at me. He seemed relieved I was there. I suddenly felt that my feet were unglued from my spot in the doorway and I finally entered the room. I saw that Plez was crying too. He stopped patting his son and held his hand out to me to come closer. He tried to talk, but sounded like he had dirt stuffed down his throat. Because he sounded like he was croaking as he spoke, I didn't understand half of what he said, and he became agitated that I didn't understand him, because he was trying so hard to communicate. Plez Jr. got up and walked to the other side of the hospital bed and just stood there watching me like I had some nerve talking to his father. That's when Plez grabbed my hand, stuttering out, "Help me!"

~ * * * ~

Plez had surgery to put metal rods into his right arm and leg. I guess the hospital needed the bed, because shortly after, he was taken to a live-in rehabilitation clinic to regain the strength and use of his limbs. I took that opportunity to move me and the boys back to our house.

While we settled back in to our lives there, I had to let them know what the deal was.

"I'm gonna tell you both right now, there's gonna be some changes around here. You two are brothers, so you better start learning to get along. Enough with the dumb shit!"

Plez Jr. went down to see his father every day, which was good because maybe it would give his father some incentive to get better.I started noticing a change in Plez Jr.. He was becoming less angry and did what I asked him to do without a lot of back talk. Both the boys did their part to help keep the house clean and I even saw them joking and talking nicely to each other.

Diallo's punk ass skipped town again and without as much as a "Screw you!"

We hadn't heard anything from him until Mama gave me a letter that was addressed to me. There wasn't any return address so I knew he was trying not to be found.

Dear Cheryl,

That motherfucker is hobbling around and got what he deserved. Well, not everything, because if I had my way he'd be in the ground. I just wanted to tell you that you were right about wrong righting itself. Lawrence was good enough to tell me about you and Plez in our phone conversations, so I had enough to get somebody to go by the house to fuck Plez up. The person to do the job was my cousin, Tom-Tom. But I didn't know Plez's stupid ass still owed Tom-Tom money. So it appears I wasn't the only one looking for revenge. Tom-Tom and his boys were kicking Plez's ass pretty good too, down at the pool hall, but the cops busted in because Tom-Tom had warrants for some guns shit. I told him to leave them guns alone, but you could never tell him anything. Plez better say a prayer that the cops were looking for my cousin because that's what saved his sorry ass from being murdered that day.

Anyway, tell our softy son thank you for running his mouth like a little girl. I was looking forward to having a son, but instead, I got another daughter. I need to stop shooting blanks out my dick because I already got three daughters with two other bitches, so, that shit ain't cool. I knew the first time he picked up the phone that he was sissified. So, I think it's time for us to go our separate ways. You've done a pretty good job raising him, and you can keep on raising him. I got my young girls to think about.

And don't think I didn't know, or forgot about what you were trying to do back in the day by using your pussy to get me to pay you some child support. That's sad that you think your pussy is so fucking magical that you were gonna hypnotize a nigga into paying you money. What you failed to realize is that you just let me get my dick wet that day and that was it. I hope Lawrence, or should I say "Loretta," enjoyed that $500 I sent him and the clothes I bought him, because that's all he's gonna get. If he cries like a little bitch, tell him that's what he gets for being like that. But when I was looking for him, I did have every intention of doing right by him, but, all that faggotry shit, I ain't down with. I see why Plez threw his ass out the house. I would have done the same thing, but I would have stomped him first.

Don't feel too bad about being played. You've spent years getting played by every man you ever laid down with, so it's what I'd expect from you.

I don't care what you tell "Loretta" about me being gone, just make some shit up.

Diallo

When I finished reading that mess, I was pissed. I knew Diallo hadn't changed, I just didn't think he'd stoop that low. Once a dog, always a dog.

As I ripped up those pages, I knew it would hurt Lawrence's feelings to know that the father he thought he'd have the chance to get to know wanted nothing more to do with him. I prayed that God would bless me to know how to handle the situation when it came time to explain to him why his sorry excuse for a father wasn't coming around or calling anymore.

When Plez was doing better, I went to talk to him about how we were gonna do things for the divorce. The people at the rehabilitation clinic said he wasn't making any progress and that if he didn't stop feeling sorry for himself, he wouldn't walk right again.He looked miserable and tired when I walked into his room. Seeing me brought a smile to his face. I knew I needed to stand firm in what I came to talk about.

"Hey, Cheryl. I thought you'd never come to see me."

"Well, truthfully, I came to talk to you about ironing some things out in the divorce."

His smile faded and he looked sad again. "Oh, the divorce?"

"Yes, Plez. We have to talk about custody, the house, bills, all of that."

Plez had been sitting in a chair, facing the window. He turned to look out of it. "I was hoping you'd rethink that."

"Plez, don't play with me."

"I'm not, Cheryl. It's fucked up that I had to wind up in this place to get me to realize that you're a good woman."

"You're damn right I'm a good woman. You needed to get beat up to see that?"

Plez looked down like a little boy, then back up and said, "I guess I deserved that."

"Look, I didn't come here to argue. I just want to get all of this over with so I can get on with my life."

"I was hoping we could work things out."

"Really? You were hoping to work things out while you had some bitch in our bed? The same bitch you told you loved, and didn't love me, but only put up with me because I gave you a child?"

"I know, I know. I must have been crazy then."

"Plez, you're crazy now. I don't know what you're gonna have to do to be right with this, but we have to talk about what we're each walking away with."

"How's Jr. treating you these days?" he asked me, completely off subject.

"He's doing fine. Why?"

Plez sighed heavily, and stopped for a second, not knowing if he wanted to say what he was about to say. "I told Jr. to stop giving you problems. All that is my fault."

"What's your fault?"

"I told him that you were a piece of shit and that you were out messing around, trying to break up our family. "And I told him that you loved Lawrence more than you loved him. I told him that because you were angry with me, you wished he was never born."

I felt my blood pressure rise. It all made sense. Plez had sabotaged my relationship with Plez Jr., just like he'd tried to sabotage my relationship with Clayton and my parents. Before I made a scene, I backed away from him, shaking my head. He stared up at me, his one good eye wet like it wanted to drop tears. "I'm leaving now. I'm gonna go and push forward with the divorce papers. I'm gonna file it as a no-fault divorce, and you're gonna sign them."

"Cheryl, I'm sorry."

"That's the most right you've ever been about anything, Plez. You're sorry and you're tired. But I'm sorry, too. I'm sorry that the cops arrested that man before he had the chance to finish your black ass off!"

CHAPTER

43

PLEZ JR. SAT AT THE kitchen table, drawing pictures on the frosted window with his fingers. We each had experienced a different Christmas in 1990. I had received assurance from Plez of signed divorce papers (I believed him), the biggest gift I could've gotten. But it was a sad holiday for Plez Jr., who spent his Christmas without his father. It didn't matter that I spent an arm and a leg on gifts to try and take his mind off the fact that while his daddy probably wanted to be at home for Christmas, he still wasn't fully recovered.

I'd been by the clinic a number of times leading up to Christmas, trying to be civil in hopes that he'd sign the damn papers when it came time, but also to be supportive for his son's sake. It wasn't that Plez couldn't walk; I'd seen firsthand the depression take over his body, as he dragged his bad leg across the floor. His pride had disappeared and he'd given up.

I ran into Rexanne at Sally's Beauty Supply. She had slimmed down a bit, and had gotten rid of the dreadlocks. Instead she was sporting a short texturized style. It didn't do much to feminize her, but she looked less angry and severe. After our hellos and a hug I said, "You look good."

"Thanks. I'm trying this liquid fast. It's supposed to help

me take some of this weight off. I figure if I'm gonna meet a woman as fine as you, I better start taking better care of myself."

"I'm glad you're working on that. You look happier." And she did. She was completely different than the mess I'd seen at the 24 hour drugstore and talked to on the phone.

"Well, you know I'm goin' to therapy. I think it's time I tried to get on with my life, for real. I need to deal with the bullshit so I can put it behind me."

I waited until we had paid for our purchases. I came to buy some Luster's Pink lotion for my hair. When we got outside, I smiled a big smile, knowing I had the news she'd been dying to hear.

"Rexanne, I got Plez for you, for us."

She didn't smile. "What are you talkin' about?"

"Plez used to kick my ass for years, but still I was desperate to save my marriage. When you told me that he raped you, I decided to divorce his ass. But I also decided to get even for what he put us through."The excitement I expected to radiate from her didn't. Instead, she shook her head slowly, almost as if she were disappointed. "What did you do to him?"

"I had somebody jack him up real good for those of us he bullied. But what difference does it make; you don't seem too enthused about it. Am I mistaken, but I thought you'd be pleased that the man who raped you finally got some kind of street justice," I said, lowering my voice as two older white ladies passed us.

"I wish you hadn't done that. Therapy is teaching me to put the blame where the blame belongs, on the perpetrator," Rexanne said, pausing for a moment. She looked off into the distance toward the parking lot. "All right, listen. I've been talking to my therapist and she said it was a good idea that I call you. I really was fixin' to call you to talk about this."

"Call me to talk about what?"

"Cheryl, Diallo did it."

"Diallo did what?"

"He raped me."

I stood there, feeling a huge rock drop in my stomach. Then I felt a wave of adrenaline come over me. "Bitch, I asked you if he did that to you and you told me no! Why would you blame Plez if he didn't do it?" I didn't care who heard me screaming at her.

"Because Diallo threatened to kill me if I told anybody."

"Yeah, right! I don't believe that!" I shouted, shaking my head."There were three of them there, like I told you before. The one guy took off running, and Plez tried to keep Diallo off me, but Diallo was crazy and took a swing at him. After Diallo was finished with me, he spit at me and said that he told me he was gonna get me for hitting him that day he dropped you off at the apartment when we lived together."

I remembered the scene from the apartment, but it still didn't make sense why she'd put Plez's name on it like he was the one who did it. And what made it so bad was how she stood there, totally at peace with it, casually sharing the news to me like she was telling me her secret to cooking a pot roast. I was glad to hear she was getting help to move past what happened to her, but lying about who did it?

"I guess maybe the reason why I pinned it on your husband was because I had feelings for you for a long time after. It was like you threw me away and went on to a better life without me."

I wanted to slap the black off her for saying that dumb shit. "Rexanne, my moving out and us not talking for *years* should've told your ass it was time to move on! And anyway, I told you, I'm not like you. You took one evening we spent together and started acting like we'd been messing around for years. You have some real head problems, sistah. I'm glad you're taking your ass to therapy to get your head checked! And I wouldn't call years of abuse a better life! But what you did, you should be ashamed of yourself. Because of you, I took an action that injured another human being."

Rexanne folded her arms while she shook her head, refusing to take responsibility for any of it. "No, no, chick. Let's get something straight right now. If you justified having your husband jumped because of me, then you do what you feel you need to do. You probably was thinkin' up shit to do to him long before we spoke, so don't try and pin that shit on me. You take responsibility for what *you* do." Then she wound her plastic bag up around her wrist and proceeded to walk out into the parking lot, leaving me standing there like BooBoo the Fool.She had tried to be all philosophical about it all, but that was probably a front. She was right on one score: I had to take a hard look at the person I'd allowed myself to become. In truth, I might have done something to Plez even if I didn't have a Rexanne as an excuse to do it. She never told me to seek vengeance on her behalf or call the police. I'd done a bad thing because I'd chosen to, and as I walked to my own car, trying not to slip and slide on the snow, I wondered if I should start making my reservation for hell now or later.

I got into my car, but before I had the chance to put the key into the ignition, I busted out crying. I cried for being made a fool of yet again. Diallo had gotten over on me three times; first by walking away from daddy duty, two, by acting like an innocent bystander when he was the one who raped Rexanne and lastly, by using me and my child to get revenge on Plez by kicking his ass over some pool debt nonsense. Then there was Plez, masquerading like he was noble. He messed with my head, my heart, and managed to put a few bruises on me too. And I was foolish for standing by while it escalated, hoping it would get better, when I knew in my heart it wouldn't. And while I wasted time, Lawrence got thrown out without a second thought and Plez Jr. witnessed and possibly picked up a few of his daddy's bad habits. And because I didn't have the sense to take my babies and run, I let hatred enter my heart. That's the reason Plez was limping around a rehabilitation clinic.When I pulled up to the house, I saw that the boys had done a better job than usual shoveling the snow out of the driveway. I made a mental note to make their favorite TV dinners, Fisherman seafood platters.Later, as I took the TV dinners out of the stove, Plez Jr. came into the kitchen in search of some juice.

"Aw, man, we're outta fruit punch again," he said, standing in front of the refrigerator as the door closed.

"That's because ya'll drink it like it's going out of style. Write it down on the list and I'll pick up some more."

"Who's *y'all?*" Lawrence asked coming into the kitchen. "I don't drink fruit punch."

"Well, whatever. Pick something out to drink and get ready for dinner," I said.

"Those dinners have to cool off first. I was in the middle of dubbing some music on a tape. Let me know when they're ready," Lawrence said, like I had wasted his time.

"Boy, don't get ahead of yourself. *I'm* the queen of the

house here, okay?" Then I thought, oh shit, what if he took offense to that? I didn't mean it like that, just that I was the head of the household. But he flashed me a smile that let me know he got the double meaning.

"Sorry, Ma," he said, "Please let me know when dinner's ready." Then he went back to his room.

"Baby, you haven't even touched the apple juice. There's plenty of that," I said to Plez Jr..

He looked at me and smiled, as though I had given him a million-dollar idea. I took the opportunity to ask him, "You remember when I told you and your brother there'd be some changes around here?"

"Yes."

"Well, your father isn't..."

"He's moving out. I already know."

"He told you?"

Plez Jr. nodded his head. "He told me he'll stay with a friend until he can walk normal again. After that, I guess he's supposed to be getting an apartment."

"What do you think about that?"

He shrugged his shoulders. "Dad said I can stay with him and help him out around the house."

"That's good. You know, just because your daddy and me aren't together doesn't mean we don't love you."

"He told me that, too," he said, jabbing his index finger into the cherry crumble dessert portion of the TV dinner to see if it was still hot.

"It's true. We both love you very much."

"Yeah, I know, Mom."

"We gotta help your daddy out. Can you help me do that?"

"I will," he said, pouring himself apple juice.

~ * * * ~

Mama was good to watch the boys while I spent an adult evening with Dino. He'd been pestering me about New Year's Eve for weeks and I finally got my fib together to tell Mama that me and some of the girls from work were going to a New Year's Eve party and would be out late, so I'd crash at one of their houses.

After I dropped the boys off at Mama's house, I drove

like a crazy lady to get to Dino's place. We enjoyed a bottle of Champagne chilling in the refrigerator while he made a fabulous dinner of salmon and asparagus. As he finished cooking, he took out what looked like a thimble-like jar of caviar and some little rye toast crackers. I didn't like it, but I was glad to say I tried it. I couldn't get past that sensation of salty little beads popping in my mouth as I chewed them. "More for me," Dino said, finishing off the rest. "I a hundred fifty bucks for it, I'm not gonna let it go to waste."

Dinner was tasty and afterward he started giving me sex looks again. But instead of dirty talk he said, "I can't wait for you to meet my family. They'll love you."

"You don't think it's a little sudden?"

"Of course not. I wouldn't have brought it up if I wasn't hoping for something a bit more serious."

I took another swig of my champagne, avoiding as much eye contact with him as I could. He could give you puppy dog eyes at the snap of fingers. But the truth was, while my feelings for him were strong, made stronger by our lovemaking; I wasn't ready to jump from one relationship into another. It wouldn't be until July of 1991 that the divorce would be finalized, and we were sitting at his dining room table, only hours before the end of 1990. Could I just enjoy my freedom first before he started expecting me to take his last name?

To be fair, New Year's Eve wasn't the beginning of the change I was going through with Dino. After the first time we made love, he asked me days later if I thought we'd make beautiful children. I hadn't thought about having anymore children. To me, divorcing Plez closed that door. It didn't have to be, but I felt like that part of my life was over. I'd had children by two different men, and it didn't work out with either.

Dino kept on with the baby talk, telling me he wanted to have a whole tribe of them, that it was important to him, being Italian and coming from such a large family. I didn't want to piss on his dreams, because I had my children, and he should be allowed to have children of his own. I just wasn't sure I was gonna be the one to give them to him.

I woke up in Dino's bed New Year's Day. Besides me, it was empty. I smelled the aroma of bacon and hash browns coming from the kitchen. I put on the robe I had brought over and went into the kitchen where he was standing in his own robe, drinking coffee.

"Good morning, sweetheart," he said, placing his coffee mug down on the counter and pulling me in to give me a morning kiss.

"Dino, not yet, I haven't brushed my teeth."

"I don't care about that. I'm just lucky to have you here. You know what my first thought of the day was?"

"No, what?"

"That whoever you're with New Year's Eve is who you'll be with forever."

I smiled politely, but I didn't believe it. I had spent many New Year's Eves with Plez and that didn't end well. "Why don't we take it one day at a time, okay?"

Dino frowned. "Am I missing something?"

"Never mind."

"No, you obviously have something on your mind."

"My divorce isn't finalized until the summertime. I like what we have, but I just want to take things slow."

Dino had a look of confusion on his face as he scratched his head, trying to make heads or tails of what I just said. "So, what am I to you— a piece of dick you can have when you want to feel more like a woman?"

"I didn't say that. Look, I don't want to start the year arguing, okay?"

"No, answer my question. You've been acting really weird since I mentioned kids. You think I haven't noticed?"

"What do you want me to say, Dino? I'm not ready for all of that. I ain't even out of my marriage and you're talking about me giving you babies. How do you know I even want any more kids?"

"I don't get you, Cheryl. I mean, you cry about your husband not treating you right, and now that you have a chance to be treated right, you're pulling away."

"You're throwing shit back in my face!"

"Am I? It's obvious from the moment I told you I loved you that you got weirded out."

"I'm not weirded out. But how in the hell are you gonna go from telling me you love me, to talking about what our babies are gonna look like? All I'm asking is that we take our time."

"Do you even love me?" Dino asked, picking up his coffee

mug in one swoop.

"I have feelings for you. Is it love? I'm not there yet."

He sucked his teeth and rolled his eyes. "I guess I'm seeing for the first time that you like to play games."

"Games? Now I'm playing games, Dino? I guess you think because you got the pussy you can just have whatever you want, huh? Well, it's not that kind of party!"

"Party? What the fuck a party! The problem I'm having with you is that you've changed. You cried to me about how bad Plez treated you, and now you have the opportunity to have a man treat you like a queen; to be all you want him to be; to give you everything you want, but I guess you'd rather be treated like a..." he stopped right there.

"Like a what? Say it, Dino. Like a what?"

Dino looked away from me and shook his head. "I don't know. Maybe you don't think you deserve any better than you've gotten. Maybe guys like Plez are all you'll ever be deserving of because you're stuck in that fucking mindset!"

"First of all, I'm not one of these women out here who expects a man to do for me. All I ask is that he has a J-O-B and can meet me halfway! And second, don't you stand up here and judge me! Who the hell do you think you are?"

"I'm a man who met a woman that I was stupid enough to fall for. Now I've got egg on my face because she's too chicken shit to give the love back!"

"And you think the best way to make me fall in love with you is to throw stuff that I've been through back in my face?"

"I'm telling you that if you want good things in this life then you have to take them when they come. Otherwise you're only gonna keep getting what you've gotten."

"I ain't gonna listen to this shit! I'm outta here." I went back into the bedroom, put my clothes on, and gathered my things. Dino watched as I made it to the door when he said, "This isn't working for me. First thing when I go back to work, I'm putting in for a transfer. Obviously we can't work together like this."

"If that's what you feel the need to do then do it. Don't let me stop you." The last thing I remember is seeing Dino bring the coffee mug to his lips and I left, closing his door behind me. As I walked down the stairs, I heard shattering sounds come from his apartment, like he had thrown something against the wall. I didn't let it stop me, or draw me back. He had done this; ruined a perfectly good morning and a good thing. He could clean up the mess.

CHAPTER

44

I N MARCH, PLEZ WENT BACK to work. He was walking better, but he would always have a slight limp. His face was still a little misshapen from being beaten, but his eyes had gone back to normal. He wasn't crossed-eyed looking anymore.

I came by his place to pick up Plez Jr. so that we could go shopping for a model kit for an after school model car class he was taking. When he got in the car his face looked sad.

"What's the matter?"

"Man, I can't stand that lady."

"What lady?"

"This blonde lady that started staying with my dad."

I immediately thought of the trailer-trash looking woman I found in my bed. I had thrown those sheets in the garbage, and I was still burning incense to get that pussy smell out of my mind, even though the smell had evaporated a long time ago. "How long has she been staying there?"

"Man, too long! At first she'd stop by and spend a couple of hours with us, you know for dinner and to watch some TV. Then she started spending the night. Now she's there every day."

"How are you eating?"

"My dad usually brings something home. If she cooks, it's usually some Pork n' Beans with chopped-up hot dogs in it. I'm gettin' sick of that, too."

"Well, that's who your daddy picked. Is she mistreating you?"

"Naw. Mostly she doesn't say much except for 'Hey' or 'See ya later.' But I don't like her. All she and my dad do is go into the bedroom and close the door and put on loud music."

"Well, as long as she's not mistreating you, there isn't much I can do. Is your daddy mistreating you?"

Plez Jr. looked at me like he didn't understand the question. Then he shrugged.

"What are you shrugging your shoulders for? Either he's mistreating you or he isn't."

"I mean, he speaks to me more than she does, but when she's there, it's like he spends all his time with her."

"Do you feel like he doesn't want you there?"

Plez Jr. shrugged again. "I'm kinda worried about him. When she's not there, I hear him talking to himself. Once I thought he was talking to me and went to see what he wanted, and I heard him saying something about being glad he killed those Vietcong or something like that. Then he started laughing."

That struck me. I remembered that a few times when we were together, I'd hear him talking to himself. But I thought he was just thinking out loud, I never thought he was having conversations with himself. Plus, he used to have periods where he had these bad dreams about Vietnam.

"I heard him saying that the nightmares were coming back and he wanted to talk to somebody about them."

"Well, Junior, some of the servicemen saw really bad things when they were in the war that messed them up. I know a girl at work whose brother was in Vietnam and he saw a lot of bad things he couldn't deal with, plus he did a lot of drugs to cope and now he's a paranoid schizophrenic."

"You think my dad might be a schizo?"

"I don't think so, but I think maybe your dad saw some things in Vietnam that shaped who he is now. Come to think of it, that answers a lot of questions." I said, with a slight laugh.

"Here, Dad wanted me to give this to you," he said,

pulling some money out of his pocket before buckling his seat belt.

I took the money from him which was about two hundred dollars. "What's this for?"

"He said for you to give it to grandfather for a debt he owed."

I smiled. It only took him five years to cough up some money. "Have you decided what kind of model car you want to buy?" I asked, placing the money into my purse.

"I dunno. Maybe a '57 Chevy. I gotta see what they have first."

"All righty then," I said, turning the ignition.

~ * * * ~

Work was a struggle to get through. Dino was waiting to hear from Hennepin County Medical. He said he'd gotten tired of geriatrics. That's what I heard from the other nurses. With the exception of anything professional, we weren't speaking. And I hated the way he looked at me when I'd have to ask him a question. He had that mix of still angry and disappointment look, and while I'd tried to move past it, I could tell his thought was, "You know why I'm pissed, Cheryl. I don't know why you're trying to act like everything is okay. We are *not* okay."I caught him giving me a sad look, like he regretted the last words we shared, but then, he'd re-position himself, and stand firm in the shit he caused. Robert, without realizing it, took care of the tension between us, because he put me back on mornings and Dino worked the 3-11 shifts. I wondered if Robert had a clue as to the drama going on between Dino and me, but I wasn't gonna ask. I still missed Dino, and what we tried to create. I knew how he felt about things but I hoped that at some point he'd see it from my perspective and realize that I was never trying to play games with him, just take things slowly. We could arrive at the same place, but why not enjoy the view getting there? Why did everything have to happen so quickly? There were nights when I wanted to call him, and I wondered if he had those nights, too? I just knew that I missed him something awful, and not having him in my life made me see how much he meant to me.

I'd been doing a lot of praying. And it wasn't necessarily

that selfish praying either. It was the "Lord, please make whatever will be...be." It had started after I last saw Rexanne, on that drive home from seeing her roll her eyes at my nonsense. As much of a burn as that was, it made me look within.

I began praying that God would remove all of the black from my heart. I had so much hatred and anger that I sometimes forgot why I was so hateful and angry. And little by little God revealed His lesson to me. I finally realized why I ran into Rexanne back in December. It was to show me what a humble heart can experience when I decided to stop holding on to what made me feel the way I felt about some of the people in my life. Rexanne of all people, showed me that she was doing what she needed to do to get to that place of forgiveness and that forgiving didn't mean that you forgot what happened to you, but that you were willing to release all of the stuff that kept you up at night crying while the people who did their dirt went to sleep. There were times in my prayer that I would bust out crying because God's truth hit me upside my head so hard. I began to learn that allowing myself to get to the same place Rexanne was trying to get to didn't make me a weak person, or say that I was okay with whatever bad things happened, but it allowed me to rid my life of unwanted mess to make room for the blessings. I recognized that it took valuable time for me to stand naked in front of a mirror and remember where Plez had left a bruise that wasn't even there anymore. Or remember a mind game he used to play on me, and yet, we no longer lived together. It took too much energy to be worried that Diallo wouldn't pay for his evil. To use his flesh and blood in a game to get revenge and then disown that flesh and blood because he isn't what Diallo wanted him to be; to rape a woman because she bruised his male ego, and who knows whatever else he did, I knew that it took a certain kind of evil to pull off. I also knew that God would see that he was brought to justice whether I was there to witness it or not.

~ * * * ~

In April of 1991, Mama called me. She sounded winded. "Cheryl, Oh my word! Did Diallo's sister call you yet?"

"No, why?"

"Diallo's dead!"

I felt like the air in the kitchen had become thinner while Mama's words disappeared into a vacuum. I was speechless.

"Girl, did you hear..."

"What happened?" I asked finally.

"His sister called over here looking for you and Lawrence. She said the cops called and that Diallo was living in Rhode Island. He was at some club, gettin' fresh with some guy's woman. A *white woman*. They had words and a fight broke out, but the security broke it up. I guess the guy was outside waiting for him afterward because they found Diallo stabbed nine times."

"Oh my God!" I said, putting a hand to my mouth in disbelief.

"Yeah, they caught the guy. Some man named Nicky Delvecchio. That's Italian, ain't it?"

"Sounds like it." I could barely comprehend what Mama had said, and in a way, I was waiting for her to come out of it by saying, "Naw, I'm just teasing!" but she never did.

"Well, all I can say is, I don't wish death on nobody, but if you think you can just get by doin' wrong to folks and there ain't gonna be any kind of consequence, then you'll find out just the opposite. I hope God has mercy on his soul," she said.

Mama was sympathetic to me when I told her about what he'd done to Lawrence and to Rexanne and how I felt like a fool. I'd even confessed to being drawn into seeking revenge on Plez.

"You better be glad Plez didn't die, otherwise the police could be finding your ass in a garbage bin somewhere. Does he know you had anything to do with it?"

"No."

"Good. Keep it that way." And while I waited for her to launch into her usual moral judgment, sounding disappointed like I'd gotten used to hearing, she didn't say anything else about it.

When I told Lawrence that his father was killed in Rhode Island, he looked at me as though I'd told him the mailman had passed away. "What happened?" he asked.

"He got into with some guy over a woman."

Lawrence shook his head, and rolled his eyes. "I'm not surprised. He looked like the type."

"Yeah, but ain't you gonna miss having your daddy around?"

"Can't miss what was hardly there. I already know what the deal is."

"What do you mean?"

"When he was at my birthday party and was talking to me, sometimes he'd get this look on his face."

"What kind of look?"

Lawrence shrugged, "I don't know, just a look."

I knew what he was talking about.

The phone rang. I reached for it, saddened that what seemed like a good thing—a father getting to know his son—had turned out so bad. "Hello," I said, barely getting the phone to my ear.

"Mom, I want to come live with you," Plez Jr. said.

"What's wrong?"

"Dad's girlfriend is pregnant. They're gonna make *my* room the nursery."

All I could do was chuckle. It didn't take them very long, did it?

CHAPTER

45

I DIDN'T DO CARTWHEELS THROUGH the streets like I thought I would the day my divorce became finalized. For months I had dreamed of how excited I would be to be a single woman, who'd have new opportunities awaiting her around the corner. Once July 23 came, that excitement was missing. God had given me what I'd wanted, which was to be free from Plez Darnell Jackson, but He also put me on the road to learning a life lesson.

For a while after Dino Taraborrelli and me fizzled out, he was always on my mind if not in my sight. The word on the street in the nursing community was that Hennepin County Medical was too big for Dino, so he settled nicely into another nursing home, this time at Truman's.I continued my prayer that God would make His will come to pass, but I started peppering my prayers with one request: that Dino would realize that I was ready for his love.

What was revealed to me was just the opposite. That's where it gets good, because in our minds we always think we know better than God about what's good for us, even though we say out loud that we don't. Our humanness, which is fueled by ego takes over and we really start believing we can cut deals with God, like he doesn't already have a plan for us. What I needed to learn was to do like my mama always said: Let go and let God.

It wasn't easy at first. I had done my best to be the best mother I could be to my boys. I had worked my ass off to get my GED and later go to school to ultimately become an RN which proved that my will was stronger than I'd thought. But I was still like a lot of women who thought of themselves as a half looking for a man to make them whole. I was already whole. I had a beating heart and a brain, blood, tissue, flesh and a personality, which made me a whole person. A man didn't complete me. The mistake I made after Diallo was to jump into something with somebody like Plez, who at the time seemed to be everything I was missing in my life. That was the problem right there. I didn't allow any space for me to grow in between Diallo and Plez. I was scared that because I was a very young single mother who had barely begun living her own life before bringing a new one into this world, that no man would want me. That if I didn't find a daddy for Lawrence, or husband for myself, then that made me a failure as a woman.

Dino was right. I wasn't ready to receive his love. I hadn't learned to love myself first. I didn't even know who Cheryl Lorraine Greene was. I was too chicken-shit to be alone with my thoughts, dreams, and fears, and be at peace with them.When July 23 came, it was a hollow victory. I'd run away from Plez the boogeyman, but I still had my own demons to deal with. That's when it hit me: I needed to work on my own stuff before I even thought about trying to get into another relationship. Never mind Dino trying to take things too quickly, I was still responsible for what I brought to the table.After some of the anger had faded, Dino called to see how I was doing. I could tell from his voice that he wasn't sure if it was even the right thing to do."I just wanted to say that I get it now," he said to me after I said hello.

"Get what?"

"I had no right to stand in judgment of you. All you were trying to say was that you wanted to take things slowly. I don't know why I took that as rejection."

"Yeah, I didn't understand that, either. I didn't say I was breaking it off."

"I guess I really messed things up, huh?"

"No. Look, it was just a breakdown in communication," I said, trying to make sense out of it.

Then I heard his voice become shaky, like he was crying. "Damn it, Cheryl, I miss you, okay? And I'm sorry if that makes you uncomfortable. I've told my friends about you and they keep telling me I should leave it alone and find myself a nice Italian girl, but I don't want that, I want you."

His words were all run together, but it was sweet that he was willing to go to that vulnerable place. Time away from him had made me realize that I loved him too, but, I still needed to get myself together. I didn't want to lose that goal.

"Why does this have to be so hard?" I asked.

"Just tell me you want to start over."

"Dino, I thought finally being free from Plez would give me my independence. But I feel just as empty as I did before, which lets me know that the problem is with me. I need to take care of myself before I can even think about being with somebody."

Dino was quiet on the other end, with the exception of a few sniffles.

"Say something, please," I said, breaking the quiet.

"I just don't understand why you think you have to work on yourself *by yourself.* You have someone that's willing to stand in your corner. I wouldn't let you lose yourself because who you are is the reason I fell in love with you in the first place. Let me stand in your corner with you."

Then it was my turn to cry. His words touched me like a beautiful song. "I don't know what to say, Dino."

"You don't have to say anything. Look, you do what you have to do, all right? I'm not gonna stop loving you overnight. If it's meant for us to be together then we'll be together. I can't believe I'm even saying this because I want us to be together, but I'm willing to wait. But I won't wait forever. No one can wait forever."

"I wouldn't expect you to."

"But your happiness is important to you. And if getting to the heart of who you are will make you an even better person, then there will be even more for me to love. Maybe somewhere in there you'll find out that you can love me back."

"Dino, I do love you," I said, without thinking. It was a truth I didn't want to reveal to him yet.

Dino sighed as though his heart had just received nourishment. "Then I'm not crazy, because I always thought you did, too."

"Yeah, I've known since the first time we made love. I don't know what this journey has in store for me, though, Dino. And part of that frightens me, because in the end it could change how I feel about you."

"Yeah, that's possible. And if that were to happen, we'll figure that one out when we come to it. But I promise you, I'll give you all the time you need. If you decide you want to try again, we'll take it one day at a time."

Somehow in his saying that, Dino made the uncertainty of the future look promising.

"Well, I gotta get ready for work," he said.

"Oh, I didn't ask, how *is* work?"

"It's fine. Same shit. But the nurses really care about the patients."

"I'm glad things are going well for you."

"Tell me we're back together and things will be going great for me," Dino said, chuckling.

"Dino..."

"I'm just kidding. I love you, Cheryl. Take care of yourself, and pick up the phone once in a while. You can work on yourself all you want but you still need support. Let me at least be that for you."

"It's a deal. And I love you, too. " I hung up the phone, my heart beating faster from both fear and excitement. I knew I could do it and I wouldn't have to be alone. And it would only take me one day at a time.

THE END

ABOUT THE AUTHOR

THIS IS LLOYD'S FIRST NOVEL. He is currently working on his second, entitled TRICKS FOR A TRADE. He lives in Connecticut with his partner of 18 years.

Made in the USA
Charleston, SC
14 April 2012